ISAAC ASIMOV is regarded as one of the greatest science fiction writers of our time, and also as a valued contributor to the world of science. He holds a Ph.D. in Chemistry from Columbia University (1948) and, though he no longer lives in the Boston area, is an Associate Professor of Biochemistry at Boston University. He has received numerous awards for his inspiring scientific articles covering a wide range of subjects.

In this collection Dr. Asimov's probing imagination has created fascinating adventures set in the not-too-distant future—adventures that could change from fiction to fact any day now.

"VINTAGE ASIMOV!" —WASHINGTON POST

"Fascinating. . . . The stories are chronologically arranged so that the development of this towering young mind becomes as engrossing as the stories themselves."
—THE NEW YORK TIMES

Fawcett Crest Books
by Isaac Asimov:

THE EARLY ASIMOV, *Book One*
THE EARLY ASIMOV, *Book Two*
PEBBLE IN THE SKY
THE STARS, LIKE DUST
THE CURRENTS OF SPACE
THE CAVES OF STEEL
THE END OF ETERNITY
THE MARTIAN WAY
THE NAKED SUN
EARTH IS ROOM ENOUGH
NINE TOMORROWS
NIGHTFALL
THE GODS THEMSELVES

And these anthologies
edited by Isaac Asimov:

THE HUGO WINNERS, Vol. I
STORIES FROM THE HUGO WINNERS, Vol. II
MORE STORIES FROM THE HUGO WINNERS, Vol. II
WHERE DO WE GO FROM HERE?

ARE THERE FAWCETT PAPERBACKS
YOU WANT BUT CANNOT FIND IN YOUR LOCAL STORES?

You can get any title in print in Fawcett Crest, Fawcett Premier,
or Fawcett Gold Medal editions. Simply send title and retail price,
plus 25¢ to cover mailing and handling costs for each book wanted, to:

MAIL ORDER DEPARTMENT,
FAWCETT PUBLICATIONS,
P.O. Box 1014
GREENWICH, CONN. 06830

Books are available at discounts in quantity lots for industrial or
sales-promotional use. For details write FAWCETT WORLD LI-
BRARY, CIRCULATION MANAGER, FAWCETT BLDG.,
GREENWICH, CONN. 06830

THE EARLY ASIMOV

Book Two

Isaac Asimov

A FAWCETT CREST BOOK

Fawcett Publications, Inc., Greenwich, Connecticut

THE EARLY ASIMOV, Book Two

This book comprises the second half of THE EARLY ASIMOV, and is reprinted by arrangement with Doubleday and Company, Inc.

Copyright © 1972 by Isaac Asimov.

All rights reserved, including the right to reproduce this book or portions thereof in any form.

All the characters in this book are fictitious, and any resemblance to actual persons living or dead is purely coincidental.

Library of Congress Catalog Card Number: 72–76116

Selection of the Science Fiction Book Club, December 1972

Printed in the United States of America

First Printing: December 1974

1 2 3 4 5 6 7 8 9 10

STORIES INCLUDED IN BOOK TWO

To the memory of

John Wood Campbell, Jr. (1910–71)

for reasons that this book will make amply obvious

What you are holding now, Gentle Reader, is the second volume of the tale of my extraordinarily slow rise to minor fame. I told it originally in a single hardback volume (Doubleday, 1972) but at sufficiently great length to make it difficult to force the whole into a paperback without having it break in two.

For that reason, the estimable people at Fawcett have published **THE EARLY ASIMOV** in two volumes. The first volume I trust you've read. If not, go out and buy it at once, and don't let go of this one which you are holding, either. Buy it also. Buy both volumes.—I'll wait.

Now if you can't find the first volume and must start this second volume from scratch, let me explain that the first volume dealt with my start as a writer and of the heroic attempts of John W. Campbell, Jr., editor of **Astounding Science Fiction,** to pummel me into shape.

By the end of the first volume, I had published 15 stories (13 of which were included in that first volume) and had, nevertheless, not yet made my name illustrious.

So now continue with the story—

On October 23, 1940, I visited Campbell and outlined to him another robot story I wanted to write, a story I planned to call "Reason." Campbell was completely enthusiastic. I had trouble writing it and had to start over several times, but eventually it was done, and on November 18 I submitted it to John. He accepted it on the twenty-second, and it appeared in the April 1941 issue of **Astounding.**

It was the third story of mine that he had accepted and the first in which he did not ask for a revision. (He told me, in fact, that he had liked it so well, he had almost decided to pay me a bonus.)

With "Reason," the "positronic robot" series was fairly launched, and my two most successful characters yet, Gregory Powell and Mike Donovan (improvements on Turner and Snead of "Ring Around the Sun") made their appearance. Eventually, "Reason" and others of the series that were to

7

follow, together with "Robbie," which Campbell had rejected, were to appear in **I, Robot.**

The success of "Reason" didn't mean that I was to have no further rejections from Campbell.

On December 6, 1940, influenced by the season and never stopping to think that a Christmas story must sell no later than July in order to make the Christmas issue, I began "Christmas on Ganymede." I submitted it to him on the twenty-third, but the holiday season did not affect his critical judgment. He rejected it.

I tried Pohl next, and, as was happening so often that year, he took it. In this case, for reasons I will describe later, the acceptance fell through. I eventually sold it the next summer (June 27, 1941, the **proper** time of year) to **Startling Stories,** the younger, sister magazine of **Thrilling Wonder Stories.**

14

Christmas on Ganymede

Olaf Johnson hummed nasally to himself and his china-blue
eyes were dreamy as he surveyed the stately fir tree in the corner of the library. Though the library was the largest single
room in the Dome, Olaf felt it none too spacious for the occasion. Enthusiastically he dipped into the huge crate at his side
and took out the first roll of red-and-green crêpe paper.

What sudden burst of sentiment had inspired the Ganymedan Products Corporation, Inc. to ship a complete collection of Christmas decorations to the Dome, he did not pause
to inquire. Olaf's was a placid disposition, and in his self-
imposed job as chief Christmas decorator, he was content
with his lot.

He frowned suddenly and muttered a curse. The General
Assembly signal light was flashing on and off hysterically.
With a hurt air Olaf laid down the tack-hammer he had just
lifted, then the roll of crêpe paper, picked some tinsel out of
his hair and left for officers quarters.

Commander Scott Pelham was in his deep armchair at the
head of the table when Olaf entered. His stubby fingers were
drumming unrhythmically upon the glass-topped table. Olaf
met the commander's hotly furious eyes without fear, for
nothing had gone wrong in his department in twenty Ganymedan revolutions.

The room filled rapidly with men, and Pelham's eyes
hardened as he counted noses in one sweeping glance.

"We're all here. Men, we face a crisis!"

There was a vague stir. Olaf's eyes sought the ceiling and he

Startling Stories, January 1942
Copyright © 1941 by Better Publications, Inc.
Copyright renewed © 1968 by Isaac Asimov

relaxed. Crises hit the Dome once a revolution, on the average. Usually they turned out to be a sudden rise in the quota of oxite to be gathered, or the inferior quality of the last batch of karen leaves. He stiffened, however, at the next words.

"In connection with the crisis. I have no question to ask." Pelham's voice was a deep baritone, and it rasped unpleasantly when he was angry. "What dirty imbecilic troublemaker has been telling those blasted Ossies fairy tales?"

Olaf cleared his throat nervously and thus immediately became the center of attention. His Adam's apple wobbled in sudden alarm and his forehead wrinkled into a washboard. He shivered.

"I—I—" he stuttered, quickly fell silent. His long fingers made a bewildered gesture of appeal. "I mean I was out there yesterday, after the last—uh—supplies of karen leaves, on account the Ossies were slow and—"

A deceptive sweetness entered Pelham's voice. He smiled. "Did you tell those natives about Santa Claus, Olaf?"

The smile looked uncommonly like a wolfish leer and Olaf broke down. He nodded convulsively.

"Oh, you did? Well, well, you told them about Santa Claus! He comes down in a sleigh that flies through the air with eight reindeer pulling it, huh?"

"Well—er—doesn't he?" Olaf asked unhappily.

"And you drew pictures of the reindeer, just to make sure there was no mistake. Also, he has a long white beard and red clothes with white trimmings."

"Yeah, that's right," said Olaf, his face puzzled.

"And he has a big bag, chock full of presents for good little boys and girls, and he brings it down the chimney and puts presents inside stockings."

"Sure."

"You also told them he's about due, didn't you? One more revolution and he's going to visit us."

Olaf smiled weakly. "Yeah, Commander, I meant to tell you. I'm fixing up the tree and—"

"Shut up!" The commander was breathing hard in a whistling sort of way. "Do you know what those Ossies have thought of?"

"No, Commander."

Pelham leaned across the table toward Olaf and shouted: "They want Santa Claus to visit *them!*"

Someone laughed and changed it quickly into a strangling cough at the commander's raging stare.

"And if Santa Claus doesn't visit them, the Ossies are going to quit work!" He repeated, "Quit cold—strike!"

There was no laughter, strangled or otherwise, after that. If there were more than one thought among the entire group, it didn't show itself. Olaf expressed that thought:

"But what about the quota?"

"Well, what about it?" snarled Pelham. "Do I have to draw pictures for you? Ganymedan Products has to get one hundred tons of wolframite, eighty tons of karen leaves and fifty tons of oxite every year, or it loses its franchise. I suppose there isn't anyone here who doesn't know that. It so happens that the current year ends in two Ganymedan revolutions, and we're five per cent behind schedule as it is."

There was pure, horrified silence.

"And now the Ossies won't work unless they get Santa Claus. No work, no quota, no franchise—no jobs! Get that, you low-grade morons. When the company loses it franchise, we lose the best-paying jobs in the System. Kiss them good-by, men, unless—"

He paused, glared steadily at Olaf, and added:

"Unless, by next revolution, we have a flying sleigh, eight reindeer and a Santa Claus. And by every cosmic speck in the rings of Saturn, we're going to have just that, especially a Santa!"

Ten faces turned ghastly pale.

"Got someone in mind, Commander?" asked someone in a voice that was three-quarters croak.

"Yes, as a matter of fact, I have."

He sprawled back in his chair. Olaf Johnson broke into a sudden sweat as he found himself staring at the end of a pointing forefinger.

"Aw, Commander!" he quavered.

The pointing finger never moved.

Pelham tramped into the foreroom, removed his oxygen nosepiece and the cold cylinders attached to it. One by one he cast off thick woolen outer garments and, with a final, weary sigh, jerked off a pair of heavy knee-high space boots.

Sim Pierce paused in his careful inspection of the latest batch of karen leaves and cast a hopeful glance over his spectacles.

"Well?" he asked.

Pelham shrugged. "I promised them Santa. What else could I do? I also doubled sugar rations, so they're back on the job—for the moment."

"You mean till the Santa we promised doesn't show up." Pierce straightened and waved a long karen leaf at the commander's face for emphasis. "This is the silliest thing I ever heard of. It can't be done. There ain't no Santa Claus!"

"Try telling that to the Ossies." Pelham slumped into a chair and his expression became stonily bleak. "What's Benson doing?"

"You mean that flying sleigh he says he can rig up?" Pierce held a leaf up to the light and peered at it critically. "He's a crackpot, if you ask me. The old buzzard went down to the sub-level this morning and he's been there ever since. All I know is that he's taken the spare lectro-dissociator apart. If anything happens to the regular, it just means that we're without oxygen."

"Well," Pelham rose heavily, "for my part I hope we *do* choke. It would be an easy way out of this whole mess. I'm going down below."

He stumped out and slammed the door behind him.

In the sub-level he gazed about in bewilderment, for the room was littered with gleaming chrome-steel machine parts. It took him some time to recognize the mess as the remains of what had been a compact, snugly built lectro-dissociator the day before. In the center, in anachronistic contrast, stood a dusty wooden sleigh atop rust-red runners. From beneath it came the sound of hammering.

"Hey, Benson!" called Pelham.

A grimy, sweat-streaked face pushed out from underneath the sleigh, and a stream of tobacco juice shot toward Benson's ever-present cuspidor.

"What are you shouting like that for?" he complained. "This is delicate work."

"What the devil is that weird contraption?" demanded Pelham.

"Flying sleigh. My own idea, too." The light of enthusiasm shone in Benson's watery eyes, and the quid in his mouth shifted from cheek to cheek as he spoke. "The sleigh was brought here in the old days, when they thought Ganymede was covered with snow like the other Jovian moons. All I have to do is fix a few gravo-repulsors from the dissociator to the bottom and that'll make it weightless when the current's on. Compressed air-jets will do the rest."

The commander chewed his lower lip dubiously.

"Will it work?"

"Sure it will. Lots of people have thought of using repulsors in air travel, but they're inefficient, especially in heavy gravity fields. Here on Ganymede, with a field of one-third gravity and a thin atmosphere, a child could run it. Even Johnson could run it, though I wouldn't mourn if he fell off and broke his blasted neck."

"All right, then, look here. We've got lots of this native purplewood. Get Charlie Finn and tell him to put that sleigh on a platform of it. He's to have it extend about twenty feet or more frontward, with a railing around the part that projects."

Benson spat and scowled through the stringy hair over his eyes.

"What's the idea, Commander?"

Pelham's laughter came in short, harsh barks.

"Those Ossies are expecting reindeer, and reindeer they're going to have. Those animals will have to stand on something, won't they?"

"Sure . . . But wait, hold on! There aren't any reindeer on Ganymede."

Commander Pelham paused on his way out. His eyes narrowed unpleasantly as they always did when he thought of Olaf Johnson.

"Olaf is out rounding up eight spinybacks for us. They've got four feet, a head on one end and a tail on the other. That's close enough for the Ossies."

The old engineer chewed this information and chuckled nastily.

"Good! I wish the fool joy of his job."

"So do I," gritted Pelham.

He stalked out as Benson, still leering, slid underneath the sleigh.

The commander's description of a spinyback was concise and accurate, but it left out several interesting details. For one thing, a spinyback has a long, mobile snout, two large ears that wave back and forth gently, and two emotional purple eyes. The males have pliable spines of a deep crimson color along the backbone that seem to delight the female of the species. Combine these with a scaly, muscular tail and a brain by no means mediocre, and you have a spinyback— or at least you have one if you can catch one.

It was just such a thought that occurred to Olaf Johnson as he sneaked down from the rocky eminence toward the herd of twenty-five spinybacks grazing on the sparse, gritty undergrowth. The nearest spinies looked up as Olaf, bundled in fur and grotesque with attached oxygen nosepiece, approached. However, spinies have no natural enemies, so they merely gazed at the figure with languidly disapproving eyes and returned to their crunchy but nourishing fare.

Olaf's notions on bagging big game were sketchy. He fumbled in his pocket for a lump of sugar, held it out and said:

"Here, pussy, pussy, pussy, pussy, pussy!"

The ears of the nearest spinie twitched in annoyance. Olaf came closer and held out the sugar again.

"Come, bossy! Come, bossy!"

The spinie caught sight of the sugar and rolled his eyes at it. His snout twitched as he spat out his last mouthful of vegetation and ambled over. With neck stretched out, he sniffed. Then, using a rapid, expert motion, he struck at the outheld palm and flipped the lump into his mouth. Olaf's other hand whistled down upon nothingness.

With a hurt expression, Olaf held out another piece.

"Here, Prince! Here, Fido!"

The spinie made a low, tremulous sound deep in his throat. It was a sound of pleasure. Evidently this strange monstrosity before him, having gone insane, intended to feed him these bits of concentrated succulence forever. He snatched and was back as quickly as the first time. But, since Olaf had held on firmly this time, the spinie almost bagged half a finger as well.

Olaf's yell lacked a bit of the nonchalance necessary at such times. Nevertheless, a bite that can be felt through thick gloves is a *bite!*

He advanced boldly upon the spinie. There are some things that stir the Johnson blood and bring up the ancient spirit of the Vikings. Having one's finger bitten, especially by an unearthly animal, is one of these.

There was an uncertain look in the spinie's eyes as he backed slowly away. There weren't any white cubes being offered any more and he wasn't quite sure what was going to happen now. The uncertainty vanished with a suddenness he did not expect, when two glove-muffled hands came down upon his ears and jerked. He let out a high-pitched yelp and charged forward.

A spinie has a certain sense of dignity. He doesn't like to have his ears pulled, particularly when other spinies, including several unattached females, have formed a ring and are looking on.

The Earthman went over backward and remained in that position for awhile. Meantime, the spinie backed away a few feet in a gentlemanly manner and allowed Johnson to get to his feet.

The old Viking blood frothed still higher in Olaf. After rubbing the hurt spot where he had landed on his oxygen cylinder, he jumped, forgetting to allow for Ganymedean gravity. He sailed five feet over the spinie's back.

There was awe in the animal's eye as he watched Olaf, for it was a stately jump. But there was a certain amount of bewilderment as well. There seemed to be no purpose to the maneuver.

Olaf landed on his back again and got the cylinder in the same place. He was beginning to feel a little embarrassed. The sounds that came from the circle of onlookers were remarkably like snickers.

"Laugh!" he muttered bitterly. "I haven't even begun to fight yet."

He approached the spinie slowly, cautiously. He circled, watching for his opening. So did the spinie. Olaf feinted and the spinie ducked. Then the spinie reared and Olaf ducked.

Olaf kept remembering new profanity all the time. The husky "Ur-r-r-r-r" that came out the spinie's throat seemed to lack the brotherly spirit that is usually associated with Christmas.

There was a sudden, swishing sound. Olaf felt something collide with his skull, just behind his left ear. This time he turned a back somersault and landed on the nape of his neck. There was a chorused whinny from the onlookers, and the spinie waved his tail triumphantly.

Olaf got rid of the impression that he was floating through a star-studded unlimited space and wavered to his feet.

"Listen," he objected, "using your tail is a foul!"

He leaped back as the tail shot forward again, then flung himself forward in a diving tackle. He grabbed at the spinie's feet and felt the animal come down on his back with an indignant yelp.

Now it was a case of Earth muscles against Ganymedan muscles, and Olaf became a man of brute strength. He struggled up, and the spinie found himself slung over the stranger's shoulders.

The spinie objected vociferously and tried to prove his objections by a judicious whip of the tail. But he was in an inconvenient position and the stroke whistled harmlessly over Olaf's head.

The other spinies made way for the Earthman with saddened expressions. Evidently they were all good friends of the captured animal and hated to see him lose a fight. They returned to their meal in philosophic resignation, plainly convinced that it was kismet.

On the other side of the rocky ledge, Olaf reached his prepared cave. There was the briefest of scrambling struggles before he managed to sit down hard on the spinie's head and put enough knots into rope to hold him there.

A few hours later, when he had corralled his eighth spinyback, he possessed the technique that comes of long practice. He could have given a Terrestrial cowboy valuable pointers on throwing a maverick. Also, he could have given a Terrestrial stevedore lessons in simple and compound swearing.

'Twas the night before Christmas—and all through the Ganymedan Dome there was deafening noise and bewildering excitement, like an exploding nova equipped for sound. Around the rusty sleigh, mounted on its huge platform of purplewood, five Earthmen were staging a battle royal with a spinie.

The spinie had definite views about most things, and one of his stubbornest and most definite views was that he would never go where he didn't want to go. He made that clear by flailing one head, one tail, three spines and four legs in every possible direction, with all possible force.

But the Earthmen insisted, and not gently. Despite loud, agonized squeaks, the spinie was lifted onto the platform, hauled into place and harnessed into hopeless helplessness.

"Okay!" Peter Benson yelled. "Pass the bottle."

Holding the spinie's snout with one hand, Benson waved the bottle under it with the other. The spinie quivered eagerly and whined tremulously. Benson poured some of the liquid down the animal's throat. There was a gurgling swallow and an appreciative whinny. The spinie's neck stretched out for more.

Benson sighed. "Our best brandy, too."

He up-ended the bottle and withdrew it half empty. The spinie, eyes whirling in their sockets rapidly, did what seemed an attempt at a gay jig. It didn't last long, however, for Ganymedan metabolism is almost immediately affected by alcohol. His muscles locked in a drunken rigor and, with a loud hiccup, he went out on his feet.

"Drag out the next!" yelled Benson.

In an hour the eight spinybacks were so many cataleptic statues. Forked sticks were tied around their heads as antlers. The effect was crude and sketchy, but it would do.

As Benson opened his mouth to ask where Olaf Johnson was, that worthy showed up in the arms of three comrades, and he was putting up a stiff a fight as any spinie. His objections, however, were highly articulate.

"I'm not going anywhere in this costume!" he roared, gouging at the nearest eye. "You hear me?"

There certainly was cause for objection. Even at his best, Olaf had never been a heart-throb. But in his present condition, he resembled a hybrid between a spinie's nightmare and a Picassian conception of a patriarch.

He wore the conventional costume of Santa. His clothes were as red as red tissue paper sewed onto his space coat could make it. The "ermine" was as white as cotton wool, which it was. His beard, more cotton wool glued into a linen foundation, hung loosely from his ears. With that below and his oxygen nosepiece above, even the strongest were forced to avert their eyes.

Olaf had not been shown a mirror. But, between what he could see of himself and what his instinct told him, he would have greeted a good, bright lightning bolt like a brother.

By fits and starts, he was hauled to the sleigh. Others pitched in to help, until Olaf was nothing but a smothered squirm and muffled voice.

"Leggo," he mumbled. "Leggo and come at me one by one. Come on!"

He tried to spar a bit, to point his dare. But the multiple grips upon him left him unable to wriggle a finger.

"Get in!" ordered Benson.

"You go to hell!" gasped Olaf. "I'm not getting into any patented short-cut to suicide, and you can take your bloody flying sleigh and—"

"Listen," interrupted Benson, "Commander Pelham is waiting for you at the other end. He'll skin you alive if you don't show up in half an hour."

"Commander Pelham can take the sleigh sideways and—"

"Then think of your job! Think of a hundred and fifty a

week. Think of every other year off with pay. Think of Hilda, back on Earth, who isn't going to marry you without a job. Think of all that!"

Johnson thought, snarled. He thought some more, got into the sleigh, strapped down his bag and turned on the gravorepulsors. With a horrible curse, he opened the rear jet.

The sleigh dashed forward and he caught himself from going backward, over and out of the sleigh, by two-thirds of a whisker. He held onto the sides thereafter, watching the surrounding hills as they rose and fell with each lurch of the unsteady sleigh.

As the wind rose, the undulations grew more marked. And when Jupiter came up, its yellow light brought out every jag and crag of the rocky ground, toward every one of which, in turn, the sleigh seemed headed. And by the time the giant planet had shoved completely over the horizon, the curse of drink—which departs from the Ganymedan organism just as quickly as it descends—began removing itself from the spinies.

The hindmost spinie came out of it first, tasted the inside of his mouth, winced and swore off drink. Having made that resolution, he took in his immediate surroundings languidly. They made no immediate impression on him. Only gradually was the fact forced upon him that his footing, whatever it was, was not the usual stable one of solid Ganymede. It swayed and shifted, which seemed very unusual.

Yet he might have attributed this unsteadiness to his recent orgy, had he not been so careless as to drop his glance over the railing to which he was anchored. No spinie ever died of heart-failure, as far as is recorded, but, looking downward, this one almost did.

His agonized screech of horror and despair brought the other spinies into full, if headachy, consciousness. For a while there was a confused blur of squawking conversation as the animals tried to get the pain out of their heads and the facts in. Both aims were achieved and a stampede was organized. It wasn't much of a stampede, because the spinies were anchored tightly. But, except for the fact that they got nowhere, they went through all the motions of a full gallop. And the sleigh went crazy.

Olaf grabbed his beard a second before it let go of his ears.

"Hey!" he shouted.

It was something like saying "Tut, tut" to a hurricane.

The sleigh kicked, bucked and did a hysterical tango. It made sudden spurts, as if inspired to dash its wooden brains out against Ganymede's crust. Meanwhile Olaf prayed, swore, wept and jiggled all the compressed air jets at once.

Ganymede whirled and Jupiter was a wild blur. Perhaps it was the spectacle of Jupiter doing the shimmy that steadied the spinies. More likely it was the fact that they just didn't give a hang any more. Whatever it was, they halted; made lofty farewell speeches to one another, confessed their sins and waited for death.

The sleigh steadied and Olaf resumed his breathing once more. Only to stop again as he viewed the curious spectacle of hills and solid ground up above, and black sky and swollen Jupiter down below.

It was at this point that he, too, made his peace with the eternal and awaited the end.

"Ossie" is short for ostrich, and that's what native Ganymedans look like, except that their necks are shorter, their heads are larger, and their feathers look as if they were about to fall out by the roots. To this, add a pair of scrawny, feathered arms with three stubby fingers apiece. They can speak English, but when you hear them, you wish they couldn't.

There were fifty of them in the low purplewood structure that was their "meeting hall." On the mound of raised dirt in the front of the room—dark with the smoky dimness of burning purplewood torches fetid to boot—sat Commander Scott Pelham and five of his men. Before them strutted the frowziest Ossie of them all, inflating his huge chest with rhythmic, booming sounds.

He stopped for a moment and pointed to a ragged hole in the ceiling.

"Look!" he squawked. "Chimney. We make. Sannycaws come in."

Pelham grunted approval. The Ossie clucked happily. He pointed to the little sacks of woven grass that hung from the walls.

"Look! Stockies. Sannycaws put presets!"

"Yeah," said Pelham unenthusiastically. "Chimney and stockings. Very nice." He spoke out of the corner of his mouth to Sim Pierce, who sat next to him: "Another half-hour in this dump will kill me. When is that fool coming?"

Pierce stirred uneasily.

"Listen," he said, "I've been doing some figuring. We're safe on everything but the karen leaves, and we're still four tons short on that. If we can get this fool business over with in the next hour, so we can start the next shift and work the Ossies at double, we can make it." He leaned back. "Yes, I think we can make it."

"Just about," replied Pelham gloomily. "That's if Johnson gets here without pulling another bloomer."

The Ossie was talking again, for Ossies like to talk. He said:

"Every year Kissmess comes, Kissmess nice, evvybody friendly. Ossie like Kissmess. You like Kissmess?"

"Yeah, fine," Pelham snarled politely. "Peace on Ganymede, good will toward men—especially Johnson. Where the devil is that idiot, anyhow?"

He fell into an annoyed fidget, while the Ossie jumped up and down a few times in a thoughtful sort of manner, evidently for the exercise of it. He continued the jumping, varying it with little hopping dance steps, till Pelham's fists began making strangling gestures. Only an excited squawk from the hole in the wall dignified by the term "window" kept Pelham from committing Ossie-slaughter.

Ossies swarmed about and the Earthmen fought for a view.

Against Jupiter's great yellowness was outlined a flying sleigh, complete with reindeer. It was only a tiny thing, but there was no doubt about it. Santa Claus was coming.

There was only one thing wrong with the picture. The sleigh, "reindeer" and all, while plunging ahead at a terrific speed, was flying upside down.

The Ossies dissolved into squawking cacophony.

"Sannycaws! Sannycaws! Sannycaws!"

They scrambled out the window like so many animated dust-mops gone mad. Pelham and his men used the low door.

The sleigh was approaching, growing larger, lurching from side to side and vibrating like an off-center flywheel. Olaf Johnson was a tiny figure holding on desperately to the side of the sleigh with both hands.

Pelham was shouting wildly, incoherently, choking on the thin atmosphere every time he forgot to breathe through his nose. Then he stopped and stared in horror. The sleigh, almost life-size now, was dipping down. If it had been an arrow shot by William Tell, it could not have aimed between Pelham's eyes more accurately.

"Everybody down!" he shrieked, and dropped.

The wind of the sleigh's passage whistled keenly and brushed his face. Olaf's voice could be heard for an instant, high-pitched and indistinct. Compressed air spurted, leaving tracks of condensing water vapor.

Pelham lay quivering, hugging Ganymede's frozen crust. Then, knees shaking like a Hawaiian hula-girl, he rose slowly. The Ossies who had scattered before the plunging vehicle had assembled again. Off in the distance, the sleigh was veering back.

Pelham watched as it swayed and hovered, still rotating. It lurched toward the dome, curved off to one side, turned back, and gathered speed.

Inside that sleigh, Olaf worked like a demon. Straddling his legs wide, he shifted his weight desperately. Sweating and cursing, trying hard not to look "downward" at Jupiter, he urged the sleigh into wilder and wilder swings. It was wobbling through an angle of 180 degrees now, and Olaf felt his stomach raise strenuous objections.

Holding his breath, he leaned hard with his right foot and felt the sleigh swing far over. At the extremity of that swing, he released the gravo-repulsor and, in Ganymede's weak gravity, the sleigh jerked downward. Naturally, since the vehicle was bottom-heavy due to the metal gravo-repulsor beneath, it righted itself as it fell.

But this was little comfort to Commander Pelham, who found himself once more in the direct path of the sleigh.

"Down!" he yelled, and dropped again.

The sleigh *whi-i-ished* overhead, came up against a huge boulder with a *crack*, bounced twenty-five feet into the air, came down with a *rush* and a *bang*, and Olaf fell over the railing and out.

Santa Claus had arrived.

With a deep, shuddering breath, Olaf swung his bag over his shoulders, adjusted his beard and patted one of the silently suffering spinies on the head. Death might be coming—in fact, Olaf could hardly wait—but he was going to die on his feet nobly, like a Johnson.

Inside the shack, into which the Ossies had once more swarmed, a *thump* announced the arrival of Santa's bag on the roof, and a second *thud* the arrival of Santa himself. A ghastly face appeared through the makeshift hole in the ceiling.

"Merry Christmas!" it croaked, and tumbled through.

Olaf landed on his oxygen cylinders, as usual, and got them in the usual place.

The Ossies jumped up and down like rubber balls with the itch.

Olaf limped heavily toward the first stocking and deposited the garishly colored sphere he withdrew from his bag, one of the many that had originally been intended as a Christmas tree ornament. One by one he deposited the rest in every available stocking.

Having completed his job, he dropped into an exhausted squat, from which position he watched subsequent proceedings with a glazed and fishy eye. The jolliness and belly-shaking good humor, traditionally characteristic of Santa Claus, were absent from this one with remarkable thoroughness.

The Ossies made up for it by their wild ecstasy. Until Olaf had deposited the last globe, they had kept their silence and seats. But when he had finished, the air heaved and writhed under the stresses of the discordant screeches that arose. In half a second the hand of each Ossie contained a globe.

They chattered among themselves furiously, handling the globes carefully and hugging them close to their chests. Then they compared one with another, flocking about to gaze at particularly good ones.

The frowziest Ossie approached Pelham and plucked at the commander's sleeve. "Sannycaws good," he cackled. "Look, he leave eggs!" He stared reverently at his sphere and said: "Pittier'n Ossie eggs. Must be Sannycaws eggs, huh?"

His skinny finger punched Pelham in the stomach.

"No!" yowled Pelham vehemently. "Hell, no!"

But the Ossie wasn't listening. He plunged the globe deep into the warmth of his feathers and said:

"Pitty colors. How long take for little Sannycaws come out? And what little Sannycaws eat?" He looked up. "We take good care. We teach little Sannycaws, make him smart and full of brain like Ossie."

Pierce grabbed Commander Pelham's arm.

"Don't argue with them," he whispered frantically. "What do you care if they think those are Santa Claus eggs? Come on! If we work like maniacs, we can still make the quota. Let's get started."

"That's right," Pelham admitted. He turned to the Ossie. "Tell everyone to get going." He spoke clearly and loudly. "Work now. Do you understand? Hurry, hurry, hurry! Come on!"

He motioned with his arms. But the frowzy Ossie had come to a sudden halt. He said slowly:

"We work, but Johnson say Kissmess come evvy.year."

"Isn't one Christmas enough for you?" Pelham rasped.

"No!" squawked the Ossie. "We want Sannycaws next year. Get more eggs. And next year more eggs. And next year. And next year, and next year. More eggs. More little Sannycaws eggs. If Sannycaws not come, we not work."

"That's a long time off," said Pelham. "We'll talk about it then. By that time I'll either have gone completely crazy, or you'll have forgotten all about it."

Pierce opened his mouth, closed it, opened his mouth, closed it, opened it, and finally managed to speak.

"Commander, they want him to come every year."

"I know. They won't remember by next year, though."

"But you don't get it. A year to them is one Ganymedan revolution around Jupiter. In Earth time, that's seven days and three hours. They want Santa Claus to come every *week*."

"Every week!" Pelham gulped. "Johnson told them—"

For a moment everything turned sparkling somersaults before his eyes. He choked, and automatically his eye sought Olaf.

Olaf turned cold to the marrow of his bones and rose to his feet apprehensively, sidling toward the door. There he stopped as a sudden recollection of tradition hit him. Beard a-dangle, he croaked:

"Merry Christmas to all, and to all a good night!"

He made for the sleigh as if all the imps of Hades were after him. The imps weren't, but Commander Scott Pelham was.

THE END

In January of 1941 (the month in which I attained my majority), I undertook something new—a collaboration.

Fred Pohl, after all, was not merely an editor. He was also a budding writer. He has since come to be a giant in the field, but in those early days he was struggling along with only the sort of meager success I was having. Alone, and in collaboration with other Futurians, he turned out stories under a variety of pseudonyms. The one he used most frequently was "James MacCreigh."

As it happened, he had written, under that pseudonym, a small fantasy called "The Little Man on the Subway," which he apparently had hopes for but couldn't get right. He asked me if I would rewrite it, and the request flattered me. Besides, I was still trying to get into **Unknown,** and if I couldn't do it on my own, maybe I could do it by way of a collaboration. I wasn't proud—at least as far as fantasy was concerned.

I took on the task and did it virtually at a sitting. Doing it easily didn't help, however. I submitted it to Campbell for **Unknown** on January 27, 1941, and he rejected it. I had to hand it back to Pohl.

Pohl, however, with the true agent's soul, never gave up, and in 1950, long after I had utterly forgotten it, he managed to place it with a small magazine called **Fantasy Book.**

15

The Little Man on the Subway
(with James MacCreigh)

Subway stations are places where people usually get out, so when no one left the first car at Atlantic Avenue station, Conductor Cullen of the I.R.T. began to get worried. In fact, no one had left the first car from the time the run to Flatbush had begun—though dozens were getting on all the time.

Odd! Very odd! It was the kind of proposition that made

Fantasy Book. Volume 1, Number 6
Copyright © 1950 by Fantasy Publishing Company, Inc.

well-bred conductors remove their caps and scratch their heads. Conductor Cullen did so. It didn't help, but he repeated the process at Bergen Street, the next station, where again the first car lost not one of its population. And at Grand Army Plaza, he added to the headscratching process a few rare old Gaelic words that had passed down from father to son for hundreds of years. They ionized the surrounding atmosphere, but otherwise did not affect the situation.

At Eastern Parkway, Cullen tried an experiment. He carefully refrained from opening the first car's doors at all. He leaned forward eagerly, twisted his head and watched—and was treated to nothing short of a miracle. The New York subway rider is neither shy, meek, nor modest, and doors that do not open immediately or sooner are helped on their way by sundry kicks. But this time there was not a kick, not a shriek, not even a modified yell. Cullen's eyes popped.

He was getting angry. At Franklin Avenue, where he again contacted the Express, he flung open the doors and swore at the crowd. Every door spouted commuters of both sexes and all ages, except that terrible first car. At those doors, three men and a very young girl got on, though Cullen could plainly see the slight bulging of the walls that the already supercrowded condition of the car had caused.

For the rest of the trip to Flatbush Avenue, Cullen ignored the first car completely, concentrating on that last stop where everyone would *have* to get off. Everyone! President, Church, and Beverly Road were visited and passed, and Cullen found himself counting the stations to the Flatbush terminus.

They seemed like such a nice bunch of passengers, too. They read their newspapers, stared into the whirling blackness out the window, or at the girl's legs across the way, or at nothing at all, quite like ordinary people. Only, they didn't want to get out. They didn't even want to get into the next car, where empty seats filled the place. Imagine New Yorkers resisting the impulse to pass from one car to the other, and missing the chance to leave the doors open for the benefit of the draft.

But it was Flatbush Avenue! Cullen rubbed his hands, slammed the doors open and yelled in his best unintelligible manner, "Lasstop!" He repeated it two or three times hoarsely and several in that damned first car looked up at him. There was reproach in their eyes. Have you never heard of the Mayor's anti-noise campaign, they seemed to say.

The last other passenger had come out of the train, and the scattered new ones were coming in. There were a few curious looks at the jammed car, but not too many. The New Yorker considers everything he cannot understand a publicity stunt.

Cullen fell back on his Gaelic once more and dashed up the platform toward the motorman's booth. He needed moral assistance. The motorman should have been out of his cab, preparing for his next trip, but he wasn't. Cullen could see him through the glass of the door, leaning on the controls and staring vacantly at the bumper-stop ahead.

"Gus!" cried Cullen. "Come out! There's a hell of—"

At this point, his tongue skidded to a halt, because it wasn't Gus. It was a little old man, who smiled politely and twiddled his fingers in greeting.

Patrick Cullen's Irish soul rebelled. With a yelp, he grabbed the edge of the door and tried to shove it open. He should have known that wouldn't work. So, taking a deep breath and commending said Irish soul to God, he made for the open door and ploughed into the mass of haunted humans in that first car. Momentum carried him six feet, and then there he stuck. Behind him, those he had knocked down picked themselves up from the laps of their fellow-travelers, apologized with true New York courtesy (consisting of a growl, a grunt, and a grimace) and returned to their papers.

Then, caught helplessly, he heard the Dispatcher's bell. It was time for his own train to be on its way. Duty called! With a superhuman effort, he inched towards the door, but it closed before he could get there, and the train commenced to move.

It occurred to Cullen that he had missed a report for the first time, and he said, "Damn!" After the train had travelled some fifty feet, it came to him that they were going the wrong way, and this time he said nothing.

After all, what was there to say—even in the purest of Gaelic.

How *could* a train go the wrong way at Flatbush Ave. There were no further tracks. There was no further tunnel. There was a bumper-stop to prevent eccentric motormen from trying to bore one. It was absurd. Even the Big Deal couldn't do it.

But there they were!

There were stations in this new tunnel, too,—cute little small ones just large enough for one car. But that was all right, because only one car was travelling. The rest had somehow become detached, presumably to make the routine trip to Bronx Park.

There were maybe a dozen stations on the line—with curious names. Cullen noticed only a few, because he found it difficult to keep his eyes from going out of focus. One was Archangel Boulevard; another Seraph Road; still another Cherub Plaza.

And then, the train slid into a monster station, that looked uncommonly like a cave, and stopped. It was huge, about three hundred feet deep, and almost spherical. The tracks ran to the exact center, without trusses, and the platform at its side likewise rested comfortably upon air.

The conductor was the only person left in the car, the rest having mostly gotten off at Hosannah Square. He hung limply from the porcelain hand-grip, staring fixedly at a lipstick advertisement. The door of the motorman's cabin opened and the little man came out. He glanced at Cullen, turned away, then whirled back.

"Hey," he said, "who are you?"

Cullen rotated slowly, still clutching the hand-grip. "Only the conductor. Don't mind me. I'm quitting anyway. I don't like the work."

"Oh, dear, dear, this is unexpected." The little man waggled his head and tch-tched. "I'm Mr. Crumley," he explained. "I steal things. People mostly. Sometimes subway cars,—but they're such big, clumsy things, don't you think?"

"Mister," groaned Cullen. "I quit thinking two hours ago. It didn't get me anywhere. Who are you, anyway?"

"I told you—I'm Mr. Crumley. I'm practicing to be a god."

"A gob?" said Cullen. "You mean a sailor?"

"Dear, no," frowned Mr. Crumley. "I said, 'god,' as in Jehovah. Look!" He pointed out the window to the wall of the cave. Where his finger pointed, the rock billowed and rose. He moved his finger and there was a neat ridge of rock describing a reversed, lower case "h."

"That's my symbol," said Crumley modestly. "Mystic, isn't it? But that's nothing. Wait till I really get things organized. Dear, dear, will I give them miracles!"

Cullen's head swivelled between the raised-rock symbol and the simpering Mr. Crumley, until he began to get dizzy, and then he stopped.

"Listen," he demanded hoarsely. "How did you get that

car out of Flatbush Avenue? Where did that tunnel come from? Are some of them foreigners—"

"Oh, my, no!" answered Mr. Crumley. "I made that myself and willed it so that no one would notice. It was quite difficult. It just wears the ectoplasm right out of me. Miracles with people mixed up in it are much harder than the other kind, because you have to fight their wills. Unless you have lots of Believers, you can't do it. Now that I've got over a hundred thousand, I can do it, but there was a time," he shook his head reminiscently, "when I couldn't even have levitated a baby—or healed a leper. Oh, well, we're wasting time. We ought to be at the nearest factory."

Cullen brightened. Factory was more prosaic. "I once had a brother," he said, "who worked in a sweater factory, but—"

"Oh, goodness, Mr. Cullen. I'm referring to my Believers' Factories. I have to educate people to believe in me, don't I, and preaching is such slow work. I believe in mass production. Some day I intend to be called the Henry Ford of Utopia. Why, I've got twelve Factories in Brooklyn alone and when I manufacture enough Believers, I'll just cover the world with them."

He sighed, "Gracious me, if I only had enough Believers. I've got to have a million before I can let things progress by themselves and until then I have to attend to every little detail myself. It is so boring! I even have to keep reminding my Believers who I am—even the Disciples. Incidentally, Cullen, —I read your mind, by the way, so that's how I know your name—you want to be a Believer, of course."

"Well, now," said Cullen nervously.

"Oh, come now. *Some* gods would have been angry at your intrusion and done away with you," he snapped his fingers, "like that. Not I, though, because I think killing people is messy and inconsiderate. Just the same, you'll have to be a Believer."

Now Patrick Cullen was an intelligent Irishman. That is to say, he admitted the existence of banshees, leprechauns, and the Little Folk, and kept an open mind on poltergeists, werewolves, vampires and such-like foreign trash. At mere supernaturalities, he was too well-educated to sneer. Still, Cullen did not intend to compromise his religion. His theology was weak, but for a mortal to claim godship smacked of heresy, not to say sacrilege and blasphemy, even to him.

"You're a faker," he cried boldly, "and you're headed

straight for Hell the way you're going."

Mr. Crumley clicked his tongue, "What terrible language you use. And so unnecessary! Of course you Believe in me."

"Oh, yeah?"

"Well, then, if you are stubborn, I'll pass a minor miracle. It's inconvenient, but now," he made vague motions with his left hand, "you Believe in me."

"Certainly," said Cullen, hurt. "I always did. How do I go about worshipping you? I want to do this properly."

"Just Believe in me, and that's enough. Now you must go to the factories and then we'll send you back home—they'll never know you were gone—and you can live your life like a Believer."

The conductor smiled ecstatically, "Oh, happy life! I *want* to go to the factories."

"Of course you would," replied Mr. Crumley. "You'd be a fine Crumleyite otherwise, wouldn't you? Come!" He pointed at the door of the car, and the door slid open. They walked out and Crumley kept on pointing. Rock faded away in front, and bit down again behind. Through the wall Cullen walked, following that little figure who was his god.

That *was* a god, thought Cullen. Any god that could do that was one hell of a damn good god to believe in.

And then he was at the factory—in another cave, only smaller. Mr. Crumley seemed to like caves.

Cullen didn't pay much attention to his surroundings. He couldn't see much anyway on account of the faint violet mist that blurred his vision. He got the impression of a slowly-moving conveyor belt, with men stationed at intervals along it. Disciples, he thought. And the parts being machined on that belt were probably non-Believers, or such low trash.

There was a man watching him, smiling. A Disciple, Cullen thought, and quite naturally made the sign to him. He had never made it before, but it was easy. The Disciple replied in kind.

"He told me you were coming," said the Disciple. "He made a special miracle for you, he said. That's quite a distinction. Do you want me to show you around the belt?"

"You bet."

"Well, this is Factory One. It's the nerve center of all the factories of the country. The others give preliminary treatment only; and make only Believers. *We* make Disciples."

Oh, boy, Disciples! "Am I going to be a Disciple?" asked Cullen eagerly.

"After being miraculated by *him*, of course! You're a *somebody*, you know. There are only five other people he ever took personal charge of."

This was a glorious way to do things. Everything Mr. Crumley did was glorious. What a god! What a god!

"You started that way, too."

"Certainly," said the Disciple, placidly, "I'm an important fellow, too. Only I wish I were more important, even."

"What for?" said Cullen, in a shocked tone of voice. "Are you murmuring against the dictates of Mr. Crumley? (may he prosper). This is sacrilege."

The Disciple shifted uncomfortably, "Well, I've got ideas, and I'd like to try them out."

"You've got ideas, huh?" muttered Cullen balefully. "Does Mr. Crumley (may he live forever) know?"

"Well—frankly, no! But just the same," the Disciple looked over each shoulder carefully and drew closer, "I'm not the only one. There are lots of us that think Mr. Crumley (on whom be blessings) is just a trifle old-fashioned. For instance, take the lights in this place."

Cullen stared upwards. The lights were the same type as those in the terminal-cave. They might have been stolen from any line of the IRT subway. Perfect copies of the stop-and-go signals and the exit markers.

"What's wrong?" he asked.

The Disciple sneered, "They lack originality. You'd think a grade A god would do something new. When he takes people, he does it through the subway, and he obeys subway rules. He waits for the Dispatcher to tell him to go; he stops at every station; he uses crude electricity and so on. What we need," the Disciple was waving his hands wildly and shouting, "is more enterprise, more git-and-go. We've got to speed up things and run them with efficiency and vim."

Cullen stared hotly, "You are a heretic," he accused. "You are doomed to damnation." He looked angrily about for a bell, whistle, gong, or drum wherewith to summon the great Crumley, but found nothing.

The other blinked in quick thought. "Say," he said, bluffly, "look at what time it is. I'm behind schedule. You better get on the belt for your first treatment.

Cullen was hot about the slovenly assistance Mr. Crumley was getting from this inferior Disciple, but a treatment is a treatment, so making the sign devoutly, he got on. He found it fairly comfortable despite its jerky motion. The Disciple motioned to Cullen's first preceptor—another Disciple—standing beside a sort of blackboard. Cullen had watched others while discussing Crumley and he had noticed the question and answer procedure that had taken place. He had noticed it particularly.

Consequently, he was surprised, when the second Disciple, instead of using his heavy pointer to indicate a question on the board, reversed it and brought it down upon his head.

The lights went out!

When he came to, he was under the belt, at the very bottom of the cave. He was tied up, and the Rebellious Disciple and three others were talking about him.

"He couldn't be persuaded," the Disciple was saying. "Crumley must have given him a double treatment or something."

"It's the last double treatment Crumley'll ever give," said the fat little man.

"Let's hope so. How's it coming?"

"Very well. Very well, indeed. We teleported ourselves to Section Four about two hours ago. It was a perfect miracle."

The Disciple was pleased. "Fine! How're they doing at Four?"

The fat little man clucked his lips. "Well, now, not so hot. For some reason, they're getting odd effects over there. Miracles are just happening. Even ordinary Crumleyites can pass them, and sometimes they—just happen. It's extremely annoying."

"Hmm, that's bad. If there are too many hitches, Crumley'll get suspicious. If he investigates there first, he can reconvert all of them in a jiffy, before he comes here and then without their support we might not be strong enough to stand up against him."

"Say, now," said the fat man apprehensively, "we're not strong enough *now,* you know. None of this going off half-cocked."

"We're strong enough," pointed out the Disciple stiffly, "to weaken him long enough to get us a new god started, and after that—"

"A new god, eh?" said another. He nodded wisely.

"Sure," said the Disciple. "A new god, created by us, can be destroyed by us. He'd be completely under our thumb and then instead of this one-man tyranny, we can have a sort of—er—council."

There were general grins and everyone looked pleased.

"But we'll discuss that further some other time," continued the Disciple briskly. "Let's Believe just a bit. Crumley isn't stupid, you know, and we don't want him to observe any slackening. Come on, now. All together."

They closed their eyes, concentrated a bit, and then opened them with a sigh.

"Well," said the little, fat man, "*that's* over. I'd better be getting back now."

From under the belt, Cullen watched him. He looked singularly like a chicken about to take off for a tree as he flexed his knees and stared upwards. Then he added to the resemblance not a little when he spread his arms, gave a little hop and fluttered away.

Cullen could follow his flight only by watching the eyes of the three remaining. Those eyes turned up and up, following the fat man to the very top of the cave, it seemed. There was an air of self-satisfaction about those eyes. They were very happy over their miracles.

Then they all went away and left Cullen to his holy indignation. He was shocked to the very core of his being at this sinful rebellion, this apostasy—this—this— There weren't any words for it, even when he tried Gaelic.

Imagine trying to create a god that would be under the thumbs of the creators. It was anthropomorphic heresy (where had he heard that word, now?) and struck at the roots of all religion. Was he going to lie there and watch anything strike at the roots of all religion? Was he going to submit to having Mr. Crumley (may be swim through seas of ecstasy) deposed?

Never!

But the ropes thought otherwise, so there he stayed.

And then there was an interruption in his thoughts. There came a low, booming sound—a sound which would have been a voice if it had not been pitched so incredibly low. There was a menace to it that got immediate attention. It got attention from Cullen, who quivered in his bonds; from the others in the cave, who quivered even harder, not being restrained by ropes; from the belt itself, which stopped dead with a jerk, and quivered mightily.

The Rebellious Disciple dropped to his knees and quivered more than any of them.

The voice came again, this time in a recognizable language, "WHERE IS THAT BUM, CRUMLEY?" it roared.

There was no wait for an answer. A cloud of shadow gathered in the center of the hall and spat a black bolt at the belt. A spot of fire leaped out from where the bolt had touched and spread slowly outward. Where it passed, the belt ceased to exist. It was far from Cullen, but there were humans nearer, and among those scurrying pandemonium existed.

Cullen wanted very much to join the flight, but unfortunately the Disciple who had trussed him up had evidently been a Boy Scout. Jerking, twisting, and writhing had no effect upon the stubborn ropes, so he fell back upon Gaelic and wishing. He wished he were free. He wished he weren't tied. He wished he were far away from that devouring flame. He wished lots of things, some unprintable, but mainly those.

And with that he felt a gentle slipping pressure and down at his feet was an untidy pile of hempen fibre. Evidently the forces liberated by the rebellion were getting out of control here as well as in Section Four. What had the little fat man said? "Miracles are just happening. Even ordinary Crumleyites can pass them, and sometimes they—just happen."

But why waste time? He ran to the rock wall and howled a wish at it to dissolve into nothing. He howled several times, with Gaelic modifications, but the wall didn't even slightly soften. He stared wildly and then saw the hole. It was on the side of the cave, diametrically across from Cullen's position at the bottom of the hall, and about three loops of the belt up. The upward spiral passed just below it.

Somehow he made the leap that grabbed the lower lip of the spiral, wriggled his way onto it and jumped into a run. The fire of disintegration was behind him and plenty far away, but it was making time. Up the belt to the third loop he ran, not taking time to be dizzy from the circular trip. But when he got there, the hole, large, black and inviting, was just the tiniest bit higher than he could jump.

He leaned against the wall panting. The spot of fire was now two spots, crawling both ways from a twenty foot break in the belt. Everyone in the cavern, some two hundred people, was in motion, and everyone made some sort of noise.

Somehow, the sight stimulated him. It nerved him to further efforts to get into the hole. Wildly, he tried walking up the sheer wall, but this didn't work.

And then Mr. Crumley stuck his head out of the hole and said, "Oh, mercy me, what a perfectly terrible mess. Dear, dear! Come up here, Cullen! Why do you stay down there!"

A great peace descended upon Cullen. "Hail, Mr. Crumley," he cried. "May you sniff the essence of roses forever."

Mr. Crumley looked pleased, "Thank you, Cullen." He waved his hand, and the conductor was beside him—a simple matter of levitation. Once again, Cullen decided in his inmost soul that here was a *god*.

"And now," said Mr. Crumley, "we must hurry, hurry, hurry. I've lost most of my power when the Disciples rebelled, and my subway car is stuck half-way. I'll need your help. Hurry!"

Cullen had no time to admire the tiny subway at the end of the tunnel. He jumped off the platform on Crumley's heels and dashed about a hundred feet down the tube to where the car was standing idle. He wafted into the open front door with the grace of a chorus-boy. Mr. Crumley took care of that.

"Cullen," said Mr. Crumley, "start this thing and take it back to the regular line. And be careful; *he* is waiting for me."

"Who?"

"He, the new god. Imagine those fools—no, idiots—thinking they could create a controllable god, when the very essence of godship is uncontrollability. Of course, when they made a god to destroy me, they made a Destroyer, and he'll just destroy everything in sight that I created, including my Disciples."

Cullen worked quickly. He knew how to start car 30990; any conductor would. He raced to the other end of the car for the control lever, snatched it off, and returned at top speed. That was all he needed. There was power in the rail; the lights were on; and there were no stop signals between him and God's Country.

Mr. Crumley lay himself down on a seat, "Be very quiet. *He* may let you get past him. I'm going to blank myself out, and maybe he won't notice me. At any rate, he won't harm you—I *hope*. Dear, dear, since this all started in section four, things are *such* a mess."

Eight stations passed before anything happened and then came Utopia Circle station and—well, nothing really *happened*. It was just an impression—an impression of people all around him for a few seconds watching him closely with a virulent hostility. It wasn't exactly people, but a person. It wasn't exactly a person either, but just a huge eye, watching—watching—watching.

But it passed, and almost immediately Cullen saw a black

and white "Flatbush Avenue" sign at the side of the tunnel. He jammed on his brakes in a hurry, for there was a train waiting there. But the controls didn't work the way they should have, and the car edged up until it was in contact with the cars before. With a soft click, it coupled and 30990 was just the last car of the train.

It was Mr. Crumley's work, of course. Mr. Crumley stood behind him, watching. "He didn't get you, did he? No—I see he didn't."

"Is there any more danger?" asked Cullen, anxiously.

"I don't think so," responded Mr. Crumley sadly. "After he has destroyed all my creation, there will be nothing left for him to destroy, and, deprived of a function, he will simply cease to exist. That's the result of this nasty, slipshod work. I'm disgusted with human beings."

"Don't say that," said Cullen.

"I will," reported Mr. Crumley savagely, "Human beings aren't fit to be god of. They're too much trouble and worry. It would give any self-respecting god grey hairs and I suppose you think a god looks very dignified all grey. Darn all humans! They can get along without me. From now on, I'm going to go to Africa and try the chimpanzees. I'll bet they make *much* better material."

"But wait," wailed Cullen. "What about me? I *believe* in you."

"Oh, dear, that would never do. Here! Return to normal."

Mr. Crumley's hand caressed the air, and Cullen, once more a God-fearing Irishman, let loose a roar in the purest Gaelic and made for him.

"Why, you blaspheming spalpeen—"

But there was no Mr. Crumley. There was only the Dispatcher, asking very impolitely—in· English—what the blankety-blank hell was the matter with him.

THE END

I am sorry to say that I have no clear memory, at this time, what parts of the story are mine and what parts are Pohl's. Going over it, I can say, "This part sounds like me, this part doesn't," but whether I'd be right or not I couldn't swear.

Fantasy Book was a very borderline publication that lasted only eight issues. "The Little Man on the Subway" was in the sixth.

An amusing fact about this issue of a small magazine that had to make do with what it could find among the rejects of the field was that it included "Scanners Live in Vain," by Cordwainer Smith. This was Smith's first published story and he was not to publish another for eight years or so. In the 1960s, Smith (a pseudonym for a man whose real identity was not made clear until after his death) became a writer of considerable importance, and this first story of his became a classic.

While working on "The Little Man on the Subway" I was also doing another "positronic robot" story, called "Liar!" In this one, my character Susan Calvin first appeared (she has been a character in ten of my stories up to the present time and I don't eliminate the possibility that she will appear yet again).

It was while Campbell and I were discussing this story, by the way, on December 16, 1940, that the "Three Laws of Robotics" were worked out in full. (I say it was Campbell who worked them out and he says it was I—but I know I'm right. It was he.)

"Liar!" was accepted at once by Campbell, at the end of January, without revision, and appeared in the May 1941 issue of **Astounding**. It was my fourth appearance in that magazine. The fact that it appeared the month after "Reason" helped fix the "positronic robot" stories in the readers' minds as a "series." "Liar!" eventually appeared in **I, Robot**.

The sale of two "positronic robot" stories, "Reason" and "Liar!" virtually back to back put me all on fire to do more of the same. When I suggested still another story of the sort to Campbell on February 3, 1941, he approved, but he said he didn't want me, this early in the game, tying myself down too completely into a rigid formula. He suggested I do other kinds of stories first. I was a good boy; I obeyed.

On that very day, in fact, I decided to try fantasy again. I wrote a short one (1,500 words) called "Masks," and

heaven only knows what it was about for I don't. I submitted
it to Campbell for **Unknown** on February 10, and he rejected
it. It is gone; it no longer exists.

Later that month I also wrote a short story called "The
Hazing," intended for Pohl. I submitted it to him on February
24, and he rejected it at once. Eventually I submitted it to
Thrilling Wonder Stories. They requested a revision, I obliged,
and they accepted it on July 29, 1941.

16

The Hazing

The Campus of Arcturus University, on Arcturus's second
planet, Eron, is a dull place during mid-year vacations and,
moreover, a hot one, so that Myron Tubal, sophomore, found
life boring and uncomfortable. For the fifth time that day,
he looked in at the Undergraduate Lounge in a desperate
attempt at locating an acquaintance, and was at last gratified
to behold Bill Sefan, a green-skinned youngster from Vega's
fifth planet.

Sefna, like Tubal, had flunked Biosociology and was staying
through vacation to study for a make-up exam. Things like
that weave strong bonds between sophomore and sophomore.

Tubal grunted a greeting, dropped his huge hairless body
—he was a native of the Arcturian System itself—into the
largest chair and said:

"Have you seen the new freshmen yet?"

"Already! It's six weeks before the fall semester starts!"

Tubal yawned. "These are a special breed of frosh. They're
the very first batch from the Solarian System—ten of them."

"Solarian System? You mean that new system that joined

Thrilling Wonder Stories, October 1942
Copyright © 1942 by Better Publications, Inc.
Copyright renewed © 1969 by Isaac Asimov

the Galactic Federation three—four years ago?"

"That's the one. Their world capital is called Earth, I think."

"Well, what about them?"

"Nothing much. They're just here, that's all. Some of them have hair on the upper lip, and very silly it looks, too. Otherwise, they look like any of a dozen or so other breeds of Humanoids."

It was at this point that the door flew open and little Wri Forase ran in. He was from Deneb's single planet, and the short, gray fuzz that covered his head and face bristled with agitation, while his large purple eyes gleamed excitedly.

"Say," he twittered breathlessly, "have you seen the Earthmen?"

Sefan sighed. "Isn't anyone ever going to change the subject? Tubal was just telling me about them."

"He was?" Forase seemed disappointed. "But—but did he tell you these were that abnormal race they made such a fuss over when the Solarian System entered the Federation?"

"They looked all right to me," said Tubal.

"I'm not talking about them from the physical standpoint," said the Denebian disgustedly. "It's the mental aspect of the case. Psychology! That's the stuff!" Forase was going to be a psychologist some day.

"Oh, that! Well, what's wrong with them?"

"Their mob psychology as a race is all wrong," babbled Forase. "Instead of becoming less emotional with numbers, as is the case with every other type of Humanoid known, they become *more* emotional! In groups, these Earthmen riot, panic, go crazy. The more there are, the worse it is. So help me, we even invented a new mathematical notation to handle the problem. Look!"

He had his pocket-pad and stylus out in one rapid motion; but Tubal's hand clamped down upon them before the stylus so much as made a mark.

Tubal said, "Whoa! I've got a walloping lulu of an idea."

"Imagine!" murmured Sefan.

Tubal ignored him. He smiled again, and his hand rubbed thoughtfully over his bald dome.

"Listen," he said, with sudden briskness. His voice dropped to a conspiratorial whisper.

Albert Williams, late of Earth, stirred in his sleep and became conscious of a prodding finger exploring the space between his second and third ribs. He opened his eyes, swiveled his head, stared stupidly; then gasped, shot upright, and reached for the light switch.

"Don't move," said the shadowy figure beside his bed. There was a muted click, and the Earthman found himself centered in the pearly beam of a pocket flash.

He blinked and said, "Who the blasted devil are you?"

"You are going to get out of bed," replied the apparition stolidly. "Dress, and come with me."

Williams grinned savagely. "Try and make me."

There was no answer, but the flash beam shifted slightly and fell upon the shadow's other hand. It held a "neuronic whip," that pleasant little weapon that paralyzes the vocal cords and twists nerves into so many knots of agony. Williams swallowed hard, and got out of bed.

He dressed in silence, and then said:

"All right, what do I do now?"

The gleaming "whip" gestured, and the Earthman moved toward the door.

"Just walk ahead," said the unknown.

Williams moved out of the room, along the silent corridor, and down eight stories without daring to look back. Out upon the campus he stopped, and felt metal probe the small of his back.

"Do you know where Obel Hall is?"

Williams, nodding, began walking. He walked past Obel Hall, turned right at University Avenue, and after half a mile stepped off the roads and past the trees. A spaceship hulked dimly in the darkness, with ports closely curtained and only a dim light showing where the airlock opened a crack.

"Get in!" He was shoved up a flight of stairs and into a small room.

He blinked, looked about him and counted aloud.

"—seven, eight, nine, and I make ten. They've got us all, I guess."

"It's no guess," growled Eric Chamberlain sourly. "It's a certainty." He was rubbing his hand. "I've been here an hour."

"What's wrong with the mitt?" asked Williams.

"I sprained it on the jaw of the rat that brought me here. He's as tough as a spaceship's hull."

Williams seated himself cross-legged upon the floor and rested his head against the wall.

"Has anyone any idea as to what this is all about?"

"Kidnaping!" said little Joey Sweeney. His teeth were chattering.

"What the devil for?" snorted Chamberlain. "If any of us are millionaires, I hadn't heard of it. I know I'm not!"

Williams said, "Look, let's not go off the deep end. Kidnaping or anything of that sort is out. These people can't be criminals. It stands to reason that a civilization that has developed psychology to the extent this Galactic Federation has, would be able to wipe out crime without raising a sweat."

"Pirates," grunted Lawrence Marsh. "I don't think so, but it's just a suggestion."

"Nuts!" said Williams. "Piracy is a frontier phenomenon. This region of space has been civilized for tens of millennia."

"Just the same, they had guns," insisted Joe, "and I don't like it." He had left his glasses in his room and peered about in near-sighted anxiety.

"That doesn't mean much," answered Williams. "Now, I've been thinking. Here we are—ten newly arrived freshmen at Arcturus U. On our first night here, we're bundled mysteriously out of our rooms and into a strange spaceship. That suggests something to me. How about it?"

Sidney Morton raised his head from his arms long enough to say sleepily:

"I've thought of it, too. It looks like we're in for one hell of a hazing. Gents, I think the local sophs are just having good, clean fun."

"Exactly," agreed Williams. "Anyone have any other ideas?"

Silence. "All right, then, so there isn't anything to do but wait. Personally, I'm going to catch up on my sleep. They can wake me up if they need me."

There was a jar at that moment and he fell off balance.

"Well, we're off—wherever we're going."

Moments later, Bill Sefan hesitated just an instant before entering the control room. When he finally did, it was to face a highly excited Wri Forase.

"How is it working?" demanded the Denebian.

"Rotten," responded Sefan sourly. "If they're panicked, then I'm damned. They're going to sleep."

"Asleep! All of them? But what were they saying?"

"How do I know? They weren't speaking Galactic, and I can't make head or tail out of their infernal foreign gibberish."

Forase threw his hands into the air in disgust.

Tubal spoke finally. "Listen, Forase, I'm cutting a class in Biosoc.—which I can't afford. You guaranteed the psychology of this stunt. If it turns out to be a flop, I'm not going to like it."

"Well, for the love of Deneb," grated Forase desperately, "you two are a fine pair of yellow-bellies! Did you expect them to start screaming and kicking right off? Sizzling Arcturus! Wait till we get to the Spican System, will you? When we maroon them overnight—"

He tittered suddenly. "This is going to be the fanciest trick since they tied those stink-bats to the chromatic organ on Concert Night."

Tubal cracked a grin, but Sefan leaned back in his chair and remarked thoughtfully.

"What if someone—say, President Wynn—hears about this?"

The Arcturian at the controls shrugged. "It's only a hazing. They'll go easy."

"Don't play dumb, M. T. This isn't kid stuff. Planet Four, Spica—the whole Spican System, in fact—is banned to Galactic ships, and you know that. It's got a sub-Humanoid race on it. They're supposed to develop entirely free of interference until they discover interstellar travel on their own. That's the law, and they're strict about it. Space! If they find out about this, we'll be in the soup for fair."

Tubal turned in his seat. "How in Arcturus do you expect Prexy Wynn—damn his thick hide!—to find out about us? Now, mind you, I'm not saying the story won't spread around the campus, because half the fun will be killed if we have to keep it to ourselves. But how will names come out? No one will squeal. You know that."

"Okay," said Sefan, and shrugged.

And then Tubal said, "Ready for hyper-space!"

He compressed keys and there was the queer internal wrench that marked the ship's departure from normal space.

The ten Earthmen were rather the worse for wear, and looked it. Lawrence Marsh squinted at his watch again.

"Two-thirty," he said. "That's thirty-six hours now. I wish they'd get this over with."

"This isn't a hazing," moaned Sweeney. "It takes too long."

Williams grew red. "What do you all look half-dead about? They've been feeding us regularly, haven't they? They haven't tied us up, have they? I should say it was pretty evident that they were taking good care of us."

"Or," came Sidney Morton's discontented drawl, "fattening us up for the slaughter."

He paused, and everyone stiffened. There was no mistaking the queer internal wrench they had felt.

"Get *that!*" said Eric Chamberlain in sudden frenzy. "We're back in normal space again, and that means we're only an hour or two from wherever we're going. We've got to do something!"

"Hear, hear," Williams snorted. "But what?"

"There are ten of us, aren't there?" shouted Chamberlain, puffing out his chest. "Well, I've only seen one of them so far. Next time he comes in, and we've got another meal due us pretty soon, we're going to mob him."

Sweeney looked sick. "What about the neuronic whip he always carries?"

"It won't kill us. He can't get us all before we pin him down, anyway."

"Eric," said Williams bluntly, "you're a fool."

Chamberlian flushed and his stub-fingered fists closed slowly.

"I'm just in the mood for a little practice persuasion. Call me that again, will you?"

"Sit down!" Williams scarcely bothered to look up. "And don't work so hard justifying my epithet. All of us are nervous and keyed-up, but that doesn't mean we ought to go altogether crazy. Not yet, anyway. First of all, even discounting the whip, mobbing our jailer won't be particularly successful.

"We've only seen one, but that one is from the Arcturian System. He's better than seven feet tall, and comfortably past the three-hundred-pound mark. He'd mop us up—all ten of us—with his bare fists. I thought you had one run-in with him already, Eric."

There was a thickish silence.

Williams added, "And even if we could knock him out and finish as many others as there may be in the ship, we still haven't the slightest idea where we are or how to get back or even how to run the ship." A pause. Then, "Well?"

"Nuts!" Chamberlain turned away, and glowered in silence.

The door kicked open and the giant Arcturian entered. With one hand, he emptied the bag he carried, and with the other kept his neuronic whip carefully leveled.

"Last meal," he grunted.

There was a general scramble for the rolling cans, still lukewarm from recent heating. Morton glared at his with disgust.

"Say," he spoke stumblingly in Galactic, "can't you give us a change? I'm tired of this rotten goulash of yours. This is the fourth can!"

"So what? It's your last meal," the Arcturian snapped, and left.

A horrified paralysis prevailed.

"What did he mean by that!" gulped someone huskily.

"They're going to kill us!" Sweeney was round-eyed, the thin edge of panic in his voice.

Williams' mouth was dry and he felt unreasoning anger grow against Sweeney's contagious fright. He paused—the kid was only seventeen—and said huskily, "Stow it, will you? Let's eat."

It was two hours later that he felt the shuddering jar that meant the landing and end of the journey. In that time, no one had spoken, but Williams could feel the pall of fear choke tighter with the minutes.

Spica had dipped crimsonly below the horizon and there was a chill wind blowing. The ten Earthmen, huddled together miserably upon the rock-strewn hilltop, watched their captors sullenly. It was the huge Arcturian, Myron Tubal, that did the talking, while the green-skinned Vegan, Bill Sefan, and the fuzzy little Denebian, Wri Forase, remained placidly in the background.

"You've got your fire," said the Arcturian gruffly, "and there's plenty of wood about to keep it going. That will keep the beasts away. We'll leave you a pair of whips before we go, and those will do as protection, if any of the aborigines of the planet bother you. You will have to use your own wits as far as food, water and shelter are concerned."

He turned away. Chamberlain let loose with a sudden roar, and leaped after the departing Arcturian. He was sent reeling back with an effortless heave of the other's arm.

The lock closed after the three other-world men. Almost at once, the ship lifted off the ground and shot upward. Williams finally broke the chilled silence.

"They've left the whips. I'll take one and you can have the other, Eric."

One by one, the Earthmen dropped into a sitting position, back to the fire, frightened, half panicky.

Williams forced a grin. "There's plenty of game about—the region is well-wooded. Come on, now, there are ten of us and they've got to come back sometime. Let's show them we Earthmen can take it. How about it, fellows?"

He was talking aimlessly now. Morton said listlessly.

"Why don't you shut up? You're not making this any easier."

Williams gave up. The pit of his own stomach was turning cold.

The twilight blackened into night, and the circle of light about the fire contracted into a little flickering area that ended in shadows. Marsh gasped suddenly, and his eyes went wide.

"There's some—something coming!"

The stir that followed froze itself into attitudes of breathless attention.

"You're crazy," began Williams huskily—and stopped dead at the unmistakable, slithering sound that reached his ears.

"Grab your whip!" he screamed to Chamberlain.

Joey Sweeney laughed suddenly—a strained, high-pitched laugh.

And then—there was a sudden shrieking in the air, and the shades charged down upon them.

Things were happening elsewhere, too.

Tubal's ship lazed outward from Spica's fourth planet, with Bill Sefan at the controls. Tubal himself was in his own cramped quarters, polishing off a huge flagon of Denebian liquor in two gulps.

Wri Forase watched the operation sadly.

"It cost twenty credits a bottle," he said, "and I only have a few left."

"Well, don't let me hog it," said Tubal magnanimously, "Match me bottle for bottle. It's all right with me."

"One swig like that," grumbled the Denebian, "and I'd be out till the Fall exams."

Tubal paid scant attention. "This," he began, "is going to make campus history as the hazing stunt—"

And at this point, there was a sharp, singing pinging *ping-g-g-g*, scarcely muffled by intervening walls, and the lights went out.

Wri Forase felt himself pressed hard against the wall. He struggled for breath and stuttered out in gasps.

"B-by Space, we're at f-full acceleration! What's wr-rong with the equalizer?"

"Damn the equalizer!" roared Tubal, heaving to his feet. "What's wrong with the ship?"

He stumbled out the door, into the equally dark corridor, with Forase crawling after him. When they burst into the control room, they found Sefan surrounded by the dim emergency lights, his green skin shining with perspiration.

"Meteor," he croaked. "It played hob with our power distributors. It's all going into acceleration. The lights, heating units and radio are all out of commission, while the ventilators are just barely limping." He added, "And Section Four is punctured."

Tubal gazed about him wildly. "Idiot! Why didn't you keep your eye on the mass indicator?"

"I did, you overgrown lump of putty," howled Sefan, "but it never registered! It—never—registered! Isn't that just what you'd expect from a second-hand jalopy, rented for two hundred credits? It went through the screen as if it were empty ether."

"Shut up!" Tubal flung open the suit-compartments and groaned. "They're all Arcturian models. I should have checked up. Can you handle one of these, Sefan?"

"Maybe." The Vegan scratched a doubtful ear.

In five minutes, Tubal swung into the lock and Sefan, stumbling awkwardly, followed after. It was half an hour before they returned.

Tubal removed his head-piece. "Curtains!"

Wri Forase gasped. "You mean—we're through?"

The Arcturian shook his head. "We can fix it, but it will take time. The radio is ruined for good, so we can't get help."

"Get help!" Forase looked shocked. "That's all we need. How would we explain being inside the Spican system? We might as well commit suicide as send out radio calls. As long as we can get back without help, we're safe. Missing a few more classes won't hurt us too much."

Sefan's voice broke in dully. "But what about those panicky Earthmen back on Spica Four?"

Forase's mouth opened, but he didn't say a word. It closed again, and if ever a Humanoid looked sick, Forase was that Humanoid.

That was only the beginning.

It took a day and a half to unscramble the space jalopy's power lines. It took two more days to decelerate to safe turn-

ing point. It took four days to return to Spica IV. Total—
eight days.

When the ship hovered once more over the place where
they had marooned the Earthmen, it was midmorning, and
Tubal's face as he surveyed the area through the tele-
visor was a study in length. Shortly he broke a silence that
had long since become sticky.

"I guess we've made every boner we could possibly have
made. We landed them right outside a native village. There's
no sign of the Earthmen."

Sefan shook his head dolefully. "This is a bad business."

Tubal buried his head in his long arms clear down to the
elbows.

"That's the finish. If they didn't scare themselves to death,
the natives got them. Violating prohibited solar systems is
bad enough—but it's just plain murder now, I guess."

"What we've go to do," said Sefan, "is to get down there
and find out if there are any still alive. We owe them that
much. After that—"

He swallowed. Forase finished in a whisper.

"After that, it's expulsion from the U., psycho-revision—
and manual labor for life."

"Forget it!" barked Tubal. "We'll face that when we have
to."

Slowly, very slowly, the ship circled downward and came
to rest on the rocky clearing where, eight days previously ten
Earthmen had been left stranded.

"How do we handle these natives?" Tubal turned to
Forase with raised eyebrow ridges (there was no hair on
them, of course). "Come on, son, give with some sub-Humanoid psychology. There are only three of us and I don't
want any trouble."

Forase shrugged and his fuzzy face wrinkled in perplexity.
"I've just been thinking about that, Tubal. I don't know any."

"What!" exploded Sefan and Tubal in twin shouts.

"No one does," added the Denebian hurriedly. "It's a fact.
After all, we don't let sub-Humanoids into the Federation till
they're fully civilized, and we quarantine them until then. Do
you suppose we have much opportunity to study their psychology?"

The Arcturian seated himself heavily. "This gets better and
better. *Think,* Fuzzy-face, will you? Suggest something!"

Forase scratched his head. "Well—uh—the best we can

do is to treat them like normal Humanoids. If we approach slowly, palms spread out, make no sudden movements and keep calm, we ought to get along. Now, remember, I'm saying we *ought* to. I can't be certain about this."

"Let's go, and damnation with certainty," urged Sefan impatiently. "It doesn't matter much, anyway. If I get knocked off here, I don't have to go back home." His face took on a haunted look. "When I think of what my family is going to say—"

They emerged from the ship and sniffed the atmosphere of Spica's fourth planet. The sun was at meridian, and loomed overhead like a large orange basketball. Off in the woods, a bird called once in a creaky caw. Utter silence descended.

"Hmph!" said Tubal, arms akimbo.

"It's enough to make you feel sleepy. No signs of life at all. Now, which way is the village?"

There was a three-way dispute about this, but it didn't last long. The Arcturian first, the other two tagging along, they strode down the slope and toward the straggling forest.

A hundred feet inside, the trees came alive, as a wave of natives dropped noiselessly from the overhanging branches. Wri Forase went under at the very first of the avalanche. Bill Sefan stumbled, stood his ground momentarily, then went over backward with a grunt.

Only huge Myron Tubal was left standing. Legs straddled wide, and whooping hoarsely, he laid about right and left. The attacking natives hit him and bounced off like drops of water from a whirling flywheel. Modeling his defense on the principle of the windmill, he backed his way against a tree.

Here he made a mistake. On the lowest branch of that tree squatted a native at once more cautious and more brainy than his fellows. Tubal had already noticed that the natives were equipped with stout, muscular tails, and had made a mental note of the fact. Of all the races in the Galaxy, only one other, Homo Gamma Cepheus, possessed tails. What he *didn't* notice, however, was that these tails were prehensile.

This he found out almost immediately, for the native in the branch above his head looped his tail downward, flashed it about Tubal's neck and contracted it.

The Arcturian threshed wildly in agony, and the tailed attacker was jerked from his tree. Suspended head-first and whirled about in huge sweeps, the native nevertheless maintained his hold and tightened that tail-grip steadily.

The world blacked out. Tubal was unconscious before he hit the ground.

Tubal came to slowly, unpleasantly aware of the stinging stiffness of his neck. He tried vainly to rub that stiffness, and it took a few seconds to realize that he was tied tightly. The fact startled him into alertness. He became aware, first, that he was lying on his stomach; second, of the horrible din about him; third, of Sefan and Forase bundled up next to him—and last, that he could not break his bonds.

"Hey, Sefan, Forase! Can you hear me?"

It was Sefan that answered joyfully. "You old Draconian goat! We thought you were out for good."

"I don't die so easy," grunted the Arcturian. "Where are we?"

There was a short pause.

"In the native village, I imagine," Wri Forase said dully. "Did you ever hear such a noise? The drum hasn't stopped a minute since they dumped us here."

"Have you seen anything of—"

Hands were upon Tubal, and he felt himself whirled about. He was in a sitting posture now and his neck hurt worse than ever. Ramshackle huts of thatch and green logs gleamed in the early afternoon sun. In a circle about them, watching in silence, were dark-skinned, long-tailed natives. There must have been hundreds, all wearing feathered head-dresses and carrying short, wickedly barbed spears.

Their eyes were upon the row of figures that squatted mysteriously in the foreground, and upon these Tubal turned his angry glare. It was plain that they were the leaders of the tribe. Dressed in gaudy, fringed robes of ill-tanned skins, they added further to their barbaric impressiveness by wearing tall wooden masks painted into caricatures of the human face.

With measured steps, the masked horror nearest the Humanoids approached.

"Hello," it said, and the mask lifted up and off. "Back so soon?"

For quite a long while, Tubal and Sefan said absolutely nothing, while Wri Forase went into a protracted fit of coughing.

Finally, Tubal drew a long breath. "You're one of the Earthmen, aren't you?"

"That's right. I'm Al Williams. Just call me Al."

"They haven't killed you yet?"

Williams smiled happily. "They haven't killed any of us. Quite the contrary. Gentlemen," he bowed extravagantly, "meet the new tribal—er—gods."

"The new tribal *what?*" gasped Forase. He was still coughing.

"—er—gods. Sorry, but I don't know the Galactic word for a god."

"What do you 'gods' represent?"

"We're sort of supernatural entities—objects to be worshipped. Don't you get it?"

The Humanoids stared unhappily.

"Yes, indeed," Williams grinned, "we're persons of great power."

"What are you talking about?" exclaimed Tubal indignantly. "Why should they think you were of great power? You Earth people are below average physically—well below!"

"It's the psychology of the thing," explained Williams. "If they see us landing in a large, gleaming vehicle that travels mysteriously through the air, and then takes off in a burst of rocket-flame—they're bound to consider us supernatural. That's elementary barbaric psychology."

Forase's eyes seemed on the point of dropping out as Williams continued.

"Incidentally, what detained you? We figure it was all a hazing of some sort, and it was, wasn't it?"

"Say," broke in Sefan, "I think you're feeding us a lot of bull! If they thought you people were gods, why didn't they think we were? We had the ship, too, and—"

"That," said Williams, "is where *we* started to interfere. We explained—via pictures and sign language—that you people were devils. When you finally came back—and say, were we glad to see that ship coming down—they knew what to do."

"What," asked Forase, with a liberal dash of awe in his voice, "are 'devils'?"

Williams sighed. "Don't you Galaxy people know anything?" Tubal moved his aching neck slowly. "How about letting us up now?" he rumbled. "I've got a crick in my neck."

"What's your hurry? After all, you were brought here to be sacrificed in our honor."

"Sacrificed!"

"Sure. You're to be carved up with knives."

There was a horror-laden silence. "Don't give us any of that comet-gas!" Tubal managed to grind out at last. "We're not Earthmen who get panicky or scared, you know."

"Oh, we know *that!* I wouldn't fool you for the world. But simple ordinary savage psychology always goes for a little human sacrifice and—"

Sefan writhed against his bonds and tried to throw himself in a rage at Forase.

"I thought you said no one knew any sub-Humanoid psychology! Trying to alibi your ignorance, weren't you, you shriveled, fuzz-covered, pop-eyed son of a half-breed Vegan lizard! A fine mess we're in now!"

Forase shrank away. "Now, wait! Just—"

Williams decided the joke had gone far enough.

"Take it easy," he soothed. "Your clever hazing blew up right in your faces—it blew up beautifully—but we're not going to carry it too far. I guess we've had enough fun out of you fellows. Sweeney is with the native chief now, explaining that we're leaving and taking you three with us. Frankly, I'll be glad to get going—Wait a while, Sweeney's calling me."

When Williams returned two seconds later, his expression was peculiar, having turned a bit greenish. In fact, he got greener by the second.

"It looks," he gulped throatily, "as if our counter-haze has blown up in *our* faces. The native chief *insists* on the sacrifice!"

Silence brooded, while the three Humanoids thought over the state of affairs. For moments, none of them could say a word.

"I've told Sweeney," Williams added, glumly, "to go back and tell the chief that if he doesn't do as we say, something terrible is going to happen to his tribe. But it's pure bluff and he may not fall for it. Uh,—I'm sorry, fellows, I guess we went too far. If it looks really bad, we'll cut you loose and join in the fight."

"Cut us loose now," growled Tubal, his blood running cold. "Let's get this over with!"

"Wait!" cried Forase frantically. "Let the Earthman try some of his psychology. Go ahead, Earthman. Think hard!"

Williams thought until his brain began to hurt.

"You see," he said weakly, "we've lost some of our god-like prestige, ever since we were unable to cure the chief's wife. She died yesterday." He nodded abstractedly to himself.

"What we need is an impressive miracle. Er—have you fellows anything in your pockets?"

He knelt beside them and began searching. Wri Forase had a stylus, a pocket-pad, a thin-toothed comb, some anti-itch powder, a sheaf of credits and a few odds and ends. Sefan had a collection of similar nondescript material.

It was from Tubal's hip pocket that Williams withdrew a small black gunlike object with a huge hand-grip and a short barrel.

"What's this?"

Tubal scowled. "Is that what I've been sitting on all this while? It's a weld-gun that I used to fix up a meteor puncture in our ship. It's no good; power's almost gone."

William's eyes kindled. His whole body galvanized with excitement.

"That's what you think! You Galaxy men never could see further than your noses. Why don't you come down to Earth for a spell—and get a new point of view?"

Williams was running toward his fellow conspirators now.

"Sweeney," he howled, "you tell that damned monkey-tailed chief that in just about one second, I'm going to get sore and pull the whole sky down over his head. Get tough!"

But the chief did not wait for the message. He gestured defiance and the natives made a united rush. Tubal roared, and his muscles cracked against the bonds. The weld-gun in Williams' hand flared into life, its feeble power beaming outward.

The nearest native hut went up in sudden flames. Another followed—and another—and the fourth—and then the weld-gun went dead.

But it was enough. Not a native remained standing. All were groveling on their faces, wailing and shrieking for pardon. The chief wailed and shrieked loudest of all.

"Tell the chief," said Williams to Sweeney, "that that's just a little, insignificant sample of what we're thinking of doing to him!"

To the Humanoids, as he cut the rawhide holding them, he added complacently,

"Just some simple, ordinary savage psychology."

It was only after they were back in their ship and off in space again that Forase locked up his pride.

"But I thought Earthmen had never developed mathematical psychology! How did you know all that sub-Humanoid stuff? No one in the Galaxy has got that far yet!"

"Well," Williams grinned, "we have a certain amount of rule-of-thumb knowledge about the workings of the uncivilized mind. You see—we come from a world where most people, in a manner of speaking, are still uncivilized. So we *have* to know!"

Forase nodded slowly. "You screwball Earthmen! At least, this little episode has taught us all one thing."

"What's that?"

"Never," said Forase, dipping a second time into Earth slang, "get tough with a bunch of nuts. They may be nuttier than you think!"

THE END

In going through my stories while preparing this book, I found "The Hazing" to be the only **published** story concerning which I could remember nothing from the title alone. Even as I reread it, nothing clicked. If I had been given the story without my name on it and had been asked to read it and guess the author, I would probably have been stumped. Maybe that means something.

It does seem to me, though, that the story is set against a "Homo Sol" background.

I had better luck with Fred Pohl with another story, "Super-Neutron," which I wrote at the end of the same February in which I did "Masks" and "The Hazing." I submitted it to him on March 3, 1941, and he accepted it on March 5.

By that time, less than three years after my first submission, I was clearly becoming rather impatient with rejections. At least, the news of the acceptance of "Super-Neutron" is greeted in my diary with an "It's about time I made a sale—five and a half weeks since the last one."

17

Super-Neutron

It was at the seventeenth meeting of the Honorable Society of Ananias that we got the greatest scare of our collective lives and consequently elected Gilbert Hayes to the office of Perpetual President.

The Society is not a large one. Before the election of Hayes there were only four of us: John Sebastian, Simon Murfree, Morris Levin and myself. On the first Sunday of every month we met at luncheon, and on these monthly occasions justified our Society's title by gambling the dinner check on our ability to lie.

It was quite a complicated process, with strict Parliamentary rules. One member spun a yarn each meeting as his turn came up, and two conditions had to be adhered to. His story had to be an outrageous, complicated, fantastic lie; *and,* it had to sound like the truth. Members were allowed to—and did—attack any and every point of the story by asking questions or demanding explanations.

Woe to the narrator who did not answer all questions immediately, or who, in answering, involved himself in a contradiction. The dinner-check was his! Financial loss was slight; but the disgrace was great.

And then came that seventeenth meeting—and Gilbert Hayes. Hayes was one of several non-members who attended occasionally to listen to the after-dinner whopper, paying his own check, and, of course, being forbidden to participate; but on this occasion he was the only one present aside from the regular members.

Astonishing Stories, September 1941
Copyright © 1941 by Fictioneers, Inc.
Copyright renewed © 1968 by Isaac Asimov

Dinner was over, I had been voted into the chair (it was my regular turn to preside), and the minutes had been read, when Hayes leaned forward and said quietly, "I'd like a chance today, gentlemen."

I frowned, "In the eyes of the Society you are non-existent, Mr. Hayes. It is impossible for you to take part."

"Then just let me make a statement," he rejoined. "The Solar System is coming to an end at exactly seventeen and a half minutes after two this afternoon."

There was a devil of a stir, and I looked at the electric clock over the television receiver. It was 1:14 P.M.

I said hesitantly, "If you have anything to substantiate that extraordinary statement, it should be most interesting. It is Mr. Levin's turn today, but if he is willing to waive it, and if the rest of the Society agrees—"

Levin smiled and nodded, and the others joined in.

I banged the gavel, "Mr. Hayes has the floor."

Hayes lit his cigar and gazed at it pensively. "I have little more than an hour, gentlemen, but I'll start at the beginning —which is about fifteen years ago. At that time, though I've resigned since, I was an astrophysicist at Yerkes Observatory —young, but promising. I was hot on the trail of the solution to one of the perennial puzzles of astrophysics—the source of the cosmic rays—and full of ambition."

He paused, and continued in a different tone, "You know, it is strange that with all our scientific advance in the last two centuries we have never found either that mysterious source or the equally mysterious reason for the explosion of a star. They are the two eternal puzzles and we know as little about them today as we did in the days of Einstein, Eddington, and Millikan.

"Still, as I say, I thought I had the cosmic ray by the tail, so I set out to check my ideas by observation, and for that I had to go out in space. It wasn't, however, as easy as all that. It was in 2129, you see, just after the last war, and the Observatory was about broke—as weren't we all?

"I made the best of it. I hired an old second-hand '07 model, piled my apparatus in, and set out alone. What's more, I had to sneak out of port without clearance papers, not wishing to go through the red tape the occupation army would have put me through. It was illegal, but I wanted my data— so I headed out at a right angle to the ecliptic, in the direction of the South Celestial Pole, approximately, and left Sol a billion miles behind me.

"The voyage I made, and the data I collected are unimportant. I never reported one or the other. It was the planet I found that makes the story."

At this point, Murfree raised those bushy eyebrows of his and grunted, "I would like to warn the gentleman, Mr. Chairman. No member has yet escaped with his skin with a phony planet."

Hayes smiled grimly, "I'll take my chance.—To continue; it was on the eighteenth day of my trip that I first detected the planet as a little orange disc the size of a pea. Naturally, a planet in that region of space is something of a sensation. I headed for it; and immediately discovered that I had not even scratched the surface of that planet's queerness. To exist there at all was phenomenal—but it likewise possessed absolutely no gravitational field."

Levin's wine-glass crashed to the floor. "Mr. Chairman," he gasped, "I demand the gentleman's immediate disqualification. No mass can exist without distorting the space in its neighborhood and thus creating a gravitational field. He has made an impossible statement, and should therefore be disqualified." His face was an angry red.

But Hayes held his hand up, "I demand time, Mr. Chairman. The explanation will be forthcoming in due course. To make it now would only complicate things. Please, may I continue?"

I considered, "In view of the nature of your story, I am disposed to be lenient. Delay is granted, but please remember that an explanation will be required eventually. You will lose without it."

"All right," said Hayes. "For the present, you will have to accept my statement that the planet had no gravity *at all*. That is definite, for I had complete astronomical equipment upon my ship, and though my instruments were very sensitive, they registered a dead zero.

"It worked the other way around as well, for the planet was not affected by the gravity of other masses. Again, I stress the point that it was not affected *at all*. This I was not able to determine at the time, but subsequent observation over a period of years, showed that the planet was traveling in a straight-line orbit and at a constant speed. As it was well within the sun's influence, the fact that its orbit was neither elliptical nor hyperbolic, and that, though approaching the

sun, it was not accelerating, showed definitely that it was independent of solar gravity."

"Wait a while, Hayes." Sebastian scowled till his gold
premolar gleamed. "What held this wonderful planet together? Without gravity, why didn't it break up and drift
apart?"

"Sheer inertia, for one thing!" was the immediate retort.
"There was nothing to *pull* it apart. A collision with another
body of comparable size might have done it—leaving out of
consideration the possibility of the existence of some other
binding force peculiar to the planet."

He sighed and continued, "That doesn't finish the properties of the body. Its red-orange color and its low reflective
power, or albedo, set me on another track, and I made the
astonishing discovery that the planet was entirely transparent
to the whole electro-magnetic spectrum from radio waves to
cosmic rays. It was only in the region of the red and yellow
portion of the visible-light octave that it was reasonably
opaque. Hence, its color."

"Why was this?" demanded Murfree.

Hayes looked at me, "That is an unreasonable question,
Mr. Chairman. I maintain that I might as well be asked to
explain why glass is entirely transparent to anything above
or below the ultra-violet region, so that heat, light, and
X-rays pass through, while it remains opaque to ultra-violet
light itself. This sort of thing is a property of the substance
itself and must be accepted as such without explanation."

I whacked my gavel, "Question declared improper!"

"I object," declared Murfree. "Hayes missed the point.
Nothing is perfectly transparent. Glass of sufficient thickness
will stop even cosmic rays. Do you mean to say that blue
light would pass through an entire planet, or heat, for
instance?"

"Why not?" replied Hayes. "That perfect transparency does
not exist in your experience does not mean it does not exist
altogether. There is certainly no scientific law to that effect.
This planet was perfectly transparent except for one small
region of the spectrum. That's a definite fact of observation."

My gavel thumped again, "Explanation declared sufficient.
Continue, Hayes."

His cigar had gone out and he paused to relight. Then,
"In other respects, the planet was normal. It was not quite
the size of Saturn—perhaps half way in diameter between it

and Neptune. Subsequent experiments showed it to possess mass, though it was hard to find out how much—certainly more than twice Earth's. With mass, it possessed the usual properties of inertia and momentum—but no gravity."

It was 1:35 now.

Hayes followed my eyes and said, "Yes, only three-quarters of an hour is left. I'll hurry! . . . Naturally, this queer planet set me to thinking, and that, together with the fact that I had already been evolving certain theories concerning cosmic rays and novae, led to an interesting solution."

He drew a deep breath, "Imagine—if you can—our cosmos as a cloud of—well, super-atoms which—"

"I beg your pardon," exclaimed Sebastian, rising to his feet, "are you intending to base any of your explanation on drawing analogies between stars and atoms, or between solar systems and electronic orbits?"

"Why do you ask?" questioned Hayes, quietly.

"Because if you do, I demand immediate disqualification. The belief that atoms are miniature solar systems is in a class with the Ptolemaic scheme of the universe. The idea has never been accepted by responsible scientists even at the very dawn of the atomic theory."

I nodded, "The gentleman is correct. No such analogy will be permitted as part of the explanation."

"*I* object," said Hayes. "In your school course in elementary physics or chemistry, you will remember that in the study of the properties of gases, it was often pretended, for the sake of illustrating a point, that the gas molecules were tiny billiard balls. Does that mean that gas molecules *are* billiard balls?"

"No," admitted Sebastian.

"It only means," drove on Hayes, "that gas molecules act similarly to billiard balls in some ways. Therefore the actions of one are better visualized by studying the actions of the other. —Well, then, I am only trying to point out a phenomenon in our universe of stars, and for the sake of ease of visualization, I compare it to a similar, and better-known, phenomenon in the world of atoms. That does not mean that stars are magnified atoms."

I was won over. "The point is well-taken," I said. "You may continue with your explanation, but if it is the judgment of the chair that the analogy becomes a false one, you will be disqualified."

"Good," agreed Hayes, "but we'll pass on to another point for a moment. Do any of you remember the first atomic power plants of a hundred and seventy years ago and how they operated?"

"I believe," muttered Levin, "that they used the classical uranium fission method for power. They bombarded uranium with slow neutrons and split it up into masurium, barium, gamma rays and more neutrons, thus establishing a cyclic process."

"That's right! Well, imagine that the stellar universe acted in ways—mind you, this is a metaphor, and not to be taken literally—like a body composed of uranium atoms, and imagine this stellar universe to be bombarded from without by objects which might act in some ways similar to the way neutrons act on an atomic scale.

"Such a super-neutron, hitting a sun, would cause that sun to explode into radiation and more super-neutrons. In other words, you would have a nova." He looked around for disagreement.

"What justification have you for that idea?" demanded Levin.

"Two; one logical, and one observational. Logic first. Stars are essentially in matter-energy equilibrium, yet suddenly, with no observable change, either spectral or otherwise, they occasionally explode. An explosion indicates instability, but where? Not within the star, for it had been in equilibrium for millions of years. Not from a point within the universe, for novae occur in even concentration throughout the universe. Hence, by elimination, only from a point *outside* the universe.

"Secondly, observation. I came across one of these super-neutrons!"

Said Murfree indignantly: "I suppose you mean that gravitationless planet you came across?"

"That's right."

"Then what makes you think it's a super-neutron? You can't use your theory as proof, because you're using the super-neutron itself to bolster the theory. We're not allowed to argue in circles here."

"I know that," declared Hayes stiffly. "I'll resort to logic again. The world of atoms possesses a cohesive force in the electro-magnetic charge on electrons and protons. The world of stars possesses a cohesive force in gravity. The two forces are only alike in a very general manner. For instance, there are two kinds of electrical charges, positive and negative, but only one kind of gravity—and innumerable minor differences. Still, an analogy this far seems to me to be permissible. A neutron on an atomic scale is a mass without the atomic cohesive force—electric charge. A super-neutron on a stellar scale *ought* to be a mass without the stellar cohesive force—gravity. Therefore, if I find a body without gravity, it seems reasonable to assume it to be a super-neutron."

"Do you consider that a rigorously scientific proof?" asked Sebastian sarcastically.

"No," admitted Hayes, "but it is logical, conflicts with no scientific fact I know of, and works out to form a consistent explanation of novae. That should be enough for our purpose at present."

Murfree was gazing hard at his fingernails, "And just where is this super-neutron of yours heading?"

"I see you anticipate," said Hayes, sombrely. "It was what I asked myself at the time. At 2:09½ today it hits the sun square, and eight minutes later, the radiation resulting from the explosion will sweep Earth to oblivion."

"Why didn't you report all this?" barked Sebastian.

"Where was the use? There was nothing to be done about it. We can't handle astronomical masses. All the power available on Earth would not have sufficed to swerve that great body from its path. There was no escape within the Solar System itself, for Neptune and Pluto will turn gaseous along with the other planets, and interstellar travel is as yet impossible. Since man cannot exist independently in space, he is doomed.

"Why tell of all this? What would result after I had convinced them that the death warrant was signed? Suicides, crime waves, orgies, messiahs, evangelists, and everything bad and futile you could think of. And after all, is death by nova so bad? It is instantaneous and clean. At 2:17 you're here. At 2:18 you are a mass of attenuated gas. It is so quick and easy a death, it is almost not death."

There was a long silence after this. I felt uneasy. There are lies and lies, but this sounded like the real thing. Hayes didn't have that little quirk of the lip or that little gleam in the eye which marks the triumph of putting over a good one. He was deadly, deadly serious. I could see the others felt the same. Levin was gulping at his wine, hand shaking.

Finally, Sebastian coughed loudly, "How long ago did you discover this super-neutron and where?"

"Fifteen years ago, a billion miles or better from the sun."

"And all that time it has been approaching the sun?"

"Yes; at a constant speed of two miles per second."

"Good, I've got you!" Sebastian almost laughed his relief. "Why haven't the astronomers spotted it in all this while?"

"My God," responded Hayes, impatiently, "it's clear you aren't an astronomer. Now, what fool would look to the Southern Celestial Pole for a planet, when they're only found in the ecliptic?"

"But," pointed out Sebastian, "the region is studied just the same. It is photographed."

"Surely! For all I know, the super-neutron has been photographed a hundred times—a thousand times if you like— though the Southern Pole is the most poorly watched region of the sky. But what's to differentiate it from a star? With its low albedo, it never passed eleventh magnitude in brightness. After all, it's hard enough to detect any planets in any case. Uranus was spotted many times before Herschel realized it was a planet. Pluto took years to find even when they were *looking* for it. Remember also that without gravity, it causes no planetary perturbations, and that the absence of these removes the most obvious indication of its presence."

"But," insisted Sebastian, desperately, "as it approached the sun, its apparent size would increase and it would begin to show a perceptible disc through a telescope. Even if its reflected light were very faint, it would certainly obscure the stars behind it."

"True," admitted Hayes. "I will not say that a really thorough mapping of the Polar Region would not have uncovered it, but such mapping has been done long ago, and the present cursory searches for novae, special spectral types, and so on are by no means thorough. Then, as the super-neutron approaches the sun, it begins to appear only in the dawn and twilight—in evening and morning star fashion— so that observation becomes much more difficult. And so, as a matter of fact, it just has not been observed—and it is what should have been expected."

Again a silence, and I became aware that my heart was pounding. It was two o'clock even, and we hadn't been able to shake Hayes' story. We had to prove it a lie fast, or I'd die of sheer suspense. We were all of us watching the clock.

Levin took up the fight. "It's an awfully queer coincidence that the super-neutron should be heading straight for the sun.

What are the chances against it? Remember, that would be the same thing as reciting the chances against the truth of the story."

I interposed, "That is an illegitimate objection, Mr. Levin. To cite improbability, however great, is not sufficient. Only outright impossibility or citation of inconsistency can serve to disqualify."

But Hayes waved his hand, "It's all right. Let me answer. Taking an individual super-neutron and an individual star, the chances of collision, head on, are all but infinitely small. However, statistically, if you shoot enough super-neutrons into the universe, then, given enough time, every star ought to be hit sooner or later. Space must be swarming with super-neutrons—say one every thousand cubic parsecs—so that in spite of the vast distances between the stars and the relative minuteness of the targets, twenty novae occur in our single Galaxy every year—that is, there are twenty collisions between super-neutrons and stars annually.

"The situation is no different really from uranium being bombarded with ordinary neutrons. Only one neutron out of a hundred million may score a hit, but, given time, every nucleus is exploded eventually. If there is an outer-universe intelligence directing this bombardment—pure hypothesis, and *not* part of my argument, please—a year to us is probably an infinitesimal fraction of a second to them. The hits, to them, may be occurring at the rate of billions to their seconds. Energy is being developed, perhaps, to the point where the material this universe composes has become heated to the gaseous state—or whatever passes for the gaseous state there. The universe *is* expanding, you know—like a gas."

"Still, for the very first super-neutron entering our system to head straight for the sun seems—" Levin ended in a weak stammer.

"Good Lord," snapped Hayes, "who told you this *was* the first? Hundreds may have passed through the system in geologic times. One or two may have passed through in the last thousand years or so. How would we know? Even when one is headed straight for the sun, astronomers don't find it. Perhaps this is the only one that's passed through since the telescope was invented, and before then, of course. . . . And never forget that, having no gravity, they can go right through the middle of the system, without affecting the planets. Only a hit on the sun registers, and then it's too late."

He looked at the clock, "2:05! We ought to see it now

against the sun." He stood up and raised the window shade. The yellow sunlight streamed in and I moved away from the dusty shaft of light. My mouth was dry as desert sand. Murfree was mopping his brow, but beads of sweat stood out all along his cheeks and neck.

Hayes took out several slips of exposed film-negative and handed them out, "I came prepared, you see." He held one up and squinted at the sun. "There it is," he remarked placidly. "My calculations showed it would be in transit with respect to Earth at the time of collision. Rather convenient!"

I was looking at the sun, too, and felt my heart skip a beat. There, quite clear against the brightness of the sun, was a little, perfectly round, black spot.

"Why doesn't it vaporize?" stammered Murfree. "It must be almost in the sun's atmosphere." I don't think he was trying to disprove Hayes' story. He had gone past that. He was honestly seeking information.

"I told you," explained Hayes, "that it is transparent to almost all solar radiation. Only the radiation it absorbs can go into heat and that's a very small percentage of all it receives. Besides, it isn't ordinary matter. It's probably much more refractory than anything on Earth, and the Solar surface is only at 6,000 degrees Centigrade."

He pointed a thumb over his shoulder, "It's 2:09½, gentlemen. The super-neutron has struck and death is on its way. We have eight minutes."

We were dumb with something that was just simply unbearable terror. I remember Hayes' voice, quite matter-of-fact, saying, "Mercury just went!" then a few minutes later, "Venus has gone!" and lastly, "Thirty seconds left, gentlemen!"

The seconds crawled, but passed at last, and another thirty seconds, and still another. . . .

And on Hayes' face, a look of astonishment grew and spread. He lifted the clock and stared at it, then peered through his film at the sun once more.

"It's gone!" He turned and faced us, "It's unbelievable. I had thought of it, but I dared not draw the atomic analogy too far. You know that not all atomic nuclei explode on being hit by a neutron. Some, cadmium, for instance, absorb them one after the other like sponges do water. I—"

He paused again, drew a deep breath, and continued musingly, "Even the purest block of uranium contains traces of all other elements. And in a universe of trillions of stars acting like uranium, what does a paltry million of cadmium-like stars amount to—nothing! Yet the sun is one of them! Mankind never deserved that!"

He kept on talking, but relief had finally penetrated and we listened no longer. In half-hysterical fashion, we elected Gilbert Hayes to the office of Perpetual President by enthusiastic acclamation, and voted the story the whoppingest lie ever told.

But there's one thing that bothers me. Hayes fills his post well; the Society is more successful than ever—but I think he should have been disqualified after all. His story fulfilled the second condition; it sounded like the truth. But I don't think it fulfilled the *first* condition.

I think it *was* the truth!

THE END

I had series on my mind by now. "Super-Neutron" was certainly intended to be but the first in a long chain of very clever and very ingenious tales to be told at the meetings of the "Honorable Society of Ananias." It didn't work out that way. There was never a second story, not even the beginnings of one, not even the idea for one.

By the time I was writing "Super-Neutron," in February of 1941, I had heard of uranium fission and had even discussed it in some detail with Campbell. I managed to refer to it in the course of the story as "the classical uranium fission method for power." I also spoke of the metal cadmium as a neutron absorber. It wasn't bad for a story that apeared in 1941, and I sometimes quote it in public to create an impression.

Notice, though, that in the same paragraph in which I mention fission, I also talk of "masurium." Actually, masurium was the name given to element #43 in 1926, but that discovery had proven a false alarm. The element was really discovered in 1937 and was given the now-accepted name of "technetium." It seems, then, that I could look years into the future and see uranium fission as a practical power source, but I couldn't look a few years into the past and see the correct name for element #43.

This brings us to March 17, 1941, and one of the key turning points of my literary career.

By that day, I had written thirty-one stories. Of these I had already sold seventeen and was yet to sell four more. Of all these stories, three perhaps, and no more, were to turn out to be of more than ephemeral value, and those were the three "positronic robots" stories I had so far written: "Robbie," "Reason," and "Liar!"

Looking back on my first three years as a writer, then, I can judge myself to be nothing more than a steady and (perhaps) hopeful third-rater. What's more, that's all I considered myself then, too. Nor did anyone else, at that time, seriously consider me a a potential first-magnitude star in the science fiction heavens—except, maybe, Campbell.

What are the odds, then, that on March 17, 1941, I would sit down and write something that for thirty years now has been considered by a surprising number of people to be the outstanding short classic of magazine science fiction? It was one of those things that couldn't possibly happen—yet it did.

It began when I walked into Campbell's office that day and, as usual, suggested an idea. What it was I don't remember, but whatever it was he turned it down instantly, not because it was such a bad idea but because he had something he wanted to show me that crowded everything else out of his mind. He had come across a quotation from Ralph Waldo Emerson that went: "If the stars should appear one night in a thousand years, how would men believe and adore, and preserve for many generations the remembrance of the city of God!"*

Campbell asked me what I thought would happen if the

*Does anyone know in what essay, and in what connection, Emerson says this? Every once in a while I make a desultory search through quotation books or through a collection of Emerson but haven't found it yet. I hope it exists and that the quote is given correctly.

stars would appear at only very long intervals. I had nothing intelligent to suggest.

"I think men would go mad," he said thoughtfully.

We talked about that notion for quite a while, and I went home to write a story on the subject, one that Campbell and I decided from the start was to be called "Nightfall."

I began it that night. I can remember the details exactly: my parents' apartment on Windsor Place in Brooklyn, across the street from the candy store; my own room, just next to the living room, is clear in my mind, with the position of my bed, my desk, my typewriter—and myself getting started.

In years to come, fans would occasionally vote in polls designed to decide the best science fiction short stories of all time. Quite frequently, "Nightfall" would finish in first place. Just a couple of years ago, the Science Fiction Writers of America polled their membership to decide the best science fiction short stories ever published, for inclusion in a Hall of Fame anthology. "Nightfall" finished in first place by a sizable margin. And, of course, it has been anthologized a dozen times so far.

With all this, one might argue that "Nightfall" is the best (or at least the most popular) short science fiction story ever to appear in the magazines. Well, I often wonder, with a shudder, what might have happened on the evening of March 17, 1941, if some angelic spirit had whispered in my ear, "Isaac, you are about to start writing the best short science fiction story of our time."

I would undoubtedly have frozen solid. I wouldn't have been able to type a word.

But we don't know the future, and I tapped away blissfully, writing the story and completing it by April 9, 1941. That day, I submitted it to Campbell. He asked for a small revision. I took care of that, and on April 24, 1941, he bought the story.

It set several records for me. It was the longest story I had yet sold, a little over thirteen thousand words. Since Campbell paid me a bonus (my first one), the word rate was one and a quarter cents a word, and the total check was for $166, more than twice as large as any single payment I had ever before received.*

Then, too, "Nightfall" appeared in the September 1941 issue of **Astounding** as the lead novelette. For the first time, I made the cover of that magazine, with "Nightfall, by Isaac Asimov" in large, bold letters.

Most important of all, the appearance of "Nightfall" graduated me by common consent (three years after I had begun my career) into the list of first-rank science fiction writers.

Alas, the story is not included here. It appears (of course) in **Nightfall and Other Stories.****

The excitement of writing "Nightfall" and Campbell's hearty and unqualified praise of it ought, one might think, to have set me furiously to work at the typewriter, but it didn't. Spring 1941 was a bad time for me.

I could at any time that half year have left Columbia with a master's degree, but that would have done me no good. I had no job to go to, so I could only mark time and try to raise my value to some prospective employer by going on to the big one, the doctorate.

But that meant I had to take a series of elaborate, interminable "qualifying examinations," which I had to pass in order to be allowed to begin the research without which I could not get the Ph.D. Passing was difficult and I didn't feel prepared at all, but I had to try it sometime, and besides,

---

*"Black Friar of the Flame" was three thousand words longer than "Nightfall," but the former was not to be sold for another half year, and since it earned merely one cent a word, it brought in only $161. Of course, first-time earnings are not the whole story, either. "Nightfall" has earned me some thousands of dollars since 1941 and will yet earn me more; "Black Friar of the Flame" has not yet earned me one cent over the original check—till its appearance in this book.
**In telling the story, in that collection, of how "Nightfall" came to be written, I mentioned that I had received $150 for it, quoting from memory. Once again, I must confess fallibility. The records say $166. It is a small point, and perhaps not worth noting, but I know my readers. By explaining this now, I fend off dozens of letters that will mention the discrepancy and demand an explanation.

if I didn't fall short by too far, I would be allowed to continue taking courses and to repeat the qualifying examinations at some future date.

So in May I absented myself from the typewriter, studied earnestly for my qualifyings, took them—and didn't pass. I did well enough to earn the option of a future repeat, and I also received my M.A. as a kind of consolation prize, but I was badly disheartened all the same.

(And in the larger world outside, though Great Britain had survived air bombardment, Hitler still seemed unstoppable. He invaded the Balkans and was again winning spectacular victories, and that was disheartening, too.)

It was not till May 24, 1941, that I could bring myself to go back to my writing. I turned out "Not Final!" which I submitted to Campbell on June 2. It was accepted on the sixth, but without a bonus.

18

Not Final!

Nicholas Orloff inserted a monocle in his left eye with all the incorruptible Briticism of a Russian educated at Oxford and said reproachfully, "But, my dear Mr. Secretary! Half a billion dollars!"

Leo Birnam shrugged his shoulders wearily and allowed his lank body to cramp up still farther in the chair, "The appropriation must go through, commissioner. The Dominion government here at Ganymede is becoming desperate. So far, I've been holding them off, but as secretary of scientific affairs, my powers are small."

Astounding Science Fiction, October 1941
Copyright © 1941 by Street & Smith Publications, Inc.
Copyright renewed © 1968 by Isaac Asimov

"I know, but—" and Orloff spread his hands helplessly.

"I suppose so," agreed Birnam. "The Empire government finds it easier to look the other way. They've done it consistently up to now. I've tried for a year now to have them understand the nature of the danger that hangs over the entire System, but it seems that it can't be done. But I'm appealing to you, Mr. Commissioner. You're new in your post and can approach this Jovian affair with an unjaundiced eye."

Orloff coughed and eyed the tips of his boots. In the three months since he had succeeded Gridley as colonial commissioner he had tabled unread everything relating to "those damned Jovian D. T.'s." That had been according to the established cabinet policy which had labeled the Jovian affair as "deadwood" long before he had entered office.

But now that Ganymede was becoming nasty, he found himself sent out to Jovopolis with instructions to hold the "blasted provincials" down. It was a nasty spot.

Birnam was speaking, "The Dominion government has reached the point where it needs the money so badly, in fact, that if they don't get it, they're going to publicize everything."

Orloff's phlegm broke completely, and he snatched at the monocle as it dropped, "My dear fellow!"

"I know what it would mean. I've advised against it, but they're justified. Once the inside of the Jovian affair is out; once the people know about it; the Empire government won't stay in power a week. And when the Technocrats come in, they'll give us whatever we ask. Public opinion will see to that."

"But you'll also create a panic and hysteria—"

"Surely! That is why we hesitate. But you might call this an ultimatum. We want secrecy, we *need* secrecy; but we need money more."

"I see." Orloff was thinking rapidly, and the conclusions he came to were not pleasant. "In that case, it would be advisable to investigate the case further. If you have the papers concerning the communications with the planet Jupiter—"

"I have them," replied Birnam, dryly, "and so has the Empire government at Washington. That won't do, commissioner. It's the same cud that's been chewed by Earth officials for the last year, and it's gotten us nowhere. I want you to come to Ether Station with me."

The Ganymedan had risen from his chair, and he glowered

down upon Orloff from his six and a half feet of height.

Orloff flushed, "Are you ordering me?"

"In a way, yes. I tell you there is no time. If you intend acting, you must act quickly or not at all." Birnam paused, then added, "You don't mind walking, I hope. Power vehicles aren't allowed to approach Ether Station, ordinarily, and I can use the walk to explain a few of the facts. It's only two miles off."

"I'll walk," was the brusque reply.

The trip upward to subground level was made in silence, which was broken by Orloff when they stepped into the dimly lit anteroom.

"It's chilly here."

"I know. It's difficult to keep the temperature up to norm this near the surface. But it will be colder outside. Here!"

Birnam had kicked open a closet door and was indicating the garments suspended from the ceiling. "Put them on. You'll need them."

Orloff fingered them doubtfully, "Are they heavy enough?"

Birnam was pouring into his own costume as he spoke. "They're electrically heated. You'll find them plenty warm. That's it! Tuck the trouser legs inside the boots and lace them tight."

He turned then and, with a grunt, brought out a double compressed-gas cylinder from its rack in one corner of the closet. He glanced at the dial reading; and then turned the stopcock. There was a thin wheeze of escaping gas, at which Birnam sniffed with satisfaction.

"Do you know how to work one of these?" he asked, as he screwed onto the jet a flexible tube of metal mesh, at the other end of which was a curiously curved object of thick, clear glass.

"What is it?"

"Oxygen nosepiece! What there is of Ganymede's atmosphere is argon and nitrogen, just about half and half. It isn't particularly breathable." He heaved the double cylinder into position, and tightened it in its harness on Orloff's back.

Orloff staggered, "It's heavy. I can't walk two miles with this."

"It won't be heavy out there," Birnam nodded carelessly upward and lowered the glass nosepiece over Orloff's head. "Just remember to breathe in through the nose and out through the mouth, and you won't have any trouble. By the way, did you eat recently?"

"I lunched before I came to your place."

Birnam sniffed dubiously, "Well, that's a little awkward." He drew a small metal container from one of his pockets and tossed it to the commissioner. "Put one of those pills in your mouth and keep sucking on it."

Orloff worked clumsily with gloved fingers and finally managed to get a brown spheroid out of the tin and into his mouth. He followed Birnam up a gently sloped ramp. The blind-alley ending of the corridor slid aside smoothly when they reached it and there was a faint soughing as air slipped out into the thinner atmosphere of Ganymede.

Birnam caught the other's elbow, and fairly dragged him out.

"I've turned your air tank on full," he shouted. "Breathe deeply and keep sucking at that pill."

Gravity had flicked to Ganymedan normality as they crossed the threshold and Orloff after one horrible moment of apparent levitation, felt his stomach turn a somersault and explode.

He gagged, and fumbled the pill with his tongue in a desperate attempt at self-control. The oxygen-rich mixture from the air cylinders burned his throat, and gradually Ganymede steadied. His stomach shuddered back into place. He tried walking.

"Take it easy, now," came Birnam's soothing voice. "It gets you that way the first few times you change gravity fields quickly. Walk slowly and get the rhythm, or you'll take a tumble. That's right, you're getting it."

The ground seemed resilient. Orloff could feel the pressure of the other's arm holding him down at each step to keep him from springing too high. Steps were longer now—and flatter, as he got the rhythm. Birnam continued speaking, a voice a little muffled from behind the leather flap drawn loosely across mouth and chin.

"Each to his own world," he grinned. "I visited Earth a few years back, with my wife, and had a hell of a time. I couldn't get myself to learn to walk on a planet's surface without a nosepiece. I kept choking—I really did. The sunlight was too bright and the sky was too blue and the grass was too green. And the buildings were right out on the surface. I'll never forget the time they tried to get me to sleep in a room twenty stories up in the air, with the window wide open and the moon shining in.

"I went back on the first spaceship going my way and don't ever intend returning. How are you feeling now?"

"Fine! Splendid!" Now that the first discomfort had gone. Orloff found the low gravity exhilarating. He looked about him. The broken, hilly ground, bathed in a drenching yellow light, was covered with ground-hugging broad-leaved shrubs that showed the orderly arrangement of careful cultivation.

Birnam answered the unspoken question, "There's enough carbon dioxide in the air to keep the plants alive, and they all have the power to fix atmospheric nitrogen. That's what makes agriculture Ganymede's greatest industry. Those plants are worth their weight in gold as fertilizers back on Earth and worth double or triple that as sources for half a hundred alkaloids that can't be gotten anywhere else in the System. And, of course, everyone knows that Ganymedan green-leaf has Terrestrial tobacco beat hollow."

There was the drone of a strato-rocket overhead, shrill in the thin atmosphere, and Orloff looked up.

He stopped—stopped dead—and forgot to breathe!

It was his first glimpse of Jupiter in the sky.

It is one thing to see Jupiter, coldly harsh, against the ebon backdrop of space. At six hundred thousand miles, it is majestic enough. But on Ganymede, barely topping the hills, its outlines softened and ever so faintly hazed by the thin atmosphere; shining mellowly from a purple sky in which only a few fugitive stars dare compete with the Jovian giant —it can be described by no conceivable combination of words.

At first, Orloff absorbed the gibbous disk in silence. It was gigantic, thirty-two times the apparent diameter of the Sun as seen from Earth. Its stripes stood out in faint washes of color against the yellowness beneath and the Great Red Spot was an oval splotch of orange near the western rim.

And finally Orloff murmured weakly, "It's beautiful!"

Leo Birnam stared, too, but there was no awe in his eyes. There was the mechanical weariness of viewing a sight often seen, and besides that an expression of sick revulsion. The chin flap hid his twitching smile, but his grasp upon Orloff's arm left bruises through the tough fabric of the surface suit.

He said slowly, "It's the most horrible sight in the System."

Orloff turned reluctant attention to his companion, "Eh?" Then, disagreeably, "Oh, yes, those mysterious Jovians."

At that, the Ganymedan turned away angrily and broke

into swinging, fifteen-foot strides. Orloff followed clumsily after, keeping his balance with difficulty.

"Here, now," he gasped.

But Birnam wasn't listening. He was speaking coldly, bitterly, "You on Earth can afford to ignore Jupiter. You know nothing of it. It's a little pin prick in your sky, a little flyspeck. You don't live here on Ganymede, watching that damned colossus gloating over you. Up and over fifteen hours—hiding God knows what on its surface. Hiding something that's waiting and waiting and *trying to get out*. Like a giant bomb just waiting to explode!"

"Nonsense!" Orloff managed to jerk out. *"Will* you slow down. I can't keep up."

Birnam cut his strides in half and said tensely, "Everyone knows that Jupiter is inhabited, but practically no one ever stops to realize what that means. I tell you that those Jovians, whatever they are, are born to the purple. *They are the natural rulers of the Solar System."*

"Pure hysteria," muttered Orloff. "The Empire government has been hearing nothing else from your Dominion for a year."

"And you've shrugged it off. Well, listen! Jupiter, discounting the thickness of its colossal atmosphere, is eighty thousand miles in diameter. That means it possesses a surface one hundred times that of Earth, and more than fifty times that of the entire Terrestrial Empire. Its population, its resources, its war potential are in proportion."

"Mere numbers—"

"I know what you mean," Birnam drove on, passionately. "Wars are not fought with numbers, but with science and with organization. The Jovians have both. In the quarter of a century during which we have communicated with them, we've learned a bit. They have atomic power and they have radio. And in a world of ammonia under great pressure—a world in other words in which almost none of the metals can exist *as* metals for any length of time because of the tendency to form soluble ammonia complexes—they have managed to build up a complicated civilization. That means they have had to work through plastics, glasses, silicates and synthetic building materials of one sort of another. *That* means a chemistry developed just as far as ours is, and I'd put odds on its having developed further."

Orloff waited long before answering. And then, "But how certain are you people about the Jovians' last message. We on

Earth are inclined to doubt that the Jovians can possibly be as unreasonably belligerent as they have been described."

The Ganymedan laughed shortly, "They broke off all communication after that last message, didn't they? That doesn't sound friendly on their part, does it? I assure you that we've all but stood on our ears trying to contact them.

"Here, now, don't talk. Let me explain something to you. For twenty-five years here on Ganymede a little group of men have worked their hearts out trying to make sense out of a static-ridden, gravity-distorted set of variable clicks in our radio apparatus, for those clicks were our only connection with living intelligence upon Jupiter. It was a job for a world of scientists, but we never had more than two dozen at the Station at any one time. I was one of them from the very beginning and, as a philologist, did my part in helping construct and interpret the code that developed between ourselves and the Jovians, so that you can see I am speaking from the real inside.

"It was a devil of a heartbreaking job. It was five years before we got past the elementary clicks of arithmetic: three and four are seven; the square root of twenty-five is five; factorial six is seven hundred and twenty. After that, months sometimes passed before we could work out and check by further communication a single new fragment of thought.

"*But*—and this is the point—by the time the Jovians broke off relations, we understood them *thoroughly*. There was no more chance of a mistake in comprehension, than there was of Ganymede suddenly cutting loose from Jupiter. And their last message was a threat, and a promise of destruction. Oh, there's no doubt—there's no doubt!"

They were walking through a shallow pass in which the yellow Jupiter light gave way to a clammy darkness.

Orloff was disturbed. He had never had the case presented to him in this fashion before. He said, "But the reason, man. What reason did we give them—"

"No reason! It was simply this: the Jovians had finally discovered from our messages—just where and how I don't know—that *we* were *not* Jovians."

"Well, of course."

"It wasn't 'of course' to them. In their experiences they had never come across intelligences that were not Jovian.

Why should they make an exception in favor of those from outer space?"

"You say they were scientists." Orloff's voice had assumed a wary frigidity. "Wouldn't they realize that alien environments would breed alien life? *We* knew it. We never thought the Jovians were Earthmen though we had never met intelligences other than those of Earth."

They were back in the drenching wash of Jupiter light again, and a spreading region of ice glimmered amberly in a depression to the right.

Birnam answered, "I said they were chemists and physicists —but I never said they were astronomers. Jupiter, my dear commissioner, has an atmosphere three thousand miles or more thick, and those miles of gas block off everything but the Sun and the four largest of Jupiter's moons. The Jovians know nothing of alien environments."

Orloff considered. "And so they decided we were aliens. What next?"

"If we weren't Jovians, then, in their eyes, we weren't people. It turned out that a non-Jovian was 'vermin' by definition."

Orloff's automatic protest was cut off short by Birnam, "In their eyes, I said, vermin we were; and vermin we are. Moreover, we were vermin with the peculiar audacity of having dared to attempt to treat with Jovians—with *human beings*. Their last message was this, word for word—'Jovians are the masters. There is no room for vermin. We will destroy you immediately.' I doubt if there was any animosity in that message—simply a cold statement of fact. But they meant it."

"But why?"

"Why did man exterminate the housefly?"

"Come, sir. You're not seriously presenting an analogy of that nature."

"Why not, since it is certain that the Jovian considers us a sort of housefly—an insufferable type of housefly that dares aspire to intelligence."

Orloff made a last attempt, "But truly, Mr. Secretary, it seems impossible for intelligent life to adopt such an attitude."

"Do you possess much of an acquaintance with any other type of intelligent life than our own?" came with immediate sarcasm. "Do you feel competent to pass on Jovian psychology? Do you know just *how* alien Jovians must be physically? Just think of their world with its gravity at two and one half

Earth normal; with its ammonia oceans—oceans that you might throw all Earth into without raising a respectable splash; with its three-thousand-mile atmosphere, dragged down by the colossal gravity into densities and pressures in its surface layers that make the sea bottoms of Earth resemble a medium-thick vacuum. I tell you we've tried to figure out what sort of life could exist under those conditions and we've given up. It's thoroughly incomprehensible. Do you expect their mentality, then, to be any more understandable? Never! Accept it as it is. They intend destroying us. That's all we know and all we need to know."

He lifted a gloved hand as he finished and one finger pointed, "There's Ether Station just ahead."

Orloff's head swiveled, "Underground?"

"Certainly! All except the Observatory. That's that steel and quartz dome to the right—the small one."

They had stopped before two large boulders that flanked an earthy embankment, and from behind either one a nose-pieced, suited soldier in Ganymedan orange, with blasters ready, advanced upon the two.

Birnam lifted his face into Jupiter's light and the soldiers saluted and stepped aside. A short word was barked into the wrist mike of one of them and the camouflaged opening between the boulders fell into two and Orloff followed the secretary into the yawning air lock.

The Earthman caught one last glimpse of sprawling Jupiter before the closing door cut off the surface altogether.

It was no longer beautiful.

Orloff did not quite feel normal again until he had seated himself in the overstuffed chair in Dr. Edward Prosser's private office. With a sigh of utter relaxation, he propped his monocle under his eyebrow.

"Would Dr. Prosser mind if I smoked in here, while we're waiting?" he asked.

"Go ahead," replied Birnam, carelessly. "My own idea would be to drag Prosser away from whatever he's fooling with just now, but he's a queer chap. We'll get more out of him if we wait until he's ready for us." He withdrew a gnarled stick of greenish tobacco from its case, and bit off the edge viciously.

Orloff smiled through the smoke of his own cigarette, "I don't mind waiting. I still have something to say. You see, for the moment, Mr. Secretary, you gave me the jitters, but, after all, granted that the Jovians intend mischief once they get at us, it remains a fact," and here he spaced his words emphatically, "that they can't get at us."

"A bomb without a fuse, hey?"

"Exactly! It's simplicity itself, and not really worth discussing. You will admit, I suppose, that under no circumstances can the Jovians get away from Jupiter."

"Under *no* circumstances?" There was a quizzical tinge in Birnam's slow reply. "Shall we analyze that?"

He stared hard at the purple flame of his cigar. "It's an old trite saying that the Jovians can't leave Jupiter. The fact has been highly publicized by the sensation mongers of Earth and Ganymede and a great deal of sentiment has been driveled about the unfortunate intelligences who are irrevocably surface-bound, and must forever stare into the Universe without, watching, watching, wondering, and never attaining.

"But, after all, what holds the Jovians to their planet? Two factors! That's all! The first is the immense gravity field of the planet. Two and a half Earth normal."

Orloff nodded. "Pretty bad!" he agreed.

"And Jupiter's gravitational potential is even worse, for because of its greater diameter the intensity of its gravitational field decreases with distance only one tenth as rapidly as Earth's field does. It's a terrible problem—*but it's been solved.*"

"Hey?" Orloff straightened.

"They've got atomic power. Gravity—even Jupiter's—means nothing once you've put unstable atomic nuclei to work for you."

Orloff crushed his cigarette to extinction with a nervous gesture. "But their atmosphere—"

"Yes, that's what's stopping them. They're living at the bottom of a three-thousand-mile-deep ocean of it, where the hydrogen of which it is composed is collapsed by sheer pressure to something approaching the density of *solid* hydrogen. It stays a gas because the temperature of Jupiter is above the critical point of hydrogen, but you just try to figure out the pressure that can make hydrogen *gas* half as heavy as water. You'll be surprised at the number of zeros you'll have to put down.

"No spaceship of metal or of any kind of matter can stand that pressure. No Terrestrial spaceship can land on Jupiter without smashing like an eggshell, and no Jovian spaceship can leave Jupiter without exploding like a soap bubble. That problem has not yet been solved, but it will be some day. Maybe tomorrow, maybe not for a hundred years, or a thousand. We don't know, but when it is solved, the Jovians will be on top of us. And it can be solved in a specific way."

"I don't see how—"

"Force fields! We've got them now, you know."

"Force fields!" Orloff seemed genuinely astonished, and he chewed the word over and over to himself for a few moments. "They're used as meteor shields for ships in the asteroid zone—but I don't see the application to the Jovian problem."

"The ordinary force field," explained Birnam, "is a feeble rarefied zone of energy extending over a hundred miles or more outside the ship. It'll stop meteors but it's just so much empty ether to an object like a gas molecule. *But* what if you took that same zone of energy and compressed it to a thickness of a tenth of an inch. Molecules would bounce off it like this—*ping-g-g-g!* And if you used stronger generators, and compressed the field to a hundredth of an inch, molecules would bounce off even when driven by the unthinkable pressure of Jupiter's atmosphere—and then if you build a ship inside—" He left the sentence dangling.

Orloff was pale. "You're not saying it can be done?"

"I'll bet you anything you like that the Jovians are *trying* to do it. And *we're* trying to do it right here at Ether Station."

The colonial commissioner jerked his chair closer to Birnam and grabbed the Ganymedan's wrist. "Why can't we bombard Jupiter with atomic bombs. Give it a thorough going-over, I mean! With her gravity, and her surface area, we can't miss."

Birnam smiled faintly, "We've thought of that. But atomic bombs would merely tear holes in the atmosphere. And even if you could penetrate, just divide the surface of Jupiter by the area of damage of a single bomb and find how many years we must bombard Jupiter at the rate of a bomb a minute before we begin to do significant damage. Jupiter's *big*. Don't ever forget that!"

His cigar had gone out, but he did not pause to relight. He continued in a low, tense voice. "No, we can't attack the Jovians as long as they're on Jupiter. We must wait for them to come out—and once they do, they're going to have the edge on us in numbers. A terrific, heart-breaking edge—

so we'll just have to have the edge on them in science."

"But," Orloff broke in, and there was a note of fascinated horror in his voice, "how can we tell in advance what they'll have?"

"We can't. We've got to scrape up everything we can lay our hands on and hope for the best. But there's one thing we *do* know they'll have, and that's force fields. They can't get out without them. And if they have them, we must, too, and that's the problem we're trying to solve here. They will not insure us victory, but without them, we will suffer certain defeat. And now you know why we need money—and more than that. We want Earth itself to get to work. It's got to start a drive for scientific armaments and subordinate everything to that. You see?"

Orloff was on his feet. "Birnam, I'm with you—a hundred percent with you. You can count on me back in Washington."

There was no mistaking his sincerity. Birnam gripped the hand outstretched toward him and wrung it—and at the moment, the door flew open and a little pixie of a man hurtled in.

The newcomer spoke in rapid jerks, and exclusively to Birnam. "Where'd you come from? Been trying to get in touch with you. Secretary said you weren't in. Then five minutes later you show up on your own. Can't understand it." He busied himself furiously at his desk.

Birnam grinned. "If you'll take time out, doc, you might say hello to Colonial Commissioner Orloff."

Dr. Edward Prosser turned on his toe like a ballet dancer and looked the Earthman up and down twice. "The new un, hey? We getting any money? We ought to. Been working on a shoestring ever since. At that, we might not be needing any. It depends." He was back at the desk.

Orloff seemed a trifle disconcerted, but Birnam winked impressively, and he contented himself with a glassy stare through the monocle.

Prosser pounced upon a black leather booklet in the recesses of a pigeonhole, threw himself into his swivel chair and wheeled about.

"Glad you came, Birnam," he said, leafing through the booklet. "Got something to show you. Commissioner Orloff, too."

"What were you keeping us waiting for?" demanded Birnam. "Where were you?"

"Busy! Busy as a pig! No sleep for three nights." He looked

up, and his small puckered face fairly flushed with delight. "Everything fell into place of a sudden. Like a jig-saw puzzle. Never saw anything like it. Kept us hopping, I tell you."

"You've gotten the dense force fields you're after?" asked Orloff in sudden excitement.

Prosser seemed annoyed. "No, not that. Something else. Come on." He glared at his watch and jumped out of his seat. "We've got half an hour. Let's go."

An electric-motored flivver waited outside and Prosser spoke excitedly as he sped the purring vehicle down the ramps into the depths of the Station.

"Theory!" he said. "Theory! Damned important, that. You set a technician on a problem. He'll fool around. Waste lifetimes. Get nowhere. Just putter about at random. A true scientist works with theory. Lets math solve his problems." He overflowed with self-satisfaction.

The flivver stopped on a dime before a huge double door and Prosser tumbled out, followed by the other two at a more leisurely pace.

"Through here! Through here!" he said. He shoved the door open and led them down the corridor and up a narrow flight of stairs onto a wall-hugging passageway that circled a huge three-level room. Orloff recognized the gleaming quartz-and-steel pipe-sprouting ellipsoid two levels below as an atomic generator.

He adjusted his monocle and watched the scurrying activity below. An earphoned man on a high stool before a control board studded with dials looked up and waved. Prosser waved back and grinned.

Orloff said, "You create your force fields here?"

"That's right! Ever see one?"

"No." The commissioner smiled, ruefully. "I don't even know what one *is*, except that it can be used as a meteor shield."

Prosser said, "It's very simple. Elementary matter. All matter is composed of atoms. Atoms are held together by interatomic forces. Take away atoms. Leave interatomic forces behind. *That's* a force field."

Orloff looked blank, and Birnam chuckled deep in his throat and scratched the back of his ear.

"That explanation reminds me of our Ganymedan method of suspending an egg a mile high in the air. It goes like this. You find a mountain just a mile high and put the egg on top. Then, keeping the egg where it is, you take the mountain away. That's all."

The colonial commissioner threw his head back to laugh, and the irascible Dr. Prosser puckered his lips in a pursed symbol of disapproval.

"Come, come. No joke, you know. Force fields most important. Got to be ready for the Jovians when they come."

A sudden rasping bur from below sent Prosser back from the railing.

"Get behind screen here," he babbled. "The twenty-millimeter field is going up. Bad radiation."

The bur muted almost into silence, and the three walked out onto the passageway again. There was no apparent change, but Prosser shoved his hand out over the railing and said, "Feel!"

Orloff extended a cautious finger, gasped, and slapped out with the palm of his hand. It was like pushing against very soft sponge rubber or superresilient steel springs.

Birnam tried, too. "That's better than anything we've done yet, isn't it?" He explained to Orloff, "A twenty-millimeter screen is one that can hold an atmosphere of a pressure of twenty millimeters of mercury against a vacuum without appreciable leakage."

The commissioner nodded, "I see! You'd need a seven-hundred-sixty-millimeter screen to hold Earth's atmosphere then."

"Yes! That would be a unit atmosphere screen. Well, Prosser, is this what got you excited?"

"This twenty-millimeter screen? Of course not. I can go up to two hundred fifty millimeters using the activated vanadium pentasulphide in the praseodymium breakdown. But it's not necessary. Technician would do it and blow up the place. Scientist checks on theory and goes slow." He winked. "We're hardening the field now. Watch!"

"Shall we get behind the screen?"

"Not necessary now. Radiation bad only at beginning."

The burring waxed again, but not as loudly as before. Prosser shouted to the man at the control board, and a spreading wave of the hand was the only reply.

Then the control man waved a clenched fist and Prosser cried, "We've passed fifty millimeters! Feel the field!"

Orloff extended his hand and poked it curiously. The sponge rubber had hardened! He tried to pinch it between finger and thumb so perfect was the illusion, but here the "rubber" faded to unresisting air.

Prosser *tch-tched* impatiently. "No resistance at right angles to force. Elementary mechanics, that is."

The control man was gesturing again. "Past seventy," explained Prosser. "We're slowing down now. Critical point is 83.42."

He hung over the railing and kicked out with his feet at the other two. "Stay away! Dangerous!"

And then he yelled, "Careful! The generator's bucking!"

The bur had risen to a hoarse maximum and the control man worked frantically at his switches. From within the quartz heart of the central atomic generator, the sullen red glow of the bursting atoms had brightened dangerously.

There was a break in the bur, a reverberant roar, and a blast of air that threw Orloff hard against the wall.

Prosser dashed up. There was a cut over his eye. "Hurt? No? Good, good! I was expecting something of the sort. Should have warned you. Let's go down. Where's Birnam?"

The tall Ganymedan picked himself up off the floor and brushed at his clothes. "Here I am. What blew up?"

"Nothing blew up. Something buckled. Come on, down we go." He dabbed at his forehead with a handkerchief and led the way downward.

The control man removed his earphones as he approached and got off his stool. He looked tired, and his dirt-smeared face was greasy with perspiration.

"The damn thing started going at 82.8, boss. It almost caught me."

"It did, did it?" growled Prosser. "Within limits of error, isn't it? How's the generator? Hey, Stoddard!"

The technician addressed replied from his station at the generator, "Tube 5 died. It'll take two days to replace."

Prosser turned in satisfaction and said, "It worked. Went exactly as presumed. Problem solved, gentlemen. Trouble over. Let's get back to my office. I want to eat. And then I want to sleep."

He did not refer to the subject again until once more behind the desk in his office, and then he spoke between huge bites of a liver-and-onion sandwich.

He addressed Birnam, "Remember the work on space strain last June. It flopped, but we kept at it. Finch got a lead last week and I developed it. Everything fell into place. Slick as goose grease. Never saw anything like it."

"Go ahead," said Birnam, calmly. He knew Prosser sufficiently well to avoid showing impatience.

"You saw what happened. When a field tops 83.42 millimeters, it becomes unstable. Space won't stand the strain. It buckles and the field blows. *Boom!*"

Birnam's mouth dropped open and the arms of Orloff's chair creaked under sudden pressure. Silence for a while, and then Birnam said unsteadily, "You mean force fields stronger than that are impossible?"

"They're possible. You can create them. But the denser they are, the more unstable they are. If I had turned on the two-hundred-and-fifty-millimeter field, it would have lasted one tenth of a second. Then, blooie! Would have blown up the Station! *And* myself! Technician would have done it. Scientist is warned by theory. Works carefully, the way I did. No harm done."

Orloff tucked his monocle into his vest pocket and said tremulously, "But if a force field is the same thing as interatomic forces, why is it that steel has such a strong interatomic binding force without bucking space? There's a flaw there."

Prosser eyed him in annoyance. "No flaw. Critical strength depends on number of generators. In steel, each atom is a force-field generator. That means about three hundred billion trillion generators for every ounce of matter. If we could use that many— As it is, one hundred generators would be the practical limit. That only raises the critical point to ninety-seven or thereabout."

He got to his feet and continued with sudden fervor, "No. Problem's over, I tell you. Absolutely impossible to create a force field capable of holding Earth's atmosphere for more than a hundredth of a second. Jovian atmosphere entirely out of the question. Cold figures say that; backed by experiment. *Space won't stand it!*

"Let the Jovians do their damnedest. They can't get out! That's final! That's final! *That's final!*"

Orloff said, "Mr. Secretary, can I send a spacegram anywhere in the Station? I want to tell Earth that I'm returning by the next ship and that the Jovian problem is liquidated— entirely and for good."

Birnam said nothing, but the relief of his face as he shook hands with the colonial commissioner, transfigured the gaunt homeliness of it unbelievably.

And Dr. Prosser repeated, with a birdlike jerk of his head, "That's *final!*"

Hal Tuttle looked up as Captain Everett of the spaceship *Transparent,* newest ship of the Comet Space Lines, entered his private observation room in the nose of the ship.

The captain said, "A spacegram has just reached me from the home offices at Tucson. We're to pick up Colonial Commissioner Orloff at Jovopolis, Ganymede, and take him back to Earth."

"Good. We haven't sighted any ships?"

"No, no! We're way off the regular space lanes. The first the System will know of us will be the landing of the *Transparent* on Ganymede. It will be the greatest thing in space travel since the first trip to the Moon." His voice softened suddenly, "What's wrong, Hal? This is *your* triumph, after all."

Hal Tuttle looked up and out into the blackness of space. "I suppose it is. Ten years of work, Sam. I lost an arm and an eye in that first explosion, but I don't regret them. It's the reaction that's got me. The problem is solved; my lifework is finished."

"So is every steel-hulled ship in the System."

Tuttle smiled. "Yes. It's hard to realize, isn't it?" He gestured outward. "You see the stars? Part of the time, there's nothing between them and us. It gives me a queazy feeling." His voice brooded, "Nine years I worked for nothing. I wasn't a theoretician, and never really knew where I was headed—just tried everything. I tried a little too hard and space wouldn't stand it. I paid an arm and an eye and started fresh."

Captain Everett balled his fist and pounded the hull—the hull through which the stars shone unobstructed. There was the muffled thud of flesh striking an unyielding surface—but no response whatever from the invisible wall.

Tuttle nodded, "It's solid enough, now—though it flicks on and off eight hundred thousand times a second. I got the idea from the stroboscopic lamp. You know them—they flash on and off so rapidly that it gives all the impression of steady illumination.

"And so it is with the hull. It's not on long enough to buckle space. It's not off long enough to allow appreciable leakage of the atmosphere. And the net effect is a strength better than steel."

He paused and added slowly, "And there's no telling how far we can go. Speed up the intermission effect. Have the field flick off and on millions of times per second—billions of times. You can get fields strong enough to hold an atomic explosion. My lifework!"

Captain Everett pounded the other's shoulder. "Snap out of it, man. Think of the landing on Ganymede. The devil! It will be great publicity. Think of Orloff's face, for instance, when he finds he is to be the first passenger in history ever to travel in a spaceship with a force-field hull. How do you suppose he'll feel?"

Hal Tuttle shrugged. "I imagine he'll be rather pleased."

THE END

With "Not Final!" I completed my third year as a writer—three years since my initial trip to Campbell's office. In that time I had earned just a hair short of a thousand dollars (not as bad as it sounds in days when college tuition was only four hundred dollars a year) and I had about a quarter of that in my savings account.

Still, you can see that there was nothing in that financial record to lead me to think that writing was a possible way of making a living—especially since I had no dream of ever writing anything but magazine science fiction.

On June 10, 1941, in the course of a talk with Fred Pohl, I mentioned my frustration at not being able to make a sale to **Unknown.** Fred said he had a good idea for a fantasy, and from that it was a short step to an agreement to go halfies. We'd talk the idea over, I would write it, and we'd split the sale, if any, fifty-fifty.

Fred must have been willing because (as I found out three days later) his magazines were doing poorly and he was being relieved of his editorial position.

It was too bad, of course, but not an irredeemable catastrophe. Pohl had had nearly two years of valuable editorial experience, and the time would come when this would stand him in good stead in a much more important and longerenduring role as editor of **Galaxy,** which during the 1950s and 1960s was to compete with **Astounding** for leadership in the field.

As for myself, I could scarcely complain. Pohl had accepted eight of my stories (over a quarter of those I had written and nearly half of those I had sold up to then). Of these, six had already been published and one ("Super-Neutron") was safely slated for publication in the forthcoming issue of **Astounding.** That left the ninth, "Christmas on Ganymede." It was not yet paid for, nor had it actually been set in type, and, regretfully, Pohl had to return it. However, I sold it within two weeks to **Thrilling Wonder Stories** for a little more than Pohl would have been able to pay me, so no harm was done even there.—And though I regretted the loss of a market, Pohl had safely seen me through the period during which I developed to the point where Campbell and **Astounding** itself could become my major market.

At first, when "Christmas on Ganymede" was returned, I thought it was because the Pohl magazines had been suspended altogether. If the publishers had intended that, they changed their minds. **Astonishing** continued a couple of years, until it was killed by the World War II paper shortage. **Super Science Stories** survived World War II and even a little past the 1940s, and was yet to publish one more story of mine.

But back to June 10— Taking Fred's fantasy idea, I wrote the story entirely on my own, calling it "Legal Rights." Once again, though, a collaboration don't succeed. On July 8, Campbell rejected it, the first rejection I had received from him in half a year.

By that time, though, Fred was agenting again. I gave him the story, rather shamefacedly, and forgot about it. He changed the name to "Legal Rites" (much better) and rewrote it quite a bit. Seven years later, he actually sold it.

19

Legal Rites
(with James MacCreigh)

I

Already the stars were out, though the sun had just dipped under the horizon, and the sky of the west was a blood-stuck gold behind the Sierra Nevadas.

"Hey!" squawked Russell Harley. "Come back!"

But the one-lunged motor of the old Ford was making too much noise; the driver didn't hear him. Harley cursed as he watched the old car career along the sandy ruts on its half-flat tires. Its taillight was saying a red *no* to him. *No,* you can't get away tonight; *no,* you'll have to stay here and fight it out.

Harley grunted and climbed back up the porch stairs of the old wooden house. It was well made, anyhow. The stairs, though half a century old, neither creaked beneath him nor showed cracks.

Harley picked up the bags he'd dropped when he experienced his abrupt change of mind—fake leather and worn out, they were—and carted them into the house. He dumped them on a dust-jacketed sofa and looked around.

It was stifling hot, and the smell of the desert outside had permeated the room. Harley sneezed.

"Water," he said out loud. "That's what I need."

He'd prowled through every room on the ground floor before he stopped still and smote his head. Plumbing—naturally there'd be no plumbing in this hole eight miles out on the desert! A well was the best he could hope for—

If that.

It was getting dark. No electric lights either, of course.

Weird Tales, September 1950
Copyright © 1950 by Weird Tales

He blundered irritatedly through the dusky rooms to the back of the house. The screen door shrieked metallically as he opened it. A bucket hung by the door. He picked it up, tipped it, shook the loose sand out of it. He looked over the "back yard"—about thirty thousand visible acres of hilly sand, rock and patches of sage and flame-tipped ocotillo.

No well.

The old fool got water from somewhere, he thought savagely. Obstinately he climbed down the back steps and wandered out into the desert. Overhead the stars were blinding, a million billion of them, but the sunset was over already and he could see only hazily. The silence was murderous. Only a faint whisper of breeze over the sand, and the slither of his shoes.

He caught a glimmer of starlight from the nearest clump of sage and walked to it. There was a pool of water, caught in the angle of two enormous boulders. He stared at it doubtfully, then shrugged. It was water. It was better than nothing. He dipped the bucket in the little pool. Knowing nothing of the procedure, he filled it with a quart of loose sand as he scooped it along the bottom. When he lifted it, brimful, to his lips, he spat out the first mouthful and swore violently.

Then he used his head. He set the bucket down, waited a second for the sand grains to settle, cupped water in his hands, lifted it to his lips. . . .

Pat. HISS. Pat. HISS. Pat. HISS—

"What the hell!" Harley stood up, looked around in abrupt puzzlement. It sounded like water dripping from somewhere, onto a red-hot stove, flashing into sizzling steam. He saw nothing, only the sand and the sage and the pool of tepid, sickly water.

Pat. HISS—

Then he saw it, and his eyes bulged. Out of nowhere it was dripping, a drop a second, a sticky, dark drop that was thicker than water, that fell to the ground lazily, in slow defiance of gravity. And when it struck each drop sizzled and skittered about, and vanished. It was perhaps eight feet from him, just visible in the starlight.

And then, "Get off my land!" said the voice from nowhere.

Harley got. By the time he got to Rebel Butte three hours later, he was barely managing to walk, wishing desperately that he'd delayed long enough for one more good drink of water, despite all the fiends of hell. But he'd run the first three miles. He'd had plenty of encouragement. He remembered with a shudder how the clear desert air had taken milky shape around the incredible trickle of dampness and had advanced on him threateningly.

And when he got to the first kerosene-lighted saloon of Rebel Butte, and staggered inside, the saloonkeeper's fascinated stare at the front of his shoddy coat showed him strong evidence that he hadn't been suddenly taken with insanity, or drunk on the unaccustomed sensation of fresh desert air. All down the front of him it was, and the harder he rubbed the harder it stayed, the stickier it got. Blood!

"Whiskey!" he said in a strangled voice, tottering to the bar. He pulled a threadbare dollar bill from his pocket, flapped it onto the mahogany.

The blackjack game at the back of the room had stopped. Harley was acutely conscious of the eyes of the players, the bartender and the tall, lean man leaning on the bar. All were watching him.

The bartender broke the spell. He reached for a bottle behind him without looking at it, placed it on the counter before Harley. He poured a glass of water from a jug, set it down with a shot glass beside the bottle.

"I could of told you that would happen," he said cautiously. "Only you wouldn't of believed me. You had to meet Hank for yourself before you'd believe he was there."

Harley remembered his thirst and drained the glass of water, then poured himself a shot of the whiskey and swallowed it without waiting for the chaser to be refilled. The whiskey felt good going down, almost good enough to stop his internal shakes.

"What are you talking about?" he said finally. He twisted his body and leaned forward across the bar to partly hide the stains on his coat. The saloonkeeper laughed.

"Old Hank," he said. "I knowed who you was right away, even before Tom came back and told me where he'd took you. I knowed you was Zeb Harley's no-good nephew, come to take Harley Hall an' sell it before he was cold in the grave."

The blackjack players were still watching him, Russell Harley saw. Only the lean man farther along the bar seemed to have dismissed him. He was pouring himself another drink, quite occupied with his task.

Harley flushed. "Listen," he said, "I didn't come in here for advice. I wanted a drink. I'm paying for it. Keep your mouth out of this."

The saloonkeeper shrugged. He turned his back and walked away to the blackjack table. After a couple of seconds one of the players turned, too, and threw a card down. The others followed suit.

Harley was just getting set to swallow his pride and talk to the saloonkeeper again—he seemed to know something about what Harley'd been through, and might be helpful—when the lean man tapped his shoulder. Harley whirled and almost dropped his glass. Absorbed and jumpy, he hadn't seen him come up.

"Young man," said the lean one, "My name's Nicholls. Come along with me, sir, and we'll talk this thing over. I think we may be of service to each other."

Even the twelve-cylinder car Nicholls drove jounced like a hay-wagon over the sandy ruts leading to the place old Zeb had—laughingly—named "Harley Hall."

Russell Harley twisted his neck and stared at the heap of paraphernalia in the open rumble seat. "I don't like it," he complained. "I never had anything to do with ghosts. How do I know this stuff'll work?"

Nicholls smiled, "You'll have to take my word for it. I've had dealings with ghosts before. You could say that I might qualify as a ghost exterminator, if I chose."

Harley growled. "I still don't like it."

Nicholls turned a sharp look on him. "You like the prospect of owning Harley Hall, don't you? And looking for all the money your late uncle is supposed to have hidden around somewhere?" Harley shrugged. "Certainly you do," said Nicholls, returning his eyes to the road. "And with good reason. The local reports put the figure pretty high, young man."

"That's where you come in, I guess," Harley said sullenly. "I find the money—that I own anyhow—and give some of it to you. How much?"

"We'll discuss that later," Nicholls said. He smiled absently as he looked ahead.

"We'll discuss it right now!"

The smile faded from Nicholl's face. "No," he said. "We won't. I'm doing you a favor, young Harley. Remember that. In return—you'll do as I say, all the way!"

Harley digested that carefully, and it was not a pleasant meal. He waited a couple of seconds before he changed the subject.

"I was out here once when the old man was alive," he said. "He didn't say nothing about any ghost."

"Perhaps he felt you might think him—well, peculiar," Nicholls said. "And perhaps you would have. When were you here?"

"Oh, a long time ago," Harley said evasively. "But I was here a whole day, and part of the night. The old man was crazy as a coot, but he didn't keep any ghosts in the attic."

"This ghost was a friend of his," Nicholls said. "The gentleman in charge of the bar told you that, surely. Your late uncle was something of a recluse. He lived in this house a dozen miles from nowhere, came into town hardly ever, wouldn't let anyone get friendly with him. But he wasn't exactly a hermit. He had Hank for company."

"Fine company."

Nicholls inclined his head seriously. "Oh, I don't know," he said. "From all accounts, they got on well together. They played pinochle and chess—Hank's supposed to have been a great pinochle player. He was killed that way, according to the local reports. Caught somebody dealing from the bottom and shot it out with him. He lost. A bullet pierced his throat and he died quite bloodily." He turned the wheel, putting his weight into the effort, and succeeded in twisting the car out of the ruts of the "road," sent it jouncing across unmarked sand to the old frame house to which they were going.

"That," he finished as he pulled up before the porch, "accounts for the blood that accompanies his apparition."

Harley opened the door slowly and got out, looking uneasily at the battered old house. Nicholls cut the motor, got out and walked at once to the back of the car.

"Come on," he said, dragging things out of the compartment. "Give me a hand with this. I'm not going to carry this stuff all by myself."

Harley came around reluctantly, regarded the curious assortment of bundles of dried faggots, lengths of colored cord, chalk pencils, ugly little bunches of wilted weeds, bleached bones of small animals and a couple of less pleasant things without pleasure.

Pat. HISS. Pat. HISS—

"He's here!" Harley yelped. "Listen! He's someplace around here watching us."

"Ha!"

The laugh was deep, unpleasant and—bodiless. Harley looked around desperately for the tell-tale trickle of blood. And he found it; from the air it issued, just beside the car, sinking gracefully to the ground and sizzling, vanishing there.

"I'm watching you, all right," the voice said grimly. "Russell, you worthless piece of corruption, I've got no more use for you than you used to have for me. Dead or alive, this is my land! I shared it with your uncle, you young scalawag, but I won't share it with you. Get out!"

Harley's knees weakened and he tottered dizzily to the rear bumper, sat on it. "Nicholls—" he said confusedly.

"Oh, brace up," Nicholls said with irritation. He tossed a ball of gaudy twine, red and green, with curious knots tied along it, to Harley. Then he confronted the trickle of blood and made a few brisk passes in the air before it. His lips were moving silently, Harley saw, but no words came out.

There was a gasp and a chopped-off squawk from the source of the blood drops. Nicholls clapped his hands sharply, then turned to young Harley.

"Take that cord you have in your hands and stretch it around the house," he said. "All the way around, and make sure it goes right across the middle of the doors and windows. It isn't much, but it'll hold him till we can get the good stuff set up."

Harley nodded, then pointed a rigid finger at the drops of blood, now sizzling and fuming more angrily than before. "What about *that?*" he managed to get out.

Nicholls grinned complacently. "I'll hold him here till the cows come home," he said. "Get moving!"

Harley inadvertently inhaled a lungful of noxious white smoke and coughed till the tears rolled down his cheeks. When he recovered he looked at Nicholls, who was reading silently from a green leather book with dog-eared pages. He said, "Can I stop stirring this now?"

Nicholls grimaced angrily and shook his head without looking at him. He went on reading, his lips contorting over syllables that were not in any language Harley had ever heard, then snapped the book shut and wiped his brow.

"Fine," he said. "So far, so good." He stepped over to windward of the boiling pot Harley was stirring on the hob over the fireplace, peered down into it cautiously.

"That's about done," he said. "Take it off the fire and let it cool a bit."

Harley lifted it down, then squeezed his aching biceps with his left hand. The stuff was the consistency of sickly green fudge.

"Now what?" he asked.

Nicholls didn't answer. He looked up in mild surprise at the sudden squawk of triumph from outside, followed by the howling of a chill wind.

"Hank must be loose," he said casually. "He can't do us any harm, I think, but we'd better get a move on." He rummaged in the dwindled pile of junk he'd brought from the car, extracted a paintbrush. "Smear this stuff around all the windows and doors. All but the front door. For that I have something else." He pointed to what seemed to be the front axle of an old Model-T. "Leave that on the doorsill. Cold iron. You can just step over it, but Hank won't be able to pass it. It's been properly treated already with the very best thaumaturgy."

"Step over it," Harley repeated. "What would I want to step over it for? *He's* out there."

"He won't hurt you," said Nicholls. "You will carry an amulet with you—that one, there—that will keep him away. Probably he couldn't really hurt you anyhow, being a low-order ghost who can't materialize to any greater density. But just to take no chances, carry the amulet and don't stay out too long. It won't hold him off forever, not for more than half an hour. If you ever have to go out and stay for any length of time, tie that bundle of herbs around your neck." Nicholls smiled. "That's only for emergencies, though. It works on the asafoetida principle. Ghosts can't come anywhere near it—but you won't like it much yourself. It has—ah—a rather definite odor."

He leaned gingerly over the pot again, sniffing. He sneezed.

"Well, that's cool enough," he said. "Before it hardens, get moving. Start spreading the stuff upstairs—and make sure you don't miss any windows."

"What are you going to do?"

"I," said Nicholls sharply, "will be here. Start."

But he wasn't. When Harley finished his disagreeable task and came down, he called Nicholls' name, but the man was gone. Harley stepped to the door and looked out; the car was gone, too.

He shrugged. "Oh, well," he said, and began taking the dust-cloths off the furniture.

II

Somewhere within the cold, legal mind of Lawyer Turnbull, he weighed the comparative likeness of nightmare and insanity.

He stared at the plush chair facing him, noted with distinct uneasiness how the strangely weightless, strangely sourceless trickle of redness disappeared as it hit the floor, but left long, mud-ochre streaks matted on the upholstery. The sound was unpleasant, too; *Pat. HISS. Pat. HISS*—

The voice continued impatiently, "Damn your human stupidity! I may be a ghost, but heaven knows I'm not trying to haunt you. Friend, you're not that important to me. Get this—I'm here on business."

Turnbull learned that you cannot wet dry lips with a dehydrated tongue. "Legal business?"

"Sure. The fact that I was once killed by violence, and have to continue my existence on the astral plane, doesn't mean I've lost my legal rights. Does it?"

The lawyer shook his head in bafflement. He said, "This would be easier on me if you weren't invisible. Can't you do something about it?"

There was a short pause. "Well, I could materialize for a minute," the voice said. "It's hard work—damn hard, for me. There are a lot of us astral entities that can do it easy as falling out of bed, but—Well, if I have to I shall try to do it once."

There was a shimmering in the air above the armchair, and a milky, thin smoke condensed into an intangible seated figure. Turnbull took no delight in noting that, through the figure, the outlines of the chair were still hazily visible. The figure thickened. Just as the features took form—just as Turnbull's bulging eyes made out a prominent hooked nose and a crisp beard—it thinned and exploded with a soft pop.

The voice said weakly, "I didn't think I was that bad. I'm way out of practice. I guess that's the first daylight materialization I've made in seventy-five years."

The lawyer adjusted his rimless glasses and coughed. *Hell's binges*, he thought, *the worst thing about this is that I'm believing it!*

"Oh, well," he said aloud. Then he hurried on before the

visitor could take offense: "Just what did you want? I'm just a small-town lawyer, you know. My business is fairly routine—"

"I know all about your business," the voice said. "You can handle my case—it's a land affair. I want to sue Russell Harley."

"Harley?" Turnbull fingered his cheek. "Any relation to Zeb Harley?"

"His nephew—and his heir, too."

Turnbull nodded. "Yes, I remember now. My wife's folks live in Rebel Butte, and I've been there. Quite a coincidence you should come to me—"

The voice laughed. "It was no coincidence," it said softly.

"Oh." Turnbull was silent for a second. Then, "I see," he said. He cast a shrewd glance at the chair. "Lawsuits cost money, Mr.—I don't think you mentioned your name?"

"Hank Jenkins," the voice prompted. "I know that. Would —let's see. Would six hundred and fifty dollars be sufficient?"

Turnbull swallowed. "I think so," he said in a relatively unemotional tone—relative to what he was thinking.

"Then suppose we call that your retainer. I happen to have cached a considerable sum of gold when I was—that is to say, before I became an astral entity. I'm quite certain it hasn't been disturbed. You will have to call it treasure trove, I guess, and give half of it to the state, but there's thirteen hundred dollars altogether."

Turnbull nodded judiciously. "Assuming we can locate your trove," he said, "I think that would be quite satisfactory." He leaned back in his chair and looked legal. His aplomb had returned.

And half an hour later he said slowly, "I'll take your case."

Judge Lawrence Gimbel had always liked his job before. But his thirteen honorable years on the bench lost their flavor for him as he grimaced wearily and reached for his gavel. This case was far too confusing for his taste.

The clerk made his speech, and the packed courtroom sat down en masse. Gimbel held a hand briefly to his eyes before he spoke.

"Is the counsel for the plaintiff ready?"

"I am, your honor." Turnbull, alone at his table, rose and bowed.

"The counsel for the defendant?"

"Ready, your honor!" Fred Wilson snapped. He looked

with a hard flicker of interest at Turnbull and his solitary table, then leaned over and whispered in Russell Harley's ear. The youth nodded glumly, then shrugged.

Gimbel said, "I understand the attorneys for both sides have waived jury trial in this case of Henry Jenkins versus Russell Joseph Harley."

Both lawyers nodded. Gimbel continued, "In view of the unusual nature of this case, I imagine it will prove necessary to conduct it with a certain amount of informality. The sole purpose of this court is to arrive at the true facts at issue, and deliver a verdict in accord with the laws pertaining to these facts. I will not stand on ceremony. Nevertheless, I will not tolerate any disturbances or unnecessary irregularities. The spectators will kindly remember that they are here on privilege. Any demonstration will result in the clearing of the court."

He looked severely at the white faces that gleamed unintelligently up at him. He suppressed a sigh and he said, "The counsel for the plaintiff will begin."

Turnbull rose quickly to his feet, faced the judge.

"Your honor," he said, "we propose to show that my client, Henry Jenkins, has been deprived of his just rights by the defendant. Mr. Jenkins, by virtue of a sustained residence of more than twenty years in the house located on Route 22, eight miles north of the town of Rebel Butte, with the full knowledge of its legal owner, has acquired certain rights. In legal terminology we define these as the rights of adverse possession. The layman would call them common-law rights—squatters' rights."

Gimbel folded his hands and tried to relax. Squatters' rights—for a ghost! He sighed, but listened attentively as Turnbull went on.

"Upon the death of Zebulon Harley, the owner of the house involved—it is better known, perhaps, as Harley Hall—the defendant inherited title to the property. We do not question his right to it. But my client has an equity in Harley Hall; the right to free and full existence. The defendant has forcefully evicted my client, by means which have caused my client great mental distress, and have even endangered his very existence."

Gimbel nodded. If the case only had a precedent somewhere. . . . But it hadn't; he remembered grimly the hours he'd spent thumbing through all sorts of unlikely law books, looking for anything that might bear on the case. It had been his better judgment that he throw the case out of court outright—a judge couldn't afford to have himself laughed at, not if he were ambitious. And public laughter was about the only certainty there was to this case. But Wilson had put up such a fight that the judge's temper had taken over. He never did like Wilson, anyhow.

"You may proceed with your witnesses," he said.

Turnbull nodded. To the clerk he said, "Call Henry Jenkins to the stand."

Wilson was on his feet before the clerk opened his mouth.

"Objection!" he bellowed. "The so-called Henry Jenkins cannot qualify as a witness!"

"Why not?" demanded Turnbull.

"Because he's dead!"

The judge clutched his gavel with one hand, forehead with the other. He banged on the desk to quiet the courtroom.

Turnbull stood there, smiling. "Naturally," he said, "you'll have proof of that statement."

Wilson snarled. "Certainly." He referred to his brief. "The so-called Henry Jenkins is the ghost, spirit or specter of one Hank Jenkins, who prospected for gold in this territory a century ago. He was killed by a bullet through the throat from the gun of one Long Tom Cooper, and was declared legally dead on September 14, 1850. Cooper was hanged for his murder. No matter what hocus-pocus you produce for evidence to the contrary now, that status of legal death remains completely valid."

"What evidence have you of the identity of my client with this Hank Jenkins?" Turnbull asked grimly.

"Do you deny it?"

Turnbull shrugged. "I deny nothing. I'm not being cross-examined. Furthermore, the sole prerequisite of a witness is that he understand the value of an oath. Henry Jenkins was tested by John Quincy Fitzjames, professor of psychology at the University of Southern California. The results—I have Dr. Fitzjames' sworn statement of them here, which I will introduce as an exhibit—show clearly that my client's intelligence quotient is well above normal, and that a psychiatric examination discloses no important aberrations which would injure his validity as a witness. I insist that my client be allowed to testify on his own behalf."

"But he's dead!" squawked Wilson. "He's invisible right now!"

"My client," said Turnbull stiffly, "is not present just

now. Undoubtedly that accounts for what you term his invisibility." He paused for the appreciative murmur that swept through the court. Things were breaking perfectly, he thought, smiling. "I have here another affidavit," he said. "It is signed by Elihu James and Terence MacRae, who respectively head the departments of physics and biology at the same university. It states that my client exhibits all the vital phenomena of life. I am prepared to call all three of my expert witnesses to the stand, if necessary."

Wilson scowled but said nothing. Judge Gimbel leaned forward.

"I don't see how it is possible for me to refuse the plaintiff the right to testify," he said. "If the three experts who prepared these reports will testify on the stand to the facts contained in them, Henry Jenkins may then take the stand."

Wilson sat down heavily. The three experts spoke briefly— and dryly. Wilson put them through only the most formal of cross-examinations.

The judge declared a brief recess. In the corridor outside, Wilson and his client lit cigarettes and looked unsympathetically at each other.

"I feel like a fool," said Russell Harley. "Bringing suit against a ghost."

"The ghost brought the suit," Wilson reminded him. "If only we'd been able to hold fire for a couple more weeks, till another judge came on the bench, I could've got this thing thrown right out of court."

"Well, why couldn't we wait?"

"Because you were in such a damn hurry!" Wilson said. "You and that idiot Nicholls—so confident that it never would come to trial."

Harley shrugged, and thought unhappily of their failure in completely exorcising the ghost of Hank Jenkins. That had been a mess. Jenkins had somehow escaped from the charmed circle they'd drawn around him, in which they'd hoped to keep him till the trial was forfeited by non-appearance.

"That's another thing," said Wilson. "Where is Nicholls?"

Harley shrugged again. "I dunno. The last I saw of him was in your office. He came around to see me right after the deputy slapped the show-cause order on me at the house. He brought me down to you—said you'd been recommended to him. Then you and him and I talked about the case for a while. He went out, after he lent me a little money to help meet your retainer. Haven't seen him since."

"I'd like to know who recommended me to him," Wilson said grimly. "I don't think he'd ever recommend anybody else. I don't like this case—and I don't much like you."

Harley growled but said nothing. He flung his cigarette away. It tasted of the garbage that hung around his neck— everything did. Nicholls had told no lies when he said Harley wouldn't much like the bundle of herbs that would ward off the ghost of old Jenkins. They smelled.

The court clerk was in the corridor, bawling something, and people were beginning to trickle back in. Harley and his attorney went with them.

When the trial had been resumed, the clerk said, "Henry Jenkins!"

Wilson was on his feet at once. He opened the door of the judge's chamber, said something in a low tone. Then he stepped back, as if to let someone through.

Pat. HISS. Pat. HISS—

There was a concerted gasp from the spectators as the weirdly appearing trickle of blood moved slowly across the open space to the witness chair. This was the ghost—the plaintiff in the most eminently absurd case in the history of jurisprudence.

"All right, Hank," Turnbull whispered. "You'll have to materialize long enough to let the clerk swear you in."

The clerk drew back nervously at the pillar of milky fog that appeared before him, vaguely humanoid in shape. A phantom hand, half transparent, reached out to touch the Bible. The clerk's voice shook as he administered the oath, and heard the response come from the heart of the cloudpillar.

The haze drifted into the witness chair, bent curiously at about hip-height, and popped into nothingness.

The judge banged his gavel wildly. The buzz of alarm that had arisen from the spectators died out.

"I'll warn you again," he declared, "that unruliness will not be tolerated. The counsel for the plaintiff may proceed."

Turnbull walked to the witness chair and addressed its emptiness.

"Your name?"

"My name is Henry Jenkins."

"Your occupation?"

There was a slight pause. "I have none. I guess you'd say I'm retired."

"Mr. Jenkins, just what connection have you with the building referred to as Harley Hall?"

"I have occupied it for ninety years."

"During this time, did you come to know the late Zebulon Harley, owner of the Hall?"

"I knew Zeb quite well."

Turnbull nodded. "When did you make his acquaintance?" he asked.

"In the spring of 1907. Zeb had just lost his wife. After that, you see, he made Harley Hall his year-round home. He became—well, more or less of a hermit. Before that we had never met, since he was only seldom at the Hall. But we became friendly then."

"How long did this friendship last?"

"Until he died last fall. I was with him when he died. I still have a few keepsakes he left me then." There was a distinct nostalgic sigh from the witness chair, which by now was literally spattered with muddy red liquid. The falling drops seemed to hesitate for a second, and their sizzling noise was muted as with a strong emotion.

Turnbull went on, "Your relations with him were good, then?"

"I'd call them excellent," the emptiness replied firmly. "Every night we sat up together. When we didn't play pinochle or chess or cribbage, we just sat and talked over the news of the day. I still have the book we used to keep records of the chess and pinochle games. Zeb made the entries himself, in his own handwriting."

Turnbull abandoned the witness for a moment. He faced the judge with a smile. "I offer in evidence," he said, "the book mentioned. Also a ring given to the plaintiff by the late Mr. Harley, and a copy of the plays of Gilbert and Sullivan. On the flyleaf of this book is inscribed, 'To Old Hank,' in Harley's own hand."

He turned again to the empty, blood-leaking witness chair.

He said, "In all your years of association, did Zebulon Harley ever ask you to leave, or to pay rent?"

"Of course not. Not Zeb!"

Turnbull nodded. "Very good," he said. "Now, just one or two more questions. Will you tell in your own words what occurred after the death of Zebulon Harley, that caused you to bring this suit?"

"Well, in January young Harley—"

"You mean Russell Joseph Harley, the defendant?"

"Yes. He arrived at Harley Hall on January fifth. I asked him to leave, which he did. On the next day he returned with another man. They placed a talisman upon the threshold of the main entrance, and soon after sealed every threshold and windowsill in the Hall with a substance which is noxious to me. These activities were accompanied by several of the most deadly spells in the Ars Magicorum. He further added an Exclusion Circle with a radius of a little over a mile, entirely surrounding the Hall."

"I see," the lawyer said. "Will you explain to the court the effects of these activities?"

"Well," the voice said thoughtfully, "it's a little hard to put in words. I can't pass the Circle without a great expenditure of energy. Even if I did I couldn't enter the building because of the talisman and the seals."

"Could you enter by air? Through a chimney, perhaps?"

"No. The Exclusion Circle is really a sphere. I'm pretty sure the effort would destroy me."

"In effect, then, you are entirely barred from the house you have occupied for ninety years, due to the wilful acts of Russell Joseph Harley, the defendant, and an unnamed accomplice of his."

"That is correct."

Turnbull beamed. "Thank you. That's all."

He turned to Wilson, whose face had been a study in dourness throughout the entire examination. "Your witness," he said.

Wilson snapped to his feet and strode to the witness chair.

He said belligerently, "You say your name is Henry Jenkins?"

"Yes."

"That is your name now, you mean to say. What was your name before?"

"Before?" There was surprise in the voice that emanated from above the trickling blood-drops. "Before when?"

Wilson scowled. "Don't pretend ignorance," he said sharply. "Before you *died,* of course."

"Objection!" Turnbull was on his feet, glaring at Wilson. "The counsel for the defense has no right to speak of some hypothetical death of my client!"

Gimbel raised a hand wearily and cut off the words that were forming on Wilson's lips. "Objection sustained," he said. "No evidence has been presented to identify the plaintiff as the prospector who was killed in 1850—or anyone else."

Wilson's mouth twisted into a sour grimace. He continued on a lower key.

"You say, Mr. Jenkins, that you occupied Harley Hall for ninety years."

"Ninety-two years next month. The Hall wasn't built—in its present form, anyhow—until 1876, but I occupied the house that stood on the site previously."

"What did you do before then?"

"Before then?" The voice paused, then said doubtfully, "I don't remember."

"You're under oath!" Wilson flared.

The voice got firmer. "Ninety years is a long time," it said. "I don't remember."

"Let's see if I can't refresh your memory. Is it true that ninety-one years ago, in the very year in which you claim to have begun your occupancy of Harley Hall, Hank Jenkins was killed in a gun duel?"

"That may be true, if you say so. I don't remember."

"Do you remember that the shooting occurred not fifty feet from the present site of Harley Hall?"

"It may be."

"Well, then," Wilson thundered, "is it not a fact than when Hank Jenkins died by violence his ghost assumed existence? That it was then doomed to haunt the site of its slaying throughout eternity?"

The voice said evenly, "I have no knowledge of that."

"Do you deny that it is well known throughout that section that the ghost of Hank Jenkins haunts Harley Hall?"

"Objection!" shouted Turnbull. "Popular opinion is not evidence."

"Objection sustained. Strike the question from the record."

Wilson, badgered, lost his control. In a dangerously uneven voice, he said, "Perjury is a criminal offense. Mr. Jenkins, do you deny that you are the ghost of Hank Jenkins?"

The tone was surprised. "Why, certainly."

"You *are* a ghost, aren't you?"

Stiffly, "I'm an entity on the astral plane."

"That, I believe, is what is called a ghost?"

"I can't help what it's called. I've heard you called a lot of things. Is that proof?"

There was a surge of laughter from the audience. Gimbel slammed his gavel down on the bench.

"The witness," he said, "will confine himself to answering questions."

Wilson bellowed, "In spite of what you say, it's true, isn't it, that you are merely the spirit of a human being who had died through violence?"

The voice from above the blood drops retorted, "I repeat that I am an entity of the astral plane. I am not aware that I was ever a human being."

The lawyer turned an exasperated face to the bench.

"Your honor," he said, "I ask that you instruct the witness to cease playing verbal hide-and-seek. It is quite evident that the witness is a ghost, and that he is therefore the relict of some human being, ipso facto. Circumstantial evidence is strong that he is the ghost of the Hank Jenkins who was killed in 1850. But this is a non-essential point. What is definite is that he is the ghost of someone who is dead, and hence is unqualified to act as witness! I demand his testimony be stricken from the record!"

Turnbull spoke up at once. "Will the counsel for the defense quote his authority for branding my client a ghost—in the face of my client's repeated declaration that he is an entity of the astral plane? What is the legal definition of a ghost?"

Judge Gimbel smiled. "Counsel for the defense will proceed with the cross-examination," he said.

Wilson's face flushed dark purple. He mopped his brow with a large bandanna, then glared at the dropping, sizzling trickle of blood.

"Whatever you are," he said, "answer me this question. Can you pass through a wall?"

"Why, yes. Certainly." There was a definite note of surprise in the voice from nowhere. "But it isn't as easy as some people think. It definitely requires a lot of effort."

"Never mind that. You can do it?"

"Yes."

"Could you be bound by any physical means? Would handcuffs hold you? Or ropes, chains, prison walls, a hermetically sealed steel chest?"

Jenkins had no chance to answer. Turnbull, scenting danger, cut in hastily. "I object to this line of questioning. It is entirely irrelevant."

"On the contrary," Wilson cried loudly, "it bears strongly on the qualifications of the so-called Henry Jenkins as a witness! I demand that he answer the question."

Judge Gimbel said, "Objection overruled. Witness will answer the question."

The voice from the chair said superciliously, "I don't mind answering. Physical barriers mean nothing to me, by and large."

The counsel for the defense drew himself up triumphantly.

"Very good," he said with satisfaction. "*Very* good." Then to the judge, the words coming sharp and fast, "I claim, your honor, that the so-called Henry Jenkins has no legal status as a witness in court. There is clearly no value in understanding the nature of an oath if a violation of the oath can bring no punishment in its wake. The statements of a man who can perjure himself freely have no worth. I demand they be stricken from the record!"

Turnbull was at the judge's bench in two strides.

"I had anticipated that, your honor," he said quickly. "From the very nature of the case, however, it is clear that my client can be very definitely restricted in his movements —spells, pentagrams, talismans, amulets, Exclusion Circles and what-not. I have here—which I am prepared to deliver to the bailiff of the court—a list of the various methods of confining an astral entity to a restricted area for periods ranging from a few moments to all eternity. Moreover, I have also signed a bond for five thousand dollars, prior to the beginning of the trial, which I stand ready to forfeit should my client be confined and make his escape, if found guilty of any misfeasance as a witness."

Gimbel's face, which had looked startled for a second, slowly cleared. He nodded. "The court is satisfied with the statement of the counsel for the plaintiff," he declared. "There seems no doubt that the plaintiff can be penalized for any misstatements, and the motion of the defense is denied."

Wilson looked choleric, but shrugged. "All right," he said. "That will be all."

"You may step down, Mr. Jenkins," Gimbel directed, and watched in fascination as the blood-dripping column rose and floated over the floor, along the corridor, out the door.

Turnbull approached the judge's bench again. He said, "I would like to place in evidence these notes, the diary of the late Zebulon Harley. It was presented to my client by Harley himself last fall. I call particular attention to the entry for April sixth, nineteen seventeen, in which he mentions the entrance of the United States into the First World War, and records the results of a series of eleven pinochle games played with a personage identified as 'Old Hank.' With the court's permission, I will read the entry for that day, and also various other entries for the next four years. Please note the references to someone known variously as 'Jenkins,' 'Hank Jenkins,' and—in one extremely significant passage—'Old Invisible.' "

Wilson stewed silently during the slow reading of Harley's diary. There was anger on his face, but he paid close attention, and when the reading was over he leaped to his feet.

"I would like to know," he asked, "if the counsel for the plaintiff is in possession of any diaries *after* nineteen twenty?"

Turnbull shook his head. "Harley apparently never kept a diary, except during the four years represented in this."

"Then I demand that the court refuse to admit this diary as evidence on two counts," Wilson said. He raised two fingers to tick off the points. "In the first place, the evidence presented is frivolous. The few vague and unsatisfactory references to Jenkins nowhere specifically describe him as what he is—ghost, astral entity or what you will. Second, the evidence, even were the first point overlooked, concerns only the years up to nineteen twenty-one. The case concerns itself only with the supposed occupation of Harley Hall by the so-called Jenkins in the last twenty years—*since* 'twenty-one. Clearly, the evidence is therefore irrelevant."

Gimbel looked at Turnbull, who smiled calmly.

"The reference to 'Old Invisible' is far from vague," he said. "It is a definite indication of the astral character of my client. Furthermore, evidence as to the friendship of my client with the late Mr. Zebulon Harley before nineteen twenty-one is entirely relevant, as such a friendship, once established, would naturally be presumed to have continued indefinitely. Unless of course, the defense is able to present evidence to the contrary."

Judge Gimbel said, "The diary is admitted as evidence."

Turnbull said, "I rest my case."

There was a buzz of conversation in the courtroom while the judge looked over the diary, and then handed it to the clerk to be marked and entered.

Gimbel said, "The defense may open its case."

Wilson rose. To the clerk he said, "Russell Joseph Harley."

But young Harley was recalcitrant. "Nix," he said, on his feet, pointing at the witness chair. "That thing's got blood all over it! You don't expect me to sit down in that large puddle of blood, do you?"

Judge Gimbel leaned over to look at the chair. The drip-drop trickle of blood from the apparition who'd been testifying had left its mark. Muddy brown all down the front of the chair. Gimbel found himself wondering how the ghost managed to replenish its supply of the fluid, but gave it up.

"I see your point," he said. "Well, it's getting a bit late anyhow. The clerk will take away the present witness chair and replace it. In the interim, I declare the court recessed till tomorrow morning at ten o'clock."

III

Russell Harley noticed how the elevator boy's back registered repulsion and disapproval, and scowled. He was not a popular guest in the hotel, he knew well. Where he made his mistake, though, was in thinking that the noxious bundle of herbs about his neck was the cause of it. His odious personality had a lot to do with the chilly attitude of the management and his fellow guests.

He made his way to the bar, ignoring the heads that turned in surprise to follow the reeking comet-tail of his passage. He entered the red-leather-and-chromium drinking room, and stared about for Lawyer Wilson.

And blinked in surprise when he saw him. Wilson wasn't alone. In the booth with him was a tall, dark figure, with his back to Harley. The back alone was plenty for recognition. Nicholls!

Wilson had seen him. "Hello, Harley," he said, all smiles and affability in the presence of the man with the money. "Come on and sit down. Mr. Nicholls dropped in on me a little while ago, so I brought him over."

"Hello," Harley said glumly, and Nicholls nodded. The muscles of his cheeks pulsed, and he seemed under a strain, strangely uncomfortable in Harley's presence. Still there was a twinkle in the look he gave young Harley, and his voice was friendly enough—though supercilious—as he said:

"Hello, Harley. How is the trial going?"

"Ask him," said Harley, pointing a thumb at Wilson as he slid his knees under the booth's table and sat down. "He's the lawyer. He's supposed to know these things."

"Doesn't he?"

Harley shrugged and craned his neck for the waitress. "Oh,

I guess so. . . . Rye and water!" He watched the girl appreciatively as she nodded and went off to the bar, then turned his attention back to Nicholls. "The trouble is," he said, "Wilson may think he knows, but I think he's all wet."

Wilson frowned. "Do you imply——" he began, but Nicholls put up a hand.

"Let's not bicker," said Nicholls. "Suppose you answer my question. I have a stake in this, and I want to know. How's the trial going?"

Wilson put on his most open-faced expression. "Frankly," he said, "not too well. I'm afraid the judge is on the other side. If you'd listened to me and stalled till another judge came along——"

"I had no time to stall," said Nicholls. "I have to be elsewhere within a few days. Even now, I should be on my way. Do you think we might lose the case?"

Harley laughed sharply. As Wilson glared at him he took his drink from the waitress' tray and swallowed it. The smile remained on his face as he listened to Wilson say smoothly:

"There is a good deal of danger, yes."

"Hum." Nicholls looked interestedly at his fingernails. "Perhaps I chose the wrong lawyer."

"Sure you did." Harley waved at the waitress, ordered another drink. "You want to know what else I think? I think you picked the wrong client, spelled s-t-o-o-g-e. I'm getting sick of this. This damn thing around my neck smells bad. How do I know it's any good, anyway? Far as I can see, it just smells bad, and that's all."

"It works," Nicholls said succinctly. "I wouldn't advise you to go without it. The late Hank Jenkins is not a very strong ghost—a strong one would tear you apart and chew up your herbs for dessert—but without the protection of what you wear about your neck, you would become a very uncomfortable human as soon as Jenkins heard you'd stopped wearing it."

He put down the glass of red wine he'd been inhaling without drinking, looked intently at Wilson. "I've put up the money in this," he said. "I had hoped you'd be able to handle the legal end. I see I'll have to do more. Now listen intently, because I have no intention of repeating this. There's an angle to this case that's got right by your blunted legal acumen. Jenkins claims to be an astral entity, which he undoubtedly is. Now, instead of trying to prove him a ghost, and legally dead, and therefore unfit to testify, which you have been doing, suppose you do this. . . ."

He went on to speak rapidly and to the point.

And when he left them a bit later, and Wilson took Harley up to his room and poured him into bed, the lawyer felt happy for the first time in days.

Russell Joseph Harley, a little hung over and a lot nervous, was called to the stand as first witness in his own behalf.

Wilson said, "Your name?"

"Russell Joseph Harley."

"You are the nephew of the late Zebulon Harley, who bequeathed the residence known as Harley Hall to you?"

"Yes."

Wilson turned to the bench. "I offer this copy of the late Mr. Zebulon Harley's will in evidence. All his possessions are left to his nephew and only living kin, the defendant."

Turnbull spoke from his desk. "The plaintiff in no way disputes the defendant's equity in Harley Hall."

Wilson continued, "You passed part of your childhood in Harley Hall, did you not, and visited it as a grown man on occasion?"

"Yes."

"At any time, has anything in the shape of a ghost, specter or astral entity manifested itself to you in Harley Hall?"

"No. I'd remember it."

"Did your late uncle ever mention any such manifestation to you?"

"Him? No."

"That's all."

Turnbull came up for the cross-examination.

"When, Mr. Harley, did you last see your uncle before his death?"

"It was in nineteen thirty-eight. In September, some time—around the tenth or eleventh of the month."

"How long a time did you spend with him?"

Harley flushed unaccountably. "Ah—just one day," he said.

"When before that did you see him?"

"Well, not since I was quite young. My parents moved to Pennsylvania in nineteen twenty."

"And since then—except for that one-day visit in nineteen thirty-eight—has any communication passed between your uncle and yourself?"

"No, I guess not. He was a rather queer duck—solitary. A little bit balmy, I think."

"Well, you're a loving nephew. But in view of what you've just said, does it sound surprising that your uncle never told you of Mr. Jenkins? He never had much chance to, did he?"

"He had a chance in nineteen thirty-eight, but he didn't," Harley said defiantly.

Turnbull shrugged. "I'm finished," he said.

Gimbel began to look bored. He had anticipated something more in the way of fireworks. He said, "Has the defense any further witnesses?"

Wilson smiled grimly. "Yes, your honor," he said. This was his big moment, and he smiled again as he said gently, "I would like to call Mr. Henry Jenkins to the stand."

In the amazed silence that followed, Judge Gimbel leaned forward. "You mean you wish to call the plaintiff as a witness for the defense?"

Serenely, "Yes, your honor."

Gimbel grimaced. "Call Henry Jenkins," he said wearily to the clerk, and sank back in his chair.

Turnbull was looking alarmed. He bit his lip, trying to decide whether to object to this astonishing procedure, but finally shrugged as the clerk bawled out the ghost's name.

Turnbull sped down the corridor, out the door. His voice was heard in the anteroom, then he returned more slowly. Behind him came the trickle of blood drops: *Pat. HISS. Pat. HISS.*

"One moment," said Gimbel, coming to life again. "I have no objection to your testifying, Mr. Jenkins, but the State should not be subjected to the needless expense of reupholstering its witness chair every time you do. Bailiff, find some sort of a rug or something to throw over the chair before Mr. Jenkins is sworn in."

A tarpaulin was hurriedly procured and adjusted to the chair; Jenkins materialized long enough to be sworn in, then sat.

"Tell me, Mr. Jenkins," he said, "just how many 'astral entities'—I believe that is what you call yourself—are there?"

"I have no way of knowing. Many billions."

"As many, in other words, as there have been human beings to die by violence?"

Turnbull rose to his feet in sudden agitation, but the ghost neatly evaded the trap. "I don't know. I only know there are billions."

The lawyer's cat-who-ate-canary smile remained undimmed. "And all these billions are constantly about us, everywhere, only remaining invisible. Is that it?"

"Oh, no. Very few remain on Earth. Of those, still fewer have anything to do with humans. Most humans are quite boring to us."

"Well, how many would you say are on Earth? A hundred thousand?"

"Even more, maybe. But that's a good guess."

Turnbull interrupted suddenly. "I would like to know the significance of these questions. I object to this whole line of questioning as being totally irrelevant."

Wilson was a study in legal dignity. He retorted, "I am trying to elicit some facts of major value, your honor. This may change the entire character of the case. I ask your patience for a moment or two."

"Counsel for the defense may continue," Gimbel said curtly.

Wilson showed his canines in a grin. He continued to the blood-dripping before him. "Now, the contention of your counsel is that the late Mr. Harley allowed an 'astral entity' to occupy his home for twenty years or more, with his full knowledge and consent. That strikes me as being entirely improbable, but shall we for the moment assume it to be the case?"

"Certainly! It's the truth."

"Then tell me, Mr. Jenkins, have you fingers?"

"Have I—what?"

"You heard me!" Wilson snapped. "Have you fingers, flesh-and-blood fingers, capable of making an imprint?"

"Why, no. I—"

Wilson rushed on. "Or have you a photograph of yourself —or specimens of your handwriting—or any sort of material identification? Have you any of these?"

The voice was definitely querulous. "What do you mean?"

Wilson's voice became harsh, menacing. "I mean, can you prove that *you* are the astral entity alleged to have occupied Zebulon Harley's home. Was it you—or was it another of the featureless, faceless, intangible unknowns—one of the hundreds of thousands of them that, by your own admission, are all over the face of the earth, rambling where they choose, not halted by any locks or bars? Can you prove that *you* are anyone in particular?"

"Your honor!" Turnbull's voice was almost a shriek as he found his feet at last. "My client's identity was never in question!"

"It is now!" roared Wilson. "The opposing counsel has presented a personage whom he styles 'Henry Jenkins.' Who is this Jenkins? What is he? Is he even an individual—or a corporate aggregation of these mysterious 'astral entities' which we are to believe are everywhere, but which we never see? If he is an individual, is he *the* individual? And how can we know that, even if he says he is? Let him produce evidence—photographs, a birth certificate, fingerprints. Let him bring in identifying witnesses who have known both ghosts, and are prepared to swear that these ghosts are the same ghost. Failing this, there is no case! Your honor, I demand the court declare an immediate judgment in favor of the defendant!"

Judge Gimbel stared at Turnbull. "Have you anything to say?" he asked. "The argument of the defense would seem to have every merit with it. Unless you can produce some sort of evidence as to the identity of your client, I have no alternative but to find for the defense."

For a moment there was a silent tableau. Wilson triumphant, Turnbull furiously frustrated.

How could you identify a ghost?

And then came the quietly amused voice from the witness chair.

"This thing has gone far enough," it said above the sizzle and splatter of its own leaking blood. "I believe I can present proof that will satisfy the court."

Wilson's face fell with express-elevator speed. Turnbull held his breath, afraid to hope.

Judge Gimbel said, "You are under oath. Proceed."

There was no other sound in the courtroom as the voice said, "Mr. Harley, here, spoke of a visit to his uncle in nineteen thirty-eight. I can vouch for that. They spent a night and a day together. They weren't alone. I was there."

No one was watching Russell Harley, or they might have seen the sudden sick pallor that passed over his face.

The voice, relentless, went on. "Perhaps I shouldn't have eavesdropped as I did, but old Zeb never had any secrets from me anyhow. I listened to what they talked about. Young Harley was working for a bank in Philadelphia at the time.

His first big job. He needed money, and needed it bad. There was a shortage in his department. A woman named Sally—"

"Hold on!" Wilson yelled. "This has nothing to do with your identification of yourself. Keep to the point!"

But Turnbull had begun to comprehend. He was shouting, too, almost too excited to be coherent. "Your honor, my client must be allowed to speak. If he shows knowledge of an intimate conversation between the late Mr. Harley and the defendant, it would be certain proof that he enjoyed the late Mr. Harley's confidence, and thus, Q.E.D., that he is no other than the astral entity who occupied Harley Hall for so long!"

Gimbel nodded sharply. "Let me remind counsel for the defense that this is his own witness. Mr. Jenkins, continue."

The voice began again, "As I was saying, the woman's name—"

"Shut up, damn you!" Harley yelled. He sprang upright, turned beseechingly toward the judge. "He's twisting it! Make him stop! Sure, I knew my uncle had a ghost. He's it, all right, curse his black soul! He can have the house if he wants it—I'll clear out of the whole damned state!"

He broke off into babbling and turned about wildly. Only the intervention of a marshal kept him from hurtling out of the courtroom.

Banging of the gavel and hard work by the court clerk and his staff restored order in the courtroom. When the room had returned almost to normalcy, Judge Gimbel, perspiring and annoyed, said, "As far as I am concerned, identification of the witness is complete. Has the defense any further evidence to present?"

Wilson shrugged morosely. "No, your honor."

"Counsel for the plaintiff?"

"Nothing, your honor. I rest my case."

Gimbel plowed a hand through his sparse hair and blinked. "In that case," he said, "I find for the plaintiff. An order is entered hereby that the defendant, Russell Joseph Harley, shall remove from the premises of Harley Hall all spells, pentagrams, talismans and other means of exorcism employed; that he shall cease and desist from making any attempts, of whatever nature, to evict the tenant in the future; and that Henry Jenkins, the plaintiff, shall be permitted to full use and occupancy of the premises designated as Harley Hall for the full term of his natural—ah—existence."

The gavel banged. "The case is closed."

"Don't take it so hard," said a mild voice behind Russell Harley. He whirled surlily. Nicholls was coming up the street after him from the courthouse, Wilson in tow.

Nicholls said, "You lost the case, but you've still got your life. Let me buy you a drink. In here, perhaps."

He herded them into a cocktail lounge, sat them down before they had a chance to object. He glanced at his expensive wrist watch. "I have a few minutes," he said. "Then I really must be off. It's urgent."

He hailed a barman, ordered for all. Then he looked at young Harley and smiled broadly as he dropped a bill on the counter to pay for the drinks.

"Harley," he said, "I have a motto that you would do well to remember at times like these. I'll make you a present of it, if you like."

"What is it?"

" 'The worst is yet to come.' "

Harley snarled and swallowed his drink without replying. Wilson said, "What gets me is, why didn't they come to us before the trial with that stuff about this charmingly illicit client you wished on me? We'd have had to settle out of court."

Nicholls shrugged. "They had their reasons," he said "After all, one case of exorcism, more or less, doesn't matter. But lawsuits set precedents. You're a lawyer, of sorts, Wilson; do you see what I mean?"

"Precedents?" Wilson looked at him slackjawed for a momen; then his eyes widened.

"I see you understand me." Nicholls nodded. "From now on is this state—and by virtue of the full-faith-and-credence clause of the Constitution, in *every* state of the country—a ghost has a legal right to haunt a house!"

"Good Lord!" said Wilson. He began to laugh, not loud, but from the bottom of his chest.

Harley stared at Nicholls. "Once and for all," he whispered, "tell me—what's your angle on all this?"

Nicholls smiled again.

"Think about it a while," he said lightly. "You'll begin to understand." He sniffed his wine once more, then sat the glass down gently—

And vanished.

THE END

As I've mentioned before, I was never a reader of **Weird Tales,** and its type of fiction did not captivate me. In 1950, though, when "Legal Rites" finally appeared, **Weird Tales** was nearing the end of its thirty-year road and I'm rather glad I made its pages at least once before its end, even if only as half of a collaboration. It was the longest story in the issue and it received the cover.

"Legal Rites" and "The Little Man on the Subway" are the only pieces of fiction I ever wrote in collaboration, and I didn't really enjoy the process. Later on in my career, I had occasion to collaborate on four or five non-fiction books and never really enjoyed that either, nor were any of the collaborations successful. I'm essentially a loner and like to take full responsibility for what I write.

In the case of "Legal Rites" it seems to me that the beginning is mostly Pohl's rewriting; the trial scene is mostly mine; the ending—I don't remember.

Fantasy was not the only type of story I kept bullheadedly trying, over and over, without much success. Another type was the broadly farcical. I never sold either type to Campbell, but I at least sold the latter elsewhere.

Even while I was writing "Legal Rites," I was working on another robot story, but a humorous one—or what I considered humor. I called it "Source of Power" and at least knew better than to waste time trying it on Campbell. I sent it directly to **Thrilling Wonder,** and when it was rejected there, I tried **Amazing.**

Amazing bought it on October 8, 1941—my first sale to that magazine since those exciting beginning days of the fall of 1938. When it appeared on the stands (two days after Pearl Harbor) in the February 1942 issue, I found that **Amazing** had retitled it "Robot AL-76 Goes Astray."

Although "Robot AL-76 Goes Astray" was a "positronic robot" story, it didn't really fit in with the other three I had thus far written. When **I, Robot,** my first collection of "positronic robot" stories, was put together, in 1950, I did not include "Robot AL-76 Goes Astray" in that volume. When, however, in 1964, **The Rest of the Robots** was put together, I felt honor-bound by the title, if nothing else, to include all the remaining robot stories published till then, and therefore "Robot AL-76 Goes Astray" was included.

August 1, 1941 ("Robot AL-76 Goes Astray" was then still working its slow way through the typewriter, because the Nazi invasion of the Soviet Union distracted me) was another important day in my writing career. I went to see John Campbell that day and, not liking to come to him without an idea, I thought hard on the subway ride there.

The fate of "Pilgrimage" (soon to become "Black Friar of the Flame") was still rankling, and I wanted to write another future-historical. I therefore suggested to him that I do a short story against the background of the slow fall of the Galactic Empire (something I intended to model quite frankly on the fall of the Roman Empire).

Campbell caught fire. We spent two hours together, and by the time it was over it was not going to be a short story at all, but an indefinitely long series of stories dealing with the fall of the First Galactic Empire and the rise of the Second.

I submitted the first story of the series, "Foundation," to Campbell on September 8, 1941, and it was accepted on the fifteenth. It appeared in the May 1942 issue of **Astounding.**

Over the next eight years I was to write seven more stories of what came to be called the "Foundation" series, and these were finally collected into three volumes, **Foundation, Foundation and Empire,** and **Second Foundation,** which collectively were called **The Foundation Trilogy.**

Of all my science fiction, these books were most successful. First published in 1951, 1952, and 1953, respectively, they have been in print constantly as hard-covers ever since, despite the appearance of numerous soft-cover editions. And in 1966, at the 24th World Science Fiction Convention, in Cleveland, the "Foundation" series received a Hugo (science fiction's equivalent of the Oscar) as the "Best All-Time Series."

After "Foundation" I was ready to try a serious positronic robot story for the first time in half a year. This one, "Runaround," was submitted to Campbell on October 20, 1941, and he accepted it on the twenty-third. It appeared in the March 1942 issue of **Astounding** and was eventually included in **I, Robot.**

I then had to get to work at once on a sequel to "Foundation." "Foundation" had been brought to an inconclusive ending on the assumption that a sequel would be forthcoming, and I had to come through. On November 17, the sequel, "Bridle and Saddle," which was the second story of the "Foundation" series, was submitted to Campbell, and he accepted it the same day—a record in speed. What's more, it was the longest story I had yet written—eighteen thousand words—and even though I received no bonus, the check, for $180, was the largest single check I had yet received. "Bridle and Saddle" was eventually included in **Foundation.**

Now, at last, I had a series of **long stories** going, together with my "positronic robot" series of short stories. I was feeling quite good.

On November 17, 1941, the day I submitted and sold "Bridle and Saddle," Campbell told me his plan for starting a new department in **Astounding,** one to be called "Probability Zero." This was to be a department of short-shorts, five hundred to one thousand words, which were to be in the nature of plausible and entertaining Munchausen-like lies. Campbell's notion was that, aside from the entertainment value of these things, they would offer a place where beginners could penetrate the market without having to compete quite so hard with established writers. It would form a stairway to professional status.

This was a good idea in theory and even worked a little. Ray Bradbury, later to be one of the best-known and successful of all science fiction writers, broke into the field with a "Probability Zero" item in the July 1942 **Astounding.** Hal Clement and George O. Smith also published in "Probability Zero" near the very start of their careers.

Unfortunately, it didn't work **enough.** Campbell had to start the department going with professionals, hoping to let the amateurs carry on once they saw what it was Campbell wanted. There were, however, never enough amateurs who could meet Campbell's standards even for short-shorts of an undemanding nature, and after twelve appearances of "Probability Zero" over a space of two and a half years, Campbell gave up.

On November 17, however, he was just beginning, and he wanted me to do a "Probability Zero" for him. I was delighted that he considered me to be at that stage of virtuosity where he could order me to do something for him according to measure. I promptly sat down and wrote a short-short called "Big Game." On November 24, 1941, I showed it to Campbell. He glanced over it and, rather to my astonishment, handed it back. It wasn't what he wanted.

I wish I could remember what "Big Game" was about, for I thought enough of it to try submitting it to **Collier's** magazine (an over-awing **slick**) in 1944—and it was, of course, rejected. The title, however, recalls nothing to my mind, and the story now no longer exists.

I tried a second time and did a humorous little positronic robot story called "First Law." I showed it to Campbell on December 1, and he didn't like that, either. This time, though, I kept the story. Thank goodness, I had finally learned that stories must be carefully saved for eternity, however many times they are rejected, and however firmly you imagine they are retired. "Big Game" was the eleventh of my stories to disappear, but it was also the **last.**

In the case of "First Law" there came a time when a magazine that did not exist in 1941 was to ask me for something. The magazine in question was **Fantastic Universe,** whose editor, Hans Stefan Santesson, asked me for a story at rates that would have been fine in 1941 but that by the mid-1950s I was reluctant to accept. I remembered "First Law," however, and sent it in. Santesson took it and ran it in the October 1956 issue of **Fantastic Universe,** and, eventually, I included it in **The Rest of the Robots.**

But back to "Probability Zero"—

I tried a third time with a short-story called "Time Pussy," which I wrote on the morning of Sunday, December 7, 1941, finishing it just before the radio went crazy with the news of Pearl Harbor. I brought it in to Campbell the next day (life goes on!), and this time he took it, but "not too enthusiastically," according to my diary.

20

Time Pussy

This was told me long ago by old Mac, who lived in a shack just over the hill from my old house. He had been a mining prospector out in the Asteroids during the Rush of '37, and spent most of his time now in feeding his seven cats.

"What makes you like cats so much, Mr. Mac?" I asked him.

The old miner looked at me and scratched his chin. "Well," he said, "they remind me o' my leetle pets on Pallas. *They* was something like cats—same kind of head, sort o'—and the cleverest leetle fellers y' ever saw. All dead!"

I felt sorry and said so. Mac heaved a sigh.

"Cleverest leetle fellers," he repeated. "They was four-dimensional pussies."

"Four-dimensional, Mr. Mac? But the fourth dimension is time." I had learned that the year before, in the third grade.

"So you've had a leetle schooling, hey?" He took out his pipe and filled it slowly. "Sure, the fourth dimension is time. These pussies was about a foot long and six inches high and four inches wide and stretched somewheres into middle o' next week. That's four dimensions, ain't it? Why, if you

Astounding Science Fiction, April 1942
Copyright © 1942 by Street & Smith Publications, Inc.

petted their heads, they wouldn't wag their tails till next day, mebbe. Some o' the big ones wouldn't wag till day after. Fact!"

I looked dubious, but didn't say anything.

Mac went on: "They was the best leetle watchdogs in all creation, too. They had to be. Why, if they spotted a burglar or any suspicious character, they'd shriek like a banshee. And when one saw a burglar today, he'd shriek yesterday, so we had twenty-four hours' notice every time."

My mouth opened. "Honest?"

"Cross my heart! Y' want to know how we used to feed them? We'd wait for them to go to sleep, see, and then we'd know they was busy digesting their meals. These leetle time pussies, they always digested their meals exactly three hours before they ate it, on account their stomachs stretched that far back in time. So when they went to sleep, we used to look at the time, get their dinner ready and feed it to them exactly three hours later."

He had lit his pipe now and was puffing away. He shook his head sadly. "Once, though, I made a mistake. Poor leetle time pussy. His name was Joe, and he was just about my favorite, too. He went to sleep one morning at nine and somehow I got the idea it was eight. Naturally, I brought him his feed at eleven. I looked all over for him, but I couldn't find him."

"What had happened, Mr. Mac?"

"Well, no time pussy's insides could be expected to handle his breakfast only *two* hours after digesting it. It's too much to expect. I found him finally under the tool kit in the outer shed. He had crawled there and died of indigestion an hour before. Poor leetle feller! After that, I always set an alarm, so I never made that mistake again."

There was a short, mournful silence after that, and I resumed in a respectful whisper: "You said they all died, before. Were they all killed like that?"

Mac shook his head solemnly. "No! They used to catch colds from us fellers and just die anywhere from a week to ten days before they caught them. They wasn't too many to start with, and a year after the miners hit Pallas they wasn't but about ten left and them ten sort o' weak and sickly. The trouble was, leetle feller, that when they died, they went all to pieces; just rotted away fast. Especially the little four-dimensional jigger they had in their brains which made them act the way they did. It cost us all millions o' dollars.

"How was that, Mr. Mac?"

"Y' see, some scientists back on Earth got wind of our leetle time pussies, and they knew they'd all be dead before they could get out there next conjunction. So they offered us all a million dollars for each time pussy we preserved for them."

"And did you?"

"Well, we tried, but they wouldn't keep. After they died, they were just no good any more, and we had to bury them. We tried packing them in ice, but that only kept the outside all right. The inside was a nasty mess, and it was the inside the scientists wanted.

"Natur'lly, with each dead time pussy costing us a million dollars, we didn't want that to happen. One of us figured out that if we put a time pussy into hot water when it was about to die, the water would soak all through it. Then, after it died, we could freeze the water so it would just be one solid chunk o' ice, and *then* it would keep."

My lower jaw was sagging. "Did it work?"

"We tried and we tried, son, but we just couldn't freeze the water fast enough. By the time we had it all iced, the four-dimensional jigger in the time pussy's brain had just corrupted away. We froze the water faster and faster but it was no go. Finally, we had only one time pussy left, and he was just fixing to die, too. We was desperate—and then one of the fellers thought o' something. He figured out a complicated contraption that would freeze all the water just like that—in a split second.

"We picked up the last leetle feller and put him into the hot water and hooked on the machine. The leetle feller gave us a last look and mad a funny leetle sound and died. We pressed the button and iced the whole thing into a solid block in about a quarter of a second." Here Mac heaved a sigh that must have weighed a ton. "But it was no use. The time pussy spoiled inside o' fifteen minutes and we lost the last million dollars."

I caught my breath. "But Mr. Mac, you just said you iced the time pussy in a quarter of a second. It didn't have *time* to spoil."

"That's just it, leetle feller," he said heavily. "We did it *too* doggoned fast. The time pussy didn't keep because we froze that hot water so derned fast that *the ice was still warm!*"

THE END

The most unusual thing about this small item is that it was not published under my own name. Campbell wanted one item in that first "Probability Zero" to appear to be by a non-professional, just to encourage the newcomers he hoped would try to break in. He had three entries in that first department and the other two were by L. Sprague de Camp and Malcolm Jameson. Both were longer-established and (despite "Nightfall") more renowned than I. As low man, it was up to me to use a pseudonym and pretend to be a newcomer.

I saw Campbell's point and, just a little sullenly, agreed. I used the name George E. Dale. It is the only time I ever used a pseudonym in the magazines. In later years I used the pseudonym Paul French on a series of six teen-age science fiction novels for reasons that are another story altogether. That was a special case, and in 1971 and 1972 those six novels appeared as paperbacks under my own name. Now "Time Pussy" appears here under my own name, and the record is at last absolutely clean.

There followed a two-month period during which I wrote nothing.

The reasons were twofold. In the first place, Pearl Harbor put the United States in the war the day I wrote "Time Pussy," and those first two months after the debacle were too disastrous and heartbreaking to allow much in the way of fiction composing.

If that in itself weren't enough, the time had come to try, once again, the qualifying examinations that would, or would not, grant me permission to do research. I very much felt myself to be dangling over the abyss. A second failure to pass would probably mean an end for me at Columbia. Consequently, during those hours when I wasn't working in my father's candy store or hanging over the radio, I had to be studying. There was time for nothing else at all.

Hedging my bets rather desperately, I registered for graduate work at New York University, just in case I did not pass once again. After I took my qualifying examinations, at the end of January 1942, I actually attended a few classes

at N.Y.U. while waiting for the results to be announced.
—But I won't keep you in suspense. On Friday, the thir-
teenth of February, the results were announced. I had
passed, this time.

During the interval between the taking of the qualifying
examinations and the annunciation, I managed to do "Victory Unintentional." This was a positronic robot story that
was a sequel to "Not Final!" which had **not** been a positronic robot story. Obviously I was trying to ride the series
notion all I could, in the hope of surer sales.

I submitted it to Campbell on February 9, 1942, and if
I thought Campbell would find himself unable to reject a
series story, I was roundly disabused. Nor was he so impressed by "Nightfall" and by my "Foundation" series as
to find himself incapable of making the rejection a severe
one.

On February 13, the very day of my passing into the
sacred list of those permitted to do research toward their
Ph.D., my spirits were somewhat dashed when I received
"Victory Unintentional" back with a cryptic rejection, which
consisted of the following, in toto, "$CH_3C_2CH_2CH_2SH$."
Campbell very well knew that this was the formula for
"butyl mercaptan," which gives the skunk its smell, and I
very well knew it, too, and Campbell very well knew I knew.

Oh, well! I managed to sell it anyway, to **Super Science
Stories** under its post-Pohl editor, on March 16, 1942, and
it appeared in the August 1942 issue of that magazine.
Though I did not include it in **I, Robot,** I did include it, of
necessity, in **The Rest of the Robots.**

After that, though, there came another dry period, the
longest I was ever to experience. Once "Victory Unintentional" was finished, fourteen months (!) were to pass before I turned back to the typewriter. It was not the
conventional "writer's block," of course, for that I have
never experienced. Rather, it was the coming of a vast,
triple change in my life.

The first change was the fact that I was now beginning
chemical research in earnest under Professor Charles R.

Dawson. Research is a full-time job and I still had to work it around, somehow, my duties in my father's candy store, so there was bound to be very little time for writing.

Then, as though that weren't enough, a second change took place simultaneously—

In January 1942 I joined an organization called "The Brooklyn Writers' Club," which had sent me a postcard of invitation. I took the invitation to be a recognition of my status as a "writer" and I couldn't possibly have refused.

The first meeting I attended was on January 19, 1942. It turned out to be rather pleasant. I welcomed the chance to get my mind off the qualifying examinations and the war disasters (though I remember spending part of that first meeting discussing the possibility that New York might be bombed).

Most of the members of the club were no further advanced in the profession than I was; nor were any of them, aside from myself, science fiction writers. The chief activity consisted of reading from our own manuscripts so that criticism from the others might be invited. Since it was quickly discovered that I read "with expression," I became chief reader, a role I enjoyed. (It was to be eight years yet before I discovered that I had a natural flair for the lecture platform.)

On February 9, 1942, the third meeting I attended, there was present a young man, Joseph Goldberger, whom I had not met before. He was a couple of years older than I was. I did most of the reading that day and Goldberger was sufficiently impressed to suggest, after the meeting had adjourned, that the two of us, with our girls, go out on a double date and get to know each other. Embarrassed, I had to explain that I had no girl. With an expansive gesture, he said he would get one for me.

And so he did. On February 14, 1942 (Valentine's Day and the day after I had passed my qualifying examinations) I met him at the Astor Hotel at 8:30 P.M. With him was his girl friend, and with her was **her** girl friend, Gertrude Blugerman, who was going to be my blind date. —I fell in love, and when I wasn't thinking of research I was thinking of her.

But there was also a third change, in a way the most drastic—

With war, the job situation suddenly changed: technically trained men of all sorts were in demand.

Robert Heinlein, for instance, was an engineer who had been trained at Annapolis. His health had retired him from active service in the Navy and had kept him retired, but his Annapolis connections made it possible for him to work as a civilian engineer at the Naval Air Experimental Station at the U. S. Navy Yard in Philadelphia. He cast about for other qualified people he might persuade to join him there, particularly among his fellow science fiction writers.

He got L. Sprague de Camp to come to the N.A.E.S., and on March 30, 1942, I received a letter from the navy yard asking if I would consider joining them.

I am rather single-minded and, having labored toward my Ph.D. for a year and a half, I would not ordinarily have considered letting go for anything short of a major force. —But the major force was there. I was in love and I wanted to get married even more than I wanted my degree. It occurred to me that I could suspend work toward my Ph.D. with full approval of the school, thanks to the war emergency, and that I could also get full permission to resume after the war. And by taking a job and postponing—merely **postponing**—my research, I could get married.

I went down to Philadelphia for an interview on April 10 and apparently met their requirements. I took the job, and on May 14, having left my father's candy store at last and (at least as a worker) forever, I moved to Philadelphia. Fortunately, Philadelphia was only an hour and a half from New York by train (in those days, I couldn't drive a car and, even if I could, I wouldn't have been able to get the gasoline because of rationing). I was therefore back in New York every weekend.

By the twenty-fourth of the month I had persuaded Gertrude to agree to marry me, and on July 26 we were married.

During those months it did not bother me that I was doing no writing. I had too much to think of—first the war, then research, then the job, then the marriage.

Besides, in the years up to early 1942, I never thought of my writing as anything but a way to help out with my college tuition. It was fun; it was exciting; and such success as I managed to achieve was deeply satisfying—but it had been done to serve a purpose and that purpose had been served. I had no notion that writing could be my career; that it could ever **possibly** be my career.

My career was to be chemistry. All the time I was writing and selling stories, I was also slaving away at Columbia. Once I earned my Ph.D., I intended to make my living by doing chemical research for some large industry at some munificent salary such as a hundred dollars a week. (As the son of a candy-store keeper, brought up in the depression, I suffered dizzy spells if I tried to think of more than a hundred dollars a week, so I confined my ambitions to that.)

My Philadelphia job, to be sure, paid me only fifty dollars a week at the beginning, but a young couple could live on that, those days, with taxes very small, with an apartment costing $42.50 a month and dinner for two at a restaurant coming to two dollars (including tip).

It wasn't the height of my dreams, but it was only a temporary war job, after all. Once the war was over, I would go back to my research and get my Ph.D. and a better job. Meanwhile, even a salary of $2,600 a year seemed to make it unnecessary for me to write. By my marriage day, I had written forty-two stories, of which twenty-eight had been sold (and three more were yet to sell). My total bachelor earnings over a space of four years had been $1,788.50 for those twenty-eight stories. This amounted to an average earning of just under $8.60 per week or $64 per story.

I never dreamed at that time that I could ever do much better. I had no intention of ever writing anything but science fiction or fantasy for the pulp magazines, which paid one cent a word at most—a cent and a quarter with bonus.

To make even the feeble fifty dollars a week that my job paid me would make it necessary for me to write and sell some forty stories a year, and, at that time, that didn't seem conceivable to me.

It had been all right to labor at the typewriter to pay my way through school, when I had no other source of income, but for what purpose ought I to be writing now? And with a six-day, fifty-four hour week, and the excitement of a new marriage, who had time?

The very existence of science fiction seemed to fade. I had left my magazine collection in New York; I no longer saw Campbell regularly, or Pohl, or any of my science fiction cronies. I scarcely even read the current magazines as they came out.

I might have let science fiction die altogether, and my writing career with it, except that there were little reminders from the outside world, and little itchings inside me that meant (though I didn't know it at the time) that writing was a great deal more to me than just a handy device to make a little spare cash.

I had hardly begun to work at the N.A.E.S., for instance, when the June 1942 issue of **Astounding** came out with my story "Bridle and Saddle." And it made the cover.

It was quite beyond my power to resist the temptation to take a copy to work and show it around. I couldn't help but feel the status I gained as a "writer." Later that summer and fall, three other stories were published: "Victory Unintentional" and "The Imaginary" in the post-Pohl **Super Science Stories** and "The Hazing" in **Thrilling Wonder Stories.** Each kept the science fiction world alive for me.

And although my New York coterie of science fiction editors, writers, and readers were gone, I was left not entirely bereft.

Working with me at the N.A.E.S. were Robert Heinlein and L. Sprague de Camp, and I kept up a close social relationship with both. To be sure, each had quit writing for the duration but they were far more successful writers than I was and I hero-worshipped them. In addition, John D. Clark, who was an ardent science fiction fan and who had written and published a couple of stories in 1937, was living in Philadelphia at the time and we frequently saw one another. All three kept the science fiction atmosphere about me.

It was on January 5, 1943, though, that the real trigger came. On that day I received a letter from Fred Pohl to the effect that he was planning to rewrite "Legal Rites" and was going to try to sell it again. That was exciting. He wasn't to succeed in selling the story for six more years, but of course I had no way of telling that. To me it seemed that another sale was in the offing and that I was an as-yet-active writer.

Besides, "Legal Rites" was a fantasy and I had never yet satisfied that long-standing desire to write and sell a fantasy to **Unknown.** Five times I had tried, and five times I had failed.

On January 13, quite suddenly, a week after the letter had come and fourteen months after my last-written story, the urge overwhelmed me. I sat down to write a fantasy called "Author! Author!"

Quickly I found there was something lacking. It was the first time I had ever tried to write something for Campbell without conferences with him. I missed the inspiration that invariably came through talks with him; I missed his encouragement. In fact, I wasn't sure that I could write at all without him. So the story limped and there were dry spells. I didn't finish the first draft till March 5, and the final version wasn't ready for mailing till April 4, 1943.

It had taken me nearly three months to write the story. To be sure, it was twelve thousand words long, but "Bridle and Saddle," which was half again as long, had taken me only three weeks.

Perhaps if "Author! Author!" had been rejected, it might have been a long time before I would have had the courage to try again. Fortunately, that was never put to the test. I mailed the story to Campbell on April 6, 1943 (the first time I ever **mailed** him a story instead of handing it to him), and on the twelfth the check of acceptance arrived. There was not even a revision requested, and what's more, Campbell paid me a bonus for the first time since "Nightfall." I received one and a quarter cents a word, or $150 in all. My sixth try at **Unknown** had succeeded.

It was the equivalent of three weeks' pay at the N.A.E.S.

for something that had taken me, off and on, three months. However, the three months' work on "Author! Author!" had been of a totally different kind than the three weeks' work at the N.A.E.S. would have been, and the receipt of the $150 check was infinitely more exciting than picking up a similar check, or even a larger one, earned in the course of a punch-the-time-clock job. (Yes, indeed, I punched a time clock at the N.A.E.S.)

As it happened, though, the happy excitement with which I greeted the sale was premature. I had scaled the heights of **Unknown** too late, and though I had the money, I didn't have the magazine. Robert Heinlein brought me the sad news on August 2, less than four months after the sale.

Unknown had been having a difficult time of it. Sales weren't high enough, and after its first two years of operation it had had to switch from monthly to bimonthly issues. Now the war had introduced a paper shortage and Street & Smith Publications decided to save what paper it could receive for the more successful **Astounding** and let **Unknown** go.

At the time I made my sale, there were only three more issues of **Unknown** fated to be issued and there was no room in any of them for "Author! Author!" The story remained in the vaults of Street & Smith indefinitely; a story sold, but not published; and the $150 check was deprived of most of its fun as a result.

There is, however, a happy ending. Twenty years later, Don Bensen of Pyramid Publications was publishing a paperback anthology of stories from **Unknown,** he asked me for an introduction. With glad nostalgia I complied, writing it on January 15, 1963, almost twenty years to the day after I had starting writing the only story I ever sold to the magazine. In the course of the introduction, I referred to the sad story of my attempts to write for **Unknown.**

The 1960s were not the 1940s. In 1963, the mere mention of an existing Asimov story that had never been published produced excitement, and Bensen wrote to me within three days, asking to see the story. I dug out the manuscript (I saved them now, you see, even for twenty years) and sent it to him.

He asked permission to include it in a second anthology of **Unknown** stories (pointing out that it had been accepted by the magazine). I explained he would also need permission from Campbell and the publisher. They very kindly granted the permission, and in January 1964, twenty-one years after it was written, "Author! Author!" was finally published and I finally—after a fashion, and glancingly—made **Unknown.**

21

Author! Author!

It occurred to Graham Dorn, and not for the first time, either, that there was one serious disadvantage in swearing you'll go through fire and water for a girl, however beloved. Sometimes she takes you at your miserable word.

This is one way of saying that he had been waylaid, shanghaied and dragooned by his fiancée into speaking at her maiden aunt's Literary Society. Don't laugh! It's not funny from the speaker's rostrum. Some of the faces you have to look at!

To race through the details, Graham Dorn had been jerked onto a platform and forced upright. He had read a speech on "The Place of the Mystery Novel in American Literature" in an appalled tone. Not even the fact that his own eternally precious June had written it (part of the bribe to get him to speak in the first place) could mask the fact that it was essentially tripe.

And then when he was weltering, figuratively speaking, in his own mental gore, the harpies closed in, for lo, it was time for the informal discussion and assorted feminine gush.

The Unknown 5, edited by D. R. Bensen
Copyright © 1964 by Isaac Asimov

—Oh, Mr. Dorn, do you work from inspiration? I mean, do you just sit down and then an idea strikes you—all at once? And you must sit up all night and drink black coffee to keep you awake till you get it down?

—Oh, yes. Certainly. (His working hours were two to four in the afternoon every other day, and he drank milk.)

—Oh, Mr. Dorn, you must do the most awful research to get all those bizarre murders. About how much must you do before you can write a story?

—About six months, usually. (The only reference books he ever used were a six-volume encyclopedia and year-before-last's World Almanac.)

—Oh, Mr. Dorn, did you make up your Reginald de Meister from a real character? You must have. He's oh, so convincing in his every detail.

—He's modeled after a very dear boyhood chum of mine. (Dorn had never known *anyone* like de Meister. He lived in continual fear of meeting someone like him. He had even a cunningly fashioned ring containing a subtle Oriental poison for use just in case he did. So much for de Meister.)

Somewhere past the knot of women, June Billings sat in her seat and smiled with sickening and proprietary pride.

Graham passed a finger over his throat and went through the pantomime of choking to death as unobtrusively as possible. June smiled, nodded, threw him a delicate kiss, and did nothing.

Graham decided to pass a stern, lonely, woman-less life and to have nothing but villainesses in his stories forever after.

He was answering in monosyllables, alternating yesses and noes. Yes, he did take cocaine on occasion. He found it helped the creative urge. No, he didn't think he could allow Hollywood to take over de Meister. He thought movies weren't true expressions of real Art. Besides, they were just a passing fad. Yes, he would read Miss Crum's manuscripts if she brought them. Only too glad to. Reading amateur manuscripts was such fun, and editors are really such brutes.

And then refreshments were announced, and there was a sudden vacuum. It took a split-second for Graham's head to clear. The mass of femininity had coalesced into a single specimen. She was four feet ten and about eighty-five pounds in weight. Graham was six-two and two hundred ten worth of brawn. He could probably have handled her without difficulty, especially since both her arms were occupied with a pachyderm of a purse. Still, he felt a little delicate, to say nothing of queasy, about knocking her down. It didn't seem quite the thing to do.

She was advancing, with admiration and fervor disgustingly clear in her eyes, and Graham felt the wall behind him. There was no doorway within armreach on either side.

"Oh, Mr. de Meister—do, do please let me call you Mr. de Meister. Your creation is so real to me, that I can't think of you as simply Graham Dorn. You don't mind, do you?"

"No, no, of course not," gargled Graham, as well as he could through thirty-two teeth simultaneously set on edge. "I often think of myself as Reginald in my more frivolous moments."

"Thank you. You can have no idea, *dear* Mr. de Meister, how I have looked *forward* to meeting you. I have read *all* your works, and I think they are wonderful."

"I'm glad you think so." He went automatically into the modesty routine. "Really nothing, you know. Ha, ha, ha! Like to please the readers, but lots of room for improvement. Ha, ha, ha!"

"But you really are, you know." This was said with intense earnestness. "I mean good, *really* good. I think it is wonderful to be an author like you. It must be almost like being God."

Graham stared blankly. "Not to editors, sister."

Sister didn't get the whisper. She continued, "To be able to create living characters out of nothing; to unfold souls to all the world; to put thoughts into words; to build pictures and create worlds. I have often thought that an author was the most gloriously gifted person in creation. Better an inspired author starving in a garret than a king upon his throne. Don't you think so?"

"Definitely," lied Graham.

"What are the crass material goods of the world to the wonders of weaving emotions and deeds into a little world of its own?"

"What, indeed?"

"And posterity, think of posterity!"

"Yes, yes. I often do."

She seized his hand. "There's only one little request. You might," she blushed faintly, "you might give poor Reginald —if you will allow me to call him that just once—a chance to marry Letitia Reynolds. You make her just a little too cruel to him. I'm sure I weep over it for hours together sometimes. But then he is too, too real to me."

And from somewhere, a lacy frill of handkerchief made its appearance, and went to her eyes. She removed it, smiled bravely, and scurried away. Graham Dorn inhaled, closed his eyes, and gently collapsed into June's arms.

His eyes opened with a jerk. "You may consider," he said severely, "our engagement frazzled to the breaking point. Only my consideration for your poor, aged parents prevents your being known henceforward as the ex-fiancée of Graham Dorn."

"Darling, you are so noble." She massaged his sleeve with her cheek. "Come, I'll take you home and bathe your poor wounds."

"All right, but you'll have to carry me. Has your precious, loveable aunt got an axe?"

"But why?"

"For one thing, she had the gall to introduce me as the brain-father, God help me, of the famous Reginald de Meister."

"And aren't you?"

"Let's get out of this creep-joint. And get this. I'm no relative by brain or otherwise, of that character. I disown him. I cast him into the darkness. I spit upon him. I declare him an illegitimate son, a foul degenerate, and the offspring of a hound, and I'll be damned if he ever pokes his lousy patrician nose into my typewriter again."

They were in the taxi, and June straightened his tie. "All right, Sonny, let's see the letter."

"What letter?"

She held out her hand. "The one from the publishers."

Graham snarled and flipped it out of his jacket pocket. "I've thought of inviting myself to his house for tea, the damned flintheart. He's got a rendezvous with a pinch of strychnine."

"You may rave later. What does he say? Hmm—uh-huh —'doesn't quite come up to what is expected—feel that de Meister isn't in his usual form—a little revision perhaps towards—feel sure the novel can be adjusted—are returning under separate cover—'"

She tossed it aside. "I told you you shouldn't have killed off Sancha Rodriguez. She was what you needed. You're getting skimpy on the love interest."

"*You* write it! I'm through with de Meister. It's getting

so clubwomen call me Mr. de Meister, and my picture is printed in newspapers with the caption Mr. de Meister. I have no individuality. No one ever heard of Graham Dorn. I'm always: Dorn, Dorn, you know, the guy who writes the de Meister stuff, *you* know."

June squealed, "Silly! You're jealous of your own detective."

"I am not jealous of my own character. Listen! I hate detective stories. I never read them after I got into the two-syllable words. I wrote the first as a clever, trenchant, biting satire. It was to blast the entire false school of mystery writers. That's why I invented this de Meister. He was the detective to end all detectives. The Compleat Ass, by Graham Dorn.

"So the public, along with snakes, vipers, and ungrateful children takes this filth to its bosom. I wrote mystery after mystery trying to convert the public—"

Graham Dorn drooped a little at the futility of it all.

"Oh, well." He smiled wanly, and the great soul rose above adversity. "Don't you see? I've got to write other things. I can't waste my life. But who's going to read a serious novel by Graham Dorn, now that I'm so thoroughly identified with de Meister?"

"You can use a pseudonym."

"I will not use a pseudonym. I'm proud of my name."

"But you can't drop de Meister. Be sensible, dear."

"A normal fiancée," Graham said bitterly, "would want her future husband to write something really worthwhile and become a great name in literature."

"Well, I do want you to, Graham. But just a little de Meister once in a while to pay the bills that accumulate."

"Ha!" Graham knocked his hat over his eyes to hide the sufferings of a strong spirit in agony. "Now you say that I can't reach prominence unless I prostitute my art to that unmentionable. Here's your place. Get out. I'm going home and write a good scorching letter on asbestos to our senile Mr. MacDunlap."

"Do exactly as you want to, cookie," soothed June. "And tomorrow when you feel better, you'll come and cry on my shoulder, and we'll plan a revision of *Death on the Third Deck* together, shall we?"

"The engagement," said Graham, loftily, "is broken."

"Yes, dear. I'll be home tomorrow at eight."

"That is of no possible interest to me. Good-bye!"

Publishers and editors are untouchables, of course. Theirs is a heritage of the outstretched hand and the well-toothed smile; the nod of the head and the slap of the back.

But perhaps somewhere, in the privacy of the holes to which authors scurry when the night falls, a private revenge is taken. There, phrases may be uttered where no one can overhear, and letters may be written that need not be mailed, and perhaps a picture of an editor, smiling pensively, is enshrined above the typewriter to act the part of bulls-eye in an occasional game of darts.

Such a picture of MacDunlap, so used, enlightened Graham Dorn's room. And Graham Dorn himself, in his usual writing costume (street-clothes and typewriter), scowled at the fifth sheet of paper in his typewriter. The other four were draped over the edge of the wastebasket, condemned for their milk-and-watery mildness.

He began:

"Dear Sir—" and added slowly and viciously, "or Madam, as the case may be."

He typed furiously as the inspiration caught him, disregarding the faint wisp of smoke curling upward from the overheated keys:

"You say you don't think much of de Meister in this story. Well, I don't think much of de Meister, period. You can handcuff your slimy carcass to his and jump off the Brooklyn Bridge. And I hope they drain the East River just before you jump.

"From now on, my works will be aimed higher than your scurvy press. And the day will come when I can look back on this period of my career with the loathing that is its just—"

Someone had been tapping Graham on the shoulder during the last paragraph. Graham twitched it angrily and ineffectively at intervals.

Now he stopped, turned around, and addressed the stranger in his room courteously: "Who the devilish damnation are you? And you can leave without bothering to answer. I won't think you rude."

The newcomer smiled graciously. His nod wafted the delicate aroma of some unobtrusive hair-oil toward Graham. His lean, hard-bitten jaw stood out keenly, and he said in a well-modulated voice:

"De Meister is the name. Reginald de Meister."

Graham rocked to his mental foundations and heard them creak.

"Glub," he said.

"Pardon?"

Graham recovered, "I said, 'glub,' a little code word meaning *which* de Meister."

"*The* de Meister," explained de Meister, kindly.

"My character? My detective?"

De Meister helped himself to a seat, and his finely-chiseled features assumed that air of well-bred boredom so admired in the best circles. He lit a Turkish cigarette, which Graham at once recognized as his detective's favorite brand, tapping it slowly and carefully against the back of his hand first, a mannerism equally characteristic.

"Really, old man," said de Meister. "This is really excruciatin'ly funny. I suppose I am your character, y'know, but let's not work on that basis. It would be so devastatin'ly awkward."

"Glub," said Graham again, by way of rejoinder.

His mind was feverishly setting up alternatives. He didn't drink, more, at the moment, was the pity, so he wasn't drunk. He had a chrome-steel digestion and he wasn't overheated, so it wasn't a hallucination. He never dreamed, and his imagination—as befitted a paying commodity—was under strict control. And since, like all authors, he was widely considered more than half a screwball, insanity was out of the question.

Which left de Meister simply an impossibility, and Graham felt relieved. It's a very poor author indeed who hasn't learned the fine art of ignoring impossibilities in writing a book.

He said smoothly, "I have here a volume of my latest work. Do you mind naming your page and crawling back into it. I'm a busy man and God knows I have enough of you in the tripe I write."

"But I'm here on business, old chap. I've got to come to a friendly arrangement with you first. Things are deucedly uncomfortable as they are."

"Look, do you know you're bothering me? I'm not in the habit of talking to mythical characters. As a general thing, I don't pal around with them. Besides which, it's time your mother told you that you really don't exist."

"My dear fellow, I always existed. Existence is such a subjective thing. What a mind thinks exists, *does* exist. I existed in your mind, for instance, ever since you first thought of me."

Graham shuddered. "But the question is, what are you doing *out* of my mind? Getting a little narrow for you? Want elbow room?"

"Not at all. Rather satisfact'ry mind in its way, but I achieved a more concrete existence only this afternoon, and so I seize the opportunity to engage you face to face in the aforementioned business conversation. You see, that thin, sentimental lady of your society—"

"What society?" questioned Graham hollowly. It was all awfully clear to him now.

"The one at which you made a speech—" de Meister shuddered in his turn—"on the detective novel. She believed in my existence, so naturally, I exist."

He finished his cigarette and flicked it out with a negligent twist of the wrist.

"The logic," declared Graham, "is inescapable. Now, what do you want and the answer is no."

"Do you realize, old man, that if you stop writing de Meister stories, my existence will become that dull, wraithlike one of all superannuated fictional detectives. I'd have to gibber through the gray mists of Limbo with Holmes, Lecocq, and Dupin."

"A very fascinating thought, I think. A very fitting fate."

Reginald de Meister's eyes turned icy, and Graham suddenly remembered the passage on page 123 of *The Case of the Broken Ashtray:*

His eyes, hitherto lazy and unattentive, hardened into twin pools of blue ice and transfixed the butler, who staggered back, a stifled cry on his lips.

Evidently, de Meister lost none of his characteristics out of the novels he adorned.

Graham staggered back, a stifled cry on his lip.

De Meister said menacingly, "It would be better for you if the de Meister mysteries continue. Do you understand?"

Graham recovered and summoned a feeble indignation. "Now, wait a while. You're getting out of hand. Remember: in a way, I'm your father. That's right. Your mental father. You can't hand me ultimatums or make threats. It isn't filial. It's lacking in the proper respect and love."

"And another thing," said de Meister, unmoved. "We've

got to straighten out this business of Letitia Reynolds. It's gettin' deucedly borin', y'know."

"Now you're getting silly. My love scenes have been widely heralded as miracles of tenderness and sentiment not found in one murder mystery out of a thousand. —Wait, I'll get you a few reviews. I don't mind your attempts to dictate my actions so much, but I'm damned if you'll criticize my writing."

"Forget the reviews. Tenderness and all that rot is what I don't want. I've been driftin' after the fair lady for five volumes now, and behavin' the most insufferable ass. This has got to stop."

"In what way?"

"I've got to marry her in your present story. Either that, or make her a good, respectable mistress. And you'll have to stop making me so damned Victorian and gentlemanly towards ladies. I'm only human, old man."

"Impossible!" said Graham, "and that includes your last remark."

De Meister grew severe. "Really, old chap, for an author, you display the most appallin' lack of concern for the well-bein' of a character who has supported you for a good many years."

Graham choked eloquently. "Supported me? In other words, you think I couldn't sell real novels, hey? Well, I'll show you. I wouldn't write another de Meister story for a million dollars. Not even for a fifty percent royalty and all television rights. How's that?"

De Meister frowned and uttered those words that had been the sound of doom to so many criminals: "We shall see, but you are not yet done with me."

With firmly jutting jaw, he vanished.

Graham's twisted face straightened out, and slowly—very slowly—he brought his hands up to his cranium and felt carefully.

For the first time in a long and reasonably ribald mental life, he felt that his enemies were right and that a good dry cleaning would not hurt his mind at all.

The *things* that existed in it!

Graham Dorn shoved the doorbell with his elbow a second time. He distinctly remembered her saying she would be home at eight.

The peep-hole shoved open. "Hello!"

"Hello!"

Silence!

Graham said plaintively, "It's raining outside. Can't I come in to dry?"

"I don't know. Are we engaged, Mr. Dorn?"

"If I'm not," was the stiff reply, "then I've been turning down the frenzied advances of a hundred passion-stricken girls—beautiful ones, all of them—for no apparent reason."

"Yesterday, you said—"

"Ah, but who listens to what I say? I'm just quaint that way. Look, I brought you posies." He flourished roses before the peep-hole.

June opened the door. "Roses! How plebeian. Come in, cookie, and sully the sofa. Whoa, whoa, before you move a step, what have you got under the other arm? Not the manuscript of *Death on the Third Deck?*"

"Correct. Not that excrescence of a manuscript. This is something different."

June's tone chilled. "That isn't your precious novel, is it?"

Graham flung his head up, "How did you know about it?"

"You slobbered the plot all over me at MacDunlap's silver anniversary party."

"I did not. I couldn't unless I were drunk."

"Oh, but you were. Stinking is the term. And on two cocktails too."

"Well, if I was drunk, I couldn't have told you the right plot."

"Is the setting a coal-mine district?"

"—Uh—yes."

"And are the people concerned real, earthy, unartificial, down-to-earth characters, speaking and thinking just like you and me? Is it a story of basic economic forces? Are the human characters lifted up and thrown down and whirled around, all at the mercy of the coal mine and mechanized industry of today?"

"—Uh—yes."

She nodded her head retrospectively. "I remember distinctly. First, you got drunk and were sick. Then you got better, and told me the first few chapters. Then I got sick."

She approached the glowering author. "Graham." She leant her golden head upon his shoulder and cooed softly. "Why don't you continue with the de Meister stories? You get such pretty checks out of them."

Graham writhed out of her grasp. "You are a mercenary

wretch, incapable of understanding an author's soul. You may consider, our engagement broken."

He sat down hard on the sofa, and folded his arms. "Unless you will consent to read the script of my novel and give me the usual story analysis."

"May I give you my analysis of *Death on the Third Deck* first?"

"No."

"Good! In the first place, your love interest is becoming sickening."

"It is not." Graham pointed his finger indignantly. "It breathes a sweet and sentimental fragrance, as of an older day. I've got the review here that says it." He fumbled in his wallet.

"Oh, bullfeathers. Are you going to start quoting that guy in the Pillsboro (Okla.) Clarion? He's probably your second cousin. You know that your last two novels were completely below par in royalties. And *Third Deck* isn't even being sold."

"So much the better—Ow!" He rubbed his head violently. "What did you do that for?"

"Because the only place I could hit as hard as I wanted to, without disabling you, was your head. Listen! The public is tired of your corny Letitia Reynolds. Why don't you let her soak her 'gleaming golden crown of hair' in kerosene and get familiar with a match?"

"But June, that character is drawn from life. From you!"

"Graham Dorn! I am not here to listen to insults. The mystery market today is swinging towards action and hot, honest love and you're still in the sweet, sentimental stickiness of five years ago."

"But that's Reginald de Meister's character."

"Well, change his character. Listen! You introduce Sancha Rodriguez. That's fine. I approve of her. She's Mexican, flaming, passionate, sultry, and in love with him. So what do you do? First he behaves the impeccable gentleman, and then you kill her off in the middle of the story."

"Hmm, I see— You really think it would improve things to have de Meister forget himself. A kiss or so—"

June clenched her lovely teeth and her lovely fists. "Oh, darling, how glad I am love is blind! If it ever peeked one tiny little bit, I couldn't stand it. Look, you squirrel's blue plate special, you're going to have de Meister and Rodriguez fall in love. They're going to have an affair through the entire book and you can put your horrible Letitia into a nunnery.

She'd probably be happier there from the way you make her sound."

"That's all *you* know about it, my sweet. It so happens that Reginald de Meister is in love with Letitia Reynolds and wants *her,* not this Rodriguez person."

"And what makes you think that?"

"He told me so."

"Who told you so?"

"Reginald de. Meister."

"What Reginald de Meister?"

"*My* Reginald de Meister."

"What do you mean, your Reginald de Meister?"

"My *character,* Reginald de Meister."

June got up, indulged in some deep-breathing and then said in a very calm voice, "Let's start all over."

She disappeared for a moment and returned with an aspirin. "Your Reginald de Meister, from your books, told you, in person, he was in love with Letitia Reynolds?"

"That's right."

June swallowed the aspirin.

"Well, I'll explain, June, the way he explained it to me. All characters really exist—at least, in the minds of the authors. But when people really begin to believe in them, they begin to exist in reality, because what people believe in, is, so far as they're concerned, and what is existence anyway?"

June's lips trembled. "Oh, Gramie, please don't. Mother will never let me marry you if they put you in an asylum."

"Don't call me Gramie, June, for God's sake. I tell you he was there, trying to tell me what to write and how to write it. He was almost as bad as you. Aw, come on, Baby, don't cry."

"I can't help it. I always thought you were crazy, but I never thought you were *crazy!*"

"All right, what's the difference? Let's not talk about it, any more. I'm never going to write another mystery novel. After all—" (he indulged in a bit of indignation)—"when it gets so that my own character—my *own* character—tries to tell me what to do, it's going too far."

June looked over her handkerchief. "How do you know it was really de Meister?"

"Oh, golly. As soon as he tapped his Turkish cigarette on the back of his hand and started dropping g's like snowflakes in a blizzard, I knew the worst had come."

The telephone rang. June leaped up. "Don't answer, Graham. It's probably from the asylum. I'll tell them you're not here. Hello. Hello. Oh, Mr. MacDunlap." She heaved a sigh of relief, then covered the mouthpiece and whispered hoarsely, "It might be a trap."

"Hello, Mr. MacDunlap! . . . No, he's not here. . . . Yes, I think I can get in touch with him. . . . At Martin's tomorrow, noon. . . . I'll tell him . . . With who? . . With who???" She hung up suddenly.

"Graham, you're to lunch with MacDunlap tomorrow."

"At his expense! Only at his expense!"

Her great blue eyes got greater and bluer, "And Reginald de Meister is to dine with you."

"What Reginald de Meister?"

"Your Reginald de Meister."

"*My* Reg—"

"Oh, Gramie, *don't.*" Her eyes misted, "Don't you see, Gramie, now they'll put us both in an insane asylum—and Mr. MacDunlap, too. And they'll probably put us all in the same padded cell. Oh, Gramie, three is such a dreadful crowd."

And her face crumpled into tears.

Grew S. MacDunlap (that the S. stands for "Some" is a vile untruth spread by his enemies) was alone at the table when Graham Dorn entered. Out of this fact, Graham extracted a few fleeting drops of pleasure.

It was not so much, you understand, the presence of Mac-Dunlap that did it, as the absence of de Meister.

MacDunlap looked at him over his spectacles and swallowed a liver pill, his favorite sweetmeat.

"Aha. You're here. What is this corny joke you're putting over on me? You had no right to mix me up with a person like de Meister without warning me he was real. I might have taken precautions. I could have hired a bodyguard. I could have bought a revolver."

"He's *not* real. God damn it! Half of him was *your* idea."

"That," returned MacDunlap with heat, "is libel. And what do you mean, he's not real? When he introduced himself, I took three liver pills at once and he didn't disappear. Do you know what three pills are? Three pills, the kind I've got (the doctor should only drop dead), could make an elephant disappear—if he weren't real. I *know.*"

Graham said wearily, "Just the same, he exists only in my mind."

"In your mind, I know he exists. Your mind should be investigated by the Pure Food and Drugs Act."

The several polite rejoinders that occurred simultaneously to Graham were dismissed almost immediately as containing too great a proportion of pithy Anglo-Saxon expletives. After all—ha, ha—a publisher is a publisher however Anglo-Saxony he may be.

Graham said, "The question arises, then, how we're to get rid of de Meister."

"Get rid of de Meister?" MacDunlap jerked the glasses off his nose in his sudden start, and caught them in one hand. His voice thickened with emotion. "Who wants to get rid of him?"

"Do you want him around?"

"God forbid," MacDunlap said between shudders. "Next to him, my brother-in-law is an angel."

"He has no business outside my books."

"For my part, he has no business inside them. Since I started reading your manuscripts, my doctor added kidney pills and cough syrups to my medicines." He looked at his watch, and took a kidney pill. "My worst enemy should be a book publisher only a year."

"Then why," asked Graham patiently, "don't you want to get rid of de Meister?"

"Because he is publicity."

Graham stared blankly.

"Look! What other writer has a real detective? All the others are fictional. Everyone knows that. But yours—*yours* is real. We can let him solve cases and have big newspaper writeups. He'll make the Police Department look silly. He'll make—"

"That," interrupted Graham, categorically, "is by all odds the most obscene proposal I have ever had my ears manured with."

"It will make money."

"Money isn't everything."

"Name one thing it isn't. . . Shh!" He kicked a near-fracture into Graham's left ankle and rose to his feet with a convulsive smile, "Mr. de Meister!"

"Sorry, old dear," came a lethargic voice. "Couldn't quite make it, you know. Loads of engagements. Must have been most borin' for you."

Graham Dorn's ears quivered spasmodically. He looked over his shoulder and reeled backward as far as a person

could reel while in a sitting position. Reginald de Meister
had sprouted a monocle since his last visitation, and his mono-
cular glance was calculated to freeze blood.

De Meister's greeting was casual. "My dear Watson! So
glad to meet you. Overjoyed deucedly."

"Why don't you go to hell?" Graham asked curiously.

"My dear fellow. Oh, my dear fellow."

MacDunlap cackled, "That's what I like. Jokes! Fun!
Makes everything pleasant to start with. Now shall we get
down to business?"

"Certainly. The dinner is on the way, I trust? Then I'll
just order a bottle of wine. The usual, Henry." The waiter
ceased hovering, flew away, and skimmed back with a bottle
that opened and gurgled into a glass.

De Meister sipped delicately, "So nice of you, old chap,
to make me a habitué of this place in your stories. It holds
true even now, and it is most convenient. The waiters all
know me. Mr. MacDunlap, I take it you have convinced Mr.
Dorn of the necessity of continuing the de Meister stories."

"Yes," said MacDunlap.

"No," said Graham.

"Don't mind him," said MacDunlap. "He's temperamental.
You know these authors.

"Don't mind him," said Graham. "He's microcephalic. You
know these publishers."

"Look, old chappie. I take it MacDunlap hasn't pointed
out to you the unpleasanter side of acting stubborn."

"For instance what, old stinkie?" asked Graham, courteously.

"Well, have you ever been haunted?"

"Like coming behind me and saying, Boo!"

"My dear fellow, I say. I'm much more subtle than that. I
can really haunt one in modern, up-to-date methods. For instance, have you ever had your individuality submerged?"

He snickered.

There was something familiar about that snicker. Graham
suddenly remembered. It was on page 103 of *Murder Rides
the Range:*

> *His lazy eyelids flicked down and up. He laughed lightly
> and melodiously, and though he said not a word, Hank Mars-
> lowe cowered. There was hidden menace and hidden power in
> that light laugh, and somehow the burly rancher did not
> dare reach for his guns.*

To Graham it still sounded like a nasty snicker, but he cowered, and did not dare reach for his guns.

MacDunlap plunged through the hole the momentary silence had created.

"You see, Graham. Why play around with ghosts? Ghosts aren't reasonable things. They're not *human!* If it's more royalties, you want—"

Graham fired up. "Will you refrain from speaking of money? From now on, I write only great novels of tearing human emotions."

MacDunlap's flushed face changed suddenly.

"No," he said.

"In fact, to change the subject just a moment—" and Graham's tone became surpassingly sweet, as the words got all sticky with maple syrup—"I have a manuscript here for you to look at."

He grasped the perspiring MacDunlap by the lapel firmly. "It is a novel that is the work of five years. A novel that will grip you with its intensity. A novel that will shake you to the core of your being. A novel that will open a new world. A novel that will—"

"No," said MacDunlap.

"A novel that will blast the falseness of this world. A novel that pierces to the truth. A novel—"

MacDunlap, being able to stretch his hand no higher, took the manuscript.

"No," he said.

"Why the bloody hell don't you read it?" inquired Graham.

"Now?"

"Well, start it."

"Look, supposing I read it tomorrow, or even the next day. I have to take my cough syrup now."

"You haven't coughed once since I got here."

"I'll let you know immediately—"

"This," said Graham, "is the first page. Why don't you begin it? It will grip you instantly.

MacDunlap read two paragraphs and said, "Is this laid in a coal-mining town?"

"Yes."

"Then I can't read it. I'm allergic to coal dust."

"But it's not real coal dust, MacIdiot."

"That," pointed out MacDunlap, "is what you said about de Meister."

Reginald de Meister tapped a cigarette carefully on the back of his hand in a subtle manner which Graham immediately recognized as betokening a sudden decision.

"That is all devastatin'ly borin', you know. Not quite gettin' to the point, you might say. Go ahead, MacDunlap, this is no time for half measures."

MacDunlap girded his spiritual loins and said, "All right Mister Dorn, with you it's no use being nice. Instead of de Meister, I'm getting coal dust. Instead of the best publicity in fifty years, I'm getting social significance. All right, Mister Smartaleck Dorn, if in one week you don't come to terms with me, *good* terms, you will be blacklisted in every reputable firm in the United States and foreign parts." He shook his finger and added in a shout, "Including Scandinavian."

Graham Dorn laughed lightly, "Pish," he said, "tush. I happen to be an officer of the Author's Union, and if you try to push me around I'll have *you* blacklisted. How do you like that?"

"I like it fine. Because supposing I can prove you're a plagiarist."

"Me," gasped Graham, recovering narrowly from merry suffocation. "Me, the most original writer of the decade."

"Is that so? And maybe you don't remember that in each case you write up, you casually mention de Meister's notebooks on previous cases."

"So what?"

"So he has them. Reginald, my boy, show Mister Dorn your notebook of your last case. —You see that. That's *Mystery of the Milestones* and it has, in detail, every incident in your book—and dated the year before the book was published. Very authentic."

"Again so what?"

"Have you maybe got the right to copy his notebook and call it an original murder mystery?"

"Why, you case of mental poliomyelitis, that notebook is my invention."

"Who says so? It's in de Meister's handwriting, as any expert can prove. And maybe you have a piece of paper, some little contract of agreement, you know, that gives you the right to use his notebooks?"

"How can I have an agreement with a mythical personage?"

"What mythical personage?"

"You and I know de Meister doesn't exist."

"Ah, but does the jury know? When I testify that I took three strong liver pills and he didn't disappear, what twelve men will say he doesn't exist?"

"This is blackmail."

"Certainly. I'll give you a week. Or in other words, seven days."

Graham Dorn turned desperately to de Meister. "You're in on this, too. In my books I give you the keenest sense of honor. Is this honorable?"

De Meister shrugged. "My dear fellow. All this—and haunting, too."

Graham rose.

"Where are you going?"

"Home to write you a letter." Graham's brows beetled defiantly. "And this time I'll mail it. I'm not giving in. I'll fight to the last ditch. And, de Meister, you let loose with one single little haunt and I'll rip your head out of its socket and spurt the blood all over MacDunlap's new suit."

He stalked out, and as he disappeared through the door, de Meister disappeared through nothing at all.

MacDunlap let out a soft yelp and then took a liver pill, a kidney pill, and a tablespoon of cough syrup in rapid succession.

Graham Dorn sat in June's front parlor, and having long since consumed his fingernails, was starting on the first knuckles.

June, at the moment, was not present, and this, Graham felt, was just as well. A dear girl; in fact, a dear, sweet girl. But his mind was not on her.

It was concerned instead with a miasmic series of flashbacks over the preceding six days:

——Say, Graham, I met your side-kick at the club yesterday. You know, de Meister. Got an awful shock. I always had the idea he was a sort of Sherlock Holmes that didn't exist. That's one on me, boy. Didn't know—— Hey, where are you going?

——Hey, Dorn, I hear your boss de Meister is back in town. Ought to have material for more stories soon. You're lucky you've got someone to grind out your plots readymade—— Huh? Well, goodbye.

——Why, Graham, darling, wherever were you last night?

Ann's affair didn't get *anywhere* without you; or at least, it wouldn't have, if it hadn't been for Reggie de Meister. He asked after you; but then, I guess he felt lost without his Watson. It must feel wonderful to Watson for such——
Mister Dorn! And the same to you, sir!

——You put one over on me. I thought you made up those wild things. Well, truth is stranger than fiction, ha, ha!

——Police officials deny that the famous amateur criminologist Reginald de Meister has interested himself in this case. Mr. de Meister himself could not be reached by our reporters for comment. Mr. de Meister is best known to the public for his brilliant solutions to over a dozen crimes, as chronicled in fiction form by his so-called "Watson," Mr. Grayle Doone.

Graham quivered and his arms trembled in an awful desire for blood. De Meister was haunting him—but good. He was losing his individuality, exactly as had been threatened.

It gradually dawned upon Graham that the monotonous ringing noise he heard was not in his head, but, on the contrary, from the front door.

Such seemed likewise the opinion of Miss June Billings, whose piercing call shot down the stairs and biffed Graham a sharp uppercut to the ear-drums.

"Hey, dope, see who's at the front door, before the vibration tears the house down. I'll be down in half an hour."

"Yes, dear!"

Graham shuffled his way to the front door and opened it.

"Ah, there. Greetin's," said de Meister, and brushed past.

Graham's dull eyes stared, and then fired high, as an animal snarl burst from his lips. He took up that gorilla posture, so comforting to red-blooded American males at moments like this, and circled the slightly-confused detective.

"My dear fellow, are you ill?"

"I," explained Graham, "am not ill, but you will soon be past all interest in that, for I am going to bathe my hands in your heart's reddest blood."

"But I say, you'll only have to wash them afterwards. It would be such an obvious clue, wouldn't it?"

"Enough of this gay banter. Have you any last words?"

"Not particularly."

"It's just as well. I'm not interested in your last words."

He thundered into action, bearing down upon the unfortunate de Meister like a bull elephant. De Meister faded to the left, shot out an arm and a foot, and Graham described a parabolic arc that ended in the total destruction of an end table, a vase of flowers, a fish-bowl, and a five-foot section of wall.

Graham blinked, and brushed away a curious goldfish from his left eyebrow.

"My dear fellow," murmured de Meister, "oh, my dear fellow."

Too late, Graham remembered that passage in *Pistol Parade:*

> *De Meister's arms were whipcord lightning, as with sure, rapid thrusts, he rendered the two thugs helpless. Not by brute force, but by his expert knowledge of judo, he defeated them easily without hastening his breath. The thugs groaned in pain.*

Graham groaned in pain.

He lifted his right thigh an inch or so to let his femur slip back into place.

"Hadn't you better get up, old chap?"

"I will stay here," said Graham with dignity, "and contemplate the floor in profile view, until such time as it suits me or until such time as I find myself capable of moving a muscle. I don't care which. And now, before I proceed to take further measures with you, what the hell do you want?"

Reginald de Meister adjusted his monocle to a nicety. "You know, I suppose, that MacDunlap's ultimatum expires tomorrow?"

"And you and he with it, I trust."

"You will not reconsider."

"Ha!"

"Really," de Meister sighed, "this is borin' no end. You have made things comfortable for me in this world. After all, in your books you've made me well-known in all the clubs and better restaurants, the bosom friend, y'know, of the mayor and commissioner of police, the owner of a Park Avenue penthouse and a magnificent art collection. And it all lingers over, old chap. Really quite affectin'."

"It is remarkable," mused Graham, "the intensity with which I am not listening and the distinctness with which I do not hear a word you say."

"Still," said de Meister. "there is no denyin' my book world suits me better. It is somehow more fascinatin', freer from dull logic, more apart from the necessities of the world. In short, I must go back, and to active participation. You have till tomorrow!"

Graham hummed a gay little tune with flat little notes.

"Is this a new threat, de Meister?"

"It is the old threat intensified. I'm going to rob you of every vestige of your personality. And eventually public opinion will force you to write as, to paraphrase you, de Meister's Compleat Stooge. Did you see the name the newspaper chappies pinned on you today, old man?"

"Yes, Mr. Filthy de Meister, and did you read a half-column item on page ten in the same paper. I'll read it *for* you: 'Noted Criminologist in 1-A. Will be inducted shortly draft board says.'"

For a moment, de Meister said and did nothing. And then one, after another, he did the following things: removed his monocle slowly, sat down heavily, rubbed his chin abstractedly, and lit a cigarette after long and careful tamping. Each of these, Graham Dorn's trained authorial eye recognized as singly representing perturbation and distress on the part of his character.

And never, in any of his books, did Graham remember a time when de Meister had gone through all four consecutively.

Finally, de Meister spoke. "Why you had to bring up draft registrations in your last book. I really don't know. This urge to be topical; this fiendish desire to be up to the minute with the news is the curse of the mystery novel. A true mystery is timeless; should have no relation to current events; should—"

"There is one way," said Graham, "to escape induction—"

"You might at least have mentioned a deferred classification on some vital ground."

"There is one way," said Graham, "to escape induction—"

"Criminal negligence," said de Meister.

"Look! Go back to the books and you'll never be filled with lead."

"Write them and I'll do it."

"Think of the war."

"Think of your ego."

Two strong men stood face to face (or would have, if Graham weren't still horizontal) and neither flinched.

Impasse!

And the sweet, feminine voice of June Billings interrupted and snapped the tension:

"May I ask, Graham Dorn, what you are doing on the

floor. It's been swept today and you're not complimenting me by attempting to improve the job."

"I am not sweeping the floor. If you looked carefully," replied Graham gently, "you would see that your own adored fiancé is lying here a mass of bruises and a hotbed of pains and aches."

"You've ruined my end table!"

"I've broken my leg."

"And my best lamp."

"And two ribs."

"And my fishbowl."

"And my Adam's apple."

"And you haven't introduced your friend."

"And my cervical verte—— What friend?"

"This friend."

"Friend! Ha!" And a mist came over his eyes. She was so young, so fragile to come into contact with hard, brutal facts of life. "This," he muttered brokenly, "is Reginald de Meister."

De Meister at this point broke a cigarette sharply in two, a gesture pregnant with the deepest emotion.

June said slowly, "Why—why, you're different from what I had thought."

"How had you expected me to look?" asked de Meister, in soft, thrilling tones.

"I don't know. Differently than you do,—from the stories I heard."

"You remind me, somehow, Miss Billings, of Letitia Reynolds."

"I think so. Graham said he drew her from me."

"A very poor imitation, Miss Billings. Devastatin'ly poor."

They were six inches apart now, eyes fixed with a mutual glue, and Graham yelled sharply. He sprang upright as memory smote him a nasty smite on the forehead.

A passage from *Case of the Muddy Overshoe* occurred to him. Likewise one from *The Primrose Murders*. Also one from *The Tragedy of Hartley Manor*, *Death of a Hunter*, *White Scorpion* and, to put it in a small nutshell, from every one of the others.

The passage read:

There was a certain fascination about de Meister that appealed irresistibly to women.

And June Billings was—as it had often, in Graham's idler moments, occurred to him—a woman.

And fascination simply gooed out of her ears and coated the floor six inches deep.

"Get out of this room, June," he ordered.

"I will not."

"There is something I must discuss with Mr. de Meister, man to man. I demand that you leave this room."

"Please go, Miss Billings," said de Meister.

June hesitated, and in a very small voice said, "Very well."

"Hold on," shouted Graham. "Don't let him order you about. I demand that you stay."

She closed the door very gently behind her.

The two men faced each other. There was that in either pair of eyes that indicated a strong man brought to bay. There was stubborn, undying antagonism; no quarter; no compromise. It was exactly the sort of situation Graham Dorn always presented his readers with, when two strong men fought for one hand, one heart, one girl.

The two said simultaneously, "Let's make a deal!"

Graham said, "You have convinced me, Reggie. Our public needs us. Tomorrow I shall begin another de Meister story. Let us shake hands and forget the past."

De Meister struggled with his emotion. He laid his hand on Graham's lapel, "My dear fellow, it is I who have been convinced by your logic. I can't allow you to sacrifice yourself for me. There are great things in you that must be brought out. Write your coal-mining novels. They count, not I."

"I couldn't, old chap. Not after all you've done for me, and all you've meant to me. Tomorow we start anew."

"Graham, my—my spiritual father, I couldn't allow it. Do you think I have no feelings, *filial* feelings—in a spiritual sort of way."

"But the war, think of the war. Mangled limbs. Blood. All that."

"I must stay. My country needs me."

"But if I stop writing, eventually you will stop existing. I can't allow that."

"Oh, that!" De Meister laughed with a careless elegance. "Things have changed since. So many people believe in my existence now that my grip upon actual existence has become too firm to be broken. I don't have to worry about Limbo any more."

"Oh." Graham clenched his teeth and spoke in searing

sibilants: "So that's your scheme, you snake. Do you suppose I don't see you're stuck on June?"

"Look here, old chap," said de Meister haughtily. "I can't permit you to speak slightingly of a true and honest love. I love June and she loves me—I know it. And if you're going to be stuffy and Victorian about it, you can swallow some nitro-glycerine and tap yourself with a hammer."

"I'll nitro-glycerine you! Because I'm going home tonight and beginning another de Meister story. You'll be part of it and you'll get back into it, and what do you think of that?"

"Nothing, because you can't write another de Meister story. I'm too real now, and you can't control me just like *that*. And what do you think of that?"

It took Graham Dorn a week to make up his mind what to think of that, and then his thoughts were completely and startlingly unprintable.

In fact, it was impossible to write.

That is, startling ideas occurred to him for great novels, emotional dramas, epic poems, brilliant essays—but he couldn't write anything about Reginald de Meister.

The typewriter was simply fresh out of Capital R's.

Graham wept, cursed, tore his hair, and anointed his finger tips with liniment. He tried typewriter, pen, pencil, crayon, charcoal, and blood.

He could not write.

The doorbell rang, and Graham threw it open.

MacDunlap stumbled in, falling over the first drifts of torn paper directly into Graham's arms.

Graham let him drop. "Hah!" he said, with frozen dignity.

"My heart!" said MacDunlap, and fumbled for his liver pills.

"Don't die there," suggested Graham, courteously. "The management won't permit me to drop human flesh into the incinerator."

"Graham, my boy," MacDunlap said, emotionally, "no more ultimatums! No more threats! I come now to appeal to your finer feelings, Graham—" he went through a slight choking interlude—"I love you like a son. This skunk de Meister must disappear. You must write more de Meister stories for my sake. Graham—I will tell you something in private. My wife is in love with this detective. She tells me I am not romantic. I! Not romantic! Can you understand it?"

"I can," was the tragic response. "He fascinates all women."

"With that face? With that monocle?"

"It says so in all my books."

MacDunlap stiffened. "Ah ha. You again. Dope! If only you ever stopped long enough to let your mind know what your typewriter was saying."

"You insisted. Feminine trade." Graham didn't care any more. Women! He snickered bitterly. Nothing wrong with any of them that a block-buster wouldn't fix.

MacDunlap hemmed. "Well, feminine trade. Very necessary. —But Graham, what shall I do? It's not only my wife. She owns fifty shares in MacDunlap, Inc. in her own name. If she leaves me, I lose control. Think of it, Graham. The catastrophe to the publishing world."

"Grew, old chap," Graham sighed a sigh so deep, his toenails quivered sympathetically. "I might as well tell you. June, my fiancée, you know, loves this worm. And he loves her because she is the prototype of Letitia Reynolds."

"The what of Letitia?" asked MacDunlap, vaguely suspecting an insult.

"Never mind. My life is ruined." He smiled bravely and choked back the unmanly tears, after the first two had dripped off the end of his nose.

"My poor boy!" The two gripped hands convulsively.

"Caught in a vise by this foul monster," said Graham.

"Trapped like a German in Russia," said MacDunlap.

"Victim of an inhuman fiend," said Graham.

"Exactly," said MacDunlap. He wrung Graham's hand as if he were milking a cow. "You've got to write de Meister stories and get him back where, next to Hell, he most belongs. Right?"

"Right! But there's one little catch."

"What?"

"I can't write. He's so real now, I *can't* put him into a book."

MacDunlap caught the significance of the massed drifts of used paper on the floor. He held his head and groaned, "My corporation! My wife!"

"There's always the Army," said Graham.

MacDunlap looked up. "What about *Death on the Third Deck*, the novel I rejected three weeks ago?"

"That doesn't count. It's past history. It's already affected him."

"Without being published?"

"Sure. That's the story I mentioned his draft board in. The one that put him in 1-A."

"I could think of better places to put him."

"MacDunlap!" Graham Dorn jumped up, and grappled MacDunlap's lapel. "Maybe it can be revised."

MacDunlap coughed hackingly, and stifled out a dim grunt.

"We can put anything we want into it."

MacDunlap choked a bit.

"We can fix things up."

MacDunlap turned blue in the face.

Graham shook the lapel and everything thereto attached, "Say something, won't you?"

MacDunlap wrenched away and took a tablespoon of cough syrup. He held his hand over his heart and patted it a bit. He shook his head and gestured with his eyebrows.

Graham shrugged. "Well, if you just want to be sullen, go ahead. I'll revise it without you.

He located the manuscript and tried his fingers gingerly on the typewriter. They went smoothly, with practically no creaking at the joints. He put on speed, more speed, and then went into his usual race, with the portable jouncing along merrily under the accustomed head of steam.

"It's working," he shouted. "I can't write new stories, but I can revise old, unpublished ones."

MacDunlap watched over his shoulder. He breathed only at odd moments.

"Faster," said MacDunlap, "faster!"

"Faster than thirty-five?" said Graham, sternly. "OPA* forbid! Five more minutes."

"Will he be there?"

"He's always there. He's been at her house every evening this week." He spat out the fine ivory dust into which he had ground the last inch of his incisors. "But God help you if your secretary falls down on the job."

"My boy, on my secretary you can depend."

"She's got to read that revision by nine."

"If she doesn't drop dead."

"With my luck, she will. Will she believe it?"

"Every word. She's seen de Meister. She *knows* he exists."

Brakes screeched, and Graham's soul cringed in sympathy with every molecule of rubber frictioned off the tires.

He bounded up the stairs, MacDunlap hobbling after.

*The Office of Price Administration was in charge of gasoline rationing at this period. Remember "A" stickers? D.R.B.

He rang the bell and burst in at the door. Reginald de Meister standing directly inside received the full impact of a pointing finger, and only a rapid backward movement of the head kept him from becoming a one-eyed mythical character.

June Billings stood aside, silent and uncomfortable.

"Reginald de Meister," growled Graham, in sinister tones, "prepare to meet your doom."

"Oh, boy," said MacDunlap, "are you going to get it."

"And to what," asked de Meister, "am I indebted for your dramatic but unilluminatin' statement? Confusin', don't you know." He lit a cigarette with a fine gesture and smiled.

"Hello, Gramie," said June, tearfully.

"Scram, vile woman."

June sniffed. She felt like a heroine out of a book, torn by her own emotions. Naturally, she was having the time of her life.

So she let the tears dribble and looked forlorn.

"To return to the subject, what is this all about?" asked de Meister, wearily.

"I have rewritten *Death on the Third Deck.*"

"Well?"

"The revision," continued Graham, "is at present in the hands of MacDunlap's secretary, a girl on the style of Miss Billings, my fiancée that was. That is, she is a girl who aspires to the status of a moron, but has not yet quite attained it. She'll believe every word."

"Well?"

Graham's voice grew ominous, "You remember, perhaps, Sancha Rodriguez?"

For the first time, Reginald de Meister shuddered. He caught his cigarette as it dropped. "She was killed by Sam Blake in the sixth chapter. She was in love with me. Really, old fellow, what messes you get me into."

"Not half the mess you're in now, old chap. Sancha Rodriguez did *not* die in the revision."

"Die!" came a sharp, but clear female voice, "I'll show him if I died. And where have *you* been this last month, you two-crosser?"

De Meister did not catch his cigarette this time. He didn't even try. He recognized the apparition. To an unprejudiced observer, it might have been merely a svelte Latin girl equipped with dark, flashing eyes, and long, glittering fingernails, but to de Meister, it was Sancha Rodriguez—*undead!*

MacDunlap's secretary had read and believed.

"Miss Rodriguez," throbbed de Meister, charmingly, "how fascinatin' to see you."

"Mrs. de Meister to you, you double-timer, you two-crosser, you scum of the ground, you scorpion of the grass. And who is this woman?"

June retreated with dignity behind the nearest chair.

"*Mrs.* de Meister," said Reginald pleadingly, and turned helplessly to Graham Dorn.

"Oh, you have forgotten, have you, you smooth talker, you low dog. I'll show you what it means to deceive a weak woman. I'll make you mince-meat with my fingernails."

De Meister back-pedaled furiously. "But darling—"

"Don't you make sweet talk. What are you doing with this woman?"

"But, darling—"

"Don't give me any explanation. What are you doing with this woman?"

"But, darling—"

"Shut up! What are you doing with this woman?"

Reginald de Meister was up in a corner, and Mrs. de Meister shook her fists at him. "Answer me!"

De Meister disappeared.

Mrs. de Meister disappeared right after him.

June Billings collapsed into real tears.

Graham Dorn folded his arms and looked sternly at her.

MacDunlap rubbed his hands and took a kidney pill.

"It wasn't my fault, Gramie," said June. "You said in your books he fascinated all women, so I couldn't help it. Deep inside, I hated him all along. You believe me, don't you?"

"A likely story!" said Graham, sitting down next to her on the sofa. "A likely story. But I forgive you, maybe."

MacDunlap said tremulously, "My boy, you have saved my stocks. Also, my wife, of course. And remember—you promised me one de Meister story each year."

Graham gritted, "Just one, and I'll henpeck him to death, and keep one unpublished story forever on hand, just in case. And you're publishing my novel, aren't you, Grew, old boy?"

"Glug," said MacDunlap.

"Aren't you?"

"Yes, Graham. Of course, Graham. Definitely, Graham. Positively, Graham."

"Then leave us now. There are matters of importance I must discuss with my fiancée."

MacDunlap smiled and tiptoed out the door.

Ah, love, love, he mused, as he took a liver pill and followed it up by a cough-syrup chaser.

THE END

I might make two points about "Author! Author!" It seems to me that I was rather easier about handling romance in this story than in any previous one. Perhaps this is a reflection of the fact that it was the first story I ever wrote as a married man.

Secondly, there are the very dated references to rationing, the draft, and other social phenomena much on the mind of anyone living through World War II. I had warned Bensen of the existence of these references and of the inability of getting them out of the story by revision since they were integral to the plot. Bensen, however, shrugged them off and in his short introduction to the story said to the readers, "And don't worry about the references to the OPA and Selective Service—consider them as part of the historical setting, just as you would a bodkin or a furbelow in a story of an earlier time."

And I second that statement here.

Had I rested on the pink cloud of gratification that came with the sale of "Author! Author!" for a few months, the death of **Unknown** might have disheartened me. It might have seemed to prove that I was not fated to reignite my career after all, and perhaps—again—everything would have turned out differently.

However, within three weeks of the sale I was at the typewriter again. The new story was "Death Sentence" and it was science fiction. Writing was still slow work; seven weeks to do a 7,200-word story. On June 29, 1943, however, I sent it off to Campbell, and on July 8, it was accepted—one and a quarter cents per word again.

This meant that when the news of **Unknown**'s demise arrived, it was cushioned by the fact that I already had another story written and sold.

22

Death Sentence

Brand Gorla smiled uncomfortably, "These things exaggerate, you know."

"No, no, no!" The little man's albino-pink eyes snapped. "Dorlis was great when no human had ever entered the Vegan System. It was the capital of a Galactic Confederation greater than ours."

"Well, then, let's say that it was an ancient capital. I'll admit that and leave the rest to an archaeologist."

"Archaeologists are no use. What I've discovered needs a specialist in its own field. And you're on the Board."

Brand Gorla looked doubtful. He remembered Theor Realo in senior year—a little white misfit of a human who skulked somewhere in the background of his reminiscences. It had been a long time ago, but the albino had been queer. *That* was easy to remember. And he was still queer.

"I'll try to help," Brand said, "if you'll tell me what you want."

Theor watched intently, "I want you to place certain facts before the Board. Will you promise that?"

Brand hedged, "Even if I help you along, Theor, I'll have to remind you that I'm junior member of the Psychological Board. I haven't much influence."

"You must do your best. The facts will speak for them-

Astounding Science Fiction, November 1943
Copyright © 1943 by Street & Smith Publications, Inc.
Copyright renewed © 1970 by Isaac Asimov

selves." The albino's hands were trembling.

"Go ahead." Brand resigned himself. The man was an old school fellow. You couldn't be *too* arbitrary about things.

Brand Gorla leaned back and relaxed. The light of Arcturus shone through the ceiling-high windows, diffused and mellowed by the polarizing glass. Even this diluted version of sunlight was too much for the pink eyes of the other, and he shaded his eyes as he spoke.

"I've lived on Dorlis twenty-five years, Brand," he said, "I've poked into places no one today knew existed, and I've found things. Dorlis was the scientific and cultural capital of a civilization greater than ours. Yes it was, and particularly in psychology."

"Things in the past always seem greater." Brand condescended a smile. "There is a theorem to that effect which you'll find in any elementary text. Freshmen invariably call it the 'GOD Theorem.' Stands for 'Good-Old-Days,' you know. But go on."

Theor frowned at the digression. He hid the beginning of a sneer. "You can always dismiss an uncomfortable fact by pinning a dowdy label to it. But tell me this. What do you know of Psychological Engineering?"

Brand shrugged, "No such thing. Anyway, not in the strict mathematical sense. All propaganda and advertising is a crude form of hit-and-miss Psych Engineering—and pretty effective sometimes. Maybe that's what you mean."

"Not at all. I mean actual experimentation, with masses of people under controlled conditions, and over a period of years."

"Such things have been discussed. It's not feasible in practice. Our social structure couldn't stand much of it, and we don't know enough to set up effective controls."

Theor suppressed excitement. "But the ancients *did* know enough. And they *did* set up controls."

Brand considered phlegmatically, "Startling and interesting, but how do you know?"

"Because I found the documents relating to it." He paused breathlessly. "An entire planet, Brand. A complete world picked to suit, peopled with beings under strict control from every angle. Studied, and charted, and experimented upon. Don't you get the picture?"

Brand noted none of the usual stigmata of mental uncontrol. A closer investigation, perhaps—

He said evenly, "You must have been misled. It's thoroughly impossible. You can't control humans like that. Too many variables."

"And that's the point, Brand. They weren't humans."

"What?"

"They were robots, positronic robots. A whole world of them, Brand, with nothing to do but live and react and be observed by a set of psychologists that were *real* psychologists."

"That's mad!"

"I have proof—because that robot world still exists. The First Confederation went to pieces, but that robot world kept on going. It still exists."

"And how do you know?"

Theor Realo stood up. "Because I've been there these last twenty-five years!"

The Board Master threw his formal red-edged gown aside and reached into a pocket for a long, gnarled and decidedly unofficial cigar.

"Preposterous," he grunted, "and thoroughly insane."

"Exactly," said Brand, "and I can't spring it on the Board just like that. They wouldn't listen. I've got to get this across to you first, and then, if you can put your authority behind it—"

"Oh, nuts! I never heard anything as— Who is the fellow?"

Brand sighed, "A crank, I'll admit that. He was in my class at Arcturus U. and a crack-pot albino even then. Maladjusted as the devil, hipped on ancient history, and just the kind that gets an idea and goes through with it by plain, dumb plugging. He's poked about in Dorlis for twenty-five years, he says. He's got the complete records of practically an entire civilization."

The Board Master puffed furiously. "Yeah, I know. In the telestat serials, the brilliant amateur always uncovers the great things. The free lance. The lone wolf. Nuts! Have you consulted the Department of Archaeology?"

"Certainly. And the result was interesting. No one bothers with Dorlis. This isn't just ancient history, you see. It's a matter of fifteen thousand years. It's practically myth. Reputable archaeologists don't waste too much time with it. It's just the thing a book-struck layman with a single-track mind *would* uncover. After this, of course, if the business turns out right, Dorlis will become an archaeologist's paradise."

The Board Master screwed his homely face into an appalling grimace. "It's very unflattering to the ego. If there's any truth in all this, the so-called First Confederation must have had a grasp of psychology so far past ours, as to make us out to be blithering imbeciles. Too, they'd have to build positronic robots that would be about seventy-five orders of magnitude above anything we've even blueprinted. Galaxy! Think of the mathematics involved."

"Look, sir, I've consulted just about everybody. I wouldn't bring this thing to you if I weren't certain that I had every angle checked. I went to Blak just about the first thing, and he's consultant mathematician to United Robots. He says there's no limit to these things. Given the time, the money, and the *advance in psychology*—get that—robots like that could be built right now."

"What proof has he?"

"Who, Blak?"

"No, no! Your friend. The albino. You said he had papers."

"He has. I've got them here. He's got documents—and there's no denying their antiquity. I've had that checked every way from Sunday. I can't read them, of course. I don't know if anyone can, except Theor Realo."

"That's stacking the deck, isn't it? We have to take his say-so."

"Yes, in a way. But he doesn't claim to be able to decipher more than portions. He says it is related to ancient Centaurian, and I've put linguists to work on it. It can be cracked and if his translation isn't accurate, we'll know about it."

"All right. Let's see it."

Brand Gorla brought out the plastic-mounted documents. The Board Master tossed them aside and reached for the translation. Smoke billowed as he read.

"Humph," was his comment. "Further details are on Dorlis, I suppose."

"Theor claims that there are some hundred to two hundred tons of blueprints altogether, on the brain plan of the positronic robots alone. They're still there in the original vault. But that's the least of it. He's been on the robot world itself. He's got photocasts, teletype recordings, all sorts of details. They're not integrated, and obviously the work of a layman who knows next to nothing about psychology. Even so, he's managed to get enough data to prove pretty conclusively that the world he was on wasn't . . . uh . . . natural."

"You've got that with you, too."

"All of it. Most of it's on microfilm, but I've brought the projector. Here are your eyepieces."

An hour later, the Board Master said, "I'll call a Board Meeting tomorrow and push this through."

Brand Gorla grinned tightly, "We'll send a commission to Dorlis?"

"When," said the Board Master dryly, "and if we can get an appropriation out of the University for such an affair. Leave this material with me for the while, please. I want to study it a little more."

Theoretically, the Governmental Department of Science and Technology exercises administrative control over all scientific investigation. Actually, however, the pure research groups of the large universities are thoroughly autonomous bodies, and, as a general rule, the Government does not care to dispute that. But a general rule is not necessarily a universal rule.

And so, although the Board Master scowled and fumed and swore, there was no way of refusing Wynne Murry an interview. To give Murry his complete title, he was under secretary in charge of psychology, psychopathy and mental technology. And he was a pretty fair psychologist in his own right.

So the Board Master might glare, but that was all.

Secretary Murry ignored the glare cheerfully. He rubbed his long chin against the grain and said, "It amounts to a case of insufficient information. Shall we put it that way?"

The Board Master said frigidly, "I don't see what information you want. The government's say in university appropriations is purely advisory, and in this case, I might say, the advice is unwelcome."

Murry shrugged, "I have no quarrel with the appropriation. But you're not going to leave the planet without government permit. That's where the insufficient information comes in."

"There is no information other than we've given you."

"But things have leaked out. All this is childish and rather unnecessary secrecy."

The old psychologist flushed. "Secrecy! If you don't know the academic way of life, I can't help you. Investigations, especially those of major importance, aren't, and can't be, made public, until definite progress has been made. When we get back, we'll send you copies of whatever papers we publish."

Murry shook his head, "Uh-uh. Not enough. You're going to Dorlis, aren't you?"

"We've informed the Department of Science of that."

"Why?"

"Why do you want to know?"

"Because it's big, or the Board Master wouldn't go himself. What's this about an older civilization and a world of robots?"

"Well, then, you know."

"Only vague notions we've been able to scrabble up. I want the details."

"There are none that we know now. We won't know until we're on Dorlis."

"Then I'm going with you."

"What!"

"You see, I want the details, too."

"Why?"

"Ah," Murry unfolded his legs and stood up, "now *you're* asking the questions. It's no use, now. I know that the universities aren't keen on government supervision; and I know that I can expect no willing help from *any* academic source. But, by Arcturus, I'm going to get help this time, and I don't care how you fight it. Your expedition is going nowhere, unless I go with you—representing the government."

Dorlis, as a world, is not impressive. It's importance to Galactic economy is nil, its position far off the great trade routes, its natives backward and unenlightened, its history obscure. And yet somewhere in the heaps of rubble that clutter an ancient world, there is obscure evidence of an influx of flame and destruction that destroyed the Dorlis of an earlier day—the greater capital of a greater Federation.

And somewhere in that rubble, men of a newer world poked and probed and tried to understand.

The Board Master shook his head and then pushed back his grizzling hair. He hadn't shaved in a week.

"The trouble is," he said, "that we have no point of reference. The language can be broken, I suppose, but nothing can be done with the notation."

"I think a great deal has been done."

"Stabs in the dark! Guessing games based on the translation of your albino friend. I won't base any hopes on that."

Brand said, "Nuts! You spent two years on the Nimian

Anomaly, and so far only two months on this, which happens to be a hundred thousand times the job. It's something else that's getting you." He smiled grimly. "It doesn't take a psychologist to see that the government man is in your hair."

The Board Master bit the end off a cigar and spat it four feet. He said slowly, "There are three things about the mule-headed idiot that make me sore. First, I don't like government interference. Second, I don't like a stranger sniffing about when we're on top of the biggest thing in the history of psychology. Third, what in the Galaxy does he want? *What is he after?*"

"I don't know."

"What *should* he be after? Have you thought of it at all?"

"No. Frankly, I don't care. I'd ignore him if I were you."

"You would," said the Board Master violently. "You would! You think the government's entrance into this affair need only be ignored. I suppose you know that this Murry calls himself a psychologist?"

"I know that."

"And I suppose you know he's been displaying a devouring interest in all that we've been doing."

"That, I should say, would be natural."

"Oh! And you know further—" His voice dropped with startling suddenness. "All right, Murry's at the door. Take it easy."

Wynne Murry grinned a greeting, but the Board Master nodded unsmilingly.

"Well, sir," said Murry bluffly, "do you know I've been on my feet for forty-eight hours! You've *got* something here. Something big."

"Thank you."

"No, no. I'm serious. The robot world exists."

"Did you think it didn't?"

The secretary shrugged amiably. "One has a certain natural skepticism. What are your future plans?"

"Why do you ask?" The Board Master grunted his words as if they were being squeezed out singly.

"To see if they jibe with my own."

"And what are your own?"

The secretary smiled. "No, no. You take precedence. How long do you intend staying here?"

"As long as it takes to make a fair beginning on the documents involved."

"That's no answer. What do you mean by a fair beginning?"

"I haven't the slightest idea. It might take years."

"Oh, damnation."

The Board Master raised his eyebrows and said nothing.

The secretary looked at his nails. "I take it you know the location of this robot world."

"Naturally. Theor Realo was there. His information up to now has proven very accurate."

"That's right. The albino. Well, why not go there?"

"Go there! Impossible!"

"May I ask why?"

"Look," said the Board Master with restrained impatience, "you're not here by our invitation, and we're not asking you to dictate our course of actions, but just to show you that I'm not looking for a fight, I'll give you a little metaphorical treatment of our case. Suppose we were presented with a huge and complicated machine, composed of principles and materials of which we knew next to nothing. It is so vast we can't even make out the relationship of the parts, let alone the purpose of the whole. Now, would you advise me to begin attacking the delicate mysterious moving parts of the machine with a detonating ray before I know what it's all about?"

"I see your point, of course, but you're becoming a mystic. The metaphor is farfetched."

"Not at all. These positronic robots were constructed along lines we know nothing of as yet and were intended to follow lines with which we are entirely unacquainted. About the only thing we know is that the robots were put aside in complete isolation, to work out their destiny by themselves. To ruin that isolation would be to ruin the experiment. If we go there in a body, introducing new, unforeseen factors, inducing unintended reactions, everything is ruined. The littlest disturbance—"

"Poppycock! Theor Realo has already gone there."

The Board Master lost his temper suddenly. "Don't you suppose I know that? Do you suppose it would ever have happened if that cursed albino hadn't been an ignorant fanatic without any knowledge of psychology at all? Galaxy knows what the idiot has done in the way of damage."

There was a silence. The secretary clicked his teeth with a thoughtful fingernail. "I don't know. . . . I don't know. But I've got to find out. And I can't wait years."

He left, and the Board Master turned seethingly to Brand,

"And how are we going to stop him from going to the robot world if he wants to?"

"I don't see how he can go if we don't let him. *He* doesn't head the expedition."

"Oh, doesn't he? *That's* what I was about to tell you just before he came in. Ten ships of the fleet have landed on Dorlis since we arrived."

"What!"

"Just that."

"But what for?"

"That, my boy, is what I don't understand, either."

"Mind if I drop in?" said Wynne Murry, pleasantly, and Theor Realo looked up in sudden anxiety from the papers that lay in hopeless disarray on the desk before him.

"Come in. I'll clear off a seat for you." The albino hustled the mess off one of the two chairs in a state of twittering nerves.

Murry sat down and swung one long leg over the other. "Are you assigned a job here, too?" He nodded at the desk.

Theor shook his head and smiled feebly. Almost automatically, he brushed the papers together in a heap and turned them face down.

In the months since he had returned to Dorlis with a hundred psychologists of various degrees of renown, he had felt himself pushed farther and farther from the center of things. There was room for him no longer. Except to answer questions on the actual state of things upon the robot world, which he alone had visited, he played no part. And even there he detected, or seemed to detect, anger that *he* should have gone, and not a competent scientist.

It was a thing to be resented. Yet, somehow, it had always been like that.

"Pardon me?" He had let Murry's next remark slip.

The secretary repeated, "I say it's surprising you're *not* put to work, then. You made the original discovery, didn't you?"

"Yes," the albino brightened. "But it went out of my hands. It got beyond me."

"You were on the robot world, though."

"That was a mistake, they tell me. I might have ruined everything."

Murry grimaced. "What really gets them, I guess, is that you've got a lot of first-hand dope that they didn't. Don't let their fancy titles fool you into thinking you're a nobody. A layman with common sense is better than a blind specialist. You and I—I'm a layman, too, you know—have to stand up for our rights. Here, have a cigarette."

"I don't sm— I'll take one, thank you." The albino felt himself warming to the long-bodied man opposite. He turned the papers face upward again, and lit up, bravely but uncertainly.

"Twenty-five years." Theor spoke carefully, skirting around urgent coughs.

"Would you answer a few questions about the world?"

"I suppose so. That's all they ever ask me about. But hadn't you better ask *them?* They've probably got it all worked out now." He blew the smoke as far from himself as possible.

Murry said, "Frankly, they haven't even begun, and I want the information without benefit of confusing psychological translations. First of all, what kind of people—or things— are these robots? You haven't a photocast of one of them, have you?"

"Well, no. I didn't like to take 'casts of them. But they're not things. They're *people!"*

"No? Do they look like—people?"

"Yes—mostly. Outside, anyway. I brought some microscopic studies of the cellular structure that I got hold of. The Board Master has them. They're different inside, you know, greatly simplified. But you'd never know that. They're interesting—and nice."

"Are they simpler than the other life of the planet?"

"Oh, no. It's a very primitive planet. And . . . and," he was interrupted by a spasm of coughing and crushed the cigarette to death as unobtrusively as possible. "They've got a protoplasmic base, you know. I don't think they have the slightest idea they're robots."

"No. I don't suppose they would have. What about their science?"

"I don't know. I never got a chance to see. And everything was so different. I guess it would take an expert to understand."

"Did they have machines?"

The albino looked surprised. "Well, of course. A good many, of all sorts."

"Large cities?"

"Yes!"

The secretary's eyes grew thoughtful. "And you like them. Why?"

Theor Realo was brought up sharply. "I don't know. They were just likable. We got along. They didn't bother me so. It's nothing I can put my finger on. Maybe it's because I have it so hard getting along back home, and they weren't as difficult as real people."

"They were more friendly?"

"N-no. Can't say so. They never quite accepted me. I was a stranger, didn't know their language at first—all that. But"—he looked up with sudden brightness—"I understood them better. I could tell what they were thinking better. I— But I don't know why."

"Hm-m-m. Well—another cigarette? No? I've got to be walloping the pillow now. It's getting late. How about a two-some at golf tomorrow? I've worked up a little course. It'll do. Come on out. The exercise will put hair on your chest."

He grinned and left.

He mumbled one sentence to himself: "It looks like a death sentence"—and whistled thoughtfully as he passed along to his own quarters.

He repeated the phrase to himself when he faced the Board Master the next day, with the sash of office about his waist. He did not sit down.

"Again?" said the Board Master, wearily.

"Again!" assented the secretary. "But real business this time. I may have to take over direction of your expedition."

"What! Impossible, sir! I will listen to no such proposition."

"I have my authority." Wynne Murry presented the metalloid cylinder that snapped open at a flick of the thumb. "I have full powers and full discretion as to their use. It is signed, as you will observe, by the chairman of the Congress of the Federation."

"So— But why?" The Board Master, by an effort, breathed normally. "Short of arbitrary tyranny, is there a reason?"

"A very good one, sir. All along, we have viewed this expedition from different angles. The Department of Science and Technology views the robot world not from the point of view of a scientific curiosity, but from the standpoint of its interference with the peace of the Federation. I don't think you've ever stopped to consider the danger inherent in this robot world."

"None that I can see. It is thoroughly isolated and thoroughly harmless."

"How can you know?"

"From the very nature of the experiment," shouted the Board Master angrily. "The original planners wanted as nearly a completely closed system as possible. Here they are, just as far off the trade routes as possible, in a thinly populated region of space. The whole idea was to have the robots develop free of interference."

Murry smiled. "I disagree with you there. Look, the whole trouble with you is that you're a theoretical man. You look at things the way they ought to be and I, a practical man, look at things as they are. No experiment can be set up and allowed to run indefinitely under its own power. It is taken for granted that somewhere there is at least an observer who watches and *modifies* as circumstances warrant."

"Well?" said the Board Master stolidly.

"Well, the observers in this experiment, the original psychologists of Dorlis, passed away with the First Confederation, and for fifteen thousand years the experiment has proceeded by itself. Little errors have added up and become big ones and introduced alien factors which induced still other errors. It's a geometric progression. And there's been no one to halt it."

"Pure hypothesis."

"Maybe. But you're interested only in the robot world, and I've got to think of the entire Federation."

"And just what possible danger can the robot world be to the Federation? I don't know *what* in Arcturus you're driving at, man."

Murry sighed. "I'll be simple, but don't blame me if I sound melodramatic. The Federation hasn't had any internal warfare for centuries. What will happen if we come into contact with these robots?"

"Are you afraid of one world?"

"Could be. What about their science? Robots can do funny things sometimes."

"What science can they have? They're not metal-electricity supermen. They're weak protoplasmic creatures, a poor imitation of actual humanity, built around a positronic brain adjusted to a set of simplified human psychological laws. If the word 'robot' is scaring you—"

"No, it isn't, but I've talked to Theor Realo. He's the only one who's seen them, you know."

The Board Master cursed silently and fluently. It came of letting a weak-minded freak of a layman get underfoot where he could babble and do harm.

He said, "We've got Realo's full story, and we've evaluated it fully and capably. I assure you, no harm exists in them. The experiment is so thoroughly academic, I wouldn't spend two days on it if it weren't for the broad scope of the thing. From what we see, the whole idea was to build up a positronic brain containing modifications of one or two of the fundamental axioms. We haven't worked out the details, but they must be minor, as it was the first experiment of this nature ever tried, and even the great mythical psychologists of that day had to progress stepwise. Those robots, I tell you, are neither supermen nor beasts. I assure you—as a psychologist."

"Sorry! I'm a psychologist, too. A little more rule-of-thumb, I'm afraid. That's all. But even little modifications! Take the general spirit of combativeness. That isn't the scientific term, but I've no patience for that. You know what I mean. We humans used to be combative. But it's being bred out of us. A stable political and economic system doesn't encourage the waste energy of combat. It's not a survival factor. But suppose the robots are combative. Suppose as the result of a wrong turn during the millennia they're been unwatched, they've become far more combative than ever their first makers intended. They'd be uncomfortable things to be with."

"And suppose all the stars in the Galaxy become novae at the same time. Let's *really* start worrying."

"And there's another point." Murry ignored the other's heavy sarcasm. "Theor Realo liked those robots. He liked robots better than he likes real people. He felt that he fitted there, and we all know he's been a bad misfit in his own world."

"And what," asked the Board Master, "is the significance of that?"

"You don't see it?" Wynne Murry lifted his eyebrows. "Theor Realo likes those robots because he is *like* them, obviously. I'll guarantee right now that a complete psychic analysis of Theor Realo will show a modification of several fundamental axioms, and the same ones as in the robots.

"And," the secretary drove on without a pause, "Theor Realo worked for a quarter of a century to prove a point, when all science would have laughed him to death if they had known about it. There's fanaticism there; good, honest, *inhuman* perserverance. *Those robots are probably like that!*"

"You're advancing no logic. You're arguing like a maniac, like a moon-struck idiot."

"I don't need strict mathematical proof. Reasonable doubt is sufficient. I've got to protect the Federation. Look, it *is* reasonable, you know. The psychologists of Dorlis weren't as super as all that. They had to advance stepwise, as you yourself pointed out. Their humanoids—let's not call them robots—were only imitations of human beings and they couldn't be good ones. Humans possess certain very, *very* complicated reaction systems—things like social consciousness, and a tendency toward the establishment of ethical systems; and more ordinary things like chivalry, generosity, fair play and so on, that simply can't possibly be duplicated. I don't think those humanoids can have them. But they *must* have perseverance, which practically implies stubborness and combativeness, if my notion on Theor Realo holds good. Well, if their science is anywhere at all, then I don't want to have them running loose in the Galaxy, if our numbers are a thousand or million times theirs. And I don't intend to permit them to do so!"

The Board Master's face was rigid. "What are your immediate intentions?"

"As yet undecided. But I think I am going to organize a small-scale landing on the planet."

"Now, wait." The old psychologist was up and around the desk. He seized the secretary's elbow. "Are you quite certain you know what you're doing? The potentialities in this massive experiment are beyond any possible precalculation by you or me. You can't know what you're destroying."

"I know. Do you think I enjoy what I'm doing? This isn't a hero's job. I'm enough of a psychologist to want to know what's going on, but I've been sent here to protect the Federation, and to the best of my ability I intend doing it—and a dirty job it is. But I can't help it."

"You can't have thought it out. What can you know of the insight it will give us into the basic ideas of psychology? This will amount to a fusion of two Galactic systems, that will send us to heights that will make up in knowledge and power a million times the amount of harm the robots could ever do, if they *were* metal-electricity supermen."

The secretary shrugged. "Now you're the one that is playing with faint possibilities."

"Listen, I'll make a deal. Blockade them. Isolate them with your ships. Mount guards. But don't touch them. Give us more time. Give us a chance. You must!"

"I've thought of that. But I would have to get Congress to agree to that. It would be expensive, you know."

The Board Master flung himself into his chair in wild impatience. "What kind of expense are you talking about? Do you realize the nature of the repayment if we succeeded?"

Murry considered; then, with a half smile, "What if they develop interstellar travel?"

The Board Master said quickly, "Then I'll withdraw my objections."

The secretary rose, "I'll have it out with Congress."

Brand Gorla's face was carefully emotionless as he watched the Board Master's stooped back. The cheerful pep talks to the available members of the expedition lacked meat, and he listened to them impatiently.

He said, "What are we going to do now?"

The Board Master's shoulders twitched and he didn't turn. "I've sent for Theor Realo. That little fool left for the Eastern Continent last week—"

"Why?"

The older man blazed at the interruption. "How can I understand anything that freak does! Don't you see that Murry's right? He's a psychic abnormality. We had no business leaving him unwatched. If I had ever thought of looking at him twice, I wouldn't have. He's coming back now, though, and he's going to stay back." His voice fell to a mumble. "Should have been back two hours ago."

"It's an impossible position, sir," said Brand, flatly.

"Think so?"

"Well— Do *you* think Congress will stand for an indefinite patrol off the robot world? It runs into money, and average Galactic citizens aren't going to see it as worth the taxes. The psychological equations degenerate into the axioms of common sense. In fact, I don't see why Murry agreed to consult Congress."

"Don't you?" The Board Master finally faced his junior. "Well, the fool considers himself a psychologist, Galaxy help us, and that's his weak point. He flatters himself that he doesn't want to destroy the robot world in his heart, but that it's the good of the Federation that requires it. And he'll jump at any reasonable compromise. Congress won't agree

to it indefinitely, you don't have to point that out to me."
He was talking quietly, patiently. "But I will ask for ten
years, two years, six months—as much as I can get. I'll get
something. In that time, we'll learn new facts about the
world. Somehow we'll strengthen our case and renew the
agreement when it expires. We'll save the project yet."

There was a short silence and the Board Master added
slowly and bitterly, "And that's where Theor Realo plays
a vital part."

Brand Gorla watched silently, and waited. The Board
Master said, "On that one point, Murry saw what we didn't.
Realo is a psychological cripple, and is our real clue to the
whole affair. If we study him, we'll have a rough picture of
what the robot is like, distorted of course, since his environment has been a hostile, unfriendly one. But we can make
allowance for that, estimate his nature in a— Ahh, I'm tired
of the whole project."

The signal box flashed, and the Board Master sighed.
"Well, he's here. All right, Gorla, sit down, you make me
nervous. Let's take a look at him."

Theor Realo came through the door like a comet and
brought himself to a panting halt in the middle of the floor.
He looked from one to the other with weak, peering eyes.

"How did all this happen?"

"All what?" said the Board Master coldly. "Sit down. I
want to ask you some questions."

"No. You first answer *me*."

"*Sit down!*"

Realo sat. His eyes were brimming. "They're going to destroy the robot world."

"Don't worry about that."

"But you said they could if the robots discovered interstellar travel. You said so. You fool. Don't you see—" He
was choking.

The Board Master frowned uneasily. "Will you calm down
and talk sense?"

The albino gritted his teeth and forced the words out. "But
they'll *have* interstellar travel before long."

And the two psychologists shot toward the little man.

"What!!"

"Well . . . well, what do you think?" Realo sprang upward
with all the fury of desperation. "Did you think I landed in
a desert or in the middle of an ocean and explored a world

all by myself? Do you think life is a storybook? I was captured as soon as I landed and taken to a big city. At least, I think it was a big city. It was different from our kind. It had— But I won't tell you."

"Never mind the city," shrieked the Board Master. "You were captured. Go ahead."

"They studied *me*. They studied my machine. And then, one night, I left, to tell the Federation. They didn't know I left. They didn't want me to leave." His voice broke. "And I would have stayed as soon as not, but the Federation had to know."

"Did you tell them anything about your ship?"

"How could I! I'm no mechanic. I don't know the theory or construction. But I showed them how to work the controls and let them look at the motors. That's all."

Brand Gorla said, to himself mostly, "Then they'll never get it. That isn't enough."

The albino's voice raised itself in sudden shrieking triumph. "Oh, yes, they will. I know them. They're machines, you know. They'll work on that problem. And they'll work. And they'll work. And they'll never quit. And they'll get it. They got enough out of me. I'll *bet* they got enough."

The Board Master looked long, and turned away—wearily. "Why didn't you tell us?"

"Because you took my world away from me. I discovered it—by myself—all by myself. And after I had done all the real work, and invited you in, you threw me out. All you had for me was complaints that I had landed on the world and might have ruined everything by interference. Why should I tell you? Find out for yourselves if you're so wise, that you could afford to kick me around."

The Board Master thought bitterly, "Misfit! Inferiority complex! Persecution mania! Nice! It all fits in, now that we've bothered to take our eyes off the horizon and see what was under our nose. And now it's all ruined."

He said, "All right, Realo, we all lose. Go away."

Brand Gorla said tightly, "All over? Really all over?"

The Board Master answered, "Really all over. The original experiment, as such, is over. The distortions created by Realo's visit will easily be large enough to make the plans we are studying here a dead language. And besides—Murry is right. If they have interstellar travel, they're dangerous."

Realo was shouting, "But you're not going to destroy them. You can't destroy them. They haven't hurt anyone."

There was no answer, and he raved on, "I'm going back. I'll warn them. They'll be prepared. I'll warn them."

He was backing toward the door, his thin, white hair bristling, his red-rimmed eyes bulging.

The Board Master did not move to stop him when he dashed out.

"Let him go. It was *his* lifetime. I don't care any more."

Theor Realo smashed toward the robot world at an acceleration that was half choking him.

Somewhere ahead was the dustspeck of an isolated world with artificial imitations of humanity struggling along in an experiment that had died. Struggling blindly toward a new goal of interstellar travel that was to be their death sentence.

He was heading toward that world, toward the same city in which he had been "studied" the first time. He remembered it well. Its name was the first words of their language he had learned.

New York!

THE END

On July 26, 1943, which was a Monday, I had one of the rare days off I could take during wartime. (It was, after all, my first wedding anniversary.) I was in New York that day, and I visited Campbell just as in the good old days. I discussed with him another story in the "Foundation" series, as well as another in the "positronic robot" series. From then on, I always saw Campbell on the rare days when I was in New York on a weekday, and of course we corresponded regularly.

I was definitely back at writing. Output was low, but during the remaining war years I wrote two positronic robot stories, "Catch That Rabbit" and "Paradoxical Escape," which appeared in the February 1944 and August 1945 issues of **Astounding**, respectively. Both were eventually included in **I, Robot**. (The latter story appears in **I, Robot** under the title of "Escape." The word "Paradoxical" had been added by Campbell in one of his few title changes, and I didn't like it.)

I also wrote no less than four stories of the "Foundation" series during those same years. These were "The Big and the Little," "The Wedge," "Dead Hand," and "The Mule." All appeared in **Astounding,** of course, the first three in the August 1944, October 1944, and April 1945 issues, respectively.

"The Mule" set several records for me. It was the longest story I had ever written up to that time—fifty thousand words long. Yet even so, and despite the fact that I had to work on it in small scraps of time left over from job and marriage, I managed to complete it in three and a half months. It was submitted on May 21, 1945, and was accepted on the twenty-ninth. (Indeed, throughout the war I never got a single rejection, or even a delayed acceptance. Nor did I submit to anyone but Campbell.)

What's more, at the beginning of 1944 Campbell raised his basic rate to one and a half cents a word and some months later to a cent and three quarters. For "The Mule" I received a check at the higher rate, for $875. It was by far the largest check I ever received for a single story. By the end of the war, in fact, I was making half as much money writing in my spare time as I was making at my N.A.E.S. job, even though I had been promoted and was receiving sixty dollars a week by the end of the war.

Then, too, "The Mule" was the first story I ever had published as a serial. It appeared in two parts in the November and December 1945 issues of **Astounding.**

Of the wartime "Foundation" stories, "The Big and the Little" and "The Wedge" are included in **Foundation,** while "Dead Hand" and "The Mule," together, make up all of **Foundation and Empire.**

During the two years between mid-1943 and mid-1945, I wrote only one story that was neither one of the "Foundation" series nor one of the "Positronic robot" series, and that one was inspired directly by the N.A.E.S. This story was "Blind Alley," which was written during September and early October of 1944. It was submitted to Campbell on October 10, and accepted on the twentieth.

23

Blind Alley

Only once in Galactic History was an intelligent race of non-Humans discovered—

"Essays on History,"
by Ligurn Vier

I.

From: Bureau for the Outer Provinces

To: Loodun Antyok, Chief Public Administrator, A-8

Subject: Civilian Supervisor of Cepheus 18, Administrative Position as,

References:

(a) Act of Council 2515, of the year 971 of the Galactic Empire, entitled, "Appointment of Officials of the Administrative Service, Methods for, Revision of."

(b) Imperial Directive, Ja 2374, dated 243/975 G.E.

1. By authorization of reference (a), you are hereby appointed to the subject position. The authority of said position as Civilian Supervisor of Cepheus 18 will extend over non-Human subjects of the Emperor living upon the planet under the terms of autonomy set forth in reference (b).

2. The duties of the subject position shall comprise the general supervision of all non-Human internal affairs, coordination of authorized government investigating and reporting committees, and the preparation of semiannual reports on all phases of non-Human affairs.

C. Morily, Chief, BuOuProv,
12/977 G.E.

Astounding Science Fiction, March 1945
Copyright © 1945 by Street & Smith Publications, Inc.

Loodun Antyok had listened carefully, and now he shook his round head mildly, "Friend, I'd like to help you, but you've grabbed the wrong dog by the ears. You'd better take this up with the Bureau."

Tomor Zamma flung himself back into his chair, rubbed his beak of a nose fiercely, thought better of whatever he was going to say, and answered quietly, "Logical, but not practical. I can't make a trip to Trantor now. You're the Bureau's representative on Cepheus 18. Are you entirely helpless?"

"Well, even as Civilian Supervisor, I've got to work within the limits of Bureau policy."

"Good," Zammo cried, "then, tell me what Bureau policy is. I head a scientific investigating committee, under direct Imperial authorization with, supposedly, the widest powers; yet at every angle in the road I am pulled up short by the civilian authorities with only the parrot shriek of 'Bureau policy' to justify themselves. What *is* Bureau policy? I haven't received a decent definition yet."

Antyok's gaze was level and unruffled. He said, "As I see it—and this is not official, so you can't hold me to it—Bureau policy consists in treating the non-Humans as decently as possible."

"Then, what authority have they—"

"*Ssh!* No use raising your voice. As a matter of fact, His Imperial Majesty is a humanitarian and a disciple of the philosophy of Aurelion. I can tell you quietly that it is pretty well-known that it is the Emperor himself who first suggested that this world be established. You can bet that Bureau policy will stick pretty close to Imperial notions. And you can bet that I can't paddle my way against *that* sort of current."

"Well, m'boy," the physiologist's fleshy eyelids quivered, "if you take that sort of attitude, you're going to lose your job. No, I won't have you kicked out. That's not what I mean at all. Your job will just fade out from under you, because nothing is going to be accomplished here!"

"Really? Why?" Antyok was short, pink, and pudgy, and his plump-cheeked face usually found it difficult to put on display any expression other than one of bland and cheerful politeness—but it looked grave now.

"You haven't been here long. I have." Zammo scowled. "Mind if I smoke?" The cigar in his hand was gnarled and strong and was puffed to life carelessly.

He continued roughly, "There's no place here for humanitarianism, administrator. You're treating non-Humans as if they were Humans, and it won't work. In fact, I don't like the word 'non-Human.' They're animals."

"They're intelligent," interjected Antyok, softly.

"Well, intelligent animals, then. I presume the two terms are not mutually exclusive. Alien intelligences mingling in the same space won't work, anyway."

"Do you propose killing them off?"

"Galaxy, no!" He gestured with his cigar. "I propose we look upon them as objects for study, and only that. We could learn a good deal from these animals if we were allowed to. Knowledge, I might point out, that would be used for the immediate benefit of the human race. *There's* humanity for you. *There's* the good of the masses, if it's this spineless cult of Aurelion that interests you."

"What, for instance, do you refer to?"

"To take the most obvious—You have heard of their chemistry, I take it?"

"Yes," Antyok admitted. "I have leafed through most of the reports on the non-Humans published in the last ten years. I expect to go through more."

"Hmp. Well— Then, all I need say is that their chemical therapy is extremely thorough. For instance, I have witnessed personally the healing of a broken bone—what passes for a broken bone with them, I mean—by the use of a pill. The bone was whole in fifteen minutes. Naturally, none of their drugs are any earthly use on Humans. Most would kill quickly. But if we found out how they worked on the non-Humans—on the animals—"

"Yes, yes. I see the significance."

"Oh, you do. Come, that's gratifying. A second point is that these animals communicate in an unknown manner."

"Telepathy!"

The scientist's mouth twisted, as he ground out, "Telepathy! Telepathy! Telepathy! Might as well say by witch brew. Nobody knows anything about telepathy except its name. What is the mechanism of telepathy? What is the physiology and the physics of it? I would like to find out, but I can't. Bureau policy, if I listen to you, forbids."

Antyok's little mouth pursed itself. "But— Pardon me, doctor, but I don't follow you. How are you prevented? Surely the Civil Administration has made no attempt to hamper scientific investigation of these non-Humans. I cannot speak for my predecessor entirely, of course, but I myself—"

"No direct interference has occurred. I don't speak of that. But by the Galaxy, administrator, we're hampered by the spirit of the entire set-up. You're making us deal with humans. You allow them their own leader and internal autonomy. You pamper them and give them what Aurelion's philosophy would call 'rights.' I can't deal with their leader."

"Why not?"

"Because he refuses to allow me a free hand. He refuses to allow experiments on any subject without the subject's own consent. The two or three volunteers we get are not too bright. It's an impossible arrangement."

Antyok shrugged helplessly.

Zammo continued, "In addition, it is obviously impossible to learn anything of value concerning the brains, physiology, and chemistry of these animals without dissection, dietary experiments, and drugs. You know, administrator, scientific investigation is a hard game. Humanity hasn't much place in it."

Loodun Antyok tapped his chin with a doubtful finger, "Must it be quite so hard? These are harmless creatures, these non-Humans. Surely, dissection— Perhaps, if you were to approach them a bit differently—I have an idea that you antagonize them. Your attitude might be somewhat overbearing."

"Overbearing! I am not one of these whining social psychologists who are all the fad these days. I don't believe you can solve a problem that requires dissection by approaching it with what is called the 'correct personal attitude' in the cant of the times."

"I'm sorry you think so. Sociopsychological training is required of all administrators above the grade of A-4."

Zammo withdrew his cud of a cigar from his mouth and replaced it after a suitably contemptuous interval, "Then you'd better use a bit of your technique on the Bureau. You know, I do have friends at the Imperial court."

"Well, now, I can't take the matter up with them, not baldly. Basic policy does not fall within my cognizance, and such things can only be initiated by the Bureau. But, you know, we might try an indirect approach on this." He smiled faintly, "Strategy."

"What sort?"

Antyok pointed a sudden finger, while his other hand fell

lightly on the rows of gray-bound reports upon the floor just next to his chair, "Now, look, I've gone through most of these. They're dull, but contain *some* facts. For instance, when was the last non-Human infant born on Cepheus 18?"

Zammo spent little time in consideration. "Don't know. Don't care either."

"But the Bureau would. There's *never* been a non-Human infant born on Cepheus 18—not in the two years the world has been established. Do you know the reason?"

The physiologist shrugged, "Too many possible factors. It would take study."

"All right, then. Suppose you write a report—"

"Reports! I've written twenty."

"Write another. Stress the unsolved problems. Tell them you must change your methods. Harp on the birth-rate problem. The Bureau doesn't dare ignore that. If the non-Humans die out, someone will have to answer to the Emperor. You see—"

Zammo stared, his eyes dark, "That will swing it?"

"I've been working for the Bureau for twenty-seven years. I know its ways."

"I'll think about it." Zammo rose and stalked out of the office. The door slammed behind him.

It was later that Zammo said to a co-worker, "He's a bureaucrat, in the first place. He won't abandon the orthodoxies of paper work and he won't risk sticking his neck out. He'll accomplish little by himself, yet maybe more than a little if we work through him."

From: Administrative Headquarters, Cepheus 18
To: BuOuProv
Subject: Outer Province Project 2563, Part II—Scientific Investigations of non-Humans of Cepheus 18, Co-ordination of,
References:
    (a) BuOuProv letr. Cep-N-CM/jg, 100132, dated 302/975 G.E.
    (b) AdHQ-Ceph18 letr. AA-LA/mn, dated 140/977 G.E.
Enclosure;
    1. SciGroup 10, Physical & Biochemical Division, Report, entitled, "Physiologic Characteristics of non-Humans of Cepheus 18, Part XI," dated 172/977 G.E.
    1. Enclosure 1, included herewith, is forwarded for the information of the BuOuProv. It is to be noted that Section XII, paragraphs 1–16 of Encl. 1, concern possible changes in present

BuOuProv policy with regard to non-Humans with a view to facilitating physical and chemical investigations at present proceeding under authorization of reference (a)

2. It is brought to the attention of the BuOuProv that reference (b) has already discussed possible changes in investigating methods and that it remains the opinion of AdHQ-Ceph18 that such changes are as yet premature. It is nevertheless suggested that the question of non-Human birth rate be made the subject of a BuOuProv project assigned to AdHQ-Ceph18 in view of the importance attached by SciGroup 10 to the problem, as evidenced in Section V of Enclosure 1.

L. Antyok, Superv. AdHQ-Ceph18,
174/977

From: BuOuProv
To: AdHQ-Ceph18
Subject: Outer Province Project 2563—Scientific Investigations of non-Humans of Cepheus 18, Co-ordination of,
Reference:

(a) AdHQ-Ceph18 letr. AA-LA/mn, dated 174/977 G.E.

1. In response to the suggestion contained in paragraph 2 of reference (a), it is considered that the question of the non-Human birth rate does not fall within the cognizance of AdHQ-Ceph18. In view of the fact that SciGroup 10 has reported said sterility to be probably due to a chemical deficiency in the food supply, all investigations in the field are relegated to SciGroup 10 as the proper authority.

2. Investigating procedures by the various SciGroups shall continue according to current directives on the subject. No changes in policy are envisaged.

C. Morily, Chief, BuOuProv,
186/977 G.E.

II.

There was a loose-jointed gauntness about the news reporter which made him appear somberly tall. He was Gustiv Bannerd, with whose reputation was combined ability—two things which do not invariably go together despite the maxims of elementary morality.

Loodun Antyok took his measure doubtfully and said, "There's no use denying that you're right. But the SciGroup report was confidential. I don't understand how—"

"It leaked," said Bannerd, callously. "Everything leaks."

Antyok was obviously baffled, and his pink face furrowed slightly, "Then I'll just have to plug the leak here. I can't pass your story. All references to SciGroup complaints have to come out. You see that, don't you?"

"No." Bannerd was calm enough. "It's important; and I have my rights under the Imperial directive. I think the Empire should know what's going on."

"But it isn't going on," said Antyok, despairingly. "Your claims are all wrong. The Bureau isn't going to change its policy. I showed you the letters."

"You think you can stand up against Zammo when he puts the pressure on?" the newsman asked derisively.

"I will—if I think he's wrong."

"If!" stated Bannerd flatly. Then, in a sudden fervor, "Antyok, the Empire has something great here; something greater by a good deal than the government apparently realizes. They're destroying it. They're treating these creatures like animals."

"Really—" began Antyok, weakly.

"Don't talk about Cepheus 18. It's a zoo. It's a high-class zoo, with your petrified scientists teasing those poor creatures with their sticks poking through the bars. You throw them chunks of meat, but you cage them up. I know! I've been writing about them for two years now. I've almost been living with them."

"Zammo says—"

"Zammo!" This with hard contempt.

"Zammo says," insisted Antyok with worried firmness, "that we treat them too like humans as it is."

The newsman's straight, long cheeks were rigid, "Zammo is rather animallike in his own right. He is a science-worshiper. We can do with less of them. Have you read Aurelion's works?" The last was suddenly posed.

"Umm. Yes. I understand the Emperor—"

"The Emperor tends towards us. That is good—better than the hounding of the last reign."

"I don't see where you're heading?"

"These aliens have much to teach us. You understand? It is nothing that Zammo and his SciGroup can use; no chemistry, no telepathy. It's a way of life; a way of thinking. The aliens have no crime, no misfits. What effort is being made to study their philosophy? Or to set them up as a problem in social engineering?"

Antyok grew thoughtful, and his plump face smoothed out,

"It is an interesting consideration. It would be a matter for psychologists—"

"No good. Most of them are quacks. Psychologists point out problems, but their solutions are fallacious. We need men of Aurelion. Men of The Philosophy—"

"But look here, we can't turn Cepheus 18 into . . . into a metaphysical study."

"Why not? It can be done easily."

"How?"

"Forget your puny test-tube peerings. Allow the aliens to set up a society free of Humans. Give them an untrammeled independence and allow an intermingling of philosophies—"

Antyok's nervous response came, "That can't be done in a day."

"We can start in a day."

The administrator said slowly, "Well, I can't prevent you from trying to start." He grew confidential, his mild eyes thoughtful, "You'll ruin your own game, though, if you publish SciGroup 10's report and denounce it on humanitarian grounds. The Scientists are powerful."

"And we of The Philosophy as well."

"Yes, but there's an easy way. You needn't rave. Simply point out that the SciGroup is not solving its problems. Do so unemotionally and let the readers think out your point of view for themselves. Take the birth-rate problem, for instance. *There's* something for you. In a generation, the non-Humans might die out, for all science can do. Point out that a more philosophical approach is required. Or pick some other obvious point. Use your judgment, eh?"

Antyok smiled ingratiatingly as he arose, "But, for the Galaxy's sake, don't stir up a bad smell."

Bannerd was stiff and unresponsive, "You may be right."

It was later that Bannerd wrote in a capsule message to a friend, "He is not clever, by any means. He is confused and has no guiding-line through life. Certainly utterly incompetent in his job. But he's a cutter and a trimmer, compromises his way around difficulties, and will yield concessions rather than risk a hard stand. He may prove valuable in that. Yours in Aurelion."

From: AdHQ-Ceph18
To: BuOuProv
Subject: Birth rate of non-Humans on Cepheus 18, News Report on.

References:

    (a) AdHQ-Ceph18 letr. AA-LA/mn, dated 174/977 G.E.

    (b) Imperial Directive, Ja2374, dated 243/975 G.E.

Enclosures:

    1-G. Bannerd news report, date-lined Cepheus 18, 201/977 G.E.

    2-G. Bannerd news report, datelined Cepheus 18, 203/977 G.E.

1. The sterility of non-Humans on Cepheus 18, reported to the BuOuProv in reference (a), has become the subject of news reports to the galactic press. The news reports in question are submitted herewith for the information of the BuOuProv as Enclosures 1 and 2. Although said reports are based on material considered confidential and closed to the public, the news reporter in question maintained his rights to free expression under the terms of reference (b).

2. In view of the unavoidable publicity and misunderstanding on the part of the general public now inevitable, it is requested that the BuOuProv direct future policy on the problem of non-Human sterility.

                      L. Antyok, Superv. AdHQ-Ceph18,
                                  209/977 G.E.

From: BuOuProv

To: AdHQ-Ceph18

Subject: Birth rate of non-Humans on Cepheus 18, Investigation of.

References:

    (a) AdHQ-Ceph18 letr. AA-LA/mn, dated 209/977 G.E.

    (b) AdHQ-Ceph18 letr. AA-LA/mn, dated 174/977 G.E.

1. It is proposed to investigate the causes and the means of precluding the unfavorable birth-rate phenomena mentioned in references (a) and (b). A project is therefore set up, entitled, "Birth rate of non-Humans on Cepheus 18, Investigation of" to which, in view of the crucial importance of the subject, a priority of AA is given.

2. The number assigned to the subject project is 2910, and all expenses incidental to it shall be assigned to Appropriation number 18/78.

                         C. Morily, Chief, BuOuProv,
                                  223/977 G.E.

III.

If Tomor Zammo's ill-humor lessened within the grounds

of SciGroup 10 Experimental Station, his friendliness had
not thereby increased. Antyok found himself standing alone
at the viewing window into the main field laboratory.

The main field laboratory was a broad court set at the
environmental conditions of Cepheus 18 itself for the discomfort of the experimenters and the convenience of the
experimentees. Through the burning sand, and the dry,
oxygen-rich air, there sparkled the hard brilliance of hot,
white sunlight. And under the blaze, the brick-red non-
Humans, wrinkled of skin and wiry of build, huddled in
their squatting positions of ease, by ones and twos.

Zammo emerged from the laboratory. He paused to drink
water thirstily. He looked up, moisture gleaming on his upper
lip, "Like to step in there?"

Antyok shook his head definitely, "No, thank you. What's
the temperature right now?"

"A hundred twenty, if there were shade. And they complain of the cold. It's drinking time now. Want to watch them
drink?"

A spray of water shot upward from the fountain in the
center of the court, and the little alien figures swayed to their
feet and hopped eagerly forward in a queer, springy half-run.
They milled about the water, jostling one another. The centers
of their faces were suddenly disfigured by the projection of
a long and flexible fleshy tube, which thrust forward into
the spray and was withdrawn dripping.

It continued for long minutes. The bodies swelled and the
wrinkles disappeared. They retreated slowly, backing away,
with the drinking tube flickering in and out, before receding
finally into a pink, wrinkled mass above a wide, lipless mouth.
They went to sleep in groups in the shaded angles, plump
and sated.

"Animals!" said Zammo, with contempt.

"How often do they drink?" asked Antyok.

"As often as they want. They can go a week if they have
to. We water them every day. They store it under their skin.
They eat in the evenings. Vegetarians, you know."

Antyok smiled chubbily, "It's nice to get a bit of firsthand
information occasionally. Can't read reports all the time."

"Yes?"—noncommittally. Then, "What's new? What about
the lacy-pants boys on Trantor?"

Antyok shrugged dubiously, "You can't get the Bureau
to commit itself, unfortunately. With the Emperor sympa-

thetic to the Aurelionists, humanitarianism is the order of the day. You know that."

There was a pause in which the administrator chewed his lip uncertainly. "But there's this birth-rate problem now. It's finally been assigned to AdHQ, you know—and double A priority, too."

Zammo muttered wordlessly.

Antyok said, "You may not realize it, but that project will now take precedence over all other work proceeding on Cepheus 18. It's important."

He turned back to the viewing window and said thoughtfully with a bald lack of preamble. "Do you think those creatures might be unhappy?"

"Unhappy!" The word was an explosion.

"Well, then," Antyok corrected hastily, "maladjusted. You understand? It's difficult to adjust an environment to a race we know so little of."

"Say—did you ever see the world we took them from?"

"I've read the reports—"

"Reports!"—infinite contempt. "I've *seen* it. This may look like desert out there to you, but it's a watery paradise to those devils. They have all the food and water they can get. They have a world to themselves with vegetation and natural water flow, instead of a lump of silica and granite where fungi were force-grown in caves and water had to be streamed out of gypsum rock. In ten years, they would have been dead to the last beast, and we saved them. Unhappy? Ga-a-ah, if they are, they haven't the decency of most animals."

"Well, perhaps. Yet I have a notion."

"A notion? What is your notion?" Zammo reached for one of his cigars.

"It's something that might help you. Why not study the creatures in a more integrated fashion? Let them use their initiative. After all, they did have a highly-developed science. Your reports speak of it continually. Give them problems to solve."

"Such as?"

"Oh . . . oh," Antyok waved his hands helplessly. "Whatever you think might help most. For instance, spaceships. Get them into the control room and study their reactions."

"Why?" asked Zammo with dry bluntness.

"Because the reaction of their minds to tools and controls adjusted to the human temperament can teach you a lot.

In addition, it will make a more effective bribe, it seems to me, than anything you've yet tried. You'll get more volunteers if they think they'll be doing something interesting."

"That's your psychology coming out. Hm-m-m. Sounds better than it probably is. I'll sleep on it. And where would I get permission, in any case, to let them handle spaceships? I've none at *my* disposal, and it would take a good deal longer than it was worth to follow down the line of red tape to get one assigned to us."

Antyok pondered, and his forehead creased lightly, "It doesn't *have* to be spaceships. But even so— If you would write up another report and make the suggestion yourself— strongly, you understand—I might figure out some way of tying it up with my birth-rate project. A double-A priority can get practically anything, you know, without questions."

Zammo's interest lacked a bit even of mildness, "Well, maybe. Meanwhile, I've some basal metabolism tests in progress, and it's getting late. I'll think about it. It's got its points."

From: AdHQ-Ceph18

To: BuOuProv

Subject: Outer Province Project 2910, Part I—Birth rate of non-Humans on Cepheus 18, Investigation of,

Reference:

(a) BuOuProv letr. Ceph-N-CM/car, 115097, 223/977 G.E.

Enclosure:

1. SciGroup 10, Physical & Biochemical Division report, Part XV, dated 220/977 G.E.

1. Enclosure 1 is forwarded herewith for the information of the BuOuProv.

2. Special attention is directed to Section V, Paragraph 3 of Enclosure 1 in which it is requested that a spaceship be assigned SciGroup 10 for use in expediting investigations authorized by the BuOuProv. It is considered by AdHQ-Ceph18 that such investigations may be of material use in aiding work now in progress on the subject project, authorized by reference (a). It is suggested, in view of the high priority placed by the BuOuProv upon the subject project, that immediate consideration be given the SciGroup's request.

L. Antyok, Superv. AdHQ-Ceph18,

240/977 G.E.

From: BuOuProv

To: AdHQ-Ceph18

Subject: Outer Province Project 2910—Birth rate of non-Humans on Cepheus 18, Investigation of.

Reference:

(a) AdHQ-Ceph18 letr. AA-LA/mn, dated 240/977 G.E.

1. Training Ship *AN-R-2055* is being placed at the disposal of AdHQ-Ceph18 for use in investigation of non-Humans on Cepheus 18 with respect to the subject project and other authorized OuProv projects, as requested in Enclosure 1 to reference (a).

2. It is urgently requested that work on the subject project be expedited by all available means.

C. Morily, Head, BuOuProv,
251/977 G.E.

IV.

The little, bricky creature must have been more uncomfortable than his bearing would admit to. He was carefully wrapped in a temperature already adjusted to the point where his human companions steamed in their open shirts.

His speech was high-pitched and careful, "I find it damp, but not unbearably so at this low temperature."

Antyok smiled, "It was nice of you to come. I had planned to visit you, but a trial run in your atmosphere out there—" The smile had become rueful.

"It doesn't matter. You other worldlings have done more for us than ever we were able to do for ourselves. It is an obligation that is but imperfectly returned by the endurance on my part of a trifling discomfort." His speech seemed always indirect, as if he approached his thoughts sidelong, or as if it were against all etiquette to be blunt.

Gustiv Bannerd, seated in an angle of the room, with one long leg crossing the other, scrawled nimbly and said, "You don't mind if I record all this?"

The Cepheid non-Human glanced briefly at the journalist, "I have no objection."

Antyok's apologetics persisted, "This is not a purely social affair, sir. I would not have forced discomfort on you for that. There are important questions to be considered, and you are the leader of your people."

The Cepheid nodded, "I am satisfied your purposes are kindly. Please proceed."

The administrator almost wriggled in his difficulty in putting thoughts into words. "It is a subject," he said, "of delicacy, and one I would never bring up if it weren't for the overwhelming importance of the . . . uh . . . question. I am only the spokesman of my government—"

"My people consider the otherworld government a kindly one."

"Well, yes, they are kindly. For that reason, they are disturbed over the fact that your people no longer breed."

Antyok paused, and waited with worry for a reaction that did not come. The Cepheid's face was motionless except for the soft, trembling motion of the wrinkled area that was his deflated drinking tube.

Antyok continued, "It is a question we have hesitated to bring up because of its extremely personal angles. Noninterference is my government's prime aim, and we have done our best to investigate the problem quietly and without disturbing your people. But, frankly, we—"

"Have failed?" finished the Cepheid, at the other's pause.

"Yes. Or at least, we have not discovered a concrete failure to reproduce the exact environment of your original world; with, of course, the necessary modification to make it more livable. Naturally, it is thought there is some chemical shortcoming. And so I ask your voluntary help in the matter. Your people are advanced in the study of your own biochemistry. If you do not choose, or would rather not—"

"No, no, I can help." The Cepheid seemed cheerful about it. The smooth flat planes of his loose-skinned, hairless skull wrinkled in an alien response to an uncertain emotion. "It is not a matter that any of us would have thought would have disturbed you other-worldlings. That is does is but another indication of your well-meaning kindness. This world we find congenial, a paradise in comparison to our old. It lacks in nothing. Conditions such as now prevail belong in our legends of the Golden Age."

"Well—"

"But there is a something; a something you may not understand. We cannot expect different intelligences to think alike."

"I shall try to understand."

The Cepheid's voice had grown soft, its liquid undertones more pronounced, "We were dying on our native world; but we were fighting. Our science, developed through a history older than yours, was losing; but it had not yet lost. Perhaps it was because our science was fundamentally biological, rather than physical as yours is. Your people discovered new forms of energy and reached the stars. Our people discovered new truths of psychology and psychiatry and built up a working society free of disease and crime.

"There is no need to question which of the two angles of approach was the more laudable, but there is no uncertainty as to which proved more successful in the end. In our dying world, without the means of life or sources of power, our biological science could but make the dying easier.

"And yet we fought. For centuries past, we had been groping toward the elements of atomic power, and slowly the spark of hope had glimmered that we might break through the two-dimensional limits of our planetary surface and reach the stars. There were no other planets in our system to serve as stepping stones. Nothing but some twenty light-years to the nearest star, without the knowledge of the possibility of the existence of other planetary systems, but rather of the contrary.

"But there is something in all life that insists on striving; even on useless striving. There were only five thousand of us left in the last days. Only five thousand. And our first ship was ready. It was experimental. It would probably have been a failure. But already we had all the principles of propulsion and navigation correctly worked out."

There was a long pause, and the Cepheid's small black eyes seemed glazed in retrospect.

The newspaperman put in suddenly, from his corner, "And then we came?"

"And then you came," the Cepheid agreed simply. "It changed everything. Energy was ours for the asking. A new world, congenial and, indeed, ideal, was ours even without asking. If our problems of society had long been solved by ourselves, our more difficult problems of environment were suddenly solved for us, no less completely."

"Well?" urged Antyok.

"Well—it was somehow not well. For centuries, our ancestors had fought towards the stars, and now the stars suddenly proved to be the property of others. We had fought for life, and it had become a present handed to us by others. There is no longer any reason to fight. There is no longer anything to attain. All the universe is the property of your race."

"This world is yours," said Antyok, gently.

"By sufferance. It is a gift. It is not ours by right."

"You have earned it, in my opinion."

And now the Cepheid's eyes were sharply fixed on the other's countenance, "You mean well, but I doubt that you understand. We have nowhere to go, save this gift of a world. We are in a blind alley. The function of life is striving, and that is taken from us. Life can no longer interest us. We have no offspring—voluntarily. It is our way of removing ourselves from your way."

Absent-mindedly, Antyok had removed the fluoro-globe from the window seat, and spun it on its base. Its gaudy surface reflected light as it spun, and its three-foot-high bulk floated with incongruous grace and lightness in the air.

Antyok said, "Is that your only solution? Sterility?"

"We might escape still," whispered the Cepheid, "but where in the Galaxy is there a place for us? It is all yours."

"Yes, there is no place for you nearer than the Magellanic Clouds if you wished independence. The Magellanic Clouds—"

"And you would not let us go of yourselves. You mean kindly, I know."

"Yes, we mean kindly—but we could not let you go."

"It is a mistaken kindness."

"Perhaps, but could you not reconcile yourselves? You have a world."

"It is something past complete explanations. Your mind is different. We could not reconcile ourselves. I believe, administrator, that you have thought of all this before. The concept of the blind alley we find ourselves trapped in is not new to you."

Antyok looked up, startled, and one hand steadied the fluoroglobe, "Can you read my mind?"

"It is just a guess. A good one, I think."

"Yes—but *can* you read my mind? The minds of humans in general, I mean. It is an interesting point. The scientists say you cannot, but sometimes I wonder if it is that you simply will not. Could you answer that? I am detaining you, unduly, perhaps."

"No . . . no—" But the little Cepheid drew his enveloping robe closer, and buried his face in the electrically-heated pad at the collar for a moment. "You other-worldings speak of reading minds. It is not so at all, but it is assuredly hopeless to explain."

Antyok mumbled the old proverb, "One cannot explain sight to a man blind from birth."

"Yes, just so. This sense which you call 'mind reading,' quite erroneously, cannot be applied to us. It is not that we cannot receive the proper sensations, it is that your people do not transmit them, and we have no way of explaining to you how to go about it."

"Hm-m-m."

"There are times, of course, of great concentration or emotional tension on the part of an other-worldling when some of us who are more expert in this sense, more sharp-eyed, so to speak, detect vaguely *something*. It is uncertain; yet I myself have at times wondered——"

Carefully, Antyok began spinning the fluoro-globe once more. His pink face was set in thought, and his eyes were fixed upon the Cepheid. Gustiv Bannerd stretched his fingers and reread his notes, his lips moving silently.

The fluoro-globe spun, and slowly the Cepheid seemed to grow tense as well, as his eyes shifted to the colorful sheen of the globe's fragile surface.

The Cepheid said, "What is that?"

Antyok started, and his face smoothed into an almost chuckling placidity, "This? A Galactic fad of three years ago; which means that it is a hopelessly old-fashioned relic this year. It is a useless device but it looks pretty. Bannerd, could you adjust the windows to non-transmission?"

There was the soft click of a contact, and the windows became curved regions of darkness, while in the center of the room, the fluoro-globe was suddenly the focus of a rosy effulgence that seemed to leap outward in streamers. Antyok, a scarlet figure in a scarlet room, placed it upon the table and spun it with a hand that dripped red. As it spun, the colors changed with a slowly increasing rapidity, blended and fell apart into more extreme contrasts.

Antyok was speaking in an eerie atmosphere of molten, shifting rainbow, "The surface is of a material that exhibits variable fluorescence. It is almost weightless, extremely fragile, but gyroscopically balanced so that it rarely falls, with ordinary care. It is rather pretty, don't you think?"

From somewhere the Cepheid's voice came, "Extremely pretty."

"But it has outworn its welcome; outlived its fashionable existence."

The Cepheid's voice was abstracted, "It is very pretty."

Bannerd restored the light at a gesture, and the colors faded.

The Cepheid said, "That is something my people would enjoy." He stared at the globe with fascination.

And now Antyok rose. "You had better go. If you stay longer, the atmosphere may have bad effects. I thank you humbly for your kindness."

"I thank you humbly for yours." The Cepheid had also risen.

Antyok said, "Most of your people, by the way, have accepted our offers to them to study the make-up of our modern spaceships. You understand, I suppose, that the purpose was to study the reactions of your people to our technology. I trust that conforms with your sense of propriety."

"You need not apologize. I, myself, have now the makings of a human pilot. It was most interesting. It recalls our own efforts—and reminds us of how nearly on the right track we were."

The Cepheid left, and Antyok sat, frowning.

"Well," he said to Bannerd, a little sharply. "You remember our agreement, I hope. This interview can't be published."

Bannerd shrugged, "Very well."

Antyok was at his seat, and his fingers fumbled with the small metal figurine upon his desk, "What do you think of all this, Bannerd?"

"I am sorry for them. I think I understand how they feel. We must educate them out of it. The Philosophy can do it."

"You think so?"

"Yes."

"We can't let them go, of course."

"Oh, no. Out of the question. We have too much to learn from them. This feeling of theirs is only a passing stage. They'll think differently, especially when we allow them the completest independence."

"Maybe. What do you think of the fluoro-globe, Bannerd? He liked them. It might be a gesture of the right sort to order several thousand of them. The Galaxy knows, they're a drug on the market right now, and cheap enough."

"Sounds like a good idea," said Bannerd.

"The Bureau would never agree, though. I know them."

The newsman's eyes narrowed, "But it might be just the thing. They need new interests."

"Yes? Well, we *could* do something. I could include your transcript of the interview as part of a report and just emphasize the matter of the globes a bit. After all, you're a member of The Philosophy and might have influence with important people, whose word with the Bureau might carry much more weight than mine. You understand—?"

"Yes," mused Bannerd. "Yes."

From: AdHQ-Ceph18
To: BuOuProv
Subject: OuProv Project 2910, Part II; Birth rate of non-Humans on Cepheus 18, Investigation of.
Reference:
    (a) BuOuProv letr. Cep-N-CM/car, 115097, dated 223/977 G.E.
Enclosure:
1. Transcript of conversation between L. Antyok of AdHQ-Ceph18, and Ni-San, High Judge of the non-Humans on Cepheus 18.

1. Enclosure 1 is forwarded herewith for the information of the BuOuProv.

2. The investigation of the subject project undertaken in response to the authorization of reference (a) is being pursued along the new lines indicated in Enclosure 1. The BuOuProv is assured that every means will be used to combat the harmful psychological attitude at present prevalent among the non-Humans.

3. It is to be noted that the High Judge of the non-Humans on Cepheus 18 expressed interest in fluoro-globes. A preliminary investigation into this fact of non-Human psychology has been initiated.

L. Antyok, Superv. AdHQ-Ceph18,
272/977 G.E.

From: BuOuProv
To: AdHQ-Ceph18
Subject: OuProv Project 2910; Birth rate of non-Humans on Cepheus 18, Investigation of.
Reference:
    (a) AdHQ-Ceph18 letr. AA-LA/mn, dated 272/977 G.E.
1. With reference to Enclosure 1 of reference (a), five thousand fluoro-globes have been allocated for shipment to Cepheus 18, by the Department of Trade.

2. It is instructed that AdHQ-Ceph18 make use of all

methods of appeasing non-Humans' dissatisfaction, consistent
with the necessities of obedience to Imperial proclamations.

C. Morily, Chief, BuOuProv,
283/977 G.E.

V.

The dinner was over, the wine had been brought in, and
the cigars were out. The groups of talkers had formed, and
the captain of the merchant fleet was the center of the largest.
His brilliant white uniform quite outsparkled his listeners.

He was almost complacent in his speech: "The trip was
nothing. I've had more than three hundred ships under me
before this. Still, I've never had a cargo quite like this. What
do you want with five thousand fluoro-globes on this desert,
by the Galaxy!"

Loodun Antyok laughed gently. He shrugged, "For the
non-Humans. It wasn't a difficult cargo, I hope."

"No, not difficult. But bulky. They're fragile, and I couldn't
carry more than twenty to a ship, with all the government
regulations concerning packing and precautions against break-
age. But it's the government's money, I suppose."

Zammo smiled grimly. "Is this your first experience with
government methods, captain?"

"Galaxy, no," exploded the spaceman. "I try to avoid it, of
course, but you can't help getting entangled on occasion.
And it's an abhorrent thing when you are, and that's the
truth. The red tape! The paper work! It's enough to stunt
your growth and curdle your circulation. It's a tumor, a can-
cerous growth on the Galaxy. I'd wipe out the whole mess."

Antyok said, "You're unfair, captain. You don't understand."

"Yes? Well, now, as one of these bureaucrats," and he
smiled amiably at the word, "suppose you explain your side
of the situation, administrator."

"Well, now," Antyok seemed confused, "government is
a serious and complicated business. We've got thousands of
planets to worry about in this Empire of ours and billions of
people. It's almost past human ability to supervise the business of governing without the tightest sort of organization.
I think there are something like four hundred million men
today in the Imperial Administrative Service alone, and in
order to co-ordinate their efforts and to pool their knowl-

edge, you *must* have what you call red tape and paper work. Every bit of it, senseless though it may seem, annoying though it may be, has its uses. Every piece of paper is a thread binding the labors of four hundred million humans. Abolish the Administrative Service and you abolish the Empire; and with it, interstellar peace, order, and civilization."

"Come—" said the captain.

"No. I mean it." Antyok was earnestly breathless. "The rules and system of the Administrative set-up must be sufficiently all-embracing and rigid so that in case of incompetent officials, and sometimes one *is* appointed—you may laugh, but there are incompetent scientists, and newsmen, and captains, too—in case of incompetent officials, I say, little harm will be done. For, at the worst, the system can move by itself."

"Yes," grunted the captain, sourly, "and if a capable administrator should be appointed? He is then caught by the same rigid web and is forced into mediocrity."

"Not at all," replied Antyok, warmly. "A capable man can work within the limits of the rules and accomplish what he wishes."

"How?" asked Bannerd.

"Well . . . well—" Antyok was suddenly ill at ease. "One method is to get yourself an A-priority project, or double-A, if possible."

The captain leaned his head back for laughter, but never quite made it, for the door was flung open and frightened men were pouring in. The shouts made no sense at first. Then:

"Sir, the ships are gone. These non-Humans have taken them by force."

"What? All?"

"Every one. Ships and creatures—"

It was two hours later that the four were together again, alone in Antyok's office now.

Antyok said coldly. "They've made no mistake. There's not a ship left behind, not even your training ship, Zammo. And there isn't a government ship available in this entire half of the Sector. By the time we organize a pursuit they'll be out of the Galaxy and halfway to the Magellanic Clouds. Captain, it was your responsibility to maintain an adequate guard."

The captain cried, "It was our first day out of space. Who could have known—"

Zammo interrupted fiercely, "Wait a while, captain. I'm beginning to understand. Antyok," his voice was hard, "you engineered this."

"I?" Antyok's expression was strangely cool, almost indifferent.

"You told us this evening that a clever administrator got an A-priority project assigned to accomplish what he wished. You got such a project in order to help the non-Humans escape."

"I did? I beg your pardon, but how could that be? It was you yourself in one of your reports that brought up the problem of the failing birth rate. It was Bannerd, here, whose sensational articles frightened the Bureau into making a double A-priority project out of it. I had nothing to do with it."

"*You* suggested that I mention the birth rate," said Zammo, violently.

"Did I?" said Antyok, composedly.

"And for that matter," roared Bannerd, suddenly, "you suggested that I mention the birth rate in my articles."

The three ringed him now and hemmed him in. Antyok leaned back in his chair and said easily, "I don't know what you mean by suggestions. If you are accusing me, please stick to evidence—legal evidence. The laws of the Empire go by written, filmed, or transcribed material, or by witnessed statements. All my letters as administrator are on file here, at the Bureau, and at other places. I never asked for an A-priority project. The Bureau assigned it to me, and Zammo and Bannerd are responsible for that. In print, at any rate."

Zammo's voice was an almost inarticulate growl, "You hoodwinked me into teaching the creatures how to handle a spaceship."

"It was *your* suggestion. I have your report proposing they be studied in their reaction to human tools on file. So has the Bureau. The evidence—the *legal* evidence, is plain. I had nothing to do with it."

"Nor with the globes?" demanded Bannerd.

The captain howled suddenly, "You had my ships brought here purposely. Five thousand globes! You knew it would require hundreds of craft."

"I never asked for globes," said Antyok, coldly. "That was

the Bureau's idea, although I think Bannerd's friends of The Philosophy helped that along."

Bannerd fairly choked. He spat out, "You were asking that Cepheid leader if he could read minds. You were telling him to express interest in the globes."

"Come, now. You prepared the transcript of the conversation yourself, and that, too, is on file. You can't prove it." He stood up, "You'll have to excuse me. I must prepare a report for the Bureau."

At the door, Antyok turned, "In a way, the problem of the non-Humans is solved, even if only to their own satisfaction. They'll breed now, and have a world they've earned themselves. It's what they wanted.

"Another thing. Don't accuse me of silly things. I've been in the Service for twenty-seven years, and I assure you that my paper work is proof enough that I have been thoroughly correct in everything I have done. And captain, I'll be glad to continue our discussion of earlier this evening at your convenience and explain how a capable administrator can work red tape and still get what he wants."

It was remarkable that such a round, smooth baby-face could wear a smile quite so sardonic.

From: BuOuProv
To: Loodun Antyok, Chief Public Administrator, A-8
Subject: Administrative Service, Standing in.
Reference:
    (a) AdServ Court Decision 22874-Q, dated 1/978 G.E.
  1. In view of the favorable opinion handed down in reference (a) you are hereby absolved of all responsibility for the flight of non-Humans on Cepheus 18. It is requested that you hold yourself in readiness for your next appointment.

                    R. Horpritt, Chief, AdServ,
                              15/978 G.E.

THE END

The letters that form a major part of this story (which contains one of my rare examples of extraterrestrial intelligences) are, you will be glad to know, based on the kind of material that routinely passed in and out of the N.A.E.S. (and, for all I know, still does). The turgid style is not my invention. I couldn't invent it if I tried.

When the story appeared, L. Sprague de Camp happily pointed out one flaw in the letter style: I had carelessly made someone in lower position, who was addressing someone in higher position, say, "it is requested" instead of "it is suggested." The underling can humbly suggest, but only an overling can harshly request.

"Blind Alley" has one distinction I would like to mention.

After the war, there began that flood of science fiction anthologies that has been growing in width and depth ever since. Few, if any, science fiction writers have been anthologized as often as I have and the first of my stories to be anthologized was not "Nightfall" or a "positronic robot" story or a "Foundation" story. It was "Blind Alley."

In early 1946 Groff Conklin was putting out the first of his many science fiction anthologies—one called **The Best of Science Fiction**—and there you will find "Blind Alley." That story, for which Campbell had paid $148.75 (1¾¢ a word) then earned another $42.50 (½¢ a word). This meant that "Blind Alley" had earned me 2¼¢ a word, which was a record high at the time.

Strictly speaking, the money for the anthologization was paid to Street & Smith, but Street & Smith had the enlightened habit of turning such money over to the author—voluntarily and without legal compulsion. And this was the first indication I ever received, by the way, that a story could earn more money than that which it earned at the time of its original sale.

On May 8, 1945, one week before "The Mule" was completed, the war ended in Europe. Naturally, there was at once a move to demobilize as many of the men who had been fighting in Europe as possible, and to draft replacements from among those who had luxuriated at home.

All through the war, till then, I had been receiving regular draft deferments as a research chemist working in a position important to the war effort. Periodically, there were revisions of the draft rules, and it was a rare month in which it did not look at one time or another as though I might be drafted. (It kept me on my toes, I can tell you, but I did not feel particularly ill-used. My predominant feeling was that of a sneaking guilt at not being drafted and some shame that I was relieved at my deferment.)

During 1944, the uncertainty went so far that I was called in for a physical examination, and it at once turned out that my nearsightedness was so bad as to render me ineligible for the draft anyway.

After V-E Day, the navy yard was ordered to retain only some percentage of those of its deferred employees, allowing the remainder to be drafted. Presumably, the navy yard would select its most important employees to keep, but they knew a better trick, according to the tale we employees heard. They retained all draftable employees who met the physical requirements, and removed protection from those who did not meet them either because of age or physical defect. In this way, they hoped to keep them all—those who were fit, because they were declared necessary, and those who were overage or unfit, because they were overage or unfit.

I, as an unfit employee, was one of those declared non-essential.

And then (you guessed it) the Army lowered its physical requirements. The result was that those navy yard employees with bad eyes or other mild deficiencies, were put in imminent peril of the draft, while others, who were in every way equivalent except that they were in good shape, were not. (You may well laugh.)

For four months after V-E Day, it was up and down with me and the draft and I never knew, on one day, whether I might not receive my induction notice on the next. While I waited, the atom bombs were dropping on Hiroshima and Nagasaki and the Japanese formally surrendered on September 2.

On September 7, 1945, I received my notice of induction. I didn't enjoy it, of course, but I tried to be philosophical. The war was over, and, whatever difficulties I might have during the two years I expected to be in, at least no one would be shooting at me. I entered the Army on November 1, 1945, as a buck private.

Naturally, during all the fuss over the draft, culminating in my induction, I did no writing. There was an eight-month hiatus, in fact, the longest in three years.

On January 7, 1946, however, while I was still working my way through basic training in Camp Lee, Virginia, I began another "positronic robot" story, called "Evidence." I made use of a typewriter in one of the administrative buildings.

Naturally, it was slow work. I didn't finish first draft till February 17, and then everything came to a halt when, the very next day, I discovered that I would be among those sent out to the South Pacific to participate in "Operation Crossroads." This was the first postwar atom bomb test, on the island of Bikini (which later gave its name to a bathing suit so skimpy as to react on the male constitution—in theory—like an atom bomb). The fact that a week later I received my check for the anthologization of "Blind Alley" did little to raise my spirits.

We left on March 2, 1946, traveling by train and ship, and arrived in Honolulu on March 15. There then began a long wait before we could go on to Bikini (the atom bomb test was postponed, of course). When time began to hang heavy enough, I returned to "Evidence." I persuaded a sympathetic librarian to lock me up in the building when it closed for lunch so that I had an hour each day absolutely alone at the typewriter. I finished the story on April 10, and mailed it off to Campbell the next day.

On April 29, I received word of its acceptance. By that time, the word rate had reached two cents.

I never did go to Bikini, by the way. Some administrative error back home ended the allotment being sent to my wife. I was sent back to the United States on May 28 to inquire into the matter; it was all straightened out by the time I was back at Camp Lee. As long as I was there, however, I applied for a "research discharge" on the ground that I was going back to my Ph.D. work. I was out of the Army, as a corporal, on July 26.

"Evidence" was the only story I wrote while in uniform.

As soon as I got out of the Army I made arrangements to return to Columbia, after an absence of a little over four years, and to resume my work toward my Ph.D. under Professor Dawson.

There was still no question in my mind that chemistry was my career, and my only career. In the four years of my marriage I had written nine science fiction stories and one fantasy and had sold them all——but all the sales had been to Campbell.

Since **Unknown** had died, I was terribly conscious that **Astounding** might die as well. If that happened, or if Campbell retired, I was not at all sure that I could continue selling.

The situation looked better postwar than prewar, to be sure. During the first four years of my marriage, I had earned $2667 as a writer, or an average of under $13 per week. This was about half again as well as I had been doing in my bachelor days, even though I was writing fewer stories.

The word rate had doubled, you see, and there was even the hope of subsidiary rights——extra money for already sold stories. "Blind Alley" had already been placed in an anthology, and on August 30, 1946, only a month after I got out of the Army, I discovered that I had made a second such sale. A new science fiction anthology "Adventures in Time and Space," edited by Raymond J. Healey and J. Francis McComas, was to include "Nightfall" and I was to receive $66.50 for that.

There was even more than anthologization sales. In that same month of August, the September 1946 issue of **Astounding** hit the stands with "Evidence." (Had I but known when writing it that by the time it was published I would be safely out of the Army!) Almost at once I received a telegram asking for the movie rights. The gentleman interested turned out to be none other than Orson Welles. In great excitement, I sold him the radio, television, and movie rights to the story on September 20, and waited to become famous. (I couldn't become wealthy, because the entire payment in full was only $250.)

Unfortunately, nothing happened. To this day, Mr. Welles has never used the story. But the check was certainly useful toward paying my tuition.

Despite everything, though, it still seemed quite out of the question that I could ever possibly depend on writing for a year-in, year-out living, especially now that I was married and hoped, eventually, to have children.

So back to school it was, with a small savings account to serve as a cushion, with some veterans' benefits supplied by the government, and, of course, with the hope that I would make a little extra cash writing.

In September I wrote still another "positronic robot" story, "Little Lost Robot," racing to complete it before the fall semester started and I grew immersed in my work. Campbell took it promptly and it appeared in the March 1947 issue of **Astounding**. Eventually, it and "Evidence" were included in **I, Robot**.

Once the semester started, it became difficult to find time to write. Toward the end of 1946, I managed to begin another "Foundation" story, "Now You See It—." I finished it on February 2, 1947, and submitted it to Campbell on the fourth. By that time I was rather sick of the "Foundation" series and I tried to write "Now You See It—" in such a way as to make it the last of the series.

Campbell would have none of that. I had to revise the ending to permit a sequel, and on the fourteenth he took it. It appeared in the January 1948 **Astounding** and eventually made up the first third of my book **Second Foundation**.

In May 1947 I wrote a story that, for the first time in over two years, was neither a "Foundation" story nor a "positronic robot" story. It was "No Connection." I submitted it to Campbell on May 26, and it was accepted on the thirty-first.

24

No Connection

Raph was a typical American of his times. Remarkably ugly, too, by American standards of our times. The bony structure of his jaws was tremendous and the musculature suited it. His nose was arched and wide and his black eyes were small and forced wide apart by the span of said nose. His neck was thick, his body broad, his fingers spatulate, with strongly curved nails.

If he had stood erect, on thick legs with large, well-padded feet, he would have topped two and a half yards. Standing or sitting, his mass neared a quarter of a ton.

Yet his forehead rose in an unrestricted arc and his cranial capacity did not stint. His enormous hand dealt delicately with a pen, and his mind droned comfortably on as he bent over his desk.

In fact, his wife and most of his fellow-Americans found him a fine-looking fellow.

Which shows the alchemy of a long displacement along the time-axis.

Raph, Junior, was a smaller edition of our typical American. He was adolescent and had not yet lost the hairy covering of childhood. It spread in a dark, close-curled mat across his chest and back, but it was already thinning and perhaps within the year he would first don the adult shirt that would cover the proudly-naked skin of manhood.

But, meanwhile, he sat in breeches alone, and scratched idly at a favorite spot just above the diaphragm. He felt curious and just a little bored. It wasn't bad to come with his father to the museum when people were there. Today was a Closed-Day, however, and the empty corridors rang lonesomely when he walked along them.

Besides, he knew everything in it—mostly bones and stones.

Junior said: "What's that thing?"

"What thing?" Raph lifted his head and looked over his shoulder. Then he looked pleased. "Oh, that's something quite new. That's a reconstruction of Primate Primeval. It was sent to me from the North River Grouping. Isn't it a nice job, though?" And he returned to his work, in the grip of a momentary twinge of pleasure. Private Primeval wasn't to go on exhibition for a week at least—not until he prepared an honorable place for it with suitable surroundings, but, for the moment, it was in his office and his own private darling.

Raph looked at the "nice job" with quite other emotions,

Astounding Science Fiction, June 1948
Copyright © 1948 by Street & Smith Publications, Inc.

however. What he saw was a spindly figure of contemptuous size, with thin legs and arms, hair-covered and owning an ugly, small-featured face with large, protruding eyes.

He said: "Well, what *is* it, Pa?"

Raph stirred impatiently: "It's a creature that lived many millions of years ago, we think. That's the way we think it looks."

"Why?" insisted the youngster.

Raph gave up. Apparently, he would have to root out the subject and do away with it.

"Well, for one thing we can tell about the muscles from the shape of the bones, and the positions where the tendons would fit and where some of the nerves would go. From the teeth we can tell the type of digestive system the animal would have, and from the foot-bones, what type of posture it would have. For the rest, we go by the principle of Analogy, that is, by the outside appearance of creatures that exist today that have the same kind of skeleton. For instance, that's why he's covered with red hair. Most of the Primates today— they're little insignificant creatures, practically extinct—are red-haired, have bare callosities on the rump—"

Junior scurried behind the figure and satisfied himself on that score.

"—have long, fleshy probosces, and short, shriveled ears. Their diets are unspecialized, hence the rather all-purpose teeth, and they are nocturnal, hence the large eyes. It's all simple, really. Now, does that dispose of you, youngster?"

And then Junior, having thought and thought about it, came out with a disparaging: "He looks just like an Eekah to me, though. Just like an ugly, old Eekah."

Raph stared at him. Apparently he had missed a point: "An Eekah?" he said, "What's an Eekah? Is that an imaginary creature you've been reading about?"

"Imaginary! Say, Pa, don't you *ever* stop at the Recorder's?"

This was an embarrassing question to answer, for "Pa" never did, or at least, never since his maturity. As a child, the Recorder, as custodian of the world's spoken, written, and recorded fiction, had, of course, had an unfailing fascination. But he had grown up—

He said, tolerantly: "Are there new stories about Eekahs? I remember none when I was young."

"You don't get it, Pa." One would almost suppose that the young Raph was on the very verge of an exasperation he was too cautious to express. He explained in wounded fashion: "The Eekahs are real things. They come from the Other World. Haven't you heard about *that?* We've been hearing about it in school, even, and in the Group Magazine. They stand upside down in their country, only they don't know it, and they look just like Ol' Primeval there."

Raph collected his astonished wits. He felt the incongruity of cross-examining his half-grown child for archaeological data and he hesitated a moment. After all, he had heard *some* things. There *had* been word of vast continents existing on the other hemisphere of Earth. It seemed to him that there were reports of life on them. It was all hazy—perhaps it wasn't always wise to stick so closely to the field of one's own interest.

He asked Junior: "Are there Eekahs here among the Groupings?"

Junior nodded rapidly: "The Recorder says they can think as good as us. They got machines that go through the air. That's how they got here."

"Junior!" said Raph severely.

"I ain't lying," Junior cried with aggrieved virtue. "You ask the Recorder and see what *he* says."

Raph slowly gathered his papers together. It was Closed-Day, but he could find the Recorder at his home, no doubt.

The Recorder was an elderly member of the Red River Gurrow Grouping and few alive could remember a time when he was not. He had succeeded to the post by general consent and filled it well, for he was Recorder for the same reason that Raph was curator of the museum. He liked to be, he wanted to be, and he could conceive no other life.

The social pattern of the Gurrow Grouping is difficult to grasp unless born into it, but there was a looseness about it that almost made the word "pattern" incongruous. The individual Gurrow took whatever job he felt an aptitude for, and such work as was left over and needed to be done was done either in common, or consecutively by each according to an order determined by lot. Put so, it sounds too simple to work, but actually the traditions that had gathered with the five thousand years since the first Voluntary Grouping of Gurrahs was supposed to have been established, made the system complicated, flexible—and workable.

The Recorder was, as Raph had anticipated, at his home, and there was the embarrassment of renewing an old and unjustly neglected acquaintanceship. He had made use of the Recorder's reference library, of course, but always indirectly—yet he had once been a child, an intimate learner at the feet of accumulated wisdom, and he had let the intimacy lapse.

The room he now entered was more or less choked with recordings and, to a lesser degree, with printed material. The Recorder interspersed greetings with apologies.

"Shipments have come from some of the other Groupings," he said. "It needs time for cataloguing, you know, and I can't seem to find the time I used to." He lit a pipe and puffed strongly. "Seems to me I'll have to find a full-time assistant. What about your son, Raph? He clusters about here the way you did twenty years ago."

"You remember those times?"

"Better than you do, I think. Think your son would like that?"

"Suppose you talk to him. He might like to. I can't honestly say he's fascinated by archaeology." Raph picked up a recording at random and looked at the identification tag: "Um-m-m—from the Joquin Valley Grouping. That's a long way from here."

"A long way." The Recorder nodded. "I have sent them some of ours, of course. The works of our own Grouping are highly regarded throughout the continent," he said, with proprietary pride. "In fact"—he pointed the stem of his pipe at the other—"your own treatise on extinct primates has been distributed everywhere. I've sent out two thousand copies and there are still requests. That's pretty good—for archaeology."

"Well, archaeology is why I am here—that and what my son says you've been telling him." Raph had a little trouble starting: "It seems you have spoken of creatures called Eekahs from the Antipodes, and I would like to have such information as you have on them."

The Recorder looked thoughtful: "Well, I could tell you what I know offhand, or we could go to the Library and look up the references."

"Don't bother opening the Library for me. It's a Closed-Day. Just give me some notions of things and I'll search the references later."

The Recorder bit at his pipe, shoved his chair back against the wall and de-focused his eyes thoughtfully. "Well," he said, "I suppose it starts with the discovery of the continents on the other side. That was five years ago. You know about that, perhaps?"

"Only the fact of it. I know the continents exist, as everyone does now. I remember once speculating on what a shining new field it would be for archaeological research, but that is all."

"Ah, then there is much else to tell you of. The new continents were never discovered by us directly, you know. It was five years ago that a group of non-Gurrow creatures arrived at the East Harbor Grouping in a machine that flew —by definite scientific principles, we found out later, based essentially on the buoyancy of air. They spoke a language, were obviously intelligent, and called themselves Eekahs. The Gurrows, of the East Harbor Grouping, learned their language—a simple one though full of unpronounceable sounds—and I have a grammar of it, if you're interested—"

Raph waved that away.

The Recorder continued: "The Gurrows of the Grouping, with the aid of those of the Iron Mountain Grouping—which specialize in steel works, you know—built duplicates of the flying machine. A flight was made across the ocean, and I should say there are several dozens of volumes on all that— volumes on the flying machine, on a new science called aerodynamics, new geographies, even a new system of philosophy based on the plurality of intelligences. All produced at the East Harbor and Iron Mountain Groupings. Remarkable work for only five years, and all are available here."

"But the Eekahs—are they still at the East Harbor Groupings?"

"Um-m-m. I'm pretty certain they are. They refused to return to their own continents. They call themselves 'political refugees.'"

"Politi . . . *what?*"

"It's their own language," said the Recorder, "and it's the only translation available."

"Well, why *political* refugees? Why not geological refugees, or oompah refugees. I should think a translation ought to make sense."

The Recorder shrugged: "I refer you to the books. They're not criminals, they claim. I know only what I tell you."

"Well, then, what do they look like? Do you have pictures?"

"At the Library."

"Did you read my 'Principles of Archaeology?' "

"I looked through it."

"Do you remember the drawings of Primate Primeval?"

"I'm afraid not."

"Then, look, let's go down to the Library, after all."

"Well, sure." The Recorder grunted as he rose.

The Administrator of the Red River Gurrow Grouping held a position in no way different in essentials from that of the Museum Curator, the Recorder or any other voluntary job holder. To expect a difference is to assume a society in which executive ability is rare.

Actually, all jobs in a Gurrow Grouping—where a "job" is defined as regular work, the fruits of which adhere to others in addition to the worker himself—are divided into two classes: one, Voluntary Jobs, and the other, Involuntary or Community Jobs. All of the first classification are equal. If a Gurrow enjoys the digging of useful ditches, his bent is to be respected and his job to be honored. If no one enjoys such burrowing and yet it is found necessary for comfort, it becomes a Community Job, done by lot or rotation according to convenience—annoying but unavoidable.

And so it was that the Administrator lived in a house no more ample and luxurious than others, sat at the head of no tables, had no particular title other than the name of his job, and was neither envied, hated, nor adored.

He liked to arrange Inter-Group trade, to supervise the common finances of the Group, and to judge the infrequent disagreements that arose. Of course, he received no additional food or energy privileges for doing what he liked.

It was not, therefore, to obtain permission, but to place his accounts in decent order, that Raph stopped in to see the Administrator. The Closed-Day had not yet ended. The Administrator sat peacefully in his after-dinner armchair, with an after-dinner cigar in his mouth, and an after-dinner book in his hand. Although there was something rather timeless about six children and a wife, even they had an after-dinner air about them.

Raph received a multiple greeting upon entering, and raised two hands to his ears, for if the various Administratelets (Only applicable title. Author.) had a job, it was noise-making. Certainly, it was what they liked to do, and certainly others reaped most of the fruits therefrom, for their own eardrums were apparently impervious.

The Administrator shooed them.

Raph accepted a cigar.

"I intend leaving the Grouping for a time, Lahr," he said. "My job necessitates it."

"We won't enjoy your going, Raph. I hope it will not be for long."

"I hope not. What have we in Common Units?"

"Oh, ample for your purposes, I'm sure. Where do you intend going?"

"To the East Harbor Grouping."

The Administrator nodded and blew out a thoughtful puff of smoke: "Unfortunately, East Harbor has a surplus in their favor registered in our books—I can verify that, if you wish—but the Common Units of Exchange on hand will take care of transportation and necessary expenses."

"Well, that's fine. But tell me, what is my status on the Community Job Roster?"

"Um-m-m—I'll have to get the rolls. You'll excuse me a moment." He trundled away, heaving his great weight across the room and out into the hallway. Raph paused to poke at the youngest of the children who rolled up to him, growling in mock ferocity with gleaming teeth—a black bundle of thick fur, with the long, childish snout that had not yet broadened away from the shape of the animal ancestry of half a million years earlier.

The Adminstrator returned with a heavy ledger and large spectacles. He opened the ledger meticulously, riffled the pages to the proper place and then drew a careful finger down the columns.

He said: "There's only the question of the water supply, Raph. You're due on the Maintenance gang for this next week. There's nothing else due for at least two months."

"I'll be back before then. Is there any chance of someone subbing for me on the Water Maintenance?"

"Um-m-m— I'll get someone. I can always send my oldest. He's getting to job age and he might as well taste everything. He may like working on the dam."

"Yes? You tell me if he does, then. He can replace me, regularly."

The Administrator smiled gently: "Don't plan on that, Raph. If he can figure out a way of making sleeping useful to all of us, he'll certainly take it up as a job. And why are you going to East Harbor Grouping, by the way, if it's something you care to talk about?"

"You'll laugh, perhaps, but I have just found out that there exist such things as Eekahs."

"Eekahs? Yes, I know." The Administrator pointed a finger. "Creatures from across the sea! Right?"

"Right! But that's not all. I've come from the Library. I've seen trimensional reproductions, Lahr, and they're *Primate Primeval*, or almost. They're primates, anyway, *intelligent* primates. They've got small eyes, flat noses, and completely different jawbones—but they're at least second cousins. I've *got* to see them, Lahr."

The Administrator shrugged. He felt no interest in the matter himself. "Why? I ask out of ignorance, Raph. Does it matter, your seeing them?"

"Matter?" Raph was obviously appalled at the question. "Don't you know what's been going on these last years? Have you read my archaeology book?"

"No," said the Administrator, definitely, "I wouldn't read it to save myself a turn at Garbage Disposal."

Raph said: "Which probably proves you more suited to Garbage Disposal than archaeology. But never mind. I've been fighting single-handed for nearly ten years in favor of my theory that Primate Primeval was an intelligent creature with a developed civilization. I have nothing on my side so far but logical necessity, which is the last thing most archaeologists will accept. They want something solid. They want the remains of a Grouping, or artifacts, structures, books—get it. All I can give them is a skeleton with a huge brainpan. Stars above, Lahr, what do they expect to survive in ten million years? Metal dies. Paper dies. Film dies.

"Only stone lasts, Lahr. And bone that's turned to stone. I've got that. A skull with room for a brain. And stone, too, old sharpened knives. Ground flints."

"Well," said Lahr, "there are your artifacts."

"Those are called eoliths, dawn stones. They won't accept them. They call them natural products, fortuitously shaped by erosion into the shapes they have, the idiots."

Then he grinned with a scientific ferocity: "But if the Eekahs are intelligent primates, I've practically proven my case."

Raph had traveled before, but never eastward, and the decline of agriculture on the road impressed him. In early history, the Gurrow Groupings had been entirely unspecialized. Each had been self-sufficient, and trade was a gesture of friendliness rather than a matter of necessity.

And so it was still in most Groupings. His own Grouping, the Red River, was perhaps typical. Some five hundred miles inland, set in lush farm land, agriculture remained centric.

The river yielded some fish and there was a well-developed dairy industry. In fact, it was food exports that provided cause for the healthy state of the store of Common Units.

As they traveled eastward, however, the Groupings through which they passed paid less and less mind to the shallowing soil and more and more to the smoking factory structures.

In the East Harbor Grouping, Raph found a trading center which depended for its prosperity primarily upon ships. It was a more populous Grouping than the average, more densely packed, with houses, on occasion, within a hundred yards of each other.

Raph felt an uncomfortable prickling at the thought of living in such close quarters. The docks were even worse, with Gurrows engaged at the huge Community Jobs of loading and unloading.

The Administrator of this East Harbor Grouping was a young man, new at his job, overwhelmed with the joy of his work, and beside himself with the pleasure of welcoming a distinguished stranger.

Raph sat through an excellent meal, and was treated to a long discourse as to the exact derivation of each dish. To his provincial ears, beef from the Prairie Grouping, potatoes from the Northeast Woods Grouping, coffee from the Isthmus Grouping, wine from the Pacific Grouping, and fruit from the Central Lakes Grouping were something strange and wonderful.

Over the cigars—South Island Grouping—he brought up the subject of the Eekahs. The East Harbor Administrator grew solemn and a little uneasy.

"The man you want to see is Lernin. He'll be glad to help you all he can. You say you know something of these Eekahs?"

"I say I would *like* to know something. They resemble an extinct species of animal I am familiar with."

"Then *that* is your field of interest. I see."

"Perhaps you can tell me some of the details of their arrival, Administrator," suggested Raph, politely.

"I was not Administrator at the time, friend, so that I lack first-hand information, but the records are plain. This group of Eekahs that arrived in their flying-machine . . . you've heard about these aeronautical devices?"

"Yes, yes."

"Yes. Well . . . apparently they were fugitives."

"So I have heard. Yet they claim not to be criminals. Isn't that so?"

"Yes. Queer, isn't it? They admitted that they had been condemned—this was after long and skillful questioning, once we had learned their language—but denied that they were evildoers. Apparently, they had disagreed with their Administrator on principles of policy."

Raph nodded his head knowingly. "Ah, and refused to abide by the common decision. Is that it?"

"More confusing than that. They insist there was no common decision. They claim that the Administrator decided on policy of his own accord."

"And was not replaced?"

"Apparently those who believe he should are considered criminals—as these were."

There was a frank pause of disbelief. Then Raph said: "Does that sound reasonable to you?"

"No, I merely relay to you their words. Of course, the Eekah language is quite a barrier. Some of the sounds can't be pronounced: words have different meanings according to position in the sentence and according to tiny differences in inflection. And it happens often that Eekah words even when best translated are a complete puzzle."

"They must have been surprised to find Gurrows here," suggested Raph, "if they are members of a different genus."

"Surprised!" The Administrator's voice sank: "I'll say they were surprised. Now, this information has not been generally published for obvious reasons, so I hope you remember that it's confidential. These Eekahs killed five Gurrows before they could be disarmed. They had an instrument that expelled metal pellets at high speeds by means of a controlled explosive chemical reaction. We have duplicated it since. Naturally, under the circumstances, we are not branding them criminals, for it is reasonable to assume that they did not realize we were intelligent beings. Apparently," and the Administrator smiled ruefully, "we resemble certain animals in their world. Or so they say."

But Raph was galvanized into a sudden enthusiasm: "Stars above! They said that, did they? Did they go into details? What kind of animals?"

The Administrator was taken aback: "Well, I don't know They give names in their language. What meaning has that? They called us giant 'bears.'"

"Giant what?"

"Bears. I haven't the slightest idea what they are, except presumably that they look like us. I know of no such in America."

"Bears. Bears." Raph stumbled over the word. "That's interesting. It's more than interesting. It's stupendous. Do you know, Administrator, that there is a great dispute among us as to the ancestry of Gurrows? Living animals related to Gurrow sapiens would be of immense importance." Raph rubbed his huge hands with pleasure.

The Administrator was pleased at the sensation he had caused. He said: "And a puzzling thing in addition is that they call themselves by two names."

"Two names?"

"Yes. No one knows the distinction yet, no matter how much the Eekahs explain it to us, except that one is a more general name, and one a more specific. The basis of the difference escapes me."

"I see. Which is 'Eekah'?"

"That is the specific one. The general one is"—the Administrator stumbled slowly over the harsh syllables—"Chim-panzee. There, that's it. There are a group called Eekahs and there are other groups with other names. But they are all called Chim . . . what I said before."

The Administrator sought through his mind for other juicy items of miscellany with which he was acquainted, but Raph interrupted him.

"May I see Lernin tomorrow?"

"Of course."

"Then I shall do so. Thank you for your courtesy, Administrator."

Lernin was a slight individual. It is doubtful if he weighed more than two hundred and fifty. There was also an imperfection in his walk, a slight lameness. But neither of these facts made much of an impression on Raph once the conversation had begun, for Lernin was a thinker who could impose his vigor upon others.

It was Raph whose eagerness dominated the first half of the conversation, and Lernin's comments were as luminous and as brief as lightning flashes. And then, there was a sudden whirl of the center of gravity, and Lernin took over.

"You will excuse me, learned friend," Lernin said with a characteristic stiffness that he could make so amiable, "if I find your problem unimportant. No, no"—he lifted a long-fingered hand—"not, in the uncomplicated talk of the times, merely unimportant to myself because my interest lies elsewhere, but unimportant to the Grouping of all the Groupings —to every single Gurrow from end to end of the world."

The concept was staggering. For a moment, Raph was offended; offended deep in his sense of individuality. It showed in his face.

Lernin added quickly: "It may sound impolite, crude, uncivilized. But I must explain because you are primarily a social scientist and will understand—perhaps better than we ourselves."

"My life-interest," said Raph angrily, "is important to myself. I cannot assume those of others in preference."

"What I talk about should be the life-interest of all—if only because it may be the means of saving the lives of all of us."

Raph was beginning to suspect all sorts of things from a queer form of joking to the unbalance of mind that sometimes came with age. Yet Lernin was not old.

Lernin said, with an impressive fervor: "The Eekahs of the other world are a danger to us, for they are not friendly to us."

And Raph replied naturally: "How do you know?"

"No one other than myself, my friend, has lived more closely with these Eekahs who have arrived here, and I find them people with minds of emotional content strange to us. I have collected queer facts which we find difficult to interpret, but which point, at any rate, in disquieting directions.

"I'll list a few: Eekahs in organized groups kill one another periodically for obscure reasons. Eekahs find it impossible to live in manner other than those of ants—that is, in huge conglomerate societies—yet find it impossible to allow for the presence of one another. Or, to use the terminology of the social scientists, they are gregarious without being social, just as we Gurrows are social without being gregarious. They have elaborate codes of behavior, which, we are told, are taught to the young, but which are disobeyed in universal practice, for reasons obscure to us. Et cetera. Et cetera. Et cetera."

"I am an archaeologist," said Raph, stiffly. "These Eekahs are of interest to me biologically only. If the curvature of the thigh bone is known to me, I care little for the curvature of their cultural processes. If I can follow the shape of the skull, it is immaterial to me that the shape of their ethics is mysterious."

"You don't think that their insanities may affect us here?"

"We are six thousand miles apart, or more, along either ocean," said Raph. "We have our world. They have theirs. There is no connection between us."

"No connection," mused Lernin, "so others have said. No connection at all. Yet Eekahs have reached us, and others may follow. We are told that the other world is dominated by a few, who are in turn dominated by their queer need for security which they confuse with an Eekah word called 'power,' which, apparently, means the prevailing of one's own will over the sum of the will of the community. What if this 'power' should extend to us?"

Raph bent his mind to the task. The matter was utterly ridiculous. It seemed impossible to picture the strange concepts.

Lernin said: "These Eekahs say that their world and ours in the long past were closer together. They say that there is a well-known scientific hypothesis in their world of a continental drift. That may interest you, since otherwise you might find it difficult to reconcile the existence of fossils of Primate Primeval closely related to living Eekahs six thousand miles away."

And the mists cleared from the archaeologist's brain as he glanced up with a live interest untroubled by insanities: "Ah, you should have said this sooner."

"I say it now as an example of what you may achieve for yourself by joining us and helping us. There is another thing. These Eekahs are physical scientists, like ourselves here in East Harbor, but with a difference dictated by their own cultural pattern. Since they live in hives, they think in hives, and their science is the result of an ant-society. Individually, they are slow and unimaginative; collectively, each supplies a crumb different from that supplied by his fellow—so that a vast structure is erected quickly. Here the individual is infinitely brighter, but he works alone. You, for instance, know nothing of chemistry, I imagine."

"A few of the fundamentals, but nothing else," admitted Raph. "I leave that, naturally, to the chemist."

"Yes, naturally. But I *am* a chemist. Yet these Eekahs, though my mental inferiors, and no chemists in their own world, know more chemistry than I. For instance, did you know that there exist elements that spontaneously disintegrate?"

"Impossible," exploded Raph. "Elements are eternal, changeless—"

Lernin laughed: "So you have been taught. So I have been taught. So I taught others. Yet the Eekahs are right, for in my laboratories I have checked them, and in every detail they are right. Uranium gives rise to a spontaneous radiation. You've heard of uranium, of course? And furthermore, I have detected radiations of energy beyond that produced by uranium which must be due to traces of elements unknown to us but described by the Eekahs. And these missing elements fit well into the so-called Periodic Tables some chemists have tried to foist upon the science. Though I do wrong to use the word 'foist' now."

"Well," said Raph, "why do you tell me this? Does this, too, help me in my problem?"

"Perhaps," said Lernin, ironically, "you will yet find it a royal bribe. You see, the energy production of uranium is absolutely constant. No known outward change in environment can affect it—and as a result of the loss in energy, uranium slowly turns to lead at an *absolutely constant rate*. A group of our men is even now using this fact as a basis for a method of determining the age of the earth. You see, to determine the age of a stratum of rock in the earth, then, it is but necesary to discover a region in it containing a trace of uranium—a widely spread element—and to determine about it the quantity of lead—and I might here add that the lead produced from uranium differs from ordinary lead and can be easily characterized—and it is then simple to determine the length of time in which that stratum has been solid. And of course, if a fossil is found in that stratum, it is of the same age, am I not correct?"

"Stars above," and Raph rose to his feet in a tremble, "you do not deceive me? It is really possible to do this?"

"It is possible. It is even easy. I tell you that our great defense, even at this late date, is co-operation in science. We are a group now of many, my friend, from many Groupings, and we want you among us. If you join us, it would be a simple matter to extend our earthage project to such regions as you may indicate—regions rich in fossils. What do you say?"

"I will help you."

It is doubtful if the Gurrow Groupings had ever before seen a community venture of such breadth as now took place. East Harbor Grouping, as has been remarked, was a shipping center, and certainly a trans-Atlantic vessel was not beyond the capacity of a Grouping that traded along the full lengths of both coasts of the Americas. What *was* unusual was the vastness of the co-operation of Gurrows from many Groupings, Gurrows of many interests.

Not that they were all happy.

Raph, for instance, on the particular morning that now concerns us, six months from the date of his first arrival in East Harbor, was searching anxiously for Lernin.

Lernin, for his part, was searching for nothing but greater speed.

They met on the docks, where Lernin, biting the end off a cigar and leading the way to a region where smoking was permitted, said: "And you, my friend, seem concerned. Not, certainly, about the progress of our ocean liner?"

"I am concerned," said Raph, gravely, "about the reports I have received of the expedition testing the age of the rocks."

"Oh— And you are unhappy about it?"

"Unhappy!" exploded Raph. "Have you seen them?"

"I have received a copy. I have looked at it. I have even read parts of it. But I have had little time and most of it bounced off. Will you please enlighten me?"

"Certainly. In the last several months, three of the regions I have indicated as being fossiliferous have been tested. The first region was in the area of East Harbor Grouping itself. Another was in the Pacific Bay Grouping, and a third in the Central Lakes Grouping. I purposely asked that those be done first because they are the richest areas and because they are widely separated. Do you know, for instance, what age they tell me the rocks upon which we stand are?"

"Two billion years, I think, is the oldest figure I noticed."

"And that's the figure for the oldest rocks—the basic igneous stratum of basalt. The upper strata, however—the recent sedimentary layers containing dozens of fossils of Primate Primeval—how old do you think *these* are supposed to be? Five—hundred—trillion—years! How is that? Do you understand?"

"Trillion?" Lernin squinted upwards and shook his head. "That's strange."

"I'll add to it. The Pacific Coast Grouping is one hundred

trillion years old—so I am told—and Central Lakes almost eighty trillion years old."

Lernin said: "And the other measurements? The ones that did not involve your strata?"

"That is the most peculiar thing of all. Most of the chosen investigations were carried on in strata that were not particularly fossiliferous. They had their own criteria of choice based on geological reasoning—and they got consistent results—one million to two billion years depending upon the depth and geological history of the particular region tested. Only *my* areas give these strange and impossible vagaries."

And Lernin said, "But what do the geologists say about all this? Can there be some error?"

"Undoubtedly. But they have fifty decent, reasonable measurements. For themselves, they have proved the method and are happy. There are three anomalies, to be sure, but they view them with equanimity as involving some unknown factors. I don't see it that way. These three measurements mean everything." Raph interrupted himself fiercely: "How sure are you that radioactivity is an absolute constant?"

"Sure? Can one ever be sure? Nothing we know of so far affects it, and such is likewise the definite testimony of our Eekahs. Besides, my friend, if you are implying that radioactivity was more extensive in the past than in the present, why only in your fossil regions? Why not everywhere?"

"Why, indeed? It's another aspect of a problem which is growing more important daily. Consider. We have regions which show a past of abnormal radioactivity. We have regions which show abnormal fossil frequencies. Why should these regions coincide, Lernin?"

"One obvious answer suggests itself, my friend. If your Primate Primeval existed at a time when certain regions were highly radioactive, certain individuals would wander into them and die. Radioactive radiation is deadly in excess, of course. Radioactivity and fossils, there you are."

"Why not other creatures," demanded Raph. "Only Primate Primeval occurs in excess, and he was intelligent. He would not be trapped by dangerous radiation."

"Perhaps he was not intelligent. That is, after all, only your theory and not a proven fact."

"Certainly, then, he was more intelligent than his small-brained contemporaries."

"Perhaps not even that. You romanticize too much."

"Perhaps I do." Raph spoke in half a whisper. "It seems

to me that I can conjure up visions of a great civilization of a million years back—or more. A great power; a great intelligence—that has vanished completely, except for the tiny whispers of ossified bones which retain that huge cavity in which a brain once existed, and a bony five-fingered hand curving into slender signs of manipulative skill—with an opposing thumb. They *must* have been intelligent."

"Then, what killed them?" Lernin shrugged. "Several million species of living things have survived."

Raph looked up, half in anger: "I cannot accompany your group, Lernin, on a Voluntary basis. To go to the other world would be useful, yes, if I could engage in my own studies. For your purposes, it can be only a Community Job to me. I cannot give my heart to it."

But Lernin's jaw was set: "That arrangement would not be fair. There are many of us, my friend, who are sacrificing our own interests. If we all placed them first and investigated the other world in terms of our own particular provincialisms only, our great purpose would be destroyed. My friend, there is not one of our men that we can spare. We must all work as if our lives depended on our instant solution of the Eekah problem, which, believe me, it does."

Raph's jaws twisted in distaste. "On your side, you have a vague apprehension of these weak, stupid little creatures. On my side I have a definite problem of great intellectual attraction to myself. And between the two I can see no connection—no possible connection at all."

"Nor can I. But listen to me a moment. A small group of our most trusted men returned last week from a visit to the other world. It was not official, as ours will be. It made no contacts. It was a frank piece of espionage, which I am telling you about now. I ask your discretion on the matter."

"Naturally."

"Our men possessed themselves of Eekah event-sheets."

"Pardon me?"

"It is a created name to describe the objects. Printed records are issued daily in the various centers of Eekah population of events and occurrences of the day, and what passes for literary efforts as well."

Raph was momentarily interested. "It strikes me as an excellent idea."

"Yes, in its essence. The Eekah notion of interesting events, however, appears to consist entirely of antisocial events.

However, leave that be. My point is that existence of the Americas is well-known there these days—and it is universally spoken of as a 'new land of opportunity.' The various divisions of Eekahs eye it with a universal desire. The Eekahs are many, they are crowded, their economy is irrational. They want new land, and that is what this is to them —new and empty land."

"Not empty," pointed out Raph, mildly.

"Empty to them," insisted Lernin terribly. "That is the vast danger. Lands occupied by Gurrows are to them empty and they mean to take it, all the more so since they have often enough striven to take the lands of one another."

Raph shrugged: "Even so, they—"

"Yes. They are weak and stupid. You said that, and so they are. But only singly. They will unite for a purpose. To be sure, they will fall apart when the purpose is done—but momentarily they will join and become strong, which we perhaps cannot do, witness yourself. And their weapons of war have been keened in the fire of conflict. Their flying machines, for instance, are superb war weapons."

"But we have duplicated it—"

"In quantity? We have also duplicated their chemical explosives, but only in the laboratory, and their firing tubes and armored vehicles, but only in experimental plants. And yet there is more—something developed within the last five years, for our own Eekahs know nothing about it."

"And what is that?"

"We don't know. Their event-sheets speak of it—the names applied to it mean nothing to us—but the context implies the terror of it, even on the part of these kill-mad Eekahs. There seems no evidence that it has been used, or that all the Eekah groups have it—but it is used as a supreme threat. It will perhaps be clearer to you when all the evidence is presented once our voyage is under way."

"But what is it? You talk of it as if it were a bogey."

"Why, *they* talk of it as if it were a bogey. And what *could* be a bogey to an Eekah? That is the most frightening aspect of it. So far, we know only that it involves the bombardment of an element they call plutonium—of which we have never heard and of which our own Eekahs have never heard either—by objects called neutrons, which our Eekahs say are subatomic particles without charge, which seems to us completely ridiculous."

"And that is all?"

"All. Will you suspend judgment till we show you the sheets?"

Raph nodded reluctantly: "Very well."

Raph's leaden thoughts revolved in their worn groove as he stood there alone.

Eekahs and Primate Primeval. A living creature of erratic habits and a dead creature that must have aspired to heights. A sordid present of explosives and neutron bombardments and a glorious, mysterious past—

No connection! No connection!

THE END

By June 1947 I had already been working on my Ph.D. research with near-total concentration (I was no longer working in the candy store; my younger brother, Stanley, had taken over) for nearly a year. I was in the homestretch and beginning to think forward to writing my Ph.D. dissertation. I rather dreaded that, since the obligatory style of dissertations is turgid in the extreme, and I had by now spent nine years trying to write well and was afraid I simply might not be able to write badly enough to qualify for my degree.

The experiments I was doing at the time required me, periodically, to dissolve a compound called catechol in water. The catechol existed in fine, feathery, fluffy needles that dissolved very readily in water. In fact, when I sprinkled catechol into the beaker of water, the individual needles dissolved as soon as they struck the water surface. Idly, it occurred to me that if the catechol were any more soluble than it was, it could dissolve **before** it struck the water surface.

Naturally, I thought at once that this notion might be the basis for an amusing story. It occurred to me, however, that instead of writing an actual story based on the idea, I might write up a fake research paper on the subject and get a little practice in turgid writing.

I did the job on June 8, 1947, even giving it the kind of long-winded title that research papers so often have—"The Endochronic Properties of Resublimated Thiotimoline"

—and added tables, graphs, and fake references to non-existent journals.

I was not at all sure that "Thiotimoline" (no use trying to quote the entire name every time) was publishable. **Astounding,** however, ran serious articles on scientific subjects of particular interest to science fiction readers and I thought it just possible Campbell might be interested in a gag article that would be on the borders of science fiction.

I brought it in to him on the tenth, and he took it almost at once.

25

The Endochronic Properties of Resublimated Thiotimoline

The correlation of the structure of organic molecules with their various properties, physical and chemical, has in recent years afforded much insight into the mechanism of organic reactions, notably in the theories of resonance and mesomerism as developed in the last decade. The solubilities of organic compounds in various solvents has become of particular interest in this connection through the recent discovery of the endochronic nature of thiotimoline.

It has been long known that the solubility of organic compounds in polar solvents such as water is enhanced by the presence upon the hydrocarbon nucleus of hydrophilic—i.e., water-loving—groups, such as the hydroxy ($-OH$), amino ($-NH_2$), or sulfonic acid (SO_3H) groups. Where the physical characteristics of two given compounds—particularly the degree of subdivision of the material—are equal, then the time of solution—expressed in seconds per gram of material

Astounding Science Fiction, March 1948
Copyright © 1948 by Street & Smith Publications, Inc.

per millileter of solvent—decreases with the number of hydrophilic groups present. Catechol, for instance, with two hydroxy groups on the benzene nucleus, dissolves considerably more quickly than does phenol, with only one hydroxy group on the nucleus. Feinschreiber and Hravlek in their studies on the problem have contended that with increasing hydrophilism, the time of solution approaches zero. That this analysis is not entirely correct was shown when it was discovered that the compound thiotimoline will dissolve in water—in the proportions of 1 gm./ml.—in *minus* 1.12 seconds. That is, it will dissolve *before* the water is added.

Previous communications from these laboratories indicated thiotimoline to contain at least fourteen hydroxy groups, two amino groups and one sulfonic acid group. The presence of a nitro group ($-NO^2$) in addition has not yet been confirmed, and no evidence as yet exists as to the nature of the hydrocarbon nucleus, though an at least partly aromatic structure seems certain.

The Endochronometer—First attempts to measure the time of solution of thiotimoline quantitatively met with considerable difficulty because of the very negative nature of the value. The fact that the chemical dissolved prior to the addition of the water made the attempt natural to withdraw the water after solution and before addition. This, fortunately for the law of Conservation of Mass-Energy, never succeeded, since solution never took place unless the water was eventually added. The question is, of course, instantly raised as to how the thiotimoline can "know" in advance whether the water will ultimately be added or not. Though this is not properly within our province as physical chemists, much recent material has been published within the last year upon the psychological and philosophical problems thereby posed.

Nevertheless, the chemical difficulties involved rest in the fact that the time of solution varies enormously with the exact mental state of the experimenter. A period of even slight hesitation in adding the water reduces the negative time of solution, not infrequently wiping it out below the limits of detection. To avoid this, a mechanical device has been constructed, the essential design of which has already been reported in a previous communication.[6] This device, termed the endochronometer, consists of a cell 2 cubic centimeters in size into which a desired weight of thiotimoline is placed, making certain that a small hollow extension at the bottom of the solution cell—1 millimeter in internal diameter —is filled. To the cell is attached an automatic pressure micro-pipette containing a specific volume of the solvent concerned. Five seconds after the circuit is closed, this solvent is automatically delivered into the cell containing the thiotimoline. During the time of action, a ray of light is focused upon the small cell-extension described above, and at the instant of solution, the transmission of this light will no longer be impeded by the presence of solid thiotimoline. Both the instant of solution—at which time the transmission of light is recorded by a photoelectric device—and the instant of solvent addition can be determined with an accuracy of better than 0.01%. If the first value is subtracted from the second, the time of solution (T) can be determined.

The entire process is conducted in a thermostat maintained at 25.00° C.—to an accuracy of 0.01° C.

Thiotimoline Purity—The extreme sensitivity of this method highlights the deviations resulting from trifling impurities present in thiotimoline. (Since no method of laboratory synthesis of the substance has been devised, it may be practically obtained only through tedious isolation from its natural source, the bark of the shrub *Rosacea Karlsbadensis rufo.*) Great efforts were therefore made to purify the material through repeated recrystallizations from conductivity water —twice re-distilled in an all-tin apparatus—and through final sublimations. A comparison of the solution times (T) at various stages of the purification process is shown in Table I.

It is obvious from Table I that for truly quantitative significance, thiotimoline purified as described must be used. After the second resublimation, for instance, the error involved in an even dozen determinations is less than 0.7%, with the extreme values being—1.119 seconds and —1.126 seconds.

TABLE I

Purification Stage	Average "T" (12 observations)	"T" extremes	% error
As isolated	—0.72	—0.25; —1.01	34.1
First recrystallization	—0.95	—0.84; —1.09	9.8
Second recrystallization	—1.05	—0.99; —1.10	4.0
Third recrystallization	—1.11	—1.08; —1.13	1.8
Fourth recrystallization	—1.12	—1.10; —1.13	1.7
First resublimation	—1.12	—1.11; —1.13	0.9
Second resublimation	—1.122	—1.12; —1.13	0.7

In all experiments described subsequently in this study, thiotimoline so purified has been used.

Time of Solution and Volume of Solvent—As would seem reasonable, experiments have shown that increasing the volume of solvent enables the thiotimoline to dissolve more quickly—i.e., with an increasingly negative time of solution. From Figure 1, however, we can see that this increase in

Figure 1

endochronic properties levels off rapidly after a volume of solvent of approximately 1.25 ml. This interesting plateau effect appeared with varying volume of solvent for all varieties of solvents used in these laboratories, just as in all cases the time of solution approaches zero with decreasing volume of solvent.

Time of Solution and Concentration of a Given Ion—In Figure 2, the results are given of the effect of the time of solution (T) of varying the volume of solvent, where the solvent consists of varying concentrations of sodium chloride solution. It can be seen that, although in each case the volume at which this plateau is reached differs markedly with the concentration, the heights of the plateau are constant (i.e.—1.13). The volume at which it is reached, hereinafter termed the Plateau Volume (PV), decreases with decreasing concentration of sodium chloride, approaching

Figure 2

the PV for water as the NaCl concentration approaches zero. It is, therefore, obvious that a sodium chloride solution of unknown concentration can be quite accurately characterized by the determination of its PV, where other salts are absent.

This usefulness of PV extends to other ions as well. Figure 3 gives the endochronic curves of 0.001 molar solutions of sodium chloride, sodium bromide, and potassium chloride.

Figure 3

Here, the PV in each case is equal within the limits of experimental error—since the concentrations in each case are equal—but the Plateau Heights (PH) *are* different.

A tentative conclusion that might be reached from this experimental data is that the PH is characteristic of the nature of the ions present in solution, whereas the PV is characteristic of the concentration of these ions. Table II gives the values of Plateau Heights and Plateau Volume for a wide variety of salts in equal concentrations, when present alone.

The most interesting variation to be noted in Table II is that of the PV with the valence type of the salt present. In the case of salts containing pairs of singly-charged ions—i.e., sodium chloride, potassium chloride, and sodium bromide— the PV is constant for all. This holds also for those salts containing one singly charged ion and one doubly charged ion—i.e. sodium sulphate, calcium chloride, and magnesium chloride—where the PV, though equal among the three, varies markedly from those of the first set. The PV is, therefore, apparently a function of the ionic strength of the solution.

This effect also exists in connection with the Plateau Height, though less regularly. In the case of singly charged ions, such as in the first three salts listed in Table II, the PH is fairly close to that of water itself. It falls considerably where doubly charged ions, such as sulphate or calcium,

TABLE II

Solvent (Salt solutions in 0.001 M concentration)	Plateau Height (PH) seconds	Plateau Volume (PV) milliliters
Water	—1.13	1.25
Sodium Chloride solution	—1.13	1.37
Sodium Bromide Solution	—1.10	1.37
Potassium Chloride solution	—1.08	1.37
Sodium Sulphate solution	—0.72	1.59
Calcium Chloride solution	—0.96	1.59
Magnesium Chloride solution	—0.85	1.59
Calcium Sulphate solution	—0.61	1.72
Sodium Phosphate solution	—0.32	1.97
Ferric Chloride solution	—0.29	1.99

are present. And when the triply charged phosphate ion or ferric ion is present, the value sinks to merely a quarter of its value in water.

Time of Solution and Mixtures of Ions—Experiments currently in progress in these laboratories are concerned with the extremely important question of the variation of these endrochronic properties of thiotimoline in the presence of mixtures of ions. The state of our data at present does not warrant very general conclusions, but even our preliminary work gives hope of the further development of the endochronic methods of analysis. Thus, in Figure 4, we have the endochronic curve where a mixture of 0.001M Sodium Chloride and 0.001M Ferric Chloride solutions is the solvent. Here, two sharp changes in slope can be seen: the first at a solution time of —0.29, and the second at—1.13, these being the PH's characteristic of Ferric Chloride and Sodium Chloride respectively—see Table II. The PH for a given salt would thus appear not to be affected by the presence of other salts.

This is definitely not the case, however, for the PV, and it is to a quantitative elucidation of the variation of PV with impurities in the solvent that our major efforts are now directed.

Figure 4

Summary—Investigations of the endochronic qualities of thiotimoline have shown that:

a—Careful purifications of the material is necessary for obtaining quantitative results.

b—Increasing the volume of solvent results in increasing the negative time of solution to a constant value known as the Plateau Height (PH), at a volume of solvent known as the Plateau Volume (PV).

c—The value of the PH is characteristic of the nature of the ions present in the solvent, varying with the ionic strength of the solution and not varying with the addition of other ions.

d—The value of the PV is characteristic of the concentration of the ions present in the solvent, being constant for different ions in solution of equal strength, but varying markedly with the admixtures of second varieties of ions.

As a result of all this, it is suggested that endochronic methods offer a means of rapid—2 minutes or less—and accurate—within 0.1% at least—analysis of inorganic, water-soluble materials.

Bibliography:

P. Krum and L. Eshkin, *Journal of Chemical Solubilities, 27,* 109–114 (1944). "Concerning the Anomalous Solubility of Thiotimoline."

E. J. Feinshreiber and Y. Hravlek. *Journal of Chemical Solubilities, 22,* 57–68 (1939), "Solubility Speeds and Hydrophilic Groupings."

P. Krum, I. Eshkin, and O. Nile. *Annals of Synthetic Chemistry, 115,* 1122–1145; 1208–1215 (1945), "Structure of Thiotimoline, Parts I & II."

G. H. Freudler, *Journal of Psychochemistry, 2,* 476–488 (1945), "Initiative and Determination: Are They Influenced by Diet?—As tested by Thiotimoline solubility Experiments."

E. Harley-Short, *Philosophical Proceedings & Reviews, 15,* 125–197 (1946). "Determinism and Free-Will. The Application of Thiotimoline Solubility to Marxian Dialectic."

P. Krum, *"Journal of Chemical Solubilities, 29,* 818–819 (1946), "A Device for the Quantitative Measurement of Thiotimoline Solubility Speed."

A. Roundin, B. Lev, and Y. J. Prutt, *Proceedings of the Society of Plant Chemistry, 80,* 11–18 (1930), "Natural Products isolated from shrubs of the genus *Rosacea."*

Tiotimolin kak Ispitatel Marksciiskoy dilektiki B. Kreschiatika, *Journal Naouki i Sovetskoy Ticorii* Vol. 11, No. 3.

Philossophia Neopredelennosti i Tiotimolin, Molvinski Pogost i Z. Brikalo. *Mir i Kultura* Vol. 2, No. 31.

THE END

When Campbell took the piece, I made one cautious stipulation. I knew it would appear in the spring and I knew that in the spring I would come up for my "oral examinations"— the last hurdle on the path to my Ph.D. I didn't want any austere member of the examining board to decide I was making fun of chemical research and to be sufficiently offended to vote against me on the grounds that I wasn't temperamentally suited to the high honor of the doctorate. —So I asked Campbell to run it under a pseudonym.

When the magazine with the article finally reached the newsstands, in mid-February 1948, I was appalled to discover that Campbell had utterly forgotten the matter of the pseudonym. The article appeared under my own name and I was scheduled to have my orals within three months. My nervousness was increased when, almost at once, copies of the magazine began circulating in the chemistry department.

On May 20, 1948, I had my orals. The examining board **had** seen the article. After I had been on the grill for an hour and twenty minutes, the last question (asked by Professor Ralph S. Halford) was, "Mr. Asimov, tell us something about the thermodynamic properties of the compound thiotimoline."

I broke into hysterical laughter out of sheer relief, for it struck me instantly that they wouldn't play good-natured jokes with me (Professor Halford sounded jovial and everyone else was smiling) if they were going to flunk me. I was led out, still laughing, and after a twenty-minute wait, the examiners emerged, shook my hand, and said, "Congratulations, Dr. Asimov."

My fellow students insisted on forcing five Manhattans down my throat that afternoon and, since I am a teetotaler under normal conditions and have no tolerance for alcohol, I was royally drunk at once. It took them three hours to sober me up.

After the official ceremonies, on June 1, 1948, I was Isaac Asimov, Ph.D.

As it turned out, Campbell's non-use of a pseudonym (and I bet he did it deliberately, because he was smarter than I was) was a lucky break indeed. Not only did the examining board **not** take it amiss, but the article became, in a minor way, famous, and I with it.

Although "Thiotimoline" appeared in **Astounding,** as did all my stories of the time, it received circulation far outside the ordinary science fiction world. It passed from chemist to chemist, by way of the magazine itself, or by reprints in small trade journals, or by copies pirated and mimeographed, even by word of mouth. People who had never heard of me at all as a science fiction writer, heard of thiotimoline. It was the very first time my fame transcended the field.

What's more, although "Thiotimoline" was essentially a work of fantasy, the **form** was that of non-fiction. Viewed from that standpoint, "Thiotimoline" was the first piece of non-fiction I had ever published professionally—the harbinger of a vast amount to come.

But what amused me most was that a surprising number of readers actually took the article seriously. I was told that in the weeks after its appearance the librarians at the New York Public Library were driven out of their minds by hordes of eager youngsters who demanded to see copies of the fake journals I had used as pseudo references.

But back to the summer of 1947—

Over a period of five years I had sold fourteen stories, every one of them to Campbell. This didn't mean that he was the only editor in the field, at all. Almost all the magazines that had been published before the war still existed (although only **Astounding** was really doing well) and would have welcomed submissions from me. Had Campbell rejected any of the stories I had submitted to him, I would certainly have tried one of those other magazines.—But he didn't, so I didn't.

The magazine **Startling Stories,** in which I had published "Christmas on Ganymede" five and a half years before, published a forty-thousand-word "short novel" in each issue. It wasn't easy to get a publishable story of that length every month though, especially since **Startling's** rate was only half that of **Astounding.**

Sometimes it was necessary, therefore, for the editor of the magazine, who at that time was Sam Merwin, Jr., to canvass those authors known to be capable of turning out such a story. About the time I was doing "Thiotimoline,"

Merwin approached me with a suggestion that I write a lead short novel.

Startling, he explained, had always published stories with the accent on adventure, but, in imitation of **Astounding's** success, he had persuaded the publisher to try the experiment of publishing stories with a heavier accent on science. Would I consider, then, doing a lead for **Startling?**

I was terribly flattered. Also, as I said earlier, I was nervous about having become a one-editor author and would have welcomed a chance to prove to myself that I could write beyond Campbell's protective shadow. I agreed, therefore, and a good part of the summer of 1947 (when I wasn't engaged in preparing my experimental data for the upcoming Ph.D., dissertation) was spent in preparing a story I called "Grow Old with Me."*

By August 3 I had completed first draft. On August 26, I had the first part of it in final copy and submitted that to Merwin. He approved. On September 23 the entire story was submitted and I had no doubt, whatever, of its acceptance. On October 15, 1947, however, Merwin told me that, alas, **Startling** had decided not to go for heavy science, after all, but for adventure, and that "Grow Old with Me" would have to be completely rewritten with no guarantee of acceptance after that.

I suppose it is an indication of how things had advanced when I tell you it was the first time that I did not accept a request for revision philosophically. Quite otherwise! It had been five years and more since even Campbell had rejected one of my stories; how, then, dare a comparative nonentity like Merwin do so? Particularly since **he** had approached **me** for the story?

I made no effort to hide my annoyance. In fact, I seized the manuscript and stalked out of the office, and in an obvious rage.** I submitted the story to Campbell, giving

---

*This was inspired by Robert Browning's poem **Rabbi Ben Ezra** and was a misquotation—which shows you the level of my culture. The first line of the poem is "Grow old along with me."
**Years afterward, as a result of the subsequent history of that story, Merwin took to apologizing for that rejection every time he met me—but he didn't have to, and I kept telling him so. He was editor, and he was completely within his rights to

him a full account of events. —I have always made it a practice to tell any editor to whom I submit a story of any rejection it has previously received. There is no necessity to do this; it is not, as far as I know, an ethical requirement for a writer. I just do it, and it has not, again as far as I know, ever cost me an acceptance.

As it happened, Campbell rejected the story, but not, I'm sure, because it had been somewhere else first. He told me enough things wrong with the story to make me feel that perhaps Merwin had not been so arbitrary in rejecting it. I thrust the story in the drawer in disgust and thought no more about it for nearly two years.

The rejection came at a bad time. More and more, I was wrapped up in trying to complete my research, in writing my dissertation, and, most of all, in anxiously looking for a job. There wasn't much time to write, and the rejection had sufficiently disheartened and humiliated me so that I withdrew from writing for nearly a year. This was the third long withdrawal of my writing career, and, to this date, the last.

I did not find a job; my expected Ph.D. degree was no passport to affluence, after all. Thas was humiliating, too.

I accepted an offer from Professor Robert C. Elderfield to do a year's postdoctoral research for him for $4,500, working on anti-malarial drugs. I accepted, though not with great enthusiasm, and started work for him on June 2, 1948, the day after I had officially gained my Ph.D.—At least it would give me another year to find a job.

By the next month, I had settled down sufficiently to consider writing a science fiction story, "The Red Queen's Race." On July 12 it was finished and I submitted it to Campbell. It was accepted on the sixteenth and once again I was back in business.

---

reject the story, and I was being pettily temperamental to be angry about it. I have made every effort, since, to avoid evident anger at any rejection, however unjustified it might seem at the time, and I think I have succeeded.

26

The Red Queen's Race

Here's a puzzle for you, if you like. Is it a crime to translate a chemistry textbook into Greek?

Or let's put it another way. If one of the country's largest atomic power plants is completely ruined in an unauthorized experiment, is an admitted accessory to that act a criminal?

These problems only developed with time, of course. We started with the atomic power plant—drained. I really mean *drained*. I don't know exactly how large the fissionable power source was—but in two flashing microseconds, it had all fissioned.

No explosion. No undue gamma ray density. It was merely that every moving part in the entire structure was fused. The entire main building was mildly hot. The atmosphere for two miles in every direction was gently warm. Just a dead, useless building which later on took a hundred million dollars to replace.

It happened about three in the morning, and they found Elmer Tywood alone in the central source chamber. The findings of twenty-four close-packed hours can be summarized quickly.

1. Elmer Tywood—Ph.D., Sc.D., Fellow of This and Honorary That, one-time youthful participant of the original Manhattan Project, and now full Professor of Nuclear Physics—was no interloper. He had a Class-A Pass—Unlimited. But no record could be found as to his purpose in being there just then. A table on casters contained equipment which had not been made on any recorded requisition. It, too, was a single fused mass—not quite too hot to touch.

Astounding Science Fiction, January 1949
Copyright © 1948 by Street & Smith Publications, Inc.

2. Elmer Tywood was dead. He lay next to the table, his face congested, nearly black. No radiation effect. No external force of any sort. The doctor said apoplexy.

3. In Elmer Tywood's office safe were found two puzzling items: i.e. twenty foolscap sheets of apparent mathematics, and a bound folio in a foreign language which turned out to be Greek, the subject matter, on translation, turning out to be chemistry.

The secrecy which poured over the whole mess was something so terrific as to make everything that touched it, *dead*. It's the only word that can describe it. Twenty-seven men and women, all told, including the Secretary of Defense, the Secretary of Science, and two or three others so top-notch that they were completely unknown to the public, entered the power plant during the period of investigation. All who had been in the plant that night, the physicist who had identified Tywood, the doctor who had examined him, were retired into virtual home arrest.

No newspaper ever got the story. No inside dopester got it. A few members of Congress got part of it.

And naturally so! Anyone or any group or any country that could suck all the available energy out of the equivalent of perhaps fifty to a hundred pounds of plutonium without exploding it, had America's industry and America's defense so snugly in the palm of the hand that the light and life of one hundred sixty million people could be turned off between yawns.

Was it Tywood? Or Tywood and others? Or just others, through Tywood?

And my job? I was decoy; or front man, if you like. Someone had to hang around the university and ask questions about Tywood. After all, he was missing. It could be amnesia, a hold-up, a kidnapping, a killing, a runaway, insanity, accident—I could busy myself with that for five years and collect black looks, and maybe divert attention. To be sure, it didn't work out that way.

But don't think I was in on the whole case at the start. I wasn't one of the twenty-seven men I mentioned a while back, though my boss was. But I knew a little—enough to get started.

Professor John Keyser was also in Physics. I didn't get to him right away. There was a good deal of routine to cover first in as conscientious a way as I could. Quite meaningless. Quite necessary. But I was in Keyser's office now.

Professors' offices are distinctive. Nobody dusts them except some tired cleaning woman who hobbles in and out at eight in the morning, and the professor never notices the dust anyway. Lots of books without much arrangement. The ones close to the desk are used a lot—lectures are copied out of them. The ones out of reach are wherever a student put them back after borrowing them. Then there are professional journals that look cheap and are darned expensive, which are waiting about and which may some day be read. And plenty of paper on the desk; some of it scribbled on.

Keyser was an elderly man—one of Tywood's generation. His nose was big and rather red, and he smoked a pipe. He had that easy-going and nonpredatory look in his eyes that goes with an academic job—either because that kind of job attracts that kind of man or because that kind of job makes that kind of man.

I said: "What kind of work is Professor Tywood doing?"

"Research physics."

Answers like that bounce off me. Some years ago they used to get me mad. Now I just said: "We know that, professor. It's the details I'm after."

And he twinkled at me tolerantly: "Surely the details can't help much unless you're a research physicist yourself. Does it matter—under the circumstances?"

"Maybe not. But he's gone. If anything's happened to him in the way of"—I gestured, and deliberately clinched—"foul play, his work may have something to do with it—unless he's rich and the motive is money."

Keyser chuckled dryly: "College professors are never rich. The commodity we peddle is but lightly considered, seeing how large the supply is."

I ignored that, too, because I know my looks are against me. Actually, I finished college with a "very good" translated into Latin so that the college president could understand it, and never played in a football game in my life. But I look rather the reverse.

I said: "Then we're left with his work to consider."

"You mean spies? International intrigue?"

"Why not? It's happened before! After all, he's a nuclear physicist, isn't he?"

"He is. But so are others. So am I."

"Ah, but perhaps he knows something you don't."

There was a stiffening to the jaw. When caught off-guard, professors can act just like people. He said, stiffly: "As I recall offhand, Tywood has published papers on the effect of liquid viscosity on the wings of the Rayleigh line, on higher-orbit field equations, and on spin-orbit coupling of two nucleons, but his main work is on quadrupole moments. I am quite competent in these matters."

"Is he working on quadrupole moments now?" I tried not to bat an eye, and I think I succeeded.

"Yes—in a way." He almost sneered, "He may be getting to the experimental stage finally. He's spent most of his life, it seems, working out the mathematical consequences of a special theory of his own."

"Like this," and I tossed a sheet of foolscap at him.

That sheet was one of those in the safe in Tywood's office. The chances, of course, were that the bundle meant nothing, if only because it was a professor's safe. That is, things are sometimes put in at the spur of the moment because the logical drawer was filled with unmarked exam papers. And, of course, nothing is ever taken out. We had found in that safe dusty little vials of yellowish crystals with scarcely legible labels, some mimeographed booklets dating back to World War II and marked "Restricted," a copy of an old college yearbook, and some correspondence concerning a possible position as Director of Research for American Electric, dated ten years back, and, of course, chemistry in Greek.

The foolscap was there, too. It was rolled up like a college diploma with a rubber band about it and had no label or descriptive title. Some twenty sheets were covered with ink marks, meticulous and small—

I had one sheet of that foolscap. I don't think any one man in the world had more than one sheet. And I'm sure that no man in the world but one knew that the loss of his particular sheet and of his particular life would be as nearly simultaneous as the government could make it.

So I tossed the sheet at Keyser, as if it were something I'd found blowing about the campus.

He stared at it and then looked at the back side, which was blank. His eyes moved down from the top to the bottom, then jumped back to the top.

"I don't know what this is about," he said, and the words seemed sour to his own taste.

I didn't say anything. Just folded the paper and shoved it back into the inside jacket pocket.

Keyser added petulantly: "It's a fallacy you laymen have that scientists can look at an equation and say, 'Ah, yes—'

and go on to write a book about it. Mathematics has no existence of its own. It is merely an arbitrary code devised to describe physical observations of philosophical concepts. Every man can adapt it to his own particular needs. For instance no one can look at a symbol and be sure of what it means. So far, science has used every letter in the alphabet, large, small and italic, each symbolizing many different things. They have used bold-faced letters, Gothic-type letters, Greek letters, both capital and small, subscripts, superscripts, asterisks, even Hebrew letters. Different scientists use different symbols for the same concept and the same symbol for different concepts. So if you show a disconnected page like this to any man, without information as to the subject being investigated or the particular symbology used, he could absolutely not make sense out of it."

I interrupted: "But you said he was working on quadrupole moments. Does that make this sensible?" and I tapped the spot on my chest where the foolscap had been slowly scorching a hole in my jacket for two days.

"I can't tell. I saw none of the standard relationships that I'd expect to be involved. At least I recognized none. But I obviously can't commit myself."

There was a short silence, then he said: "I'll tell you. Why don't you check with his students?"

I lifted my eyebrows: "You mean in his classes?"

He seemed annoyed: "No, for Heaven's sake. His research students! His doctoral candidates! They've been working with him. They'll know the details of that work better than I, or anyone in the faculty, could possibly know it."

"It's an idea," I said, casually. It was, too. I don't know why, but I wouldn't have thought of it myself. I guess it's because it's only natural to think that any professor knows more than any student.

Keyser latched onto a lapel as I rose to leave. "And, besides," he said, "I think you're on the wrong track. This is in confidence, you understand, and I wouldn't say it except for the unusual circumstances, but Tywood is not thought of too highly in the profession. Oh, he's an adequate teacher, I'll admit, but his research papers have never commanded respect. There has always been a tendency towards vague theorizing, unsupported by experimental evidence. That paper of yours is probably more of it. No one could possibly want to . . . .er, kidnap him because of it."

"Is that so? I see. Any ideas, yourself, as to why he's gone, or where he's gone?"

"Nothing concrete," he said pursing his lips, "but everyone knows he is a sick man. He had a stroke two years ago that kept him out of classes for a semester. He never did get well. His left side was paralyzed for a while and he still limps. Another stroke would kill him. It could come any time."

"You think he's dead, then?"

"It's not impossible."

"But where's the body, then?"

"Well, really— That is *your* job, I think."

It was, and I left.

I interviewed each one of Tywood's four research students in a volume of chaos called a research laboratory. These student research laboratories usually have two hopefuls working therein, said two constituting a floating population, since every year or so they are alternately replaced.

Consequently, the laboratory has its equipment stack in tiers. On the laboratory benches is the equipment immediately being used, and in three or four of the handiest drawers are replacements or supplements which are likely to be used. In the farther drawers, in the shelves reaching up to the ceiling, in odd corners, are fading remnants of the past student generations—oddments never used and never discarded. It is claimed, in fact, that no research student ever knew all the contents of his laboratory.

All four of Tywood's students were worried. But three were worried mainly by their own status. That is, by the possible effect the absence of Tywood might have on the status of their "problem." I dismissed those three—who all have degrees now, I hope—and called back the fourth.

He had the most haggard look of all, and had been least communicative—which I considered a hopeful sign.

He now sat stiffly in the straight-backed chair at the right of the desk, while I leaned back in a creaky old swivel-chair and pushed my hat off my forehead. His name was Edwin Howe and *he* did get his degree later on; I know that for sure, because he's a big wheel in the Department of Science now.

I said: "You do the same work the other boys do, I suppose?"

"It's all nuclear work, in a way."

"But it's not all exactly the same?"

He shook his head slowly. "We take different angles. You have to have something clear-cut, you know, or you won't be able to publish. We've got to get our degrees."

He said it exactly the way you or I might say, "We've got to make a living." At that, maybe it's the same thing for them.

"I said: "All right. What's *your* angle?"

He said: "I do the math. I mean, with Professor Tywood."

"What kind of math?"

And he smiled a little, getting the same sort of atmosphere about him that I had noticed in Professor Keyser's case that morning. A sort of, "Do-you-really-think-I-can-explain-all-my-profound-thoughts-to-stupid-little-you?" sort of atmosphere.

All he said aloud, however, was: "That would be rather complicated to explain."

"I'll help you," I said. "Is that anything like it?" And I tossed the foolscap sheet at him.

He didn't give it any once-over. He just snatched it up and let out a thin wail: "Where'd you get this?"

"From Tywood's safe."

"Do you have the rest of it, too?"

"It's safe," I hedged.

He relaxed a little—just a little: "You didn't show it to anybody, did you?"

"I showed it to Professor Keyser."

Howe made an impolite sound with his lower lip and front teeth, *"That* jackass. What did he say?"

I turned the palms of my hands upward and Howe laughed. Then he said, in an offhand manner: "Well, that's the sort of stuff I do."

"And what's it all about? Put it so I can understand it."

There was distinct hesitation. He said: "Now, look. This is confidential stuff. Even Pop's other students don't know anything about it. I don't even think *I* know *all* about it. This isn't just a degree I'm after, you know. It's Pop Tywood's Nobel Prize, and it's going to be an Assistant Professorship for me at Cal Tech. This has got to be published before it's talked about."

And I shook my head slowly and made my words very soft: "No, son. You have it twisted. You'll have to talk about it before it's published, because Tywood's gone and maybe he's dead and maybe he isn't. And if he's dead, maybe he's murdered. And when the department has a suspicion of murder, everybody talks. Now, it will look bad for you, kid, if you try to keep some secrets."

It worked. I knew it would, because everyone reads murder mysteries and knows all the clichés. He jumped out of his chair and rattled the words off as if he had a script in front of him.

"Surely," he said, "you can't suspect *me* of . . . of anything like that. Why . . . why, my career—"

I shoved him back into his chair with the beginnings of a sweat on his forehead. I went into the next line: "I don't suspect anybody of anything *yet*. And you won't be in any trouble, if you talk, chum."

He was ready to talk. "Now this is all in strict confidence."

Poor guy. He didn't know the meaning of the word "strict." He was never out of eyeshot of an operator from that moment till the government decided to bury the whole case with the one final comment of "?" Quote. Unquote. (I'm not kidding. To this day, the case is neither opened nor closed. It's just "?")

He said, dubiously, "You know what time travel is, I suppose?"

Sure I knew what time travel was. My oldest kid is twelve and he listens to the afternoon video programs till he swells up visibly with the junk he absorbs at the ears and eyes.

"What about time travel?" I said.

"In a sense, we can do it. Actually, it's only what you might call micro-temporal-translation—"

I almost lost my temper. In fact, I think I did. It seemed obvious that the squirt was trying to diddle me; and without subtlety. I'm used to having people think I look dumb; but not *that* dumb.

I said through the back of my throat: "Are you going to tell me that Tywood is out somewhere in time—like Ace Rogers, the Lone Time Ranger?" (That was Junior's favorite program—Ace Rogers was stopping Genghis Khan single-handed that week.)

But he looked as disgusted as I must have. "No," he yelled. "I don't know where Pop is. If you'd *listen* to me—I said micro-temporal-translation. Now, this isn't a video show and it isn't magic; this happens to be science. For instance, you know about matter-energy equivalence, I suppose."

I nodded sourly. Everyone knows about that since Hiroshima in the last war but one.

"All right, then," he went on, "that's good for a start. Now, if you take a brown mass of matter and apply temporal translation to it—you know, send it back in time—you are, in effect, creating matter at the point in time to which you are sending it. To do that, you must use an amount of energy equivalent to the amount of matter you have created. In other words, to send a gram—or, say, an ounce—of anything back in time, you have to disintegrate an ounce of matter completely, to furnish the energy required."

"Hm-m-m," I said, "that's to create the ounce of matter in the past. But aren't you destroying an ounce of matter by removing it from the present? Doesn't that *create* the equivalant amount of energy?"

And he looked just about as annoyed as a fellow sitting on a bumblebee that wasn't quite dead. Apparently laymen are never supposed to question scientists.

He said: "I was trying to simplify it so you would understand it. Actually, it's more complicated. It would be very nice if we could use the energy of disappearance to cause it to appear, but that would be working in a circle, believe me. The requirements of entropy would forbid it. To put it more rigorously, the energy is required to overcome temporal inertia and it just works out so that the energy in ergs required to send back a mass, in grams, is equal to that mass times the square of the speed of light in centimeters per second. Which just happens to be the Einstein Mass-Energy Equivalence Equation. I can give you the mathematics, you know."

"I know," I waxed some of that misplaced eagerness back. "But was all this worked out experimentally? Or is it just on paper?"

Obviously, the thing was to keep him talking.

He had that queer light in his eye that every research student gets, I am told, when he is asked to discuss his problem. He'll discuss it with anyone, even with a "dumb flatfoot"—which was convenient at the moment.

"You see," he said like a man slipping you the inside dope on a shady business deal, "what started the whole thing was this neutrino business. They've been trying to find that neutrino since the late thirties and they haven't succeeded. It's a subatomic particle which has no charge and has a mass much less than even an electron. Naturally, it's next to impossible to spot, and hasn't been spotted yet. But they keep looking because, without assuming that a neutrino exists, the energetics of some nuclear reactions can't be balanced. So Pop Tywood got the idea about twenty years ago that some energy was disappearing, in the form of matter, back into time. We got working on that—or he did—and I'm the first student he's ever had tackle it along with him.

"Obviously, we had to work with tiny amounts of material and . . . well, it was just a stroke of genius on Pop's part to think of using traces of artificial radioactive isotopes. You could work with just a few micrograms of it, you know, by following its activity with counters. The variation of activity with time should follow a very definite and simple law which has never been altered by any laboratory condition known.

"Well, we'd send a speck back fifteen minutes, say, and fifteen minutes before we did that—everything was arranged automatically, you see—the count jumped to nearly double what it should be, fell off normally, and then dropped sharply at the moment it was sent back below where it would have been normally. The material overlapped itself in time, you see, and for fifteen minutes we counted the doubled material—"

I interrupted: "You mean you had the same atoms existing in two places at the same time."

"Yes," he said, with mild surprise, "why not? That's why we use so much energy—the equivalent of creating those atoms." And then he rushed on, "Now I'll tell you what my particular job is. If you send back the material fifteen minutes, it is apparently sent back to the same spot relative to the Earth despite the fact that in fifteen minutes, the Earth moved sixteen thousand miles around the Sun, and the Sun itself moves more thousand miles and so on. But there are certain tiny discrepancies which I've analyzed and which turn out to be due, possibly, to two causes.

"First, there is a frictional effect—if you can use such a term—so that matter does drift a little with respect to the Earth, depending on how far back in time it is sent, and on the nature of material. Then, too, some of the discrepancy can only be explained by the assumption that passage through time itself takes time."

"How's that?" I said.

"What I mean is that some of the radioactivity is evenly spread throughout the time of translation as if the material tested had been reacting during backward passage through time by a constant amount. My figures show that—well, if you were to be moved backward in time, you would age one day for every hundred years. Or, to put it another way, if you could watch a time dial which recorded the time outside a 'time-machine,' your watch would move forward twenty-four hours while the time dial moved back a hundred years. That's a universal constant, I think, because the speed of light is a universal constant. Anyway, that's my work."

After a few minutes, in which I chewed all this, I asked: "Where did you get the energy needed for your experiments?"

"They ran out a special line from the power plant. Pop's a big shot there, and swung the deal."

"Hm-m-m. What was the heaviest amount of material you sent into the past?"

"Oh"—he sent his eyes upward—"I think we shot back one hundredth of a milligram once. That's ten micrograms."

"Ever try sending anything into the future?"

"That won't work," he put in quickly. "Impossible. You can't change signs like that, because the energy required becomes more than infinite. It's a one-way proposition."

I looked hard at my fingernails: "How much material could you send back in time if you fissioned about . . . oh, say, one hundred pounds of plutonium." Things, I thought, were becoming, if anything, too obvious.

The answer came quickly: "In plutonium fission," he said, "not more than one or two percent of the mass is converted into energy. Therefore, one hundred pounds of plutonium when completely used up would send a pound or two back into time."

"Is that all? But could you handle all that energy? I mean, a hundred pounds of plutonium can make quite an explosion."

"All relative," he said, a bit pompously. "If you took all that energy and let it loose a little at a time, you could handle it. If you released it all at once, but used it just as fast as you released it, you could still handle it. In sending back material through time, energy can be used much faster than it can possibly be released even through fission. Theoretically, anyway."

"But how do you get rid of it?"

"It's spread through time, naturally. Of course, the minimum time through which material could be transferred would, therefore, depend on the mass of the material. Otherwise, you're liable to have the energy density with time too high."

"All right, kid," I said. "I'm calling up headquarters, and they'll send a man here to take you home. You'll stay there a while."

"But— What for?"

"It won't be for long."

It wasn't—and it was made up to him afterwards.

I spent the evening at Headquarters. We had a library there—a very special kind of library. The very morning after the explosion, two or three operators had drifted quietly into the chemistry and physics libraries of the University. Experts in their way. They located every article Tywood had ever published in any scientific journal and had snapped each page. Nothing was disturbed otherwise.

Other men went through magazine files and through book lists. It ended with a room at Headquarters that represented a complete Tywoodana. Nor was there a definite purpose in doing this. It merely represented part of the thoroughness with which a problem of this sort is met.

I went through that library. Not the scientific papers. I knew there'd be nothing there that I wanted. But he had written a series of articles for a magazine twenty years back, and I read those. And I grabbed at every piece of private correspondence they had available.

After that, I just sat and thought—and got scared.

I got to bed about four in the morning and had nightmares.

But I was in the Boss' private office at nine in the morning just the same.

He's a big man, the Boss, with iron-gray hair slicked down tight. He doesn't smoke, but he keeps a box of cigars on his desk and when he doesn't want to say anything for a few seconds, he picks one up, rolls it about a little, smells it, then sticks it right into the middle of his mouth and lights it in a very careful way. By that time, he either has something to say or doesn't have to say anything at all. Then he puts the cigar down and lets it burn to death.

He used up a box in about three weeks, and every Christmas, half his gift-wraps held boxes of cigars.

He wasn't reaching for any cigars now, though. He just folded his big fists together on the desk and looked up at me from under a creased forehead. "What's boiling?"

I told him. Slowly, because micro-temporal-translation doesn't sit well with anybody, especially when you call it time travel, which I did. It's a sign of how serious things were that he only asked me once if I were crazy.

Then I was finished and we stared at each other.

He said: "And you think he tried to send something back

in time—something weighing a pound or two—and blew an entire plant doing it?"

"It fits in," I said.

I let him go for a while. He was thinking and I wanted him to keep on thinking. I wanted him, if possible, to think of the same thing I was thinking, so that I wouldn't have to tell him—

Because I hated to have to tell him—

Because it was nuts, for one thing. And too horrible, for another.

So I kept quiet and he kept on thinking and every once in a while some of his thoughts came to the surface.

After a while, he said: "Assuming the student, Howe, to have told the truth—and you'd better check his notebooks, by the way, which I hope you've impounded—"

"The entire wing of that floor is out of bounds, sir. Edwards has the notebooks."

He went on: "All right. Assuming he told us all the truth he knows, why did Tywood jump from less than a milligram to a pound?"

His eyes came down and they were hard: "Now you're concentrating on the time-travel angle. To you, I gather, that is the crucial point, with the energy involved as incidental— purely incidental."

"Yes, sir," I said grimly. "I think exactly that."

"Have you considered that you might be wrong? That you might have matters inverted?"

"I don't quite get that."

"Well, look. You say you've read up on Tywood. All right. He was one of that bunch of scientists after World War II that fought the atom bomb; wanted a world state— You know about that, don't you?"

I nodded.

"He had a guilt complex," the Boss said with energy. "He'd helped work out the bomb, and he couldn't sleep nights thinking of what he'd done. He lived with that fear for years. And even though the bomb wasn't used in World War III, can you imagine what every day of uncertainty must have meant to him? Can you imagine the shriveling horror in his soul as he waited for others to make the decision at every crucial moment till the final Compromise of Sixty-Five?

"We have a complete psychiatric analysis of Tywood and several others just like him, taken during the last war. Did you know that?"

"No, sir."

"It's true. We let up after Sixty-Five, of course, because with the establishment of world control of atomic power, the scrapping of the atomic bomb stockpile in all countries, and the establishment of research liaison among the various spheres of influence on the planet, most of the ethical conflict in the scientific mind was removed.

"But the findings at the time were serious. In 1964, Tywood had a morbid subconscious hatred for the very concept of atomic power. He began to make mistakes, serious ones. Eventually, we were forced to take him off research of any kind. And several others as well, even though things were pretty bad at the time. We had just lost India, if you remember."

Considering that I was in India at the time, I remembered. But I still wasn't seeing his point.

"Now, what," he continued. "if dregs of that attitude remained buried in Tywood to the very end? Don't you see that time-travel is a double-edged sword? Why throw a pound of anything into the past, anyway? For the sake of proving a point? He had proved his case just as much when he sent back a fraction of a milligram. That was good enough for the Nobel Prize, I suppose.

"But there was *one* thing he could do with a pound of matter that he couldn't do with a milligram, and that was *to drain a power plant*. So that was what he must have been after. He had discovered a way of consuming inconceivable quantities of energy. By sending back eighty pounds of dirt, he could remove all the existing plutonium in the world. End atomic power for an indefinite period."

I was completely unimpressed, but I tried not to make that too plain. I just said: "Do you think he could possibly have thought he could get away with it more than once?"

"This is all based on the fact that he wasn't a normal man. How do I know what he could imagine he could do? Besides, there may be men behind him—with less science and more brains—who are quite ready to continue upwards from this point."

"Have any of these men been found yet? Any evidence of such men?"

A little wait, and his hand reached for the cigar box. He stared at the cigar and turned it end for end. Just a little wait more. I was patient.

Then he put it down decisively without lighting it.

"No," he said.

He looked at me, and clear through me, and said: "Then, you still don't go for that?"

I shrugged, "Well— It doesn't sound right."

"Do you have a notion of your own?"

"Yes. But I can't bring myself to talk about it. If I'm wrong, I'm the wrongest man that ever was; but if I'm right, I'm the rightest."

"I'll listen," he said, and he put his hand under the desk.

That was the pay-off. The room was armored, sound-proof, and radiation-proof to anything short of a nuclear explosion. And with that little signal showing on his secretary's desk, the President of the United States couldn't have interrupted us.

I leaned back and said: "Chief, do you happen to remember how you met your wife? Was it a little thing?"

He must have thought it a *non sequitur*. What else could he have thought? But he was giving me my head now; having his own reasons, I suppose.

He just smiled and said: "I sneezed and she turned around. It was at a street corner."

"What made you be on that street corner just then? What made her be? Do you remember just why you sneezed? Where you caught the cold? Or where the speck of dust came from? Imagine how many factors had to intersect in just the right place at just the right time for you to meet your wife."

"I suppose we would have met some other time, if not then?"

"But you can't *know* that. How do you know whom you *didn't* meet, because once when you might have turned around, you didn't; because once when you might have been late, you weren't. Your life forks at every instant, and you go down one of the forks almost at random, and so does everyone else. Start twenty years ago, and the forks diverge further and further with time.

"You sneezed, and met a girl, and not another. As a consequence, you made certain decisions, and so did the girl, and so did the girl you didn't meet, and the man who did meet her, and the people you all met thereafter. And your family, her family, their family—and your children.

"Because you sneezed twenty years ago, five people, or fifty, or five hundred, might be dead now who would have been alive, or might be alive who would have been dead. Move it two hundred years ago: two thousand years ago, and a sneeze—even by someone no history ever heard of—might have meant that no one now alive would have been alive."

The Boss rubbed the back of his head: "Widening ripples. I read a story once—"

"So did I. It's not a new idea—but I want you to think about it for a while, because I want to read to you from an article by Professor Elmer Tywood in a magazine twenty years old. It was just before the last war."

I had copies of the film in my pocket and the white wall made a beautiful screen, which was what it was meant to do. The boss made a motion to turn about, but I waved him back.

"No, sir," I said. "I want to read this to you. And I want you to listen to it."

He leaned back.

"The article," I went on, "is entitled: 'Man's First Great Failure!' Remember, this was just before the war, when the bitter disappointment at the final failure of the United Nations was at its height. What I will read are some excerpts from the first part of the article. It goes like this:

" '. . . That Man, with his technical perfection, has failed to solve the great sociological problems of today is only the second immense tragedy that has come to the race. The first, and perhaps the greater, was that, once, these same great sociological problems *were* solved; and yet these solutions were not permanent, because the technical perfection we have today did not then exist.

" 'It was a case of having bread without butter, or butter without bread. Never both together. . . .

" 'Consider the Hellenic world, from which our philosophy, our mathematics, our ethics, our art, our literature—our entire culture, in fact—stem . . . In the days of Pericles, Greece, like our own world in microcosm, was a surprisingly modern potpourri of conflicting ideologies and ways of life. But then Rome came, adopting the culture, but bestowing, and enforcing, peace. To be sure, the *Pax Romana* lasted only two hundred years, but no like period has existed since. . . .

" 'War was abolished. Nationalism did not exist. The Roman citizen was Empire-wide. Paul of Tarsus and Flavius Josephus were Roman citizens. Spaniards, North Africans, Illyrians assumed the purple. Slavery existed, but it was an indiscriminate slavery, imposed as a punishment, incurred as the price of economic failure, brought on by the fortunes of war. No man was a *natural* slave—because of the color of his skin or the place of his birth.

" 'Religious toleration was complete. If an exception was made early in the case of the Christians, it was because they refused to accept the principles of toleration; because they insisted that only they themselves knew truth—a principle abhorrent to the civilized Roman. . . .

" 'With all of Western culture under a single *polis*, with the cancer of religious and national particularism and exclusivism absent; with a high civilization in existence—why could not Man hold his gains?

" 'It was because, technologically, ancient Hellenism remained backward. It was because without a machine civilization, the price of leisure—and hence civilization and culture —for the few, was slavery for the many. Because the civilization could not find the means to bring comfort and ease to *all* the population.

" 'Therefore, the depressed classes turned to the other world, and to religions which spurned the material benefits of this world—so that science was made impossible in any true sense for over a millennium. And further, as the initial impetus of Hellenism waned, the Empire lacked the technological powers to beat back the barbarians. In fact, it was not till after 1500 A.D. that war became sufficiently a function of the industrial resources of a nation to enable the settled people to defeat invading tribesmen and nomads with ease. . . .

" 'Imagine, then, if somehow the ancient Greeks had learned just a hint of modern chemistry and physics. Imagine if the growth of the Empire had been accompanied by the growth of science, technology and industry. Imagine an Empire in which machinery replaced slaves, in which all men had a decent share of the world's goods, in which the legion became the armored column against which no barbarians could stand. Imagine an Empire which would therefore spread all over the world, *without* religious or national prejudices.

" 'An Empire of all men—all brothers—eventually all free. . . .

" 'If history could be changed. If that first great failure could have been prevented—' "

And I stopped at that point.

"Well?" said the Boss.

"Well," I said, "I think it isn't difficult to connect all that with the fact that Tywood blew an entire power plant in his anxiety to send something back to the past, while in his office safe we found sections of a chemistry textbook translated into Greek."

His face changed, while he considered.

Then he said heavily: "But nothing's happened."

"I know. But then I've been told by Tywood's student that it takes a day to move back a century in time. Assuming that ancient Greece was the target area, we have twenty centuries, hence twenty days."

"But can it be stopped?"

"*I* wouldn't know. Tywood might, but he's dead."

The enormity of it all hit me at once, deeper than it had the night before—

All humanity was virtually under sentence of death. And while that was merely horrible abstraction, the fact that reduced it to a thoroughly unbearable reality was that I was, too. And my wife, and my kid.

Further, it was a death without precedence. A ceasing to exist, and no more. The passing of a breath. The vanishing of a dream. The drift into eternal non-space and non-time of a shadow. I would not be dead at all, in fact. I would merely never have been born.

Or would I? Would I exist—my individuality—my ego—my soul, if you like? Another life? Other circumstances?

I thought none of that in words then. But if a cold knot in the stomach could ever speak under the circumstances, it would sound like that, I think.

The Boss moved in on my thoughts—hard.

"Then, we have about two and a half weeks. No time to lose. Come on."

I grinned with one side of my mouth: "What do we do? Chase the book?"

"No," he replied coldly, "but there are two courses of action we must follow. First, you may be wrong—altogether. All of this circumstantial reasoning may still represent a false lead, perhaps deliberately thrown before us, to cover up the real truth. That must be checked.

"Secondly, you may be right—but there may be some way of stopping the book: other than chasing it in a time machine, I mean. If so, we must find out how."

"I would just like to say, sir, if this is a false lead, only a madman would consider it a believable one. So suppose I'm right, and suppose there's no way of stopping it?"

"Then, young fellow, I'm going to keep pretty busy for two and a half weeks, and I'd advise you to do the same.

The time will pass more quickly that way."

Of course he was right.

"Where do we start?" I asked.

"The first thing we need is a list of all men and women on the government payroll under Tywood."

"Why?"

"Reasoning. Your specialty, you know. Tywood doesn't know Greek, I think we can assume with fair safety, so someone else must have done the translating. It isn't likely that anyone would do a job like that for nothing, and it isn't likely that Tywood would pay out of his personal funds— not on a professor's salary."

"He might," I pointed out, "have been interested in more secrecy than a government payroll affords."

"Why? Where was the danger? Is it a crime to translate a chemistry textbook into Greek? Who would ever deduce from that a plot such as you've described?"

It took us half an hour to turn up the name of Mycroft James Boulder, listed as "Consultant," and to find out that he was mentioned in the University Catalogue as Assistant Professor of Philosophy and to check by telephone that among his many accomplishments was a thorough knowledge of Attic Greek.

Which was a coincidence—because with the Boss reaching for his hat, the interoffice teletype clicked away and it turned out that Mycroft James Boulder was in the anteroom, at the end of a two-hour continuing insistence that he see the Boss.

The Boss put his hat back and opened his office door.

Professor Mycroft James Boulder was a gray man. His hair was gray and his eyes were gray. His suit was gray, too.

But most of all, his expression was gray; gray with a tension that seemed to twist at the lines in his thin face.

Boulder said, softly: "I've been trying for three days to get a hearing, sir, with a responsible man. I can get no higher than yourself."

"I may be high enough," said the Boss. "What's on your mind?"

"It is quite important that I be granted an interview with Professor Tywood."

"Do you know where he is?"

"I am quite certain that he is in government custody."

"Why?"

"Because I know that he was planning an experiment which would entail the breaking of security regulations. Events since, as nearly as I can make them out, flow naturally from the supposition that security regulations have indeed been broken. I can presume, then, that the experiment has at least been attempted. I must discover whether it has been successfully concluded."

"Professor Boulder," said the Boss, "I believe you can read Greek."

"Yes, I can,"—coolly.

"And have translated chemical texts for Professor Tywood on government money."

"Yes—as a legally employed consultant."

"Yet such translation, under the circumstances, constitutes a crime, since it makes you an accessory to Tywood's crime."

"You can establish a connection?"

"Can't you? Or haven't you heard of Tywood's notions on time travel, or . . . what do you call it . . . micro-temporal-translation?"

"Ah?" and Boulder smiled a little. "He's told you, then."

"No, he hasn't," said the Boss, harshly. "Professor Tywood is dead."

"What?" Then—"I don't believe you."

"He died of apoplexy. Look at this."

He had one of the photographs taken the first night in his wall safe. Tywood's face was distorted but recognizable—sprawled and dead.

Boulder's breath went in and out as if the gears were clogged. He stared at the picture for three full minutes by the electric clock on the wall. "Where is this place?" he asked.

"The Atomic Power Plant."

"Had he finished his experiment?"

The Boss shrugged: "There's no way of telling. He was dead when we found him."

Boulder's lips were pinched and colorless. "That must be determined, somehow. A commission of scientists must be established, and, if necessary, the experiment must be repeated—"

But the Boss just looked at him, and reached for a cigar. I've never seen him take longer—and when he put it down, curled in its unused smoke, he said: "Tywood wrote an article for a magazine twenty years ago—"

"Oh," and the professor's lips twisted, "is *that* what gave you your clue? You may ignore that. The man is only a physical scientist and knows nothing of either history or sociology. A schoolboy's dreams and nothing more."

"Then, you don't think sending your translation back will inaugurate a Golden Age, do you?"

"Of course not. Do you think you can graft the developments of two thousand years of slow labor onto a child society not ready for it? Do you think a great invention or a great scientific principle is born full-grown in the mind of a genius divorced from his cultural *milieu?* Newton's enunciation of the Law of Gravity was delayed for twenty years because the then-current figure for the Earth's diameter was wrong by ten percent. Archimedes almost discovered calculus, but failed because Arabic numerals, invented by some nameless Hindu or group of Hindus, were unknown to him.

"For that matter, the mere existence of a slave society in ancient Greece and Rome meant that machines could scarcely attract much attention—slaves being so much cheaper and more adaptable. And men of true intellect could scarcely be expected to spend their energies on devices intended for manual labor. Even Archimedes, the greatest engineer of antiquity, refused to publish any of his practical inventions —only mathematic abstractions. And when a young man asked Plato of what use geometry was, he was forthwith expelled from the Academy as a man with a mean, unphilosophic soul.

"Science does not plunge forward—it inches along in the directions permitted by the greater forces that mold society and which are in turn molded by society. And no great man advances but on the shoulders of the society that surrounds him—"

The Boss interrupted him at that point. "Suppose you tell us what your part in Tywood's work was, then. We'll take your word for it that history cannot be changed."

"Oh it can, but not purposefully— You see, when Tywood first requested my services in the matter of translating certain textbook passages into Greek, I agreed for the money involved. But he wanted the translation on parchment; he insisted on the use of ancient Greek terminology—the language of Plato, to use his words—regardless of how I had to twist the literal significance of passages, and he wanted it handwritten in rolls.

"I was curious. I, too, found his magazine article. It was difficult for me to jump to the obvious conclusion, since the achievements of modern science transcend the imaginings of philosophy in so many ways. But I learned the truth eventually, and it was at once obvious that Tywood's theory of changing history was infantile. There are twenty million variables for every instant of time, and no system of mathematics—no mathematic psychohistory, to coin a phrase—has yet been developed to handle that ocean of varying functions.

"In short, any variation of events two thousand years ago would change all subsequent history, but in *no predictable way.*"

The boss suggested, with a false quietness: "Like the pebble that starts the avalanche, right?"

"Exactly. You have some understanding of the situation, I see. I thought deeply for weeks before I proceeded, and then I realized how I must act—*must* act."

There was a low roar. The Boss stood up and his chair went over backward. He swung around his desk, and he had a hand on Boulder's throat. I was stepping out to stop him, but he waved me back—

He was only tightening the necktie a little. Boulder could still breathe. He had gone very white, and for all the time that the Boss talked, he restricted himself to just that—breathing.

And the Boss said: "Sure, I can see how you decided you must act. I know that some of you brain-sick philosophers think the world needs fixing. You want to throw the dice again and see what turns up. Maybe you don't even care if you're alive in the new setup—or that no one can possibly know what you've done. But you're going to create, just the same. You're going to give God another chance, so to speak.

"Maybe I just want to live—but the world could be worse. In twenty million different ways, it could be worse. A fellow named Wilder once wrote a play called *The Skin of Our Teeth.* Maybe you've read it. Its thesis was that Mankind survived by just that skin of their teeth. No, I'm not going to give you a speech about the Ice Age nearly wiping us out. I don't know enough. I'm not even going to talk about the Greeks winning at Marathon; the Arabs being defeated at Tours; the Mongols turning back at the last minute without even being defeated—because I'm no historian.

"But take the Twentieth Century. The Germans were stopped at the Marne twice in World War I. Dunkirk happened in World War II, and somehow the Germans were stopped at Moscow and Stalingrad. We could have used the atom bomb in the last war and we didn't, and just when it looked as if both sides would have to, the Great Compromise happened—just because General Bruce was delayed in taking off from the Ceylon airfield long enough to receive the message directly. One after the other, just like that, all through history—lucky breaks. For every 'if' that didn't come true that would have made wonder-men of all of us if it had, there were twenty 'ifs' that didn't come true that would have brought disaster to all of us if they had.

"You're gambling on that one-in-twenty chance—gambling every life on Earth. And you've succeeded, too, because Tywood *did* send that text back."

He ground out that last sentence, and opened his fist, so that Boulder could fall out and back into his chair.

And Boulder laughed.

"You fool," he gasped, bitterly, "How close you can be and yet how widely you can miss the mark. Tywood *did* send his book back, then? You are sure of that?"

"No chemical textbook in Greek was found on the scene," said the Boss, grimly, "and millions of calories of energy had disappeared. Which doesn't change the fact, however, that we have two and a half weeks in which to—make things interesting for you."

"Oh, nonsense. No foolish dramatics, please. Just listen to me, and try to understand. There were Greek philosophers once, named Leucippus and Democritus, who evolved an atomic theory. All matter, they said, was composed of atoms. Varieties of atoms were distinct and changeless and by their different combinations with each other formed the various substances found in nature. That theory was not the result of experiment or observation. It came into being, somehow, full-grown.

"The didactic Roman poet Lucretius, in his *'De Rerum Natura,'*—'On the Nature of Things'—elaborated on that theory and throughout manages to sound startlingly modern.

"In Hellenistic times, Hero built a steam engine and weapons of war became almost mechanized. The period has been referred to as an abortive mechanical age, which came to nothing because, somehow, it neither grew out of nor fitted into its social and economic *milieu*. Alexandrian science was a queer and rather inexplicable phenomenon.

"Then one might mention the old Roman legend about the books of the Sibyl that contained mysterious information direct from the gods—

"In other words, gentlemen, while you are right that any

change in the course of past events, however trifling, would have incalculable consequences, and while I· also believe that you are right in supposing that any random change is much more likely to be for the worse than for the better, I must point out that you are nevertheless wrong in your final conclusions.

"Because THIS *is the world in which the Greek chemistry text* WAS *sent back.*

"This has been a Red Queen's race, if you remember your 'Through the Looking Glass.' In the Red Queen's country, one had to run as fast as one could merely to stay in the same place. And so it was in this case! Tywood may have thought he was creating a new world, but it was I who prepared the translations, and I took care that only such passages as would account for the queer scraps of knowledge the ancients apparently got from nowhere would be included.

"And my only intention, for all my racing, was to stay in the same place."

Three weeks passed, three months; three years. Nothing happened. When nothing happens, you have no proof. We gave up trying to explain, and we ended, the Boss and I, by doubting it ourselves.

The case never ended. Boulder could not be considered a criminal without being considered a world savior as well, and vice versa. He was ignored. And in the end, the case was neither solved, nor closed out; merely put in a file all by itself, under the designation "?" and buried in the deepest vault in Washington.

The Boss is in Washington now; a big wheel. And I'm Regional Head of the Bureau.

Boulder is still assistant professor, though. Promotions are slow at the University.

THE END

"The Red Queen's Race," my fifty-eighth story, was the first to be written by Dr. Asimov.

In September I began another story, "Mother Earth," and submitted it to Campbell on October 12, 1948. After a comparatively small revision of the ending, he took that one, too.

27

Mother Earth

"But can you be certain? Are you sure that even a professional historian can always distinguish between victory and defeat?"

Gustav Stein, who delivered himself of that mocking question with a whiskered smile and a gentle wipe at the gray mustache from the neighborhood of which he had just removed an empty glass, was not an historian. He was a physiologist.

But his companion *was* an historian, and he accepted the gentle thrust with a smile of his own.

Stein's apartment was, for Earth, quite luxurious. It lacked the empty privacy of the Outer Worlds, of course, since from its window there stretched outward a phenomenon that belonged only to the home planet—a city. A large city, full of people, rubbing shoulders, mingling sweat—

Nor was Stein's apartment fitted with its own power and its own utility supply. It lacked even the most elementary quota of positronic robots. In short, it lacked the dignity of self-sufficiency, and like all things on Earth, it was merely part of a community, a pendant unit of a cluster, a portion of a mob.

But Stein was an Earthman by birth and used to it. And after all, by Earth standards the apartment was still luxurious.

It was just that looking outward through the same windows before which lay the city, one could see the stars and among them the Outer Worlds, where there were no cities but only gardens; where the lawns were streaks of emerald, where

Astounding Science Fiction, May 1949
Copyright © 1949 by Street & Smith Publications, Inc.

all human beings were kings, and where all good Earthmen earnestly and vainly hoped to go some day.

Except for a few who knew better—like Gustav Stein.

The Friday evenings with Edward Field belonged to that class of ritual which comes with age and quiet life. It broke the week pleasantly for two elderly bachelors, and gave them an innocuous reason to linger over the sherry and the stars. It took them away from the crudities of life, and, most of all, it let them talk.

Field, especially, as a lecturer, scholar and man of modest means quoted chapter and verse from his still uncompleted history of Terrestrian Empire.

"I wait for the last act," he explained. "Then I can call it the 'Decline and Fall of Empire' and publish it."

"You must expect the last act to come soon, then."

"In a sense, it has come already. It is just that it is best to wait for all to recognize that fact. You see, there are three times when an Empire or an Economic System or a Social Institution falls, you skeptic—"

Field paused for effect and waited patiently for Stein to say, "And those times are?"

"First," Field ticked off a right forefinger, "there is the time when just a little nub shows up that points an inexorable way to finality. It can't be seen or recognized until the finality arrives, when the original nub becomes visible to hindsight."

"And you can tell what that little nub is?"

"I think so, since I already have the advantage of a century and a half of hindsight. It came when the Sirian sector colony, Aurora, first obtained permission of the Central Government at Earth to introduce positronic robots into their community life. Obviously, looking back at it, the road was clear for the development of a thoroughly mechanized society based upon robot labor and not human labor. And it is this mechanization that has been and will yet be the deciding factor in the struggle between the Outer Worlds and Earth."

"It is?" murmured the physiologist. "How infernally clever you historians are. What and where is the second time the Empire fell?"

"The second point in time," and Field gently bent his right middle finger backward, "arrives when a signpost is raised for the expert so large and plain that it can be seen even without the aid of perspective. And that point has been passed, too, with the first establishment of an immigration quota against Earth by the Outer Worlds. The fact that Earth found itself unable to prevent an action so obviously detrimental to itself was a shout for all to hear, and that was fifty years ago."

"Better and better. And the third point?"

"The third point?" Down went the ring finger. "That is the least important. That is when the signpost becomes a wall with a huge 'The End' scrawled upon it. The only requirement for knowing that the end has come, then, is neither perspective nor training, but merely the ability to listen to the video."

"I take it that the third point in time has not yet come."

"Obviously not, or you would not need to ask. Yet it may come soon; for instance, if there is war."

"Do you think there will be?"

Field avoided commitment. "Times are unsettled, and a good deal of futile emotion is sweeping Earth on the immigration question. And if there should be a war, Earth would be defeated quickly and lastingly, and the wall would be erected."

"Can you be certain? Are you sure that even a professional historian can always distinguish between victory and defeat?"

Field smiled. He said: "You may know something I do not. For instance, they talk about something called the 'Pacific Project.'"

"I never heard of it." Stein refilled the two glasses, "Let us speak of other things."

He held up his glass to the broad window so that the far stars flickered rosily in the clear liquid and said: "To a happy ending to Earth's troubles."

Field held up his own, "To the Pacific Project."

Stein sipped gently and said: "But we drink to two different things."

"Do we?"

It is quite difficult to describe any of the Outer Worlds to a native Earthman, since it is not so much a description of a world that is required as a description of a state of mind. The Outer Worlds—some fifty of them, originally colonies, later dominions, later nations—differ extremely among themselves in a physical sense. But the state of mind is somewhat the same throughout.

It is something that grows out of a world not originally congenial to mankind, yet populated by the cream of the difficult, the different, the daring, the deviant.

If it is to be expressed in a word, that word is "individuality."

There is the world of Aurora, for instance, three parsecs from Earth. It was the first planet settled outside the Solar System, and represented the dawn of interstellar travel. Hence its name.

It had air and water to start with, perhaps, but on Earthly standards it was rocky and infertile. The plant life that did exist, sustained by a yellow-green pigment completely unrelated to chlorophyll and not as efficient, gave the comparatively fertile regions a decidedly bilious and unpleasant appearance to unaccustomed eyes. No animal life higher than unicellular, and the equivalent of bacteria as well, were present. Nothing dangerous, naturally, since the two biological systems, of Earth and Aurora, were chemically unrelated.

Aurora became, quite gradually, a patchwork. Grains and fruit trees came first; shrubs, flowers, and grass afterwards. Herds of livestock followed. And, as if it were necessary to prevent too close a copy of the mother planet, positronic robots also came to build the mansions, carve the landscapes, lay the power units. In short, to do the work, and turn the planet green and human.

There was the luxury of a new world and unlimited mineral resources. There was the splendid excess of atomic power laid out on new foundations with merely thousands, or, at most, millions, not billions, to service. There was the vast flowering of physical science, in worlds where there was room for it.

Take the home of Franklin Maynard, for instance, who, with his wife, three children, and twenty-seven robots, lived on an estate more than forty miles away, in distance, from the nearest neighbor. Yet by community-wave he could, if he wished, share the living room of any of the seventy-five million on Aurora—with each singly; with all simultaneously.

Maynard knew every inch of his valley. He knew just where it ended, sharply, and gave way to the alien crags, along whose undesirable slopes the angular, sharp leaves of native furze clung sullenly—as if in hatred of the softer matter that had usurped its place in the sun.

Maynard did not have to leave that valley. He was a

deputy in the Gathering, and a member of the Foreign Agents Committee, but he could transact all business but the most extremely essential, by community-wave, without ever sacrificing the precious privacy he had to have in a way no Earthman could understand.

Even the present business could be performed by community-wave. The man, for instance, who sat with him in his living room, was Charles Hijkman, and he, actually, was sitting in his own living room on an island in an artificial lake stocked with fifty varieties of fish, which happened to be twenty-five hundred miles distant, in space.

The connection was an illusion, of course. If Maynard were to reach out a hand, he could feel the invisible wall.

Even the robots were quite accustomed to the paradox, and when Hijkman raised a hand for a cigarette, Maynard's robot made no move to satisfy the desire, though a half-minute passed before Hijkman's own robot could do so.

The two men spoke like Outer Worlders, that is, stiffly and in syllables too clipped to be friendly, and yet certainly not hostile. Merely undefinably lacking in the cream—however sour and thin at times—of human sociability which is so forced upon the inhabitants of Earth's ant heaps.

Maynard said: "I have long wanted a private communion, Hijkman. My duties in the Gathering, this year—"

"Quite. That is understood. You are welcome now, of course. In fact, especially so, since I have heard of the superior nature of your grounds and landscaping. Is it true that your cattle are fed on imported grass?"

"I'm afraid that is a slight exaggeration. Actually, certain of my best milkers feed on Terrestrial imports during calving time, but such a procedure would be prohibitively expensive, I'm afraid, if made general. It yields quite extraordinary milk, however. May I have the privilege of sending you a day's output?"

"It would be most kind of you." Hijkman bent his head, gravely. "You must receive some of my salmon in return."

To a Terrestrial eye, the two men might have appeared much alike. Both were tall, though not unusually so for Aurora, where the average height of the adult male is six feet one and one half inches. Both were blond and hard-muscled, with sharp and pronounced features. Though neither was younger than forty, middle-age as yet sat lightly upon them.

So much for amenities. Without a change in tone, Maynard

proceeded to the serious purpose of his call.

He said: "The Committee, you know, is now largely engaged with Moreanu and his Conservatives. We would like to deal with them firmly, we of the Independents, that is. But before we can do so with the requisite calm and certainty, I would like to ask you certain questions."

"Why me?"

"Because you are Aurora's most important physicist."

Modesty is an unnatural attitude, and one which is only with difficulty taught to children. In an individualistic society it is useless and Hijkman was, therefore, unencumbered with it. He simply nodded objectively at Maynard's last words.

"And," continued Maynard, "as one of us. You are an Independent."

"I am a member of the Party. Dues-paying, but not very active."

"Nevertheless safe. Now, tell me, have you heard of the Pacific Project."

"The Pacific Project?" There was a polite inquiry in his words.

"It is something which is taking place on Earth. The Pacific is a Terrestrial ocean, but the name itself probably has no significance."

"I have never heard of it."

"I am not surprised. Few have, even on Earth. Our communion, by the way, is via tight-beam and nothing must go further."

"I understand."

"Whatever Pacific Project is—and our agents are extremely vague—it might conceivably be a menace. Many of those who on Earth pass for scientists seem to be connected with it. Also, some of Earth's more radical and foolish politicians."

"Hm-m-m. There was once something called the Manhattan Project."

"Yes," urged Maynard, "what about it?"

"Oh, it's an ancient thing. It merely occurred to me because of the analogy in names. The Manhattan Project was before the time of extra-terrestrial travel. Some petty war in the dark ages occurred, and it was the name given to a group of scientists who developed atomic power."

"Ah," Maynard's hand became a fist, "and what do you think the Pacific Project can do, then?"

Hijkman considered. Then, softly: "Do you think Earth is planning war?"

On Maynard's face there was a sudden expression of distaste. "Six billion people. Six billion half-apes, rather, jammed into one system to a near-explosion point, facing only some millions of us, total. Don't you think it is a dangerous situation?"

"Oh, numbers!"

"All right. Are we safe despite the numbers? Tell me. I'm only an administrator, and you're a physicist. *Can* Earth win a war in any way?"

Hijkman sat solemnly in his chair and thought carefully and slowly. Then he said: "Let us reason. There are three broad classes of methods whereby an individual or group can gain his ends against opposition. On an increasing level of subtlety, those three classes can be termed the physical, the biological, and the psychological.

"Now, the physical can be easily eliminated. Earth does not have an industrial background. It does not have a technical know-how. It has very limited resources. It lacks even a single outstanding physical scientist. So it is as impossible as anything in the Galaxy can be that they can develop any form of physico-chemical application that is not already known to the Outer Worlds. Provided, of course, that the conditions of the problem imply single-handed opposition on the part of Earth against any or all of the Outer Worlds. I take it that none of the Outer Worlds intends leaguing with Earth against us."

Maynard indicated violent opposition even to the suggestion, "No, no, no. There is no question of that. Put it out of your mind."

"Then, ordinary physical surprise weapons are inconceivable. It is useless to discuss it further."

"Then, what about your second class, the biological?"

Slowly, Hijkman lifted his eyebrows: "Now, that is less certain. Some Terrestrial biologists are quite competent, I am told. Naturally, since I am myself a physicist, I am not entirely qualified to judge this. Yet I believe that in certain restricted fields, they are still expert. In agricultural science, of course, to give an obvious example. And in bacteriology. Um-m-m——"

"Yes, what about bacteriological warfare?"

"A thought! But no, no, quite inconceivable. A teeming, constricted world such as Earth cannot afford to fight an open latticework of fifty sparse worlds with germs. They are infinitely more subject to epidemics, that is, to retaliation in kind. In fact, I would say that given our living conditions here on Aurora and on the other Outer Worlds, no contagious disease could really take hold. No, Maynard. You can check with a bacteriologist, but I think he'll tell you the same."

Maynard said: "And the third class?"

"The psychological? Now, that is unpredictable. And yet the Outer Worlds are intelligent and healthy communities and not amenable to ordinary propaganda, or for that matter to any form of unhealthy emotionalism. Now, I wonder—"

"Yes?"

"What if the Pacific Project is just that? I mean, a huge device to keep us off balance. Something top-secret, but meant to leak out in just the right fashion, so that the Outer Worlds yield a little to Earth, simply in order to play safe."

There was a longish silence.

"Impossible," burst out Maynard, angrily.

"*You* react properly. *You* hesitate. But I don't seriously press the interpretation. It is merely a thought."

A longer silence, then Hijkman spoke again: "Are there any other questions?"

Maynard started out of a reverie, "No . . . no—"

The wave broke off and a wall appeared where space had been a moment before.

Slowly, with stubborn disbelief, Franklin Maynard shook his head.

Ernest Keilin mounted the stairs with a feeling for all the past centuries. The building was old, cobwebbed with history. In once housed the Parliament of Man, and from it words went out that clanged throughout the stars.

It was a tall building. It soared—stretched—strained. Out and up to the stars, it reached; to the stars that had now turned away.

It no longer even housed the Parliament of Earth. That had now been switched to a newer, neoclassical building, one that imperfectly aped the architectural stylisms of the ancient pre-Atomic age.

Yet the older building still held its great name. Officially, it was still Stellar House, but it only housed the functionaries of a shriveled bureaucracy now.

Keilin got out at the twelfth floor, and the lift dropped quickly down behind him. The radiant sign said smoothly and quietly: Bureau of Information. He handed a letter to the receptionist. He waited. And eventually, he passed through the door which said, "L. Z. Cellioni—Secretary of Information."

Cellioni was little and dark. His hair was thick and black, his mustache thin and black. His teeth, when he smiled, were startlingly white and even—so he smiled often.

He was smiling now, as he rose and held out his hand. Keilin took it, then an offered seat, then an offered cigar.

Cellioni said: "I am very happy to see you, Mr. Keilin. It is kind of you to fly here from New York on such short notice."

Keilin curved the corners of his lips down and made a tiny gesture with one hand, deprecating the whole business.

"And now," continued Cellioni, "I presume you would like an explanation of all this."

"I wouldn't refuse one," said Keilin.

"Unfortunately, it is difficult to know exactly how to explain. As Secretary of Information, my position is difficult. I must safeguard the security and well-being of Earth and, at the same time, observe our traditional freedom of the press. Naturally, and fortunately, we have no censorship, but just as naturally, there are times when we could almost wish we did have."

"Is this," asked Keilin, "with reference to me? About censorship, I mean?"

Cellioni did not answer directly. Instead, he smiled again, slowly, and with a remarkable absence of joviality.

He said: "You, Mr. Keilin, have one of the most widely heard and influential telecasts on the video. Therefore, you are of peculiar interest to the government."

"The time is mine," said Keilin, stubbornly. "I pay for it. I pay taxes on the income I derive from it. I adhere to all the common-law rulings on taboos. So I don't quite see of what interest I can be to the government."

"Oh, you misunderstand me. It's my fault, I suppose, for not being clearer. You have committed no crime, broken no laws. I have only admiration for your journalistic ability. What I refer to is your editorial attitude at times."

"With respect to what?"

"With respect," said Cellioni, with a sudden harshness about his thin lips, "to our policy toward the Outer Worlds."

"My editorial attitude represents what I feel and think, Mr. Secretary."

"I allow this. You have your right to your feelings and your thoughts. Yet it is injudicious to spread them about nightly to an audience of half a billion."

"Injudicious, according to you, perhaps. But legal, according to anybody."

"It is sometimes necessary to place good of country above a strict and selfish interpretation of legality."

Keilin tapped his foot twice and frowned blackly.

"Look," he said, "put this frankly. What is it you want?"

The Secretary of Information spread his hands out before him. "In a word—co-operation! Really, Mr. Keilin, we can't have you weakening the will of the people. Do you appreciate the position of Earth? Six billions, and a declining food supply! It is insupportable! And emigration is the only solution. No patriotic Earthman can fail to see the justice of our position. No reasonable human being anywhere can fail to see the justice of it."

Keilin said: "I agree with your premise that the population problem is serious, but emigration is not the only solution. In fact, emigration is the one sure way of hastening destruction."

"Really? And why do you say that?"

"Because the Outer Worlds will not permit emigration, and you can force their hand by war only. *And we cannot win a war.*"

"Tell me," said Cellioni softly, "have *you* tried emigrating? It seems to me you could qualify. You are quite tall, rather light-haired, intelligent—"

The video-man flushed. He said, curtly: "I have hay fever."

"Well," and the secretary smiled, "then you must have good reason for disapproving their arbitrary genetic and racist policies."

Keilin replied with heat: "I won't be influenced by personal motives. I would disapprove their policies, if I qualified perfectly for emigration. But my disapproval would alter nothing. Their policies *are* their policies, and they can enforce them. Moreover, their policies have some reason even if wrong. Mankind is starting again on the Outer Worlds, and they—the ones who got there first—would like to eliminate some of the flaws of the human mechanism that have become obvious with time. A hay fever sufferer *is* a bad egg —genetically. A cancer prone even more so. Their prejudices against skin and hair colors are, of course, senseless, but I can grant that they are interested in uniformity and homogeneity. And as for Earth, we can do much even without the help of the Outer Worlds."

"For instance, what?"

"Positronic robots and hydroponic farming should be introduced, and—most of all—birth control must be instituted. An intelligent birth control, that is, based on firm psychiatric principles intended to eliminate the psychotic trends, congenital infirmities—"

"As they do in the Outer Worlds—"

"Not at all. I have mentioned no racist principles. I talk only of mental and physical infirmities that are held in common by all ethnic and racial groups. And most of all, births must be held below deaths until a healthful equilibrium is reached."

Celloni said, grimly: "We lack the industrial techniques and the resources to introduce a robot-hydroponic technology in anything less than five centuries. Furthermore, the traditions of Earth, as well as current ethical beliefs, forbid robot labor and false foods. Most of all, they forbid the slaughter of unborn children. Now, come, Keilin, we can't have you pouring this out over video. It won't work: it distracts the attention; it weakens the will."

Keilin broke in, impatiently: "Mr. Secretary, do you want war?"

"Do I *want* war? That is an impudent question."

"Then, who are the policy-makers in the government who *do* want war? For instance, who is responsible for the calculated rumor of the Pacific Project?"

"The Pacific Project? And where did you hear of that?"

"My sources are my secret."

"Then, I'll tell you. You heard of this Pacific Project from Moreanu of Aurora on his recent trip to Earth. We know more about you than you suppose, Mr. Keilin."

"I believe that, but I do not admit that I received information from Moreanu. Why do you think I could get information from him? Is it because he was deliberately allowed to learn of this piece of trumpery?"

"Trumpery?"

"Yes. I think Pacific Project is a fake. A fake meant to inspire confidence. I think the government plans to let the so-called secret leak out in order to strengthen its war policy. It is part of a war of nerves on Earth's own people, and it will be the ruin of Earth in the end.

"And I will take this theory of mine to the people."

"You will not, Mr. Keilin," said Cellioni, quietly.

"I will."

"Mr..Keilin, your friend, Ion Moreanu is having his troubles on Aurora, perhaps for being too friendly with you. Take care that you do not have equal trouble for being too friendly with him."

"I'm not worried." The video man laughed shortly, lunged to his feet and strode to the door.

Keilin smiled very gently when he found the door blocked by two large men: "You mean, I am under arrest right now."

"Exactly," said Cellioni.

"On what charge?"

"We'll think of some later."

Keilin left—under escort.

On Aurora, the mirror image of the afore-described events was taking place, and on a larger scale.

The Foreign Agents Committee of the Gathering had been meeting now for days—ever since the session of the Gathering in which Ion Moreanu and his Conservative Party made their great bid to force a vote of no confidence. That it had failed was in part due to the superior political generalship of the Independents, and in some part due to the activity of this same Foreign Agents Committee.

For months now, the evidence had been accumulating, and when the vote of confidence turned out to be sizably in favor of the Independents, the Committee was able to strike in its own way.

Moreanu was subpoenaed in his own home, and placed under house arrest. Although this procedure of house arrest was not, under the circumstances, legal—a fact emphatically pointed out by Moreanu—it was nevertheless successfully accomplished.

For three days Moreanu was cross-examined thoroughly, in polite, even tones that scarcely ever veered from unemotional curiosity. The seven inquisitors of the Committee took turns in questioning, but Moreanu had respite only for ten-minute intervals during the hours in which the Committee sat.

After three days, he showed the effects. He was hoarse with demanding that he be faced with his accusers; weary with insisting that he be informed of the exact nature of the charges; throat-broken with shouting against the illegality of the procedure.

The Committee finally read statements at him—

"Is this true or not? Is this true or not?"

Moreanu could merely shake his head wearily as the structure spidered about him.

He challenged the competency of the evidence and was smoothly informed that the proceedings constituted a Committee Investigation and not a trial—

The chairman clapped his gavel, finally. He was a broad man of tremendous purpose. He spoke for an hour in his final summing up of the results of the inquiry, but only a relatively short portion of it need be quoted.

He said: "If you had merely conspired with others on Aurora, we could understand you, even forgive you. Such a fault would have been held in common with many ambitious men in history. It is not that at all. What horrifies us and removes all pity is your eagerness to consort with the disease-ridden, ignorant and subhuman remnants of Earth.

"You, the accused, stand here under a heavy weight of evidence showing you to have conspired with the worst elements of Earth's mongrel population—".

The chairman was interrupted by an agonized cry from Moreanu, "But the motive! What motive can you possibly attribute—"

The accused was pulled back into his seat. The chairman pursed his lips and departed from the slow gravity of his prepared speech to improvise a bit.

"It is not," he said, "for this Committee to go into your motives. We have shown the facts of the case. The Committee *does* have evidence—" He paused, and looked along the line of the members to the right and the left, then continued. "I think I may say that the Committee has evidence that points to your intentions to use Earth man power to engineer a coup that would leave you dictator over Aurora. But since the evidence has not been used, I will go no further into that, except to say that such a consummation is not inconsistent with your character as displayed at these hearings."

He went back to his speech. "Those of us who sit here have heard, I think, of something termed the 'Pacific Project,' which, according to rumors, represents an attempt on the part of Earth to retrieve its lost dominions.

"It is needless to emphasize here that any such attempt must be doomed to failure. And yet defeat for us is not entirely inconceivable. One thing can cause us to stumble, and that one thing is an unsuspected internal weakness. Genetics is, after all, still an imperfect science. Even with twenty generations behind us, undesirable traits may crop up at scattered points, and each represents a flaw in the steel shield of Aurora's strength.

"*That* is the Pacific Project—the use of our own criminals and traitors against us; and if they can find such in our inner councils, the Earthmen might even succeed.

"The Foreign Agents Committee exists to combat that threat. In the accused, we touch the fringes of the web. We must go on—"

The speech did, at any rate.

When it was concluded, Moreanu, pale, wide-eyed, pounded his fist, "I demand my say—"

"The accused may speak," said the chairman.

Moreanu rose and looked about him for a long moment. The room, fitted for an audience of seventy-five million by Community Wave, was unattended. There were the inquisitors, legal staff, official recorders— And with him, in the actual flesh, his guards.

He would have done better with an audience. To whom could he otherwise appeal? His glance fled hopelessly from each face it touched, but could find nothing better.

"First," he said, "I deny the legality of this meeting. My constitutional rights of privacy and individuality have been denied. I have been tried by a group without standing as a court, by individuals convinced, in advance, of my guilt. I have been denied adequate opportunity to defend myself. In fact, I have been treated throughout as an already convicted criminal requiring only sentence.

"I deny, completely and without reservation, that I have been engaged in any activity detrimental to the state or tending to subvert any of its fundamental institutions.

"I accuse, vigorously and unreservedly, this Committee of deliberately using its powers to win political battles. I am guilty not of treason, but of disagreement. I disagree with a policy dedicated to the destruction of the larger part of the human race for reasons that are trivial and inhumane.

"Rather than destruction, we owe assistance to these men who are condemned to a harsh, unhappy life solely because it was our ancestors and not theirs who happened to reach the Outer Worlds first. With our technology and resources, they can yet re-create and redevelop—"

The chairman's voice rose above the intense near-whisper of Moreanu, "You are out of order. The Committee is quite prepared to hear any remarks you make in your own defense, but a sermon on the rights of Earthmen is outside the legitimate realm of the discussion."

The hearings were formally closed. It was a great political victory for the Independents; all would agree to that. Of the members of the Committee, only Franklin Maynard was not completely satisfied. A small, nagging doubt remained.

He wondered—

Should he try, one last time? Should he speak once more and then no more to that queer little monkey ambassador from Earth? He made his decision quickly and acted upon it instantly. Only a pause to arrange a witness, since even for himself an unwitnessed private communion with an Earthman might be dangerous.

Luiz Moreno, Ambassador to Aurora from Earth, was, to put not too fine a point on it, a miserable figure of a man. And that wasn't exactly an accident. On the whole, the foreign diplomats of Earth tended to be dark, short, wizen, or weakly—or all four.

That was only self-protection, since the Outer Worlds exerted strong attraction for any Earthman. Diplomats exposed to the allure of Aurora, for instance, could not but be exceedingly reluctant to return to Earth. Worse, and more dangerous, exposure meant a growing sympathy with the demigods of the stars and a growing alienation from the slum-dwellers of Earth.

Unless, of course, the ambassador found himself rejected. Unless he found himself somewhat despised. And then, no more faithful servant of Earth could be imagined, no man less subject to corruption.

The Ambassador from Earth was only five foot two, with a bald head and receding forehead, a pinkish affectation of beard and red-rimmed eyes. He was suffering from a slight cold, the occasional results whereof he smothered in a handkerchief. And yet, withal, he was a man of intellect.

To Franklin Maynard, the sight and sound of the Earthman was distressing. He grew queasy at each cough and shuddered when the ambassador wiped his nose.

Maynard said: "Your excellency, we commune at my request because I wish to inform you that the Gathering has decided to ask your recall by your government."

"That is kind of you, councilor. I had an inkling of this. And for what reason?"

"The reason is not within the bounds of discussion. I believe it is the prerogative of a sovereign state to decide for itself whether a foreign representative shall be *persona grata* or not. Nor do I think you really need enlightenment on this matter."

"Very well, then." The ambassador paused to wield his handkerchief and murmur an apology. "Is that all?"

Maynard said: "Not quite. There are matters I would like to mention. Remain!"

The ambassador's reddened nostrils flared a bit, but he smiled, and said: "An honor."

"Your world, excellency," said Maynard, superciliously, "displays a certain belligerence of late that we on Aurora find most annoying and unnecessary. I trust that you will find your return to Earth at this point a convenient opportunity to use your influence against further displays such as recently occurred in New York, where two Aurorans were man-handled by a mob. The payment of an indemnity may not be enough the next time."

"But that is emotional overflow, Councilor Maynard. Surely, you cannot consider youngsters shouting in the streets to be adequate representations of belligerence."

"It is backed by your government's actions in many ways. The recent arrest of Mr. Ernest Keilin, for instance."

"Which is a purely domestic affair," said the ambassador, quietly.

"But not one to demonstrate a reasonable spirit toward the Outer Worlds. Keilin was one of the few Earthmen who until recently could yet make their voices heard. He was intelligent enough to realize that no divine right protects the inferior man simply because he is inferior."

The ambassador arose: "I am not interested in Auroran theories on racial differences."

"A moment. Your government may realize that much of their plans have gone awry with the arrest of your agent, Moreanu. Stress the fact that we of Aurora are much wiser than we have been prior to this arrest. It may serve to give them pause."

"Is Moreanu *my* agent? Really, councilor, if I am dis-accredited, I shall leave. But surely the loss of diplomatic immunity does not affect my personal immunity as an honest man from charges of espionage."

"Isn't that your job?"

"Do Aurorans take it for granted that espionage and diplomacy are identical? My government will be glad to hear it. We shall take appropriate precautions."

"Then, you defend Moreanu? You deny that he has been working for Earth?"

"I defend only myself. As to Moreanu, I am not stupid enough to say anything."

"Why stupid?"

"Wouldn't a defense by myself be but another indictment against him? I neither accuse nor defend him. Your government's quarrel with Moreanu, like my government's with Keilin—whom you, by the way, are most suspiciously eager to defend—is an internal affair. I will leave now."

The communion broke, and almost instantly the wall faded again. Hijkman was looking thoughtfully at Maynard.

"What do you think of him?" asked Maynard, grimly.

"Disgraceful that such a travesty of humanity should walk Aurora, I think."

"I agree with you, and yet . . . and yet—"

"Well?"

"And yet I can almost find myself able to think that he is the master and that we dance to his piping. You know of Moreanu?"

"Of course."

"Well, he will be convicted, sent to an asteroid. His party will be broken. Offhand, anyone would say that such actions represent a horrible defeat for Earth."

"Is there doubt in your mind that such is the case?"

"I'm not sure. Committee Chairman Hond insisted on airing his theory that Pacific Project was the name Earth gave to a device for using internal traitors on the Outer Worlds. But I don't think so. I'm not sure the facts fit that. For instance, where did we get our evidence against Moreanu?"

"I certainly can't say."

"Our agents, in the first place. But how did they get it? The evidence was a little *too* convincing. Moreanu could have guarded himself better—"

Maynard hesitated. He seemed to be attempting a blush, and failing. "Well, to put it quickly, I think it was the Terrestrian Ambassador who somehow presented us with the most evidence. I think that he played on Moreanu's sympathy for Earth first to befriend him and then to betray him."

"Why?"

"I don't know. To insure war, perhaps—with this Pacific Project waiting for us."

"I don't believe it."

"I know. I have no proof. Nothing but suspicion. The Committee wouldn't believe me either. It seemed to me, perhaps, that a last talk with the ambassador might reveal something, but his mere appearance antagonizes me, and I find I spend most of my time trying to remove him from my sight."

"Well, you are becoming emotional, my friend. It is a disgusting weakness. I hear that you have been appointed a delegate to the Interplanetary Gathering at Hesperus. I congratulate you."

"Thanks," said Maynard, absently.

Luiz Moreno, ex-Ambassador to Aurora, had been glad to return to Earth. He was away from the artificial landscapes that seemed to have no life of their own, but to exist only by virtue of the strong will of their possessors. Away from the too-beautiful men and women and from their ubiquitous, brooding robots.

He was back to the hum of life and the shuffle of feet; the brushing of shoulders and the feeling of breath in the face.

Not that he was able to enjoy these sensations entirely. The first days had been spent in lively conferences with the heads of Earth's government.

In fact, it was not till nearly a week had passed, that an hour came in which he could consider himself truly relaxed.

He was in the rarest of all appurtenances of Terrestrial Luxury—a roof garden. With him was Gustav Stein, the quite obscure physiologist, who was, nevertheless, one of the prime movers of the Plan, known to rumor as the Pacific Project.

"The confirmatory tests," said Moreno, with an almost dreadful satisfaction, "all check so far, do they not?"

"So far. *Only* so far. We have miles to go."

"Yet they will continue to go well. To one who has lived on Aurora for nearly a year, as I have, there can be no doubt but that we're on the right track."

"Um-m-m. Nevertheless, I will go only by the laboratory reports."

"And quite rightly." His little body was almost stiff with gloating. "Some day, it will be different. Stein, you have not met these men, these Outer Worlders. You may have come across the tourists, perhaps, in their special hotels, or riding through the streets in inclosed cars, equipped with the purest of private, air-conditioned atmospheres for their well-bred nostrils; observing the sights through a movable periscope and shuddering away from the touch of an Earthman.

"But you have not met them on their own world, secure in their own sickly, rotting greatness. Go, Stein, and be despised a while. Go, and find how well you can compete with their own trained lawns as something to be gently trod upon.

"And yet, when I pulled the proper cords, Ion Moreanu fell—Ion Moreanu, the only man among them with the capacity to understand the workings of another's mind. It is the crisis that we have passed now. We front a smooth path now."

Satisfaction! Satisfaction!

"As for Keilin," he said suddenly, more to himself than to Stein, "he can be turned loose now. There's little he can say, hereafter, that can endanger anything. In fact, I have an idea. The Interplanetary Conference opens on Hesperus within the month. He can be sent to report the meeting. It will be an earnest of our friendliness—and keep him away for the summer. I think it can be arranged."

It was.

Of all the Outer Worlds, Hesperus was the smallest, the latest settled, the furthest from Earth. Hence the name. In a physical sense, it was not best suited to a great diplomatic gathering, since its facilities were small. For instance, the available community-wave network could not possibly be stretched to cover all the delegates, secretarial staff, and administrators necessary in a convocation of fifty planets. So meetings in person were arranged in buildings impressed for the purpose.

Yet there was a symbolism in the choice of meeting place that escaped practically nobody. Hesperus, of all the Worlds, was furthest removed from Earth. But the spatial distance—one hundred parsecs or more—was the least of it. The important point was that Hesperus had been colonized not by Earthmen, but by men from the Outer World of Faunus.

It was therefore of the second generation, and so it had no "Mother Earth." Earth to it was but a vague grandmother, lost in the stars.

As is usual in all such gatherings, little work is actually done on the session floors. That space is reserved for the official soundings of whatever is primarily intended for home ears. The actual swapping and horse-trading takes place in the lobbies and at the lunch-tables and many an irresolvable conflict has softened over the soup and vanished over the nuts.

And yet particular difficulties were present in this particular case. Not in all worlds was the community-wave as paramount and all-pervading as it was on Aurora, but it was prominent in all. It was, therefore, with a certain sense of outrage and loss that the tall, dignified men found it necessary to approach one another in the flesh, without the comforting privacy of the invisible wall between, without the warm knowledge of the breakswitch at their fingertips.

They faced one another in uneasy semi-embarrassment and tried not to watch one another eat; tried not to shrink at the unmeant touch. Even robot service was rationed.

Ernest Keilin, the only accredited video-representative from Earth, was aware of some of these matters only in the vague way they are described here. A more precise insight he could not have. Nor could anyone brought up in a society where human beings exist only in the plural, and where a house need only be deserted to be feared.

So it was that certain of the most subtle tensions escaped him at the formal dinner party given by the Hesperian government during the third week of the conference. Other tensions, however, did not pass him by.

The gathering after the dinner naturally fell apart into little groups. Keilin joined the one that contained Franklin Maynard of Aurora. As the delegate of the largest of the Worlds, he was naturally the most newsworthy.

Maynard was speaking casually between sips at the tawny Hesperian cocktail in his hand. If his flesh crawled slightly at the closeness of the others, he masked the feeling masterfully.

"Earth," he said, "is, in essence, helpless against us if we avoid unpredictable military adventures. Economic unity is actually a necessity, if we intend to avoid such adventures. Let Earth realize to how great an extent her economy depends upon us, on the things that we alone can supply her, and there will be no talk of living space. And if we are united, Earth would never dare attack. She will exchange her barren longings for atomic motors—or not, as she pleases."

And he turned to regard Keilin with a certain hauteur as the other found himself stung to comment:

"But your manufactured goods, councilor—I mean those you ship to Earth—they are not *given* us. They are exchanged for agricultural products."

Maynard smiled silkily. "Yes, I believe the delegate from Tethys has mentioned that fact at length. There is a delusion prevalent among some of us that only Terrestrial seeds grow properly—"

He was interrupted calmly by another, who said: "Now, I am not from Tethys, but what you mention is not a delusion. I grow rye on Rhea, and I have never yet been able to duplicate Terrestrial bread. It just hasn't got the same taste." He addressed the audience in general, "In fact, I imported half a dozen Terrestrians five years back on agricultural laborer visas so they could oversee the robots. Now, they can do wonders with the land, you know. Where they spit, corn grows fifteen feet high. Well, that helped a little. And using Terrestrian seed helped. But even if you grow Terrestrian grain, its seed won't hold the next year."

"Has your soil been tested by your government's agricultural department?" asked Maynard.

The Rhean grew haughty in his turn: "No better soil in the sector. And the rye is top-grade. I even sent a hundredweight down to Earth for nutritional clearance, and it came back with full marks." He rubbed one side of his chin, thoughtfully: "It's flavor I'm talking about. Doesn't seem to have the right—"

Maynard made an effort to dismiss him. "Flavor is dispensable temporarily. They'll be coming to us on our terms, these little-menhordes of Earth, when they feel the pinch. We give up only this mysterious flavor, but they will have to give up atom-powered engines, farm machinery, and ground cars. It wouldn't be a bad idea, in fact, to attempt to get along without the Terrestrian flavors you are so concerned about. Let us appreciate the flavor of our home-grown products instead—which could stand comparison if we gave it a chance."

"That so?" the Rhean smiled. "I notice you're smoking Earth-grown tobacco."

"A habit I can break if I have to."

"Probably by giving up smoking. I wouldn't use Outer World tobacco for anything but killing mosquitoes."

He laughed a trifle too boisterously, and left the group. Maynard stared after him, a little pinch-nosed.

To Keilin, the little byplay over rye and tobacco brought a certain satisfaction. He regarded such personalities as the tiny reflection of certain Galactopolitical realities. Tethys and Rhea were the largest planets in the Galactic south, as Aurora was the largest in the Galactic north. All three planets were identically racist, identically exclusivist. Their views on

Earth were similar and completely compatible. Ordinarily, one would think that there was no room to quarrel.

But Aurora was the oldest of the Outer Worlds, the most advanced, the strongest militarily—and, therefore, aspired to a sort of moral leadership of all the Worlds. That was sufficient in itself to arouse opposition, and Rhea and Tethys served as focal points for those who did not recognize Auroran leadership.

Keilin was somberly grateful for that situation. If Earth could but lean her weight properly, first in one direction, then in the other, an ultimate split, or even fragmentation—

He eyed Maynard cautiously, almost furtively, and wondered what effect this would have on the next day's debate. Already, the Auroran was more silent than was quite polite.

And then some under-secretary or sub-official threaded his way through the clusters of guests in finicking fashion, and beckoned to Maynard.

Keilin's following eyes watched the Auroran retreat with the newcomer, watched him listen closely, mouth a startled "What!" that was quite visible to the eye, though too far off to be heard, and then reach for a paper that the other handed him.

And as a result, the next day's session of the conference went entirely differently than Keilin would have predicted.

Keilin discovered the details in the evening video-casts. The Terrestrian government, it seemed, had sent a note to all the governments attending the conference. It warned each one bluntly that any agreement among them in military or economic affairs would be considered an unfriendly act against Earth and that it would be met with appropriate countermeasures. The note denounced Aurora, Tethys, and Rhea all equally. It accused them of being engaged in an imperialist conspiracy against Earth, and so on—and on—and on.

"Fools!" gritted Keilin, all but butting his head against the wall out of sheer chagrin. "Fools! Fools! Fools!" And his voice died away still muttering the same, one word.

The next session of the conference was well and early attended by a set of angry delegates who were only too eager to grind into nothingness the disagreements still outstanding. When it ended, all matters concerning trade between Earth and the Outer Worlds had been placed in the hands of a commission with plenary powers.

Not even Aurora could have expected so complete and easy a victory, and Keilin, on his way back to Earth, longed for his voice to reach the video, so that it could be to others, and not to himself only, that he could shout his disgust.

Yet, on Earth, some men smiled.

Once back on Earth, the voice of Keilin slowly swirled under and down—lost in the noisier clamor that shouted for action.

His popularity sank in proportion as trade restrictions grew. Slowly, the Outer Worlds drew the noose tighter. First, they instituted a strict application of a new system of export licensing. Secondly, they banned the export to Earth of all materials capable of being "used in a war effort." And finally they applied a very broad interpretation indeed of what could be considered usable in such a connection.

Imported luxuries—and imported necessities, too, for that matter—vanished or priced themselves upwards out of the reach of all but the very few.

So the people marched, and the voices shouted and the banners swung about in the sunlight, and the stones flew at the consulates—

Keilin shouted hoarsely and felt as if he were going mad.

Until suddenly, Luiz Moreno, quite of his own accord, offered to appear on Keilin's program and submit to unrestricted questioning in his capacity as ex-Ambassador to Aurora and present Secretary without Portfolio.

To Keilin it had had all the possibilities of a rebirth. He knew Moreno—no fool, he. With Moreno on his program, he was assured an audience as great as his greatest. With Moreno answering questions, certain misapprehensions might be removed, certain confusions might be straightened. The mere fact that Moreno wished to use his—*his*—program as sounding-board might well mean that already a more pliant and sensible foreign policy might have been decided upon. Perhaps Maynard was correct, and the pinch was being felt and was working as predicted.

The list of questions had, of course, been submitted to Moreno in advance, but the ex-Ambassador had indicated that he would answer all of them, and any follow-up questions that might seem necessary.

It seemed quite ideal. Too ideal, perhaps, but only a criminal fool could worry over minutiae at this point.

There was an adequate ballyhoo—and when they faced

one another across the little table, the red needle that indicated the number of video sets drawing power on that channel hovered well over the two hundred million mark. And there was an average of 2.7 listeners per video set. Now the theme; the official introduction.

Keilin rubbed his cheek slowly, as he waited for the signal. Then, he began:

Q. Secretary Moreno, the question which interests all Earth at the moment, concerns the possibility of war. Suppose we start with that. Do you think there will be war?

A. If Earth is the only planet to be considered, I say: No, definitely not. In its history, Earth has had too much war, and has learned many times over how little can be gained by it.

Q. You say, "If Earth is the only planet to be considered—" Do you imply that factors outside our control will bring war?

A. I do not say "will"; but I could say "may." I cannot, of course speak for the Outer Worlds. I cannot pretend to know their motivations and intentions at this critical moment in Galactic history. They *may* choose war. I hope not. If so be that they do, however, we will defend ourselves. But in any case, *we* will never attack; *we* will not strike the first blow.

Q. Am I right in saying, then, that in your opinion there are no basic differences between Earth and the Outer Worlds which cannot be solved by negotiation?

A. You certainly are. If the Outer Worlds were sincerely desirous of a solution, no disagreement between them and us could long exist.

Q. Does that include the question of immigration?

A. Definitely. Our own role in the matter is clear and beyond reproach. As matters stand, two hundred million human beings now occupy ninety-five percent of the available land in the universe. Six billions—that is, ninety-seven percent of all mankind—are squeezed into the other five percent. Such a situation is obviously unjust and, worse, unstable. Yet Earth, in the face of such injustice, has always been willing to treat this problem as soluble by degrees. It is still so willing. We should agree to reasonable quotas and reasonable restrictions. Yet the Outer Worlds have refused to discuss this matter. Over a space of five decades, they have rebuffed all efforts on the part of Earth to open negotiations.

Q. If such an attitude on the part of the Outer Worlds continues, do you *then* think there will be war?

A. I cannot believe that this attitude will continue. Our

government will not cease hoping that the Outer Worlds will eventually reconsider their stand on the matter; that their sense of justice and right is not dead, but only sleeping.

Q. Mr. Secretary, let us pass on to another subject. Do you think that the United Worlds Commission set up by the Outer Worlds recently to control trade with Earth represents a danger to peace?

A. In the sense that its actions indicate a desire on the part of the Outer Worlds to isolate Earth, and to weaken it economically, I can say that it does.

Q. To what actions do you refer, sir?

A. To its actions in restricting interstellar trade with Earth to the point where, in credit values, the total stands now at less than ten percent of what it did three months ago.

Q. But do such restrictions really represent an economic danger to Earth? For instance, is it not true that trade with the Outer Worlds represents an almost insignificant part of total Terrestrial trade? And is it not true that the importations from the Outer Worlds reach only a tiny minority of the population at best?

A. Your questions now are representative of a profound fallacy which is very common among our isolationists. In credit values, it is true that interstellar trade represents only five percent of our total trade, but ninety-five percent of our atomic engines are imported. Eighty percent of our thorium, sixty-five percent of our cesium, sixty percent of our molybdenum and tin are imported. The list can be extended almost indefinitely, and it is quite easy to see that the five percent is an extremely important, a vital, five percent. Furthermore, if a large manufacturer receives a shipment of atomic steel-shapers from Rhea, it does not follow that the benefit redounds only to him. Every man on Earth who uses steel implements or objects manufactured by steel implements benefits.

Q. But is it not true that the current restrictions on Earth's interstellar trade have cut our grain and cattle exports to almost nothing? And far from harming Earth, isn't this really a boon to our own hungry people?

A. This is another serious fallacy. That Earth's good food supply is tragically inadequate is true. The government would be the last to deny it. But our food exports do not represent any serious drain upon this supply. Less than one fifth of one percent of Earth's food is exported, and in return we obtain, for instance, fertilizers and farm machinery which more than make up for that small loss by increasing agricultural efficiency. Therefore, by buying less food from us, the Outer Worlds are engaged, in effect, in cutting our already inadequate food supply.

Q. Are you ready to admit, then, Secretary Moreno, that at least part of the blame for this situation should rest with Earth itself? In other words, we come to my next question: Was it not a diplomatic blunder of the first magnitude for the government to issue its inflammatory note denouncing the intentions of the Outer Worlds before those intentions had been made clear at the Interplanetary Conference?

A. I think those intentions were quite clear at the time.

Q. I beg pardon, sir, but I was at the conference. At the time the note was issued, there was almost a stalemate among the Outer World delegates. Those of Rhea and Tethys strongly opposed economic action against Earth, and there was considerable chance that Aurora and its block might have been defeated. Earth's note ended that possibility instantly.

A. Well, what is your question, Mr. Keilin?

Q. In view of my statements, do you or do you not think Earth's note to have been a criminal error of diplomacy which can now be made up only by a policy of intelligent conciliation?

A. You use strong language. However, I cannot answer the question directly, since I do not agree with your major premise. I cannot believe that the delegates of the Outer Worlds could behave in the manner you describe. In the first place, it is well known that the Outer Worlds are proud of their boast that the percentage of insanity, psychoses, and even relatively minor maladjustments of personality are almost at the vanishing point in their society. It is one of their strongest arguments against Earth, that we have more psychiatrists than plumbers and yet are more pinched for want of the former. The delegates to the conference represented the best of this so-stable society. And now you would have me believe that these demigods would, in a moment of pique, have reversed their opinions and instituted a major change in the economic policy of fifty worlds. I cannot believe them capable of such childish and perverse activity, and must therefore insist that any action they took was based not upon any note from Earth, but upon motivations that go deeper.

Q. But I saw the effect upon them with my own eyes, sir. Remember, they were being scolded in what they considered to be insolent language from an inferior people. There can be no doubt, sir, that as a whole, the men of the Outer Worlds are a remarkably stable people, despite your sarcasm, but their attitude toward Earth represents a weak point in this stability.

A. Are you asking me questions, or are you defending the racist views and policies of the Outer Worlds?

Q. Well, accepting your viewpoint that Earth's note did no harm, what good could it have done? Why should it have been sent?

A. I think we were justified in presenting our side of the question before the bar of Galactic public opinion. I believe we have exhausted the subject. What is your next question, please? It is the last, isn't it?

Q. It is. It has recently been reported that the Terrestrian government will take stern measures against those dealing in smuggling operations. Is this consistent with the government's view that lowered trade relations are detrimental to Earth's welfare?

A. Our primary concern is peace, and not our own immediate welfare. The Outer Worlds have adopted certain trade restrictions. We disapprove of them, and consider them a great injustice. Nevertheless, we shall adhere to them, so that no planet may say that we have given the slightest pretext for hostilities. For instance, I am privileged to announce here for the first time that in the past month, five ships, traveling under false Earth registry, were stopped while being engaged in the smuggling of Outer World matériel into Earth. Their goods were confiscated and their personnel imprisoned. This is an earnest of our good intentions.

Q. Outer World ships?

A. Yes. But traveling under false Earth registry, remember.

Q. And the men imprisoned are citizens of the Outer Worlds?

A. I believe so. However, they were breaking not only our laws, but those of the Outer Worlds as well, and therefore doubly forfeited their interplanetary rights. I think the interview had better close, now.

Q. But this—

It was at this point that the broadcast came to a sudden end. The conclusion of Keilin's last sentence was never heard by anyone but Moreno. It ended like this:

"—means war."

But Luiz Moreno was no longer on the air. So as he drew

on his gloves, he smiled and, with infinite meaning, shrugged his shoulders in a little gesture of indifference.

There were no witnesses to that shrug.

The Gathering at Aurora was still in session. Franklin Maynard had dropped out for the moment in utter weariness. He faced his son, whom he now saw for the first time in naval uniform.

"At least *you're* sure of what will happen, aren't you?"

In the young man's response, there was no weariness at all, no apprehension; nothing but utter satisfaction. "This is it, dad!"

"Nothing bothers you, then? You don't think we've been maneuvered into this."

"Who cares if we have? It's Earth's funeral."

Maynard shook his head: "But you realize that we've been put in the wrong. The Outer World citizens they hold are law-breakers. Earth is within its rights."

His son frowned: "I hope you're not going to make statements like that to the Gathering, dad. I don't see that Earth is justified at all. All right, what if smuggling was going on? It was just because some Outer Worlders are willing to pay black market prices for Terrestrial food. If Earth had any sense, she could look the other way, and everyone would benefit. She makes enough noise about how she needs our trade, so why doesn't she do something about it? Anyway, I don't see that we ought to leave any good Aurorans or other Outer Worlders in the hands of those apemen. Since they won't give them up, we'll make them. Otherwise, none of us will be safe next time."

"I see that you've adopted the popular opinions, anyway."

"The opinions are my own. If they're popular opinion also, it's because they make sense. Earth *wants* a war. Well, they'll get it."

"But why do they want a war, eh? Why do they force our hands? Our entire economic policy of the past months was only intended to force a change in their attitude without a war."

He was talking to himself, but his son answered with the final argument: "I don't care why they wanted war. They've *got* it now, and we're going to smash them."

Maynard returned to the Gathering, but even as the drone of debate refilled the room, he thought, with a twinge, that there would be no Terrestrian alfalfa that year. He regretted the milk. In fact, even the beef seemed, somehow, to be just a little less savory—

The vote came in the early hours of the morning. Aurora declared war. Most of the worlds of the Aurora bloc joined it by dawn.

In the history books, the war was later known as the Three Weeks' War. In the first week, Auroran forces occupied several of the trans-Plutonian asteroids, and at the beginning of the third week, the bulk of Earth's home fleet was all but completely destroyed in a battle within the orbit of Saturn by an Auroran fleet not one-quarter its size, numerically.

Declarations of war from the Outer Worlds yet neutral followed like the *pop-pop* of a string of firecrackers.

On the twenty-first day of the war, lacking two hours, Earth surrendered.

The negotiations of peace terms took place among the Outer Worlds. Earth's activities were concerned with signing only. The conditions of peace were unusual, perhaps unique, and under the force of an unprecedented humiliation, all the hordes of Earth seemed suddenly struck with a silence that came from a shamed anger too strong for words.

The terms mentioned were perhaps best commented upon by a voice on the Auroran video two days after they were made public. It can be quoted in part:

". . . There is nothing in or on Earth that we of the Outer Worlds can need or want. All that was ever worthwhile on Earth left it centuries ago in the persons of our ancestors.

"They call us the children of Mother Earth, but that is not so, for we are the descendants of a Mother Earth that no longer exists, a Mother that we brought with us. The Earth of today bears us at best a cousinly relation. No more.

"Do we want their resources? Why, they have none for themselves. Can we use their industry or science? They are almost dead for lack of ours. Can we use their man power? Ten of them are not worth a single robot. Do we even want the dubious glory of ruling them? There is no such glory. As our helpless and incompetent inferiors, they would be only a drag upon us. They would divert from our own use food, labor, and administrative ability.

"So they have nothing to give us but the space they occupy in our thought. They have nothing to free us from but themselves. They cannot benefit us in any way other than in their absence.

"It is for that reason that the peace terms have been defined as they have been. We wish them no harm, so let them have their own solar system. Let them live there in peace. Let them mold their own destiny in their own way, and we will not disturb them there by even the least hint of our presence. But we in turn want peace. We in turn would guide our own future in our own way. So we do not want *their* presence. And with that end in view, an Outer World fleet will patrol the boundaries of their system, Outer World bases will be established on their outermost asteroids, so that we may make sure they do not intrude on our territory.

"There will be no trade, no diplomatic relationships, no travel, no communications. They are fenced off, locked out, hermetically sealed away. Out here we have a new universe, a second creation of Man, a higher Man—

"They ask us: What will become of Earth? We answer: That is Earth's problem. Population growth can be controlled. Resources can be efficiently exploited. Economic systems can be revised. We know, for we have done so. If they cannot, let them go the way of the dinosaur, and make room.

"Let them make room, instead of forever demanding room!"

And so an impenetrable curtain swung slowly shut about the Solar System. The stars in Earth's sky became only stars again, as in the long-dead days before the first ship had penetrated the barrier of light's speed.

The government that had made war and peace resigned, but there was no one, really, to take their place. The legislature elected Luiz Moreno—ex-Ambassador to Aurora, ex-Secretary without Portfolio—as President *pro tem,* and the Earth as a whole was too numbed to agree or disagree. There was only a widespread relief that someone existed who would be willing to take the job of trying to guide the destinies of a world in prison.

Very few realized how well-planned an ending this was, or with what calculation Moreno found himself in the president's chair.

Ernest Keilin said hopelessly from the video screen: "We are only ourselves now. For us, there is no universe and no past—only Earth, and the future."

That night we heard from Luiz Moreno once again, and before morning he left for the capital.

Moreno's presence seemed incongruent within the stiffly formal president's mansion. He was suffering from a cold again, and snuffled when he talked.

Keilin regarded him with a self-terrifying hostility; an almost singeing hatred in which he could feel his fingers begin to twitch in the first gestures of choking. Perhaps he shouldn't have come— Well, what was the difference; the orders had been plain. If he had not come, he would have been brought.

The new president looked at him sharply: "You have to alter your attitude toward me, Keilin. I know you regard me as one of the Gravediggers of Earth—isn't that the phrase you used last night?—but you must listen to me quietly for a while. In your present state of suppressed rage, I doubt if you could hear me."

"I will hear whatever you have to say, Mr. President."

"Well—the external amenities, at least. That's hopeful. Or do you think a video-tracer is attached to the room?"

Keilin merely lifted his eyebrows.

Moreno said: "It isn't. We are quite alone. We *must* be alone; otherwise, how could I tell you safely that it is being arranged for you to be elected president under a constitution now being devised? Eh, what's the matter?"

Then he grinned at the look of bloodless amazement in Keilin's face. "Oh, you don't believe it. Well, it's past your stopping. And before an hour is up, you'll understand."

"I'm to be president?" Keilin struggled with a strange, hoarse voice. Then, more firmly: "You are mad."

"No. Not I. Those out there, rather. Out there in the Outer Worlds." There was a sudden vicious intensity in Moreno's eyes, and face, and voice, so that you forgot he was a little monkey of a man with a perpetual cold. You didn't notice the wrinkled, sloping forehead. You forgot the baldish head and ill-fitting clothes. There was only the bright and luminous look in his eyes, and the hard incision in his voice. *That* you noticed.

Keilin reached blindly backward for a chair, as Moreno came closer and spoke with increasing intensity.

"Yes," said Moreno. "Those out among the Stars. The godlike ones. The stately supermen. The strong, handsome master-race. *They* are mad. But only we on Earth know it.

"Come, you have heard of the Pacific Project. I know

you have. You denounced it to Cellioni once, and called it a fake. But it isn't a fake. And almost none of it is a secret. In fact, the only secret about it was that almost none of it was a secret.

"You're no fool, Keilin. You just never stopped to work it all out. And yet you were on the track. You had the feel of it. What was it you said that time you were interviewing me on the program? Something about the attitude of the Outer Worlding toward the Earthman being the only flaw in the former's stability. That was it, wasn't it? Or something like that? Very well, then; good! You had the first third of the Pacific Project in your mind at the time, and it was no secret after all, was it?

"Ask yourself, Keilin—what was the attitude of the typical Auroran to a typical Earthman? A feeling of superiority? That's the first thought, I suppose. But, tell me, Keilin, if he really felt superior, *really* superior, would it be so necessary for him to call such continuous attention to it? What kind of superiority is it that must be continuously bolstered by the constant repetition of phrases such as 'apemen,' 'submen,' 'half-animals of Earth,' and so on? That is not the calm internal assurance of superiority. Do you waste epithets on earthworms? No, there is something else there.

"Or let us approach it from another tack. Why do Outer World tourists stay in special hotels, travel in inclosed ground-cars, and have rigid, if unwritten, rules against social intermingling? Are they afraid of pollution? Strange, then, that they are not afraid to eat our food and drink our wine and smoke our tobacco.

"You see, Keilin, there are no psychiatrists on the Outer Worlds. The supermen are, so they say, too well adjusted. But here on Earth, as the proverb goes, there are more psychiatrists than plumbers, and they get lots of practice. So it is we, and not they, who know the truth about this Outer World superiority-complex, who know it to be simply a wild reaction against an overwhelming feeling of *guilt*.

"Don't you think that can be so? You shake your head as though you disagree. You don't see that a handful of men who clutch a Galaxy while billions starve for lack of room *must* feel a subconscious guilt, no matter what? And, since they won't share the loot, don't you see that the only way they can justify themselves is to try to convince themselves that Earthmen, after all, are inferior, that they do not deserve the Galaxy, that a new race of men have been created out there and that we here are only the diseased remnants of an old race that should die out like the dinosaur, through the working of inexorable natural laws?

"Ah, if they could only convince themselves of that, they would no longer be guilty, but merely superior. Only, it doesn't work; it never does. It requires constant bolstering; constant repetition, constant reinforcement. And still it doesn't quite convince.

"Best of all, if only they could pretend that Earth and its population do not exist at all. When you visit Earth, therefore, avoid Earthmen; or they might make you uncomfortable by not looking inferior enough. Sometimes they might look miserable instead, and nothing more. Or worse still, they might even seem intelligent—as I did, for instance, on Aurora.

"Occasionally, an Outer Worlder like Moreanu did crop up, and was able to recognize guilt for what it was without being afraid to say so out loud. He spoke of the duty the Outer Worlds owed Earth—and so he was dangerous to us. For if others listened to him and had offered token assistance to Earth, their guilt might have been assuaged in their own minds; and that without any lasting help to Earth. So Moreanu was removed through our web-weaving, and the way left clear to those who were unbending, who refused to admit guilt, and whose reaction could therefore be predicted and manipulated.

"Send them an arrogant note, for instance, and they automatically strike back with a useless embargo that merely gives us the ideal pretext for war. Then lose a war quickly, and you are sealed off by the annoyed supermen. No communication, no contact. You no longer exist to annoy them. Isn't that simple? Didn't it work out nicely?"

Keilin finally found his voice, because Moreno gave him time by stopping. He said: "You mean that all this was planned? You *did* deliberately instigate the war for the purpose of sealing Earth off from the Galaxy? You sent out the men of the Home Fleet to sure death because you wanted defeat? Why, you're a monster, a . . . a—"

Moreno frowned: "Please relax. It was not as simple as you think, and I am not a monster. Do you think the war could simply be—instigated? It had to be nurtured gently in just the right way and to just the right conclusion. If we had made the first move, if we had been the aggressor, if we had in any way put the fault on our side—why, they of the Outer Worlds would have occupied Earth and ground it under.

They would no longer feel guilty, you see, if *we* committed a crime against *them*. Or, again, if we fought a protracted war, or one in which we inflicted damage, they could succeed in shifting the blame.

"But we didn't. We merely imprisoned Auroran smugglers, and were obviously within our rights. They had to go to war over it because only so could they protect their superiority, which in turn protected them against the horrors of guilt. Aud we lost quickly. Scarcely an Auroran died. The guilt grew deeper and resulted in exactly the peace treaty our psychiatrists had predicted.

"And as for sending men out to die, that is a commonplace in every war—and a necessity. It was necessary to fight a battle, and, naturally, there were casualties."

"But why?" interrupted Keilin, wildly. "Why? *Why?* Why does all this gibberish seem to make sense to you? What have we gained? What can we possibly gain out of the present situation?"

"Gained, man? You ask what we've gained? Why, we've gained the universe. What has held us back so far? *You* know what Earth has needed these last centuries. You yourself once outlined it forcefully to Cellioni. We need a positronic robot society and an atomic power technology. We need chemical farming and we need population control. Well, what's prevented that, eh? Only the customs of centuries which said robots were evil since they deprived human beings of jobs, that population control was merely the murder of unborn children, and so on. And worse, there was always the safety valve of emigration either actual or hoped-for.

"But now we cannot emigrate. We're *stuck* here. Worse than that, we have been humiliatingly defeated by a handful of men out in the stars, and we've had a humiliating treaty of peace forced upon us. What Earthman wouldn't subconsciously burn for revenge? Self-preservation has frequently knuckled under to that tremendous yearning to 'get even.'

"And that is the second third of the Pacific Project, the recognition of the revenge motive. As simple as that.

"And how can we know that this is really so? Why, it has been demonstrated in history scores of times. Defeat a nation, but don't crush it entirely, and in a generation or two or three it will be stronger than it was before. Why? Because in the interval, sacrifices will have been made for revenge that would not have been made for mere conquest.

"Think! Rome beat Carthage rather easily the first time,

but was almost defeated the second. Every time Napoleon defeated the European coalition, he laid the groundwork for another just a little bit harder to defeat, until he himself was crushed by the eighth. It took four years to defeat Wilhelm of medieval Germany, and six much more dangerous years to stop his successor, Hitler.

"There you are! Until now, Earth needed to change its way of life only for greater comfort and happiness. A minor item like that could always wait. But now it must change for revenge, and that will not wait. And I want that change for its own sake.

"Only—I am not the man to lead. I am tarred with the failure of yesteryear, and will remain so until, long after I am bone-dust, Earth learns the truth. But you . . . *you*, and others like you, have always fought for the road to modernization. *You* will be in charge. It may take a hundred years. Grandchildren of men unborn may be the first to see its completion. But at least you will see the start.

"Eh, what do you say?"

Keilin was fumbling at the dream. He seemed to see it in a misty distance—a new and reborn Earth. But the change in attitude was too extreme. It could not be done just yet. He shook his head.

He said: "What makes you think the Outer Worlds would allow such a change, supposing what you say to be true? They will be watching, I am sure, and they will dectect a growing danger and put a stop to it. Can you deny that?"

Moreno threw his head back and laughed noiselessly. He gasped out: "But we have still a third left to the Pacific Project, a last, subtle and ironic third—

"The Outer Worlders call the men of Earth the subhuman dregs of a great race, but *we* are the men of *Earth*. Do you realize what that means? We live on a planet upon which, for a billion years, life—the life that has culminated in Mankind—has been adapting itself. There is not a microscopic part of Man, not a tiny working of his mind, that has not as its reason some tiny facet of the physical make-up of Earth, or of the biological make-up of Earth's other life-forms, or of the sociological make-up of the society about him.

"No other planet can substitute for Earth, *in Man's present shape.*

"The Outer Worlders exist as they do, only because pieces of Earth have been transplanted. Soil has been brought out there; plants; animals; men. They keep themselves surrounded by an artificial Earthborn geology which has within it, for instance, those traces of cobalt, zinc, and copper which human chemistry must have. They surround themselves by Earth-born bacteria and algae which have the ability to make those inorganic traces available in just the right way and in just the right quantity.

"And they maintain that situation by continued imports— luxury imports, they call it—from Earth.

"But on the Outer Worlds, even with Terrestrian soil laid down to bedrock, they cannot keep rain from falling and rivers from flowing, so that there is an inevitable, if slow, admixture with the native soil; an inevitable contamination of Terrestrian soil bacteria with the native bacteria, and an exposure, in any case, to a different atmosphere and to solar radiations of different types. Terrestrian bacteria disappear or change. And then plant life changes. And then animal life.

"No great change, mind you. Plant life would not become poisonous or nonnutritious in a day, or year, or decade. But already, the men of the Outer Worlds can detect the loss or change of the trace compounds that are responsible for that infinitely elusive thing we call 'flavor.' It has gone that far.

"And it will go further. Do you know, for instance, that on Aurora, nearly one half the native bacterial species known have a protoplasm based on a fluorocarbon rather than hydrocarbon chemistry? Can you imagine the essential foreignness of such an environment?

"Well, for two decades now, the bacteriologists and physiologists of Earth have studied various forms of Outer World life—the only portion of the Pacific Project that has been truly secret—and the transplanted Terrestrian life is already beginning to show certain changes on the subcellular level. *Even among the humans.*

"And here is the irony. The Outer Worlders, by their rigid racism and unbending genetic policies, are consistently eliminating from among themselves any children that show signs of adapting themselves to their respective planets in any way that departs from the norm. They are maintaining—they *must* maintain as a result of their own thought-processes— an artifical criterion of 'healthy' humanity, which is based on Terrestrian chemistry and not their own.

"But now that Earth has been cut off from them; now that not even a trickle of Terrestrian soil and life will reach them, change will be piled on change. Sicknesses will come, mortality will increase, child abnormalities will become more frequent—"

"And then?" asked Keilin, suddenly caught up.

"And then? Well, they are physical scientists—leaving such inferior sciences as biology to us. And they cannot abandon their sensation of superiority and their arbitrary standard of human perfection. They will never detect the change till it is too late to fight it. Not all mutations are clearly visible, and there will be an increasing revolt against the mores of those stiff Outer World societies. There will be a century of increasing physical and social turmoil which will prevent any interference on their part with us.

"We will have a century of rebuilding and revitalization, and at the end of it, we shall face an outer Galaxy which will either be dying or changed. In the first case, we will build a second Terrestrian Empire, more wisely and with greater knowledge than we did the first; one based on a strong and modernized Earth.

"In the second case, we will face perhaps ten, twenty, or even all fifty Outer Worlds, each with a slightly different variety of Man. Fifty humanoid species, no longer united against us, each increasingly adapted to its own planet, each with a sufficient tendency toward atavism to love Earth, to regard it as the great and original Mother.

"And racism will be dead, for variety will then be the great fact of Humanity, and not uniformity. Each type of Man will have a world of its own, for which no other world could quite substitute, and on which no other type could live quite as well. And other worlds can be settled to breed still newer varieties, until out of the grand intellectual mixture, Mother Earth will finally have given birth not to merely a Terrestrian, but to a *Galactic* Empire."

Keilin said, fascinated, "You foresee all this so certainly."

"Nothing is *truly* certain; but the best minds on Earth agree on this. There may be unforeseen stumbling blocks on the way, but to remove those will be the adventure of our great-grandchildren. Of *our* adventure, one phase has been successfully concluded; and another phase is beginning. Join us, Keilin."

Slowly, Keilin began to think that perhaps Moreno was not a monster after all—

THE END

What interests me most about "Mother Earth" is that it seems to show clear premonitions of the novels **Caves of Steel** and **The Naked Sun,** which I was to write in the 1950s.

One thing about the story that I can't explain is the fact that I have two characters in it, one of whom is named Moreno and one Moreanu. I haven't the slightest idea why I used such similar names. There was no significance in it, I assure you, only carelessness. There was also a Maynard.

Somehow, in reading and rereading the manuscript, the sloppiness of the situation never struck me. It did, however, just as soon as I saw the story in print. Why Campbell didn't notice and make me change the names, I haven't the faintest idea.

I had no sooner sold "Mother Earth" than I began a new "Foundation" story entitled ". . . And Now You Don't." It was to be the last. Like "The Mule," it was fifty thousand words long, and I didn't finish it till March 29, 1949. I submitted it to Campbell the next day and he took it at once. At two cents a word, it netted me a check of one thousand dollars, the first four-figure check I ever received.

It appeared as a three-part serial in the November 1949, December 1949, and January 1950 issues of **Astounding,** and it made up the final two thirds of my book **Second Foundation.**

By then, though, a great change was coming over the field of science fiction. The atom bomb had altered science fiction from a disregarded field of crazy stories into a literature of dreadful perception. Slowly, it was mounting in readership and esteem. New magazines were about to come into being, and the large publishing houses were about to consider putting out regular lines of hardback science fiction novels (hitherto the domain of small specialty houses no more affluent than the magazines and no more hopeful as a source of income).

The matter of hardback novels was of particular interest to Doubleday & Company, Inc. (though, of course, I didn't know it at the time). On February 5, 1949, while I was working on the last of the "Foundation" stories, I attended a meeting of the Hydra Club—a group of science fiction professionals who lived in New York. There I met a Double-day editor, Walter I. Bradbury, for the first time. It was he who was trying to build up a science fiction line for Double-day, and he expressed some interest in "The Mule."

I paid little attention to this, however. The thought of publishing a **book**, a real **book,** as opposed to magazine stories, was so outlandish that I simply couldn't cram it into my head.

But Fred Pohl could. He had been in the Army, serving in Italy and rising to the rank of sergeant. After discharge, he became an agent again. I had indignantly told him the story of Merwin's rejection of "Grow Old with Me," so when Bradbury continued searching, Pohl suggested to him that he look at that story of mine.

Bradbury was interested and, after considerable trouble, Pohl managed to pry the story out of me. ("It's no good," I kept saying—having never really recovered from the double rejection.)

But on March 24, 1949, I received the word that Brad-bury wanted "Grow Old with Me" if I would expand it to seventy thousand words. What's more, he paid me a $250 option, which I could keep even if the revision was unsatis-factory. That was the first time anyone had paid me anything **in advance,** and I was flabbergasted.

On April 6, I began the revision, and on May 25, 1949; I finished it and retitled it **Pebble in the Sky.** On May 29, Doubleday accepted it, and I had to grasp the fact that I was going to have a **book** published.

But even as I struggled with that, another change was taking place simultaneously.

There was still the matter of a job. All the time I was working for Professor Elderfield, I was still searching for one that I could take after that temporary position reached its natural end in May 1949. I was having no success at all.

But then, on January 13, 1949, Professor William C. Boyd of Boston University School of Medicine was visiting New York, and we met.

Professor Boyd was a science fiction reader of long standing and had liked my stories. For a couple of years we had been corresponding and we had grown quite friendly. Now he told me that there was an opening in the biochemistry department at his school and would I be interested? I **was** interested, of course, but Boston is twice as far from New York as Philadelphia is, and I hated to leave New York again.

I refused the offer, but not very hard.

And I continued to look for a job, and I continued to fail.

I therefore reconsidered my refusal of the position at Boston University School of Medicine and wrote a letter to Professor Boyd, saying that perhaps I might be interested, after all.

On March 9, 1949, I traveled to Boston for the first time in my life (on a sleeper—but I didn't sleep). I met Professor Burnham S. Walker, head of the department of biochemistry, the next day and he offered me a position on the faculty at five thousand per year. I saw no way out of my jobless dilemma but to accept.

Did I have to? Was there no chance that I might have made my living as a writer?

How could I honestly come to a decision that I could? In mid-1949, I had been writing for exactly eleven years. In all that time, my **total** earnings had come to $7,821.75, averaging a little over $710 per year, or $13.70 per week. In my better years, such as the seventh (mid-1944 to mid-1945, when I had sold four stories, including "The Mule"), I had earned $1,600, and in the tenth and eleventh together I had earned $3,300. It looked as though, even in good years, I could not count on much more than thirty dollars per week, and that just wasn't enough.

Of course, now that I was going to be publishing a **book**—

But books were unknown quantities. Besides, the book sale had come too late. By the time Bradbury accepted **Pebble in the Sky**, I was committed to the new job, and two days later, on June 1, 1949, I left for Boston.

It is at this point I must come to a halt, for the multiple changes put a final end to the first stage of my writing career.

I had left Campbell, this time forever. Oh, I saw him

occasionally, and we corresponded, but the steady drizzle of near-weekly visits was never to take place again. Though I wrote for him and continued to publish in **Astounding,** new magazines appeared, including **The Magazine of Fantasy and Science Fiction** in 1949, **Galaxy Science Fiction** in 1950, and others. My market broadened, and the word rate went up still further, to three cents and even four cents a word.

The appearance of my first book, **Pebble in the Sky,** on January 10, 1950, introduced a new dimension to my self-image, to my prestige in the field, and to my earnings. Other books followed—some new novels, some collections of older stories.

My position at Boston University School of Medicine led me to publish non-fiction. The first attempt was a textbook for medical students called **Biochemistry and Human Metabolism.** This was begun in 1950 in collaboration with Professors Walker and Boyd. It went through three editions and, though rather a failure, allowed me to discover that I enjoyed non-fiction writing at least as much as fiction writing and helped me start on a new phase of my writing career.

With all this taken into account, it is not surprising that my earnings as a writer began to rise rapidly almost as soon as I came to Boston. By 1952 I was making considerably more money as a writer than as a professor, and the discrepancy grew larger—in favor of writing—each succeeding year. By 1957, I'd decided (still somewhat to my surprise) that I had been a writer all along and that that was all I was.

On July 1, 1958, I gave up my salary and my duties but, with the agreement of the school, kept my title, which was then Associate Professor of Biochemistry. I keep that title to this day. I give an occasional lecture at the school when asked to do so, and I also lecture elsewhere when asked to do so (and charge a fee). For the rest, I became a full-time free-lance writer.

Writing is easy now, and is ever more satisfying. I keep what amounts to a seventy-hour week, if you count all the ancillary jobs of proofreading, indexing, research, and so on. I average seven or eight books a year, and this book, **The Early Asimov,** is my 125th book.

And yet, I must admit there has never been, since 1949, anything like the real excitement of those first eleven "Campbell years," when I wrote only in my spare time, and sometimes not even then, when every submission meant unbearable suspense, when every rejection meant misery and every acceptance ecstasy, and every fifty-dollar check was the wealth of Croesus.

And on July 11, 1971, John Campbell, at the still-early age of sixty-one, while watching television, died at 7:30 p.m. quietly and peacefully, without any pain at all.

There is no way at all to express how much he meant to me and how much he did for me except, perhaps, to write this book evoking, once more, those days of a quarter century ago.

APPENDIX

The Later Stories of the Campbell Years

STORY (WORDS)	MAGAZINE ISSUE	COLLECTION
26. CHRISTMAS ON GANY-MEDE (6,000)	*Startling Stories* January 1942	*The Early Asimov*
27. THE LITTLE MAN ON THE SUBWAY (4,000)	*Fantasy Book* Vol. 1, No. 6	*The Early Asimov*
28. Liar! (7,000)	*Astounding Science Fiction* May 1941	*I, Robot*
29. Masks (1,500)	———	———
30. THE HAZING (5,000)	*Thrilling Wonder Stories* October 1942	*The Early Asimov*
31. SUPER-NEUTRON (5,000)	*Astonishing Stories* September 1941	*The Early Asimov*
32. Nightfall (13,200)	*Astounding Science Fiction* September 1941	*Nightfall and Other Stories*
33. NOT FINAL! (7,000)	*Astounding Science Fiction* October 1941	*The Early Asimov*
34. LEGAL RITES (7,500)	*Weird Tales* September 1950	*The Early Asimov*
35. Robot AL-76 Goes Astray (5,000)	*Amazing Stories* February 1942	*The Rest of the Robots*
36. Foundation (12,500)	*Astounding Science Fiction* May 1942	*Foundation*

37. Runaround (7,000)	*Astounding Science Fiction* March 1942	*I, Robot*
38. Bridle and Saddle (18,000)	*Astounding Science Fiction* June 1942	*Foundation*
39. Big Game (1,000)	———	———
40. First Law (1,000)	*Fantastic Universe* October 1956	*The Rest of the Robots*
41. TIME PUSSY (1,000)	*Astounding Science Fiction* April 1942	*The Early Asimov*
42. Victory Unintentional (7,000)	*Super Science Stories* August 1942	*The Rest of the Robots*
43. AUTHOR! AUTHOR! (12,000)	———	*The Early Asimov*
44. DEATH SENTENCE (7,000)	*Astounding Science Fiction* November 1943	*The Early Asimov*
45. Catch That Rabbit (7,000)	*Astounding Science Fiction* February 1944	*I, Robot*
46. The Big and the Little (22,500)	*Astounding Science Fiction* August 1944	*Foundation*
47. The Wedge (6,000)	*Astounding Science Fiction* October 1944	*Foundation*
48. Dead Hand (25,000)	*Astounding Science Fiction* April 1945	*Foundation and Empire*
49. BLIND ALLEY (8,500)	*Astounding Science Fiction* March 1945	*The Early Asimov*
50. Escape (Paradoxical Escape) (7,000)	*Astounding Science Fiction* August 1945	*I, Robot*

51.	The Mule (50,000)	*Astounding Science Fiction* November 1945 December 1945	*Foundation and Empire*
52.	Evidence (7,000)	*Astounding Science Fiction* September 1946	*I, Robot*
53.	Little Lost Robot (10,000)	*Astounding Science Fiction* March 1947	*I, Robot*
54.	Now You See It— (25,000)	*Astounding Science Fiction* January 1948	*Second Foundation*
55.	NO CONNECTION (7,000)	*Astounding Science Fiction* June 1948	*The Early Asimov*
56.	THE ENDO-CHRONIC PROPERTIES OF RESUBLIMATED THIOTIMOLINE (3,000)	*Astounding Science Fiction* March 1948	*The Early Asimov*
57.	Grow Old with Me (Pebble in the Sky) (70,000)	————	*Pebble in the Sky*
58.	THE RED QUEEN'S RACE (7,000)	*Astounding Science Fiction* January 1949	*The Early Asimov*
59.	MOTHER EARTH (15,000)	*Astounding Science Fiction* May 1949	*The Early Asimov*
60.	—And Now You Don't (50,000)	*Astounding Science Fiction* November 1949 December 1949 January 1950	*Second Foundation*

(Note: Stories in capital letters appear in this volume.)